EX LIBRIS

VINTAGE CLASSICS

ROBERTO BOLAÑO

Roberto Bolaño was born in Santiago, Chile, in 1953. He grew up in Chile and Mexico City, where he was a founder of the Infrarealism poetry movement. Described by the *New York Times* as 'the most significant Latin American literary voice of his generation', he was the author of over twenty works, including *The Savage Detectives*, which received the Herralde Prize and the Rómulo Gallegos Prize when it appeared in 1998, and *2666*, which posthumously won the 2008 National Book Critics Circle Award for Fiction. Bolaño died in Blanes, Spain, at the age of fifty, just as his writing found global recognition.

ALSO BY ROBERTO BOLAÑO

NOVELS

The Savage Detectives

2666

Nazi Literature in the Americas

The Skating Rink

Woes of the True Policeman

The Spirit of Science Fiction

NOVELLAS

By Night in Chile

Distant Star

Amulet

Antwerp

Monsieur Pain

A Little Lumpen Novelita

Cowboy Graves

STORIES

Last Evenings on Earth

The Insufferable Gaucho

The Return

POETRY

The Romantic Dogs

Tres

The Unknown University

ROBERTO BOLAÑO
THE THIRD REICH

TRANSLATED FROM THE SPANISH BY
Natasha Wimmer

VINTAGE CLASSICS

1 3 5 7 9 10 8 6 4 2

Vintage Classics is part of the Penguin Random House
group of companies whose addresses can be found
at global.penguinrandomhouse.com

Penguin
Random House
UK

This edition published in Vintage Classics in 2024
First published in Spain with the title *El Tercer Reich* by Editorial Anagrama in 2010
First published in the United States of America with the title
The Third Reich by Farrar, Straus and Giroux in 2011

This book was serialized, in slightly different form, in the *Paris Review*.

Designed by Jonathan D. Lippincott

penguin.co.uk/vintage-classics

Printed and bound in Great Britain by Clays Ltd, Elcograf S.p.A.

The authorised representative in the EEA is
Penguin Random House Ireland,
Morrison Chambers, 32 Nassau Street, Dublin D02 YH68

A CIP catalogue record for this book is available from the British Library

ISBN 9781784879556

Penguin Random House is committed to a sustainable future
for our business, our readers and our planet. This book is made
from Forest Stewardship Council® certified paper.

For Carolina López

Sometimes we played with traveling salesmen, other times with vacationers, and two months ago we were even able to condemn a German general to twenty years of imprisonment. He happened by with his wife, and only my wiles saved him from the gallows.

—Friedrich Dürrenmatt, *Traps*

Through the window comes the murmur of the sea mingled with the laughter of the night's last revelers, a sound that might be the waiters clearing the tables on the terrace, an occasional car driving slowly along the Paseo Marítimo, and a low and unidentifiable hum from the other rooms in the hotel. Ingeborg is asleep, her face placid as an angel's. On the night table stands an untouched glass of milk that by now must be warm, and next to her pillow, half hidden under the sheet, a Florian Linden detective novel of which she read only a few pages before falling asleep. The heat and exhaustion have had the opposite effect on me: I'm wide-awake. I usually sleep well, seven or eight hours a night, though I hardly ever go to bed tired. In the mornings I wake up ready to go and I can keep going for eight or ten hours straight. As far as I know, it's always been like that; it's how I was made. No one taught me to be this way, it's just how I am, and by that I don't mean to suggest that I'm better or worse than anybody else, than Ingeborg herself, for example, who on Saturdays and Sundays doesn't get up until after noon and who during the week needs two cups of coffee—and a cigarette—before she manages to really wake up and get off to work. Tonight, though, I'm too hot and tired to sleep. Also, the urge to write, to set down the events of the day, keeps me from getting into bed and turning out the light.

The trip came off without any mishaps worth mentioning. We

stopped in Strasbourg, a pretty town, though I'd been there before. We ate at a kind of roadside market. At the border, despite what we'd been told to expect, we didn't have to stand in line or wait more than ten minutes to cross over. Everything was quick and efficient. After that I drove because Ingeborg doesn't trust the drivers here, I think because she had a bad experience on a Spanish highway years ago when she was a girl on vacation with her parents. Also, she was tired, as is only natural.

At the hotel reception desk we were helped by a very young girl who spoke decent German, and there was no problem finding our reservations. Everything was in order, and as we were on our way up I spotted Frau Else in the dining room; I recognized her right away. She was setting a table as she made some remark to a waiter who stood next to her holding a tray full of salt shakers. She was wearing a green suit, and pinned on her chest was a metal brooch with the hotel logo.

The years had scarcely touched her.

The sight of Frau Else brought back my adolescence, its dark and bright moments: my parents and my brother at breakfast on the hotel terrace, the music that at seven in the evening began to drift across the main floor from the restaurant speakers, the idle laughter of the waiters, and the plans made by the kids my age to go night swimming or out to the clubs. What was my favorite song back then? Each summer there was a new one, resembling in some way the songs from previous summers, hummed and whistled constantly and played at the end of the night by all the clubs in town. My brother, who has always been particular when it comes to music, would carefully choose what tapes to bring along on vacation; I preferred to pick up some new tune at random, inevitably the song of the summer. I had only to hear it two or three times, purely by chance, in order for its notes to follow me through sunny days and the new friendships that enlivened our vacations. Fleeting friendships, when I look back today, existing only to banish the faintest hint of boredom. Of all those faces only a few linger in memory. First, that of Frau Else, who won me over from the start, which made me the butt of jokes and teasing by my parents, who even made fun of me in front of Frau Else and her husband, a Spaniard whose name I can't recall, with references to my supposed jealousy and the precocity of youth that made me blush to the roots of my hair and that inspired in Frau Else an affectionate sense of camaraderie. After that I thought she showed a special warmth in her treatment of me. Also, although it is a very different case, there was José (was that his name?), a boy my age who worked at the hotel and who took us, my brother and me, to places where we'd never have gone without him. When we said good-bye for the last time, possibly guessing that we wouldn't spend the next summer at the Del Mar, my brother gave him a couple of rock tapes and I gave him an old pair of jeans. Ten years have gone by and I still remember the tears that filled José's eyes as he clutched the folded jeans in one hand and the tapes in the other, not knowing what to do or say, murmuring (in an English that my brother was always making fun of): Good-bye, dear friends, good-bye, dear friends, etc., while we told him in Spanish—a language that we spoke with some fluency; not for nothing had our parents vacationed in Spain for years—not to worry, the next summer we'd be like the Three Musketeers again, and that he should stop crying. We got two postcards from José. I answered the first one in my name and my brother's. Then we forgot about José and never heard from him again. There was also a boy from Heilbronn called Erich, the best swimmer of the season, and Charlotte, who liked to lie on the beach with me although it was my brother who was crazy about her. Then there was poor Aunt Giselle, my mother's youngest sister, who came with us on the second-to-last summer we spent at the Del Mar. More than anything else, Aunt Giselle loved bullfighting, and she couldn't get enough of the fights. Indelible memory: my brother driving my father's car with complete impunity and me sitting next to him, smoking, without a word from anyone, and Aunt Giselle in the backseat staring in ecstasy at the foam-splashed cliffs and the deep green of the sea beneath us with a smile of satisfaction on her pale lips and three posters, three treasures, on her lap, proof that she, my brother, and I had rubbed shoulders with the bullfighting greats at the Plaza de Toros in Barcelona. I know my parents disapproved of many of the activities that Aunt Giselle pursued with such passion, just as they weren't pleased by the freedoms she permitted us, excessive for children, as they saw it, although by then I was nearly fourteen. At the same time, I've always suspected that it was we who looked after Aunt Giselle, a task my mother assigned us without anyone realizing, surreptitiously and with great trepidation. In any case, Aunt Giselle was with us for only one summer, the summer before the last we spent at the Del Mar.

That's almost all I remember. I haven't forgotten the laughter at the tables on the terrace, the galleons of beer that were emptied as I looked on in astonishment, the dark, sweaty waiters crouched in a corner of the bar talking in low voices. Random images. My father's happy smile and approving nods, a shop where we rented bicycles, the beach at nine thirty at night, still with a faint glow of sunlight. The room we had then was different from the one we're in now; whether better or worse I can't say, different, on a lower floor, and bigger, big enough to fit four beds, and with a large balcony facing the sea, where my parents would settle in the afternoons after lunch to play infinite card games. I'm not sure whether we had a private bathroom or not. Probably some summers we did and others we didn't. Our room now does have its own bathroom and also a nice big closet, and a huge bed, and rugs, and a marble table on the terrace, and green curtains of a fabric silky to the touch, and white wooden shutters, very modern, and direct and indirect lights, and some well-concealed speakers that play soft music at the touch of a button . . . No doubt about it, the Del Mar has come up in the world. The competition, to judge from the quick glance I got from the car as we were driving along the Paseo Marítimo, hasn't been left behind either. There are hotels that I don't remember, and apartment buildings have sprung up on once vacant lots. But this is all speculation. Tomorrow I'll try to talk to Frau Else and I'll take a walk around town.

Have I come up in the world too? Absolutely. Back then I hadn't met Ingeborg and today we're a couple; my friendships are more interesting and deeper (with Conrad, for example, who is like a second brother to me and who will read what's written here); I know what I want and I have a better sense of perspective; I'm financially independent; I'm never bored now, which wasn't true in my adolescence. According to Conrad, the true test of health is lack of boredom, which means that I must be in excellent health. I don't think it's an exaggeration to say that my life has never been better.

Most of the credit goes to Ingeborg. Meeting her was the best thing that ever happened to me. Her sweetness, her charm, her soft gaze, put everything else—my own daily struggles and the back-stabbing of those who envy me—into perspective, allowing me to face facts and rise above them. Where will our relationship lead? I ask this because relationships between young people today are so fragile. I'd rather not give it too much thought. Better to focus on the positive: loving her and taking care of her. Of course, if we end up getting married, so much the better. A life at Ingeborg's side: could I ask for anything more in matters of the heart?

Time will tell. For now her love is . . . But not to wax poetic. These vacation days will also be workdays. I have to ask Frau Else for a bigger table, or two small tables, to set up the game. Just thinking about the possibilities of my new opening strategy and all the various outcomes makes me want to get the game out right now and test it. But I won't. I have the energy only to write a little more. The trip was long and yesterday I hardly slept, partly because it was Ingeborg's and my first trip together and partly because it would be my first time back at the Del Mar in ten years.

Tomorrow we'll have breakfast on the terrace. When? Ingeborg will probably get up late. Was there a set time for breakfast? I can't remember; I don't think so. In any case we could also have breakfast at a certain café in town, an old place that always used to be full of fishermen and tourists. When I was here with my parents we always ate there or at the Del Mar. Will it have closed? Anything can happen in ten years. I hope it's still open.

Twice I've talked to Frau Else. Our encounters haven't been all I hoped. The first took place around eleven in the morning. I had just left Ingeborg at the beach and come back to the hotel to arrange a few things. I found Frau Else at the reception desk helping a few Danes who seemed to be checking out, judging by their luggage and their ostentatiously perfect tans. Their children were hauling enormous Mexican sombreros across the reception hall. Once they'd said their good-byes and promised to return without fail the following year, I introduced myself. Udo Berger, I said, extending my hand with an admiring smile, well deserved, because at that instant, viewed from up close, Frau Else seemed even more beautiful and at least as enigmatic as I remembered her from my adolescence. And yet she didn't recognize me. It took me five minutes to explain who I was, who my parents were, how many summers we'd spent at the hotel. I even dredged up some rather evocative incidents that I would have preferred to keep to myself. All of this while standing at the reception desk as clients came and went in bathing suits (I myself was wearing only shorts and sandals), constantly interrupting my efforts to nudge her memory. Finally she said she did remember us: the Berger family, from Munich? No, from Reutlingen, I corrected her, though now I live in Stuttgart. Of course, she said, your mother was a lovely person; she also remembered my father and even Aunt Giselle. You've grown so much, you're a real man now, she said in a tone that seemed to betray a hint of shyness, and that unsettled me, though I can't really say why. She asked how long I planned to stay and whether I found the town much changed. I answered that I hadn't had time to walk around yet, I had arrived the night before, quite late, and I planned to be in town for two weeks, here, at the Del Mar, of course. She smiled and that was the end of our conversation. I went right up to my room, feeling slightly agitated without knowing quite why. From there I called and had a table brought up; I made it very clear that it should be at least five feet long. As I was waiting I read the first pages of this journal. Not bad, especially for a beginner. I think Conrad is right. The daily practice, compulsory or near compulsory, of setting down one's ideas and the day's events in a diary allows a virtual autodidact like myself to learn how to reflect, how to exercise the memory by focusing deliberately rather than randomly on images, and especially how to cultivate certain aspects of the sensibility that may seem fully formed but that in reality are only seeds that may or may not develop into character. The initial reason for the diary, however, was much more practical in nature: to exercise my prose so that in the future no clumsiness of expression or defective syntax will detract from the insights offered by my articles, which are being published in an increasing number of specialized journals and have lately been subjected to all sorts of criticism, in the form of either comments in Readers Respond columns or else of cuts and revisions by the magazines' editors. And no matter how I protest or how many championships I win, I continue to be blatantly censored based solely on claims of faulty grammar (as if *they* wrote so well). In the interest of honesty, I should point out that this is happily not always the case; there are magazines that receive a piece of mine and in response send a polite little note, offering perhaps two or three respectful comments, and after a while my text appears in print, as written. Others fall all over themselves with compliments; they're the ones Conrad calls Bergerian publications. Really, my only problems are with a fraction of the Stuttgart group and some pompous asses from Cologne; I creamed them once and they still haven't forgiven me. In

Stuttgart there are three magazines and I've published in all of them; my problems there are all in the family, as they say. In Cologne there's only one journal, but it's better designed and distributed nationally, and—last but not least—it pays its writers. It even allows itself the luxury of employing a small but professional stable of regular contributers, who receive a respectable monthly stipend for doing just what they like. Whether they do it well or badly—and I would say they do it badly—is another question. I've published two articles in Cologne. The first, "How to Win in the Bulge," was translated into Italian and published in a Milanese journal, which impressed my circle of friends and put me in direct contact with the gamers of Milan. The two articles were published, as I said, although I noticed that slight revisions or small changes had been made to each, everything from whole sentences eliminated on the pretext of lack of space—though all the illustrations that I requested were included!—or corrections for style, this last a task performed by some nobody whom I never had the pleasure of meeting, even by phone, and regarding whose real existence I have grave doubts. (His name doesn't appear anywhere in the magazine. I have no doubt that this apocryphal copy chief is used as camouflage by the contributing editors in their sins against writers.) The last straw came when I turned in the third article: they simply refused to publish it despite the fact that they had specifically assigned it to me. My patience has limits; a few short hours after receiving the rejection letter I telephoned the editor in chief to express my astonishment at the decision and my anger at the editorial board for wasting my time—although this was a lie. The time I use to solve gaming problems is never wasted, much less when the campaign I'm thinking and writing about is of particular interest. To my surprise the editor responded with a barrage of insults and threats that minutes before I couldn't have imagined coming from his prissy little duck's beak of a mouth. Before I hung up on him—although in the end it was he who hung up on me—I promised that if we ever met I would kick his ass. Among the many insults I had to endure, perhaps the one that stung most concerned the alleged clumsiness of my writing. If I think about it calmly it's clear that the poor man was mistaken, because if he wasn't, why do other German magazines, and some foreign ones, keep publishing my articles? Why do I get letters from Rex Douglas, Nicky Palmer, and Dave Rossi? Is it just because I'm the champ? At this point, which I refuse to call a crisis point, Conrad told me exactly what I needed to hear: he advised me to forget the Cologne crowd (the only one of them worth anything there is Heimito, and he has nothing to do with the magazine) and to start keeping a journal, because it's never a bad idea to have a place to set down the events of the day and develop ideas for future articles, which is exactly what I plan to do.

I was deep in these thoughts when there was a knock at the door and a maid came in, just a girl, who muttered something in a made-up German—the only word she said that actually meant anything was "no"—that upon reflection I realized meant that no table was coming. I explained to her, in Spanish, that it was absolutely necessary that I have a table, and not just any table but one that was at least five feet long, or two tables half that length, and that I wanted it now.

The girl went away saying that she'd do what she could. A while later she appeared again, accompanied by a man of about forty, dressed in brown trousers as wrinkled as if he'd slept in them and a white shirt with a dirty collar. The man, without introducing himself or asking permission, came into the room and inquired what I wanted the table for. With his chin he motioned at the table that was already in the room, which was too low and too small for my needs. I chose not to answer. In the face of my silence, he explained that he couldn't put two tables in one room. He seemed to worry that I wouldn't understand, and every so often he gestured with his hands as if he were describing a pregnant woman.

A little tired by now of so much pantomime, I swept everything that was on the table onto the bed and ordered him to take the table away and come back with one that matched my specifications. The man made no move to leave; he seemed frightened. The girl, on the other hand, smiled at me in a sympathetic way. The next moment I grabbed the table and put it out in the hallway.

9

The man left the room nodding in confusion, as if he didn't understand what had just happened. Before he left he said that it wouldn't be easy to find a table like the one I wanted. I gave him an encouraging smile: everything is possible if one makes an effort.

Sometime later a call came from the reception desk. An unidentifiable voice said in German that they didn't have tables like the one I had demanded, did I want them to return the one that had been in the room? I asked with whom I had the pleasure of speaking. This is Miss Nuria, the receptionist, said the voice. In the most persuasive tone I could muster, I explained to Miss Nuria that for my work—yes, I worked on vacation—a table was absolutely indispensable, but not the one that was there already, the standard table that I supposed all the rooms had, but one that was higher and, especially, longer, if that wasn't too much to ask. What kind of work do you do, Mr. Berger? asked Miss Nuria. Why should that matter to you? Just tell someone to send up a table like the one I've requested and let that be the end of it. The receptionist faltered, then in a faint voice she said that she'd see what could be done and hung up abruptly. With that, I recovered my good humor and dropped onto the bed, laughing.

Frau Else's voice woke me. She was standing next to the bed and her eyes, curiously intense, observed me with concern. Right away I realized that I had fallen asleep, and I was embarrassed. I fumbled about for something to cover myself up—though very slowly, as if I were still dreaming—because even though I was wearing shorts I felt completely naked. How could she have come in without my hearing her? Did she have a master key to all the hotel rooms and did she use it freely?

I thought you were sick, she said. Do you know what a fright you gave our receptionist? She was just following hotel regulations, she shouldn't have to put up with rudeness from the guests.

"That's inevitable at any hotel," I said.

"Are you saying you know more than I do about my own business?"

"No, of course not."

"Well, then?"

I murmured a few words of apology, unable to tear my eyes

away from the perfect oval of Frau Else's face, upon which I thought I spied the faintest of ironic smiles, as if the situation that I had created struck her as funny.

Behind her was the table.

I knelt on the bed. Frau Else didn't make the slightest effort to move so that I could examine the table to my satisfaction. Nevertheless I could see that it was everything I had wanted, and more. I hope it suits you, I had to go down to the basement to find it, it belonged to my husband's mother. There was still an ironic edge to her voice: Will you be able to use it for your work? And are you really planning to work all summer? If I were as pale as you I'd spend all day at the beach. I promised that I would do both things in moderation, that I'd work and also spend time at the beach. And won't you go out clubbing at night? Doesn't your girlfriend like the clubs? And speaking of her, where is she? At the beach, I said. She must be a smart girl, she doesn't waste time, said Frau Else. I'll introduce you this afternoon, if you're free, I said. Actually, I'm busy and may have to spend all day in the office, so it will have to be some other time, said Frau Else. I smiled. The longer I spent with her, the more interesting I found her.

"You're choosing work over the beach too," I said.

Before she left she warned me to treat the staff more politely.

I set the table by the window, in a spot where it would get as much natural light as possible. Then I went out on the balcony and spent a long time scanning the beach, trying to spot Ingeborg among the half-naked bodies lying in the sun.

We ate at the hotel. Ingeborg's skin was flushed. She's very blond and it's not good for her to get so much sun all at once. I hope she won't get sunstroke; that would be terrible. When we went up to the room she asked where the table had come from and I had to explain, in the perfect stillness of the room, me sitting at the table, her lying on the bed, that I had asked the management to exchange the old one for a bigger one because I planned to set up the game. Ingeborg just looked at me. She didn't say a word, but in her eyes I glimpsed a hint of disapproval.

I can't say when she fell asleep. Ingeborg sleeps with her eyes half open. On tiptoe, I picked up my journal and started to write.

•

We're back from the Ancient Egypt, a club. We had dinner at the hotel. During her siesta (how quickly one picks up Spanish habits!), Ingeborg talked in her sleep. Random words like "bed," "mother," "highway," "ice cream" . . . When she woke up we took a stroll along the Paseo Marítimo, away from town, carried along by the flow of people. Then we sat on the seawall and talked.

Dinner was light. Ingeborg changed clothes. A white dress, white high heels, a mother-of-pearl necklace, and her hair pulled up in a loose twist. I dressed in white too, though not as elegantly.

The club was on the side of town near the campgrounds, a neighborhood of clubs, burger stands, and restaurants. Ten years ago there was nothing here but a few places to camp and a pine forest that stretched all the way to the train tracks; today apparently it's the town's main tourist district. The bustle of its single street, which runs along the shore, is like that of a big city at rush hour. With the difference that here rush hour begins at nine in the evening and doesn't end until after three. The crowd that gathers on the pavement is motley and cosmopolitan: white, black, yellow, Indian, mixed, as if all the races had agreed to vacation here, although I suppose not everyone is on vacation.

Ingeborg was at her most radiant, and when we walked into the club we were greeted with covert admiring glances. Admiring of Ingeborg and envious of me. Envy is something I always pick up on right away. Anyway, we didn't plan to spend much time there. And yet, as fate would have it, before long a German couple sat down at our table.

Let me explain how it happened. I'm not crazy about dancing. I do dance, especially since I met Ingeborg, but first I have to loosen up with a couple of drinks and grow accustomed to the discomfort I feel among so many strange faces in a room that usually isn't very well lit. Ingeborg, meanwhile, has no qualms about going out alone to dance. She might head to the dance floor for a few songs, stop back at the table, take a sip of her drink, return to the dance floor, and so on all night until she drops from exhaustion. I've gotten used to it. While she's gone I think about my work and meaning-less things, or I hum the tune that's playing over the sound system, or I meditate on the unknown fates of the amorphous masses and the shadowy faces that surround me. Sometimes Ingeborg, igno-rant of all this, comes up and gives me a kiss. Or she appears with new friends—like the German couple tonight—with whom she has barely exchanged a few words in the shuffle of the dance floor. Words that when taken together with our common state as vaca-tioners are enough to establish something resembling friendship.

Karl—though he prefers to be called Charly—and Hanna are from Oberhausen. She works as a secretary at the company where he's a mechanic; both are twenty-five. Hanna is divorced. She has a three-year-old son, and she plans to marry Charly as soon as she can. She told all this to Ingeborg in the ladies' room and Ingeborg told it to me when we got back to the hotel. Charly likes soccer, sports in general, and windsurfing: he brought his board, which he raves about, from Oberhausen. At one point, while Ingeborg and Hanna were on the dance floor, he asked me what my favorite sport was. I said I liked to run. Alone.

Both of them had had a lot to drink. So had Ingeborg, to tell the truth. Under the circumstances, it was easy to agree that we would get together the next day. Their hotel is the Costa Brava, which is just a few steps from ours. We planned to meet around noon, on the beach, next to the place where they rent the pedal boats.

It was close to two in the morning when we left the club. On our way out, Charly bought a last round. He was happy; he told me they'd been in town for ten days and hadn't made any friends. The Costa Brava was full of English tourists, and the few Germans he'd met at bars were either unfriendly or single men traveling in groups, which excluded Hanna.

On the way home, Charly began to sing songs that I'd never heard before. Most of them were crude; some referred to what he planned to do to Hanna when they got back to their room, by which I deduced that the lyrics, at least, were made up. Now and then Hanna, who was walking arm in arm with Ingeborg a little way ahead of us, would laugh. My Ingeborg laughed too. For an instant

I imagined her in Charly's arms and I shuddered. My stomach shrank to the size of a fist.

Along the Paseo Marítimo a cool breeze was blowing, and it helped to clear my head. The only people to be seen were tourists returning to their hotels, stumbling or singing, and the few cars to pass in either direction moved slowly, as if the whole world were suddenly exhausted or sick and everything now flowed toward bed and dark rooms.

When we got to the Costa Brava, Charly insisted on showing me his surfboard. He had it strapped with a web of cords to the luggage rack of his car in the outdoor parking lot of the hotel. What do you think? he asked. There was nothing special about it, it was a board like a million others. I confessed that I knew nothing about windsurfing. If you want I can teach you, he said. We'll see, I answered, without making any promises.

We refused to let them walk us back to our hotel, and Hanna was in complete agreement. Still, the farewell was prolonged. Charly was much drunker than I realized and insisted that we come up to see their room. Hanna and Ingeborg laughed at the silly things he said, but I remained unmoved. When at last we had convinced him that it was best if we all went to bed, he pointed at something on the beach and went running off into the darkness. We all followed him: first Hanna (who was surely used to this kind of scene), then Ingeborg, then me reluctantly bringing up the rear. Soon the lights of the Paseo Marítimo were behind us. On the beach the only sound was the noise of the sea. Far away to the left I made out the lights of the port where my father and I went one morning, very early, in a fruitless attempt to buy fish: in those days, at least, the selling took place in the afternoon.

We began to call his name. Our shouts were all that could be heard in the darkness. Without meaning to, Hanna stepped in the water and soaked her pants up to the knee. It was then, more or less, as we listened to Hanna curse—her pants were satin and the salt water would ruin them—that Charly answered our calls: he was between us and the Paseo Marítimo. Where are you, Charly? shouted Hanna. Here, over here, follow my voice, said Charly. We set out again toward the lights of the hotels.

"Watch out for the pedal boats," warned Charly.

Like creatures of the deep, the pedal boats formed a black island in the uniform darkness of the beach. Sitting on the floater of one these strange vehicles, with his shirt unbuttoned and his hair disheveled, Charly was waiting for us.

"I just wanted to show Udo the exact place we're meeting tomorrow," he said, when Hanna and Ingeborg scolded him for the fright he'd given them and for his childish behavior.

As the women helped Charly up, I observed the group of pedal boats. I couldn't say exactly what it was about them that caught my attention. Maybe it was the strange way that they were arranged, which was unlike anything I'd seen before in Spain, though Spain is hardly a regimented country. At the very least, the way they were set up was illogical and impractical. The normal thing, even accounting for the whims of the average pedal boat proprietor, is to point them away from the sea, in rows of three or four. Of course, there are those who point them toward the sea, or arrange them in a single long line, or don't line them up, or drag them against the seawall that separates the beach from the Paseo Marítimo. The way that these were positioned, however, defied explanation. Some faced the sea and others the Paseo, though most lay on their sides with their noses toward the port or the campground zone in a kind of jagged row. But even odder was that some had been turned on their sides, balancing only on a floater, and there was even one that had been overturned entirely, with the floaters and the paddles pointing skyward and the seats buried in the sand, a position that not only was unusual but must have required considerable physical strength, and that—if it hadn't been for the strange symmetry, for the clear intent that emanated from the collection of boats half covered by old tarps—might have been taken as the work of a bunch of hooligans, the kind who roam the beaches at midnight.

Of course, neither Charly nor Hanna nor even Ingeborg noticed anything out of the ordinary about the pedal boats.

When we got back to the hotel, I asked Ingeborg what she thought of Charly and Hanna.

Good people, she said. I agreed, with reservations.

The next morning we ate at the café, La Sirena. Ingeborg had an English breakfast of milky tea, a fried egg, two strips of bacon, baked beans, and a grilled tomato, all for 350 pesetas, much cheaper than at the hotel. On the wall behind the bar there's a wooden mermaid with red hair and bronzed skin. Old fishing nets still hang from the ceiling. Otherwise, everything is different. The waiter and the woman behind the bar are young. Ten years ago an old man and an old woman, dark skinned and very wrinkled, worked here; they used to talk to my parents. I couldn't bring my-self to ask after them. What good would it do? The new people speak Catalan.

We met Charly and Hanna at the agreed-upon place, near the pedal boats. They were asleep. After we spread our towels out next to them, we woke them up. Hanna opened her eyes right away but Charly grunted something unintelligible and kept sleeping. Hanna explained that he'd had a rough night. When Charly drank, accord-ing to Hanna, he didn't know when to stop, which wasn't good for him or his health. She said that at eight, after hardly sleeping, he had gone out windsurfing. And there was the board, lying next to Charly. Then Hanna compared suntan lotions with Ingeborg, and after a while, with the sun toasting their backs, their conversation turned to some guy from Oberhausen, a manager who it seemed had taken a serious interest in Hanna although she liked him only "as a friend." I stopped listening and spent the next few minutes examining the pedal boats that had so disturbed me the night before.

There weren't many of them on the beach; most, already rented, were moving about slowly and erratically on the water, which was calm and deep blue. Certainly there was nothing disturbing about the pedal boats still waiting to be rented. They were old, outdated even in comparison to the boats at neighboring rental spots, and the sun seemed to glint off their pitted and peeling surfaces. A rope, strung from a few sticks driven into the sand, separated bathers from the area set aside for the boats. The rope hung scarcely a foot from the ground and in some places the sticks were listing and about to fall over completely. On the shore I could make out the rental guy helping a group of vacationers launch their boat, at the same time making sure it didn't hit one of the countless children splashing around. The renters, about six of them, all perched on the pedal boat and carrying plastic bags that might hold sandwiches and cans of beer, waved toward the beach or slapped each other on the back in jubilation. When the pedal boat had made its way through the fringe of children, the rental guy came out of the water and headed our way.

"Poor man," I heard Hanna say.

I asked to whom she was referring; I was told to take a closer look without being obvious about it. The rental guy was dark, with long hair and a muscular build, but the most noticeable thing about him by far were the burns—I mean burns from a fire, not the sun—that covered most of his face, neck, and chest, and that he displayed openly, dark and corrugated, like grilled meat or the crumpled metal of a downed plane.

For an instant, I must admit, I was hypnotized, until I realized that he was looking at us too and that there was an indifference in his gaze, a kind of coldness that suddenly struck me as repulsive.

After that I avoided looking at him.

Hanna said that she would kill herself if she ended up like that, scarred by fire. Hanna is a pretty girl, with blue eyes and brown hair, and her breasts—neither Hanna nor Ingeborg was wearing her bikini top—are large and shapely, but it didn't take much effort for me to imagine her covered in burns, screaming and wandering blindly around her hotel room. (Why, precisely, around her hotel room?)

"Maybe it's a birthmark," said Ingeborg.

"Maybe. You see the strangest things," said Hanna. "Charly met a woman in Italy who was born without hands."

"Really?"

"I swear. Ask him. He slept with her."

Hanna and Ingeborg laughed. Sometimes I don't understand how Ingeborg can find this kind of talk funny.

"Maybe it was a birth defect."

I don't know whether Ingeborg was talking about the woman without hands or the rental guy. Either way I tried to convince her that she was wrong. No one is born like that, with such ravaged skin. At the same time, it was clear that the burns weren't recent. They probably dated back five years, or even more to judge by the attitude of the poor guy (I wasn't looking at him), who had clearly grown used to attracting the same interest and stares as monsters and the mutilated, glances of involuntary revulsion, of pity at a great misfortune. To lose an arm or a leg is to lose a part of oneself, but to be burned like that is to be transformed, to become someone else.

When Charly woke up at last, Hanna told him she thought the rental guy was good-looking. Great biceps! Charly laughed and we all went swimming.

After lunch that afternoon I set up the game. Ingeborg, Hanna, and Charly headed to the old part of town to go shopping. During lunch, Frau Else came over to our table to ask whether we were enjoying ourselves. She gave Ingeborg a frank and open smile, although when she spoke to me I thought I detected a certain irony, as if she were saying: you see, I care about your well-being, I haven't forgotten you. Ingeborg thought she was a pretty woman and wondered how old she was. I said I didn't know.

How old must Frau Else be? I remember my parents said that she had married the Spaniard—whom incidentally I still haven't seen—when she was very young. The last summer that we were here she must have been about twenty-five, around the same age as Hanna, Charly, and me. Now she's probably thirty-five.

After lunch the hotel lapses into a strange lethargy. Those who aren't going to the beach or on an outing fall asleep, overcome by the heat. The staff, except for those stoically tending bar, vanish and aren't seen on the hotel grounds until past six. A sticky silence reigns on every floor, interrupted from time to time by the low voices of children and the hum of the elevator. At times one has the impression that a group of children has gotten lost, but that's not the case; it's just that their parents can't bring themselves to speak.

If it weren't for the heat, barely mitigated by the air-conditioning, this would be the best time of day to work. There is natural light, the restlessness of morning has worn off, and there are still many hours ahead. Conrad—my dear Conrad—prefers to work at night, which explains the frequent circles under his eyes and his sometimes alarming pallor, which makes us wonder whether he's sick when he's simply sleep deprived. He claims to be unable to work, unable to think, unable to sleep, and yet it's he who has bestowed upon us many of the best variants for any number of campaigns, as well as countless analytical, historical, and methodological studies, and even simple introductions and reviews of new games. Without him, Stuttgart's gaming scene would be different—smaller and with a lower level of play. In some sense he has been our protector (mine, Alfred's, Franz's), recommending books that we never would have read otherwise and passionately addressing us on the most disparate subjects. What holds him back is his lack of ambition. Ever since I've known him—and for a long time before that, as far as I can tell—Conrad has worked at a small-time construction company, in one of the lowest-ranking jobs, beneath nearly all the office staff and construction workers, performing tasks that used to be handled by office boys and messengers-without-motorbikes, the latter the title he likes to claim for himself. He makes enough to pay for his room, he eats at a cheap restaurant where he's practically one of the family, and every once in a while he buys some clothes. The rest of his money goes to pay for games, subscriptions to European and American magazines, club dues, some books (only a few, because he usually borrows from the library, saving up his money for more games), and donations to the city's fanzines, for virtually all of which he writes. It goes without saying that many of these fanzines would collapse without Conrad's generosity, and in this too one can see his lack of ambition: the best that some of them deserve is to vanish without a trace, putrid little ditto sheets spawned by adolescents more interested in role-playing games or even computer games than the rigors of the hexagonal board. But that doesn't matter to Conrad and he supports them. Many of his best articles, including his piece on the Ukrainian Gambit—which Conrad calls General Marcks's Dream—were not only published by such a magazine but in fact written expressly for it.

Curiously, it was Conrad who encouraged me to write for publications with a broader circulation and who persuaded me to go semipro. It's to him that I owe my first contacts with *Front Line*, *Jeux de Simulation*, *Stockade*, *Casus Belli*, *The General*, etc. According-ing to Conrad—and we spent an afternoon working this out—if I write regularly for ten magazines, some of them monthly, most bi-monthly or trimonthly, I could give up my job and still get by while devoting myself entirely to writing. When I asked why he didn't try it, since his job was worse than mine and he could write as well as I could, or better, he answered that he was so shy that it was painful for him, if not impossible, to establish business relation-ships with people he didn't know, and that the work required a certain command of English, a language that Conrad could only just barely decipher.

On that memorable day we set the goals to realize our dreams, and we got straight to work. Our friendship was cemented.

Then came the Stuttgart tournament, preceding by a few months the Interzonal (essentially the national championship), to be held in Cologne. We both entered, promising half in earnest and half in jest that if fate pitted us against each other, we would be ruthless despite our steadfast friendship. Around that time Conrad had just published his Ukrainian Gambit in the fanzine *Tötenkopf.*

At first the matches went well. We both made it through the first round without too much trouble. In the second round, Conrad was slated to play Mathias Müller, Stuttgart's boy wonder, eighteen years old, editor of the fanzine *Forced Marches* and one of the fastest players we knew. The match was tough, one of the hardest fought of the tournament, and in the end Conrad was defeated. But this in no way discouraged him: with the enthusiasm of a scientist who after a resounding failure is at last able to see things clearly, he explained to me the initial flaws of the Ukrainian Gambit and its hidden virtues, how to use armored and mountain corps from the start, and where one could or couldn't apply the Schwerpunkt, etc. In short, he became my adviser.

I faced Mathias Müller in the semifinals and eliminated him. In the finals, I was pitted against Franz Grabowski, of the Model Kit Club, a good friend of Conrad's and mine. That was how I won the right to represent Stuttgart. Then I went on to Cologne, where I competed against players of the caliber of Paul Huchel or Heimito Gerhardt, the latter of whom, at sixty-five, is the oldest of Germany's gamers, a real role model for the sport. Conrad, who came with me, amused himself by giving nicknames to everyone gathered in Cologne, but when it came to Heimito Gerhardt he was at a loss, no longer so clever or boisterous. When he talked about him he called him the Old Man or Mr. Gerhardt; in front of Heimito he scarcely opened his mouth. Clearly he was afraid of saying something stupid.

One day I asked him why he had such respect for Heimito. He answered that Heimito was a man of steel. That's all he said. Rusty steel, he added with a smile, but steel even so. I thought he was referring to Heimito's military past, and said so. No, said Conrad, I'm talking about the courage it takes for him to play. Nowadays, old men usually spend their time in front of the television or going for strolls with their wives. Heimito, however, was brave enough to walk into a room full of kids, brave enough to sit at a table in front of a complicated game, and brave enough to ignore the mocking looks that many of those kids gave him. Old men with that kind of character, with that kind of purity, according to Conrad, were a uniquely German phenomenon. And their numbers were dwindling. Maybe. And maybe not. In any case, as I later saw for myself, Heimito was an excellent player. We faced each other just before the championship finals, in an especially brutal round of a poorly calibrated game in which I was assigned the weaker force. It was *Fortress Europa* and I was playing the Wehrmacht. To the surprise of nearly everyone at the table, I won.

After the match, Heimito invited a few people back to his house. His wife served sandwiches and beer, and the party, which lasted late into the night, was a delight, full of colorful tales. Heimito had served in the 352nd Infantry Division, 915th Regiment, 2nd Battalion, but according to him, his general was no match for me in maneuvering the troops—or, in my case, the counters— under his command. Though flattered, I felt obliged to point out that it was the way I had positioned my mobile divisions that had decided the match. We toasted General Marcks and General Eberbach and the Fifth Panzer Army. As the evening was drawing to a close, Heimito swore that I would be the next champion of Germany. I think that was when the Cologne group started to hate me. As for me, I felt happy, mostly because I knew that I had made a friend.

And I did win the championship. The semifinals and the final were fought with the tournament version of *Blitzkrieg*, a fairly well-calibrated game in which the map as well as the opposing powers (Great Blue and Big Red) are imaginary, which, if both players are good, makes for very long games that tend toward stalemate. Not so this time. I dispatched Paul Huchel in six hours, and in the last game, timed by Conrad, it was only three and a half hours before my opponent claimed second place and gracefully conceded.

We spent one more day in Cologne; the magazine people suggested that I write an article, and Conrad spent the time wandering around taking pictures of streets and churches. I hadn't met Ingeborg yet and already life was beautiful, or so I thought, unaware that true beauty had yet to manifest itself. But back then I saw beauty all around me. The federation of war games players might be the smallest sports federation in Germany, but I was the champion and no one could claim otherwise. The sun shone for me alone.

One more thing happened that last day in Cologne that would later have important consequences. Heimito Gerhardt, a fan of gaming by mail, presented Conrad and me with our own play-by-mail kits as he accompanied us to the bus station. It so happened that Heimito corresponded with Rex Douglas (one of Conrad's idols), the great American gamer and star writer for one of the most prestigious of the specialized journals, *The General*. After confessing that he had never been able to beat Douglas (in six years they had played three long-distance matches), Heimito suggested that I write to Rex and get a game started with him. I have to confess that at first the idea held little interest. If I had to play by mail, I'd rather do it with people like Heimito or other members of my circle; nevertheless, before the bus reached Stuttgart, Conrad had convinced me of the importance of writing to Rex Douglas and challenging him to a game.

Ingeborg is asleep now. Before she fell asleep, she asked me not to get out of bed, to hold her in my arms all night. I asked whether she was scared. It came out naturally, unthinkingly. I just said: Are you scared? And she answered yes. Why? Of what? She didn't know. I'm right beside you, I said, there's no need to be scared.

Then she fell asleep and I got up. All the lights in the room were off except for the lamp that I'd placed on the table, next to the game. This afternoon I hardly worked. In town, Ingeborg bought a necklace of yellowish stones that they call *filipino*, which the kids here wear on the beach and at the clubs. We had dinner with Hanna and Charly at a Chinese restaurant in the tourist district. When Charly started to get drunk, we left. Really, a pointless evening. The restaurant, of course, was jam-packed and it was hot; the waiter was sweating; the food was good but nothing out of this world; the conversation centered on Hanna's and Charly's favorite subjects, in other words love and sex, respectively. Hanna is a woman made for love, as she puts it, although when she talks about love one gets the strange feeling that she's talking about security, or even specific brands of cars and appliances. Charly, meanwhile, talked about legs, asses, breasts, pubic hair, necks, navels, sphincters, etc., to the great delight of Hanna and Ingeborg, who constantly burst out laughing. Frankly, I can't see what they find so funny. Maybe it's nervous laughter. As for me, I can say that I ate in silence, with my mind elsewhere.

When we got back to the hotel we spotted Frau Else. She was in the dining room, at the end that becomes a dance floor at night, next to the stage, talking to two men dressed in white. Ingeborg felt slightly unwell, maybe it was the Chinese food, so we ordered a chamomile tea at the bar. That was when we saw Frau Else. She was gesticulating like a Spaniard and shaking her head. The men in white stood as still as statues. It's the musicians, said Ingeborg, she's scolding them. I didn't care who they were, although I knew they weren't the musicians, whom I'd happened to see the night before, and who were younger. When we left, Frau Else was still there: a perfect figure in a green skirt and black blouse. The men in white, impassive, had only bowed their heads.

AUGUST 23

A relatively uneventful day. In the morning, after breakfast, Ingeborg left for the beach and I went up to the room ready to start work in earnest. A little while later, it was so hot that I put on my bathing suit and went out onto the balcony, where there were a couple of comfortable lounge chairs. Though it was early, the beach was already crowded. When I came back inside I found the bed freshly made, and sounds from the bathroom informed me that the maid was still here. It was the same girl from whom I'd requested the table. This time I didn't think she looked so young. Her face shone with exhaustion, and her sleepy eyes were like those of an animal unaccustomed to the light of day. Evidently she didn't expect to see me. For a moment she seemed about to run away. Before she did I asked what her name was. She said it was Clarita and she smiled in a way that was disturbing, to say the least. I think it was the first time I'd seen anyone smile like that.

Perhaps too brusquely, I ordered her to wait, then I found a thousand-peseta note and put it in her hand. The poor girl gazed at me, perplexed, not knowing whether she should accept the money or what in the world I was giving it to her for. It's a tip, I said. Then came the most astonishing part: first she bit her lower lip, like a nervous schoolgirl, and then she gave a little curtsy, surely copied from some Three Musketeers movie. I didn't know what to do, how to interpret her gesture; I thanked her and said she could go, though in German, not in Spanish, which I'd been speaking before. The girl obeyed immediately. She left as silently as she'd come.

The rest of the morning I spent writing in what Conrad calls my Campaign Notebook, outlining a draft of my variant.

At noon I joined Ingeborg on the beach. I was, I must admit, in a state of exaltation after having spent a productive morning with the game board, and I did something I don't usually do: I gave a detailed account of my opening strategy, until Ingeborg interrupted me, saying that people were listening.

I contended that this was only to be expected, since thousands of people were crowded on the beach, nearly shoulder to shoulder.

Later I realized that Ingeborg was *ashamed* of me, of the words coming out of my mouth (infantry corps, armored corps, air combat factors, naval combat factors, preemptive strikes on Norway, the possibility of launching an offense against the Soviet Union in the winter of '39, the possibility of obliterating France in the spring of '40), and it was as if an abyss opened up at my feet.

We ate at the hotel. After dessert, Ingeborg suggested a boat ride. At the reception desk they had given her the schedules of the little boats that make the trip between our beach and two neighboring towns. I said I couldn't come, claiming work as my excuse. When I told her that I planned to sketch out the first two turns that afternoon, she gave me the same look that I had already witnessed on the beach.

With true horror I realize that something is beginning to come between us.

A boring afternoon otherwise. At the hotel there are hardly any more pale-skinned guests to be seen. All of them, even the ones who have been here just a few days, boast perfect tans, the fruit of many hours spent on the beach and of the lotions and creams that our technology produces in abundance. In fact, the only guest who's kept his natural color is me. Not coincidentally, I'm also the one who spends the most time at the hotel. Me and an old lady who hardly ever ventures off the terrace. This fact seems to arouse the curiousity of the staff, who have begun to watch me with mounting interest, though from a prudent distance, and with something that at the risk of exaggeration I'll call fear. Word of the table incident must have spread at lightning speed. The difference between the old lady and me is that she sits placidly on the terrace, watching the sky and the beach, and I'm constantly emerging like a sleepwalker from my room to head to the beach to see Ingeborg or have a beer at the hotel bar.

It's odd: sometimes I'm convinced that the old lady was here back in the days when I used to come to the Del Mar with my parents. But ten years is a long time, at least in this instance, and her face doesn't ring a bell. Maybe if I went up to her and asked whether she remembered me . . .

But what are the odds? In any case I don't know whether I could bring myself to talk to her. There's something about her that repels me. And yet, at first glance she's an ordinary old lady: more thin than fat, very wrinkled, dressed all in white, wearing sunglasses and a little straw hat. This afternoon, after Ingeborg left, I watched her from the balcony. She always claims the same spot on the terrace, in a corner near the sidewalk. There, half hidden under an enormous white umbrella, she whiles away the time watching the few cars that pass by along the Paseo Marítimo, like a jointed doll, content. And, strangely, essential to my own happiness: when I can no longer stand the stuffy air of the room I come out and there she is, a kind of font of energy that boosts my spirits so I'm able to sit back down at the table and go on working.

And what if she, in turn, sees me every time I come out onto the balcony? What must she think of me? Who must she think I am? She never tilts her head up, but with those sunglasses it's hard to say what she's watching. She might have glimpsed my shadow on the tile floor of the terrace. There aren't many people at the hotel and surely she would consider it unseemly for a young man to keep appearing and disappearing. The last time I came out she was writing a postcard. Might she have mentioned me in it? I don't know. But if she did, how did she describe me? And from what perspective? As a pale young man with a smooth brow? Or a nervous young man, clearly in love? Or maybe an ordinary young man with a skin condition?

I don't know. What I do know is that I'm getting off the subject, losing myself in pointless speculation that only upsets me. I don't understand how my dear friend Conrad could ever say that I write like Karl Bröger. If only.

Thanks to Conrad I was introduced to the literary group Workers of Nyland House. It was he who put Karl Bröger's *Soldaten der Erde* in my hands, and who pushed me, after I had read it, to embark on an ever more dizzying and arduous search through the libraries of Stuttgart for Bröger's *Bunker 17*, Heinrich Lersch's *Hammerschläge*, Max Barthel's *Das vergitterte Land*, Gerrit Engelke's *Rhythmus des neuen Europa*, Lersch's *Mensch im Eisen*, etc.

Conrad knows our national literature. One night in his room he reeled off the names of two hundred German writers. I asked if he'd read them all. He said yes. He especially loved Goethe, and of the moderns, Ernst Jünger. There were two books by Jünger that he was always rereading: *Der Kampf als inneres Erlebnis* and *Feuer und Blut*. And yet he didn't turn his nose up at more obscure writers; hence his fervent regard—which we would soon share—for the Nyland Circle.

How many nights after that did I go to bed late, busy not just deciphering the tricky rules of new games but immersed in the joys and miseries, the heights and depths, of German literature!

Of course, I'm talking about the literature written in blood, not Florian Linden novels, which, according to Ingeborg, just keep getting more far-fetched. On the same subject, I feel it's appropriate to air a grievance here: the few times that I've talked in public to Ingeborg about my work, going into some detail about the progress of a game, she's gotten angry or embarrassed, and yet she's always telling me (during breakfast, at the club, in the car, in bed, during dinner, and even over the phone) about the riddles that Florian Linden has to solve. And I haven't gotten angry at her or been embarrassed by what she has to say. On the contrary, I've tried to take a broad and objective view (in vain), and then I've suggested possible logical solutions to the fairy-tale detective puzzles.

A month ago, not to put too fine a point on it, I dreamed about Florian Linden. That was the limit. I remember it vividly: I was in bed, because I was very cold, and Ingeborg was saying to me: "The room is hermetically sealed." Then, from the hallway, we heard the voice of Florian Linden, who warned us of the presence in the room of a poisonous spider, a spider that could bite us and then vanish, even though the room was "hermetically sealed." Ingeborg started to cry and I held her tight. After a while she said: "It's impossible, how did Florian do it this time?" I got up and looked around, going through drawers in search of the spider, but I couldn't find anything; of course there were many places where it could hide. Ingeborg shouted, Florian, Florian, Florian, what should we do? but no one answered. I think we both knew we were on our own.

That was all. In fact, it was a nightmare, not a dream. If it meant anything, I can't say what. I don't usually have nightmares. During my adolescence, I did, plenty of them, and all different, but nothing that would have given my parents or the school psychologist cause to worry. Really, I've always been a well-balanced person.

It would be interesting to remember the dreams I had here, at the Del Mar, more than ten years ago. I probably dreamed about girls and punishment, the way all boys that age do. A few times my brother described a dream to me. I don't know whether we were alone or whether our parents were there too. I never did anything like that. When Ingeborg was little she often woke up crying and needed to be consoled. In other words, she woke up afraid, and with a terrible sense of loneliness. That's never happened to me, or it's happened so few times that I've forgotten.

For a few years now I've dreamed about games. I go to bed, close my eyes, and a board lights up full of incomprehensible counters, and thus, little by little, I lull myself to sleep. But my real dreams must be different because I don't remember them.

I've dreamed only a few times about Ingeborg, though she's the central figure in one of my most vivid dreams. It's a dream that doesn't take long to tell, and this may be its greatest virtue. She's sitting on a stone bench brushing her hair with a glass hairbrush; her hair, of the purest gold, falls to her waist. It's getting dark. In the background, still very far away, is a dust cloud. Suddenly I realize that next to her is a huge wooden dog—and I wake up. I think I dreamed this just after we met. When I described it to her she said that the dust cloud meant the dawning of love. I told her I'd had the same thought. We both were happy. All of this happened at a club in Stuttgart, the Detroit, and it's possible that I still remember that dream because I told it to her and she understood it.

Sometimes Ingeborg calls me late at night. She confesses that this is one of the reasons she loves me. Some of her ex-boyfriends couldn't handle the phone calls. A guy called Erich broke up with her after she woke him up at three in the morning. A week later he wanted to get back together, but Ingeborg said no. None of them understood that she needed someone to talk to after she woke up from a nightmare, especially if she was alone and the nightmare was particularly horrible. In these cases I'm the ideal person: I'm a light sleeper; in a second I can talk as if the call were at five in the afternoon (an unlikely circumstance, since I'm still at work then); I don't mind getting calls at night; finally, when the phone rings sometimes I'm not even asleep.

It goes without saying that her calls fill me with happiness. A serene happiness that doesn't keep me from falling back to sleep as quickly as I woke up. And with Ingeborg's words of farewell echoing in my ears: "Sweet dreams, dear Udo."

Dear Ingeborg. I've never loved anyone so much. Why, then, these glances of mutual distrust? Why can't we just love each other as children do, accepting each other fully?

When she gets back I'll tell her that I love her, that I've missed her, ask her to forgive me.

This is the first time that we've traveled together, gone away together, and naturally it's hard for us to mold ourselves to each other. I should avoid talking about games, especially war games, and try to be more attentive. If I have time, as soon as I'm done writing this, I'll go down to the hotel souvenir shop and buy her something, a little thing that will make her smile and forgive me. I can't stand to think I might lose her. I can't stand to think I might hurt her.

I bought a silver necklace inlaid with ebony. Four thousand pesetas. I hope she likes it. I also picked up a tiny clay figurine of a peasant in a red hat, kneeling, in the act of defecating; according to the salesgirl it's typical of the region, or something. I'm sure Inge-borg will think it's funny.

At the reception desk I spotted Frau Else. I approached cau-tiously, and before I said hello I caught a glimpse over her shoulder of an accounting book full of zeros. Something must be bothering her because when she realized I was there she seemed annoyed. I tried to show her the necklace but she wouldn't let me. Leaning on the reception desk, her hair illuminated by the late afternoon sun coming in through the big window in the hall, she asked about Ingeborg and "your friends." I lied, saying I had no idea what friends she was talking about. That young German couple, said Frau Else. I answered that they were summer acquaintances, not friends, and they're guests of the competition, I added. Frau Else didn't seem to appreciate my irony. Since it was clear that she didn't plan to con-tinue the conversation and I didn't want to go up to my room yet, I quickly pulled out the clay figurine and showed it to her. Frau Else smiled and said:

"You're a child, Udo."

I don't know why, but that simple sentence, spoken in Frau Else's melodious voice, was enough to make me blush. Then she made it clear that she was busy and I should leave her alone. Before I left I asked her what time it usually got dark. At ten, said Frau Else.

From the balcony I can see the little boats that ply the tourist route; they leave every hour from the old fishing port, head east, then turn north and vanish behind a big outcropping that they call the Punta de la Virgen. It's nine o'clock and only now is the night be-ginning to creep in, slow and bright.

The beach is almost empty. Only children and dogs cross the golden sand. Singly first, and then in a pack, the dogs race toward the pine forest and the campgrounds, then they return and little by little the pack breaks apart. The children play in one spot. In the distance, near the old town and the cliffs, a little white boat ap-pears. Ingeborg is on board, I'm sure. But the boat hardly seems to move. On the beach, between the Del Mar and the Costa Brava, the pedal boat guy begins to pull the boats up away from the shore.

Although it must be heavy work, no one helps him. But seeing the ease with which he drags the huge things, leaving deep tracks in the sand, it's clear that he can handle it himself. From here no one would guess that most of his body is horribly burned. He's wearing only a pair of shorts and the wind tosses his too-long hair. He's a character, all right. And I don't say that because of the burns but because of his singular way of arranging the pedal boats. What I had already discovered the night that Charly ran off down the beach I see again, but this time I watch the operation from the beginning, and, as I imagined, it's slow, complicated, serving no practical purpose, absurd. The pedal boats face in different directions, assembled not in a traditional row or double row but in a circle, or rather a blunt-pointed star. An arduous task, as evidenced by the fact that by the time he's half finished, all the other pedal boat guys are done. And yet he doesn't seem to care. He must like working at this time of day, in the cool evening breeze, the beach empty except for a few children playing in the sand far from the pedal boats. Well, if I were a kid I don't think I'd get close either.

It's strange: for a second it looked to me as if he was building a fortress with the pedal boats. A fortress like the ones that children build, in fact. The difference is that the poor brute isn't a child. So why build a fortress? It's obvious, I think: to have a place to spend the night.

Ingeborg's little boat has docked. She must be heading for the hotel now. I imagine her smooth skin, her cool, sweet-smelling hair, her confident steps crossing the old town. Soon it will be completely dark.

The rental guy still hasn't finished building his star. I wonder why no one has complained; like a tumbledown shack, the pedal boats spoil the charm of the beach. Though I suppose it isn't the poor guy's fault, and maybe the unpleasant effect, the strong resemblance to a hut or den, is clear only from up here. From the Paseo Marítimo does no one notice what a mess is being made of the beach?

I've closed the door to the balcony. Where is Ingeborg?

I have so much to write. I met the Burn Victim. I'll try to sum up what's happened in the last few hours.

Ingeborg was radiant and happy when she got home last night. The excursion was a success and nothing needed to be said in order for us to proceed to a reconciliation that was all the lovelier for being completely natural. We had dinner at the hotel and then we met Hanna and Charly at a bar on the Paseo Marítimo called the Andalusia Lodge. Deep down I would rather have spent the rest of the night alone with Ingeborg, but I couldn't refuse to go out at the risk of disturbing our newfound peace.

Charly was excited and on edge, and it wasn't long before I learned why: that night the soccer match between the German and Spanish selections was on TV and he wanted the four of us to watch it at the bar, along with the many Spaniards who were waiting for the match to begin. When I pointed out that we would be more comfortable at the hotel, he argued that it wasn't the same. The audience at the hotel would almost certainly be German, whereas at the bar we would be surrounded by "enemies," which made the match twice as much fun. Surprisingly Hanna and Ingeborg took his side.

Although I disagreed, I didn't insist, and soon afterward we gave up our seats on the terrace and went inside to sit near the TV.

That was how we met the Wolf and the Lamb.

I won't describe the inside of the Andalusia Lodge; let me just say that it was big, it stank, and a single glance was enough to confirm my fears: we were the only foreigners.

The audience, scattered in a rough half circle in front of the television, was more or less all young men with the look of laborers who had just finished work for the day and who hadn't yet had time to shower. In winter it would probably be an ordinary scene; in summer it was unsettling.

To heighten the difference between them and us, the patrons all seemed to be old friends and they showed it by slapping each other on the back, yelling back and forth, making jokes that were increasingly off-color. The noise was deafening. The tables were overflowing with beer bottles. One group was playing a loud game of foosball, and the sound of clanging metal rose above the general din like the rifle shots of a sharpshooter in the middle of a battle waged with swords and knives. It was clear that our presence had raised expectations that had little or nothing to do with the match. The glances, some more discreet than others, converged on Ingeborg and Hanna, who, in contrast to those around them, looked like two storybook princesses, Ingeborg especially.

Charly was in heaven. This was clearly his kind of place. He liked the shouting, the vulgar jokes, the air filled with smoke and nauseating smells; and if he could watch our selection play, all the better. But nothing is perfect. Just as we were being served sangria for four, we discovered that the team was East German. Charly took it hard, and from that moment on his mood grew unpredictable. To begin with, he wanted to leave right away. Later I would find out how exaggerated and absurd his fears really were. Among them was the following: that the Spaniards would mistake us for East Germans.

In the end we decided to leave as soon as we were done with the sangria. Naturally, we paid no attention to the match, busy as we were drinking and laughing. It was at this point that the Wolf and the Lamb sat down at our table.

How it happened, I can't say. With no explanation, they simply sat down with us and started to talk. They knew a few words of English, insufficient by any measure, though they made up for any language deficiencies with their great skills as mimes. At first the conversation covered all the usual topics (work, the weather, wages, etc.) and I acted as interpreter. They were, I gathered, amateur local tour guides, but that was surely a joke. Then, as the night wore on and everyone felt more at ease, my expertise was required only at difficult moments. Alcohol works miracles, it's true.

We all left the Andalusia Lodge in Charly's car, heading for a club on the edge of town, near the Barcelona highway. The prices were quite a bit lower than in the tourist zone, the clubgoers were almost all people like our new friends, and the atmosphere was festive, lending itself to camaraderie, though with a hint of something dark and murky, a quality particular to Spain that, paradoxically, inspires no misgivings. As always, Charly was quick to get drunk. How, I don't know, but at some point during the night we learned that the East German selection had lost two to zero. I remember it as something strange, because I have no interest in soccer and yet I experienced the announcement of the results as a turning point, as if from that moment on all the clamor of the club might turn into something else entirely, a horror show.

We left at four in the morning. One of the Spaniards was driving because Charly, in the backseat, puked the whole way, his head out the window. Frankly, he was in terrible shape. When we got to the hotel he took me aside and started to cry. Ingeborg, Hanna, and the two Spaniards watched curiously, though I motioned for them to go away. Between hiccups, Charly confessed that he was afraid of dying; it was almost impossible to understand what he was saying, though it was clear that his fears were unjustified. Then, without transition, he was laughing and boxing with the Lamb. The Lamb, who was quite a bit shorter and thinner, just dodged him, but Charly was too drunk and he lost his balance or fell on purpose. As we were picking him up one of the Spaniards suggested that we get coffee at the Andalusia Lodge.

The terrace of the bar, seen from the Paseo Marítimo, had the aura of a den of thieves, the hazy air of a bar asleep in the morning damp and fog. The Wolf explained that although it looked closed, the owner was usually inside watching movies on his new video player until dawn. We decided to give it a try. After a moment a man with a flushed face and a week's growth of beard opened the door.

It was the Wolf himself who made our coffee. At the tables, with their backs to us, were just two people watching TV, the owner and another man, sitting separately. It took me a moment to recognize the other man. I might have been a little drunk myself. Anyway, I took my coffee and sat down at his table. I had just enough time to exchange a few commonplaces (suddenly I felt awkward and nervous) before the others joined us. The Wolf and the Lamb knew him, of course. They introduced us formally.

"Ingeborg, Hanna, Charly, and Udo here, friends from Germany."

"And this is our mate El Quemado."

I translated for Hanna. The Burn Victim.

"How can they call him El Quemado?" she asked.

"Because that's what he is. And anyway, that's not the only thing they call him. You can call him Muscles; either name suits him."

"I think it's very bad manners," said Ingeborg.

Charly, who was slurring his words, said:

"Or an excess of honesty. They simply face the truth head-on. That's how it was in wartime, soldiers called things by their names, without frills, and it wasn't disrespect, or bad manners, though, of course—"

"It's horrible," Ingeborg interrupted, giving me a disgusted look.

The Wolf and the Lamb hardly noticed our exchange, busy as they were explaining to Hanna that a glass of cognac could hardly make Charly any drunker. Hanna, sitting between them, seemed extremely animated one moment and despairing the next, ready to go running out, though I don't think she really felt much like going back to the hotel. At least not with Charly, who had reached the point at which all he could do was mumble incoherently. Only El

Quemado was sober, and he looked at us as if he understood German. Ingeborg noticed it too and got nervous, which is typical. She can't stand it when people's feelings are hurt. But really, how could he have been hurt by what we said?

Later I asked him whether he spoke German and he said no.

At seven in the morning, with the sun already high in the sky, we got in bed. The room was cold and we made love. Then we fell asleep with the windows open and the curtains drawn. But first . . . first we had to haul Charly to the Costa Brava. He was determined to sing songs that the Wolf and the Lamb whispered in his ear (the two of them were laughing like maniacs and clapping); later, on the way to the hotel, he insisted on swimming for a while. Hanna and I were against it, but the Spaniards backed him up and all three of them went in the water. Poor Hanna hesitated briefly between going in herself or waiting on the shore with us; finally she decided on the latter course.

We hadn't noticed when El Quemado left the bar, but now we spotted him walking on the beach. He stopped about fifty yards from us, and there he stayed, squatting, looking out to sea.

Hanna explained that she was afraid that something bad would happen to Charly. She was an excellent swimmer and therefore felt that it was her duty to go in with him, but—she said with a crooked smile—she didn't want to get undressed in front of our new friends.

The sea was as smooth as a rug. The three swimmers kept getting farther away. Soon we couldn't tell who was who; Charly's blond head and the dark heads of the Spaniards became indistinguishable.

"Charly is the one who's farthest out," said Hanna.

Two of the heads turned back toward the beach. The third kept heading out to sea.

"That's Charly," said Hanna.

We had to stop her from undressing and going in after him. Ingeborg looked at me as if I should volunteer, but she didn't say so. I'm not a strong swimmer, and he was already too far out for me to catch up. The returning swimmers were moving extremely slowly. One of them turned around every few strokes as if to see whether Charly was following. For an instant I thought about what Charly had said to me: that he was afraid of dying. It was ridiculous. Just then I looked over toward where El Quemado had been, and he was gone. To the left of us, halfway between the sea and the Paseo Marítimo, the pedal boats loomed, bathed in a faintly bluish light, and I realized that he was there now, inside his fortress, sleeping or perhaps watching us, and the very idea that he was hidden there was more exciting to me than the swimming display to which we'd been subjected by that idiot Charly.

At last the Wolf and the Lamb reached the shore, where they dropped, exhausted, one next to the other, unable to get up. Hanna, unconcerned by *their* nakedness, ran to them and began to fire questions at them in German. The Spaniards laughed and said they couldn't understand a thing. The Wolf tried to tackle her and then splashed water on her. Hanna gave a leap backward (an electric leap) and covered her face with her hands. I thought she would start to cry or hit them, but she didn't do anything. She came back over to us and sat on the sand, next to the little pile of clothes that Charly had left scattered and that she had gathered and carefully folded.

"Son of a bitch," she whispered.

Then, with a deep sigh, she got up and began to scan the horizon. Charly was nowhere to be seen. Ingeborg suggested that we call the police. I went over to the Spaniards and asked them how we could get in touch with the police or with some rescue team from the port.

"Not the police," said the Lamb.

"The kid's a joker. He'll be back, no sweat. He's just messing with us."

"But don't call the police," insisted the Lamb.

I informed Ingeborg and Hanna that we couldn't count on the Spaniards if we needed to ask for help, which probably wouldn't be necessary anyway. Really, Charly could show up at any moment.

The Spaniards dressed quickly and joined us. The color of the beach was shifting from blue to reddish and some early-bird tourists were jogging along the Paseo Marítimo. We were all standing except for Hanna, who'd dropped down again next to Charly's clothes and was squinting, as if the growing light hurt her eyes.

It was the Lamb who spotted him first. Cutting smoothly through the water with perfect, measured strokes, Charly came in to shore some hundred yards from where we stood. With shouts of jubilation, the Spaniards ran to welcome him, not caring that their trousers were getting wet. Meanwhile Hanna burst into tears, clutching Ingeborg, and said that she felt sick. Charly was almost sober when he emerged from the water. He kissed Hanna and Ingeborg and shook hands with the rest of us. There was something unreal about the scene.

We parted in front of the Costa Brava. As Ingeborg and I walked toward our hotel, I spied El Quemado as he came out from under the pedal boats and then began to disassemble them, getting ready for another workday.

It was after three when we woke up. We showered and had a light meal at the hotel restaurant. From the bar we watched the scene on the Paseo Marítimo through the tinted windows. It was like a post-card: old men perched on the wall along the sidewalk, half of them wearing little white hats, and old women with their skirts pulled up over their knees so the sun could lick at their thighs. That was all. We had a soda and went up to the room to put on our bathing suits. Charly and Hanna were in the usual spot near the pedal boats. That morning's incident was the subject of conversation for a while: Hanna said that when she was twelve her best friend had died of a heart attack while she was swimming; Charly, completely recovered now, told how he and some guy called Hans Krebs used to be the champions of the Oberhausen town pool. They had learned to swim in the river and they believed that anyone who learned to swim in rivers could never drown in the sea. In rivers, he said, you have to swim as hard as you can and keep your mouth closed, especially if the river is radioactive. He was glad he'd shown the Spaniards how far he could go. He said that at a certain point they'd begged him to swim back, or so he thought, at least. Anyway, even if that wasn't what they'd said, he could tell by the tone of their voices that they were scared. You weren't scared because you were drunk, said Hanna, kissing him. Charly smiled, showing two rows of big white teeth. No, he said, I wasn't scared because I know how to swim.

Inevitably we saw El Quemado. He was moving slowly and wore only cutoff jeans. Ingeborg and Hanna waved. He didn't come over.

"Since when are you friends with that guy?" asked Charly.

El Quemado waved back and headed toward the shore dragging a pedal boat. Hanna asked whether it was true that they called him El Quemado. I said it was. Charly said he hardly remembered him. Why didn't he come in the water with me? For the same reason that Udo didn't, said Ingeborg, because he isn't stupid. Charly shrugged. (I think he loves it when women scold him.) He's probably a better swimmer than you, said Hanna. I doubt it, said Charly, I'd bet anything he isn't. Hanna then observed that El Quemado had bigger muscles than either of us, and in fact than anyone on the beach just now. A bodybuilder? Ingeborg and Hanna started to laugh. Then Charly confessed that he didn't remember a thing about the night before. The trip back from the club, the vomiting, the tears—all had been erased from his memory. And yet he knew more about the Wolf and the Lamb than any of us. One of them worked in a supermarket next to the campground and the other waited tables at a café in the old town. Great guys.

At seven we left the beach and stopped for beers on the terrace of the Andalusia Lodge. The owner was behind the bar talking to a couple of locals, both tiny old men, almost dwarves. He greeted us with a nod. It was nice there. The breeze was soft and cool, and although the tables were full, the patrons hadn't quite yet devoted themselves entirely to making noise. Like us, they were people on their way back from the beach and they were worn-out from swimming and lying in the sun.

We separated without making plans for that night.

When we got back to the hotel, we took a shower and then Ingeborg decided to go lie on the balcony to write postcards and finish reading the Florian Linden novel. I spent a moment scanning my game and then went down to the restaurant to have a beer. After a while I came up for my notebook and I found Ingeborg asleep, wrapped in her black robe, the postcards clutched against her hip. I gave her a kiss and suggested that she get into bed, but she didn't want to. I think she had a bit of a fever. I decided to go back down to the bar. On the beach, El Quemado repeated his evening ritual. One by one the pedal boats were returned to their places and the hut began to take shape, to rise, if a hut can be said to rise. (A hut can't; but a fortress can.) Without thinking I raised a hand and waved. He didn't see me.

Frau Else was at the bar. She asked what I was writing. Nothing important, I said, just the first draft of an essay. Ah, you're a writer, she said. No, no, I said, my face flushing. To change the subject I asked about her husband, whom I hadn't had the pleasure of seeing.

"He's sick."

She said it with a gentle smile, her eyes on me and at the same time glancing around as if she didn't want to miss anything that was going on in the bar.

"I'm so sorry."

"It isn't anything serious."

I made some remark about summer illnesses, idiotic, I'm sure. Then I got up and asked if she would let me buy her a drink.

"No, thank you, I'm fine, and I've got work to do too. Always busy!"

But she made no move to leave.

"Has it been a long time since you were last in Germany?" I asked, to say something.

"No, my dear, I was there for a few weeks in January."

"And how did you find it?" As I said it I realized that it was a stupid thing to say and I blushed again.

"The same as always."

"Yes, of course," I murmured.

Frau Else looked at me in a friendly way for the first time and then she left. I watched a waiter stop her, and then a guest, and then a couple of old men, until she disappeared behind the stairs.

Our friendship with Charly and Hanna is beginning to be a burden. Yesterday, after I'd finished writing in my journal and when I thought I would spend a quiet evening alone with Ingeborg, they appeared. It was ten o'clock; Ingeborg had just woken up. I told her I'd rather stay at the hotel, but after talking on the phone with Hanna (Charly and Hanna were at the reception desk), she decided that we should go out. As she changed clothes, we argued. When we came downstairs I was astounded to see the Wolf and the Lamb. The Lamb, leaning on the counter, was whispering something in the receptionist's ear that made her dissolve in helpless laughter. I was extremely put off. I assumed it was the same girl who had tattled to Frau Else about the misunderstanding with the table, though considering the hour and the possibility that the receptionists worked in two shifts, it could have been someone else. In any case she was very young and silly: when she saw us she gave us a knowing smirk, as if we shared a secret. Everyone else applauded. It was the last straw.

We left town in Charly's car, with the Wolf sitting up front next to Hanna to show Charly the way. On the drive to the club, if a dump like that deserves the name, I saw huge pottery shops erected in rudimentary fashion alongside the highway. Actually, they were probably warehouses or wholesale showrooms. All night they were lit up by spotlights, and anyone who drove by got a view of endless junk, urns, pots of all sizes, and a few random pieces of statuary behind the fences. Coarse Greek imitations covered in dust. Fake Mediterranean crafts frozen in an in-between moment, neither day nor night. The yards were empty, save for the occasional guard dog.

Almost everything about the night was the same as the night before. The club had no name, though the Lamb said people called it the Crap Club. Like the other club, it was intended more for workers from the surrounding area than for tourists. The music and lighting were terrible; Charly drank and Hanna and Ingeborg danced with the Spaniards. Everything would have ended the same way if it hadn't been for an incident, the kind of thing that often happened at the club, according to the Wolf, who advised us to leave right away. I'll try to reconstruct the story. It starts with a guy who was pretending to dance between the tables and along the edge of the dance floor. Apparently he hadn't paid for his drinks and he was high. This last point, however, is pure supposition. The most distinctive thing about him, which I noticed long before the scuffle began, was a thick rod that he brandished in one hand, though later the Wolf said it was a cane made of pig's intestines, the blow of which left a scar for life. In any case, the bogus dancer's behavior was threatening, and soon he was approached by two waiters who didn't happen to be in uniform and who were indistinguishable from the rest of the clientele, though they were given away by their manner and faces: they were goons. Words were exchanged between them and the man with the rod, and the discussion grew more and more heated.

I could hear the man with the rod say:

"My rapier comes everywhere with me," referring in that peculiar way to his stick, in response to being forbidden to carry it in the club.

The waiter replied:

"I have something much *harder* than your rapier." Straightaway there came a deluge of curses that I didn't understand, and finally the waiter said: "Do you want to see it?"

The guy with the stick was silent; I'd venture to say that he grew suddenly pale.

Then the waiter raised his forearm, muscular and hairy as a gorilla's, and said:

"See? This is harder."

The guy with the stick laughed, not insolently but in relief, though I doubt the waiters registered the difference, and raised his cane, flexing it like a bow. He had a stupid laugh, the laugh of a drunk and a loser. At that moment, as if triggered by a spring, the waiter's arm shot out and grabbed the stick. It all happened very quickly. Immediately, turning red with the effort, he broke it in two. Applause came from one of the tables.

Just as swiftly, the guy with the stick hurled himself on the waiter, bent his arm behind his back before anyone could stop him, and, in the blink of an eye, broke it. Despite the music, which had continued to play during the whole altercation, I think I heard the sound of bone snapping.

People started to scream. First it was the howls of the waiter whose arm had just been broken, then the shouts of those flinging themselves into a brawl in which, at least from my table, it was impossible to tell who was on which side, and finally the general clamor of all those present, including the ones who didn't even know what was going on.

We decided to beat a retreat.

On the way back we passed two police cars. The Wolf wasn't with us. It had been impossible to find him in the crush on the way out, and the Lamb, who had followed us without protest, now felt bad about having left his friend behind and urged us to go back for him. On this point Charly was adamant: if he wanted to go back, he could hitchhike. We agreed to wait for the Wolf at the Andalusia Lodge.

The bar was still open when we got there. I mean open to everyone, the lights on outside, with a big crowd despite the late hour. The kitchen was closed, but at the Lamb's request the owner brought us a couple of chickens that we accompanied with a bottle of red wine; then, since we were still hungry, we polished off a platter of spicy sausage and cured ham and bread with tomato and olive oil. When the terrace was closed and we were the only ones left inside, along with the owner, who at that time of night devoted himself to his favorite pursuit, which was watching cowboy movies and having a leisurely dinner, the Wolf came in.

When he saw us he was furious, and surprisingly, his recriminations—"You left me," "You forgot me," "A person can't trust his own friends," etc.—were directed at Charly. The Lamb, who, frankly speaking, was his only real friend present, responded to his words by cowering in shame and mute submission. And Charly, even more surprisingly, nodded and said he was sorry, treating the whole thing as a joke but making it understood that he felt honored by the hurt that the Wolf was expressing so vehemently and in such poor taste. Charly was loving it, he really was! Maybe he saw it as an expression of true friendship! Absurd! I should clarify that the Wolf didn't say a thing to me, and that his treatment of the girls was the same as always, somewhere between gallant and crude.

I think I was ready to leave when El Quemado came in. He nodded at us and took a seat at the bar, with his back to us. I left the Wolf to finish explaining what had happened at the Crap Club, probably with further accounts of bloodletting and arrests, and I went to sit next to El Quemado. Half of his upper lip was one big scar, but after a while a person got used to it. I asked if he suffered from insomnia and he smiled. No, he wasn't an insomniac; he could do his work, which was enjoyable and not too taxing, on just a few hours of sleep. He wasn't much of a talker, though he was much less silent than I had imagined. His teeth were small, as if they'd been filed down, and they were in terrible shape, which in my ignorance I didn't know whether to attribute to the fire or simply to deficiencies in oral hygiene. I suppose that someone whose face is covered in burns doesn't worry too much about the state of his teeth.

He asked where I was from. He spoke in a deep, clear voice, certain of being understood. I answered that I was from Stuttgart and he nodded as if he knew the city, although I can't imagine that he'd ever been there. He was dressed the same as during the day, in shorts, T-shirt, and rope-soled shoes. He has a notable physique—broad chest and bulging biceps—though sitting at the bar (drinking tea!) he seemed thinner than me. Or shyer. Certainly, despite his limited wardrobe, it was evident that he took at least basic care of himself: his hair was clean and he didn't stink. This last point could be considered a minor feat, because living on the beach, the only bathroom to which he had access was the sea. (If one sharpened one's sense of smell, he smelled like salt water.) For a moment I imagined him, day after day or night after night, washing his clothes (those shorts, a few T-shirts) in the sea, scrubbing himself in the sea, doing his business in the sea or on the beach, the same beach where hundreds of tourists lay, among them Ingeborg . . . Overcome by a wave of disgust, I imagined reporting his shameful behavior to the police, but that would be out of character, of course. And yet, how to explain that a person with a paying job isn't capable of finding a decent place to sleep? Can all the rentals in town be out of his reach? Aren't there any cheap boardinghouses or campgrounds, if not on the seafront? Or by not paying rent does our friend El Quemado intend to save a few pesetas for summer's end?

There's something of the Noble Savage about him; but I can also see the Noble Savage in the Wolf and the Lamb, and they manage things differently. Maybe living rent-free means living alone, far from people and curious stares. If so, in a way I understand it. And then there are the benefits of life in the open air, although his life, as I imagine it, doesn't exactly qualify if "open air" is understood as "healthy living," since the latter is diametrically opposed to damp beach air and the sandwiches that I'm sure are his daily fare. How does El Quemado live? All I know is that during the day he's like a zombie dragging pedal boats from the shore to his small roped-off area and back again to the shore. That's all. Though he must take time to eat and he must meet with his boss at some point to hand over his earnings. Does this boss I've never seen know that El Quemado sleeps on the beach? Does the owner of the Andalusia Lodge know it? Are the Lamb and the Wolf in on the secret, or am I the only one who has discovered his refuge? I don't dare ask.

At night El Quemado does whatever he wants, or at least he tries to. But what does he do exactly besides sleep? He sits until late at the Andalusia Lodge, he goes for walks on the beach, maybe he has friends he talks to, he drinks tea, he buries himself under his great hulks . . . Yes, sometimes I see the fortress of pedal boats as a kind of mausoleum. As long as it's light out, the impression of a hut lingers; at night, by the light of the moon, a romantic soul might mistake it for a barbarian burial mound.

Nothing else worthy of mention happened the night of the 24th. We left the Andalusia Lodge relatively sober. El Quemado and the owner were still there, the former sitting across from his empty cup of tea and the latter watching another cowboy movie.

Today, as was to be expected, I saw him on the beach. Ingeborg and Hanna were lying out next to the pedal boats, and El Quemado, on the other side, was leaning against a plastic floater, gazing at the horizon where some of his boats were barely visible. At no point did he turn around to look at Ingeborg, who, I think it's fair to say, was a feast for the eyes. Both girls were wearing new orange thongs, a bright, happy color. But El Quemado avoided looking at them.

I wasn't at the beach. I stayed in the room going over my abandoned game, though every so often I went out on the balcony or looked out the window. Love, as everyone knows, is an exclusive passion, although in my case I hope to be able to reconcile my passion for Ingeborg with my dedication to gaming. According to the plans I had made in Stuttgart, by now I should have half of the strategic variant plotted out and written down, and at least a first draft of the lecture to be given in Paris. But I have yet to write a single word. If Conrad could see me I'm sure he'd have some scathing comment to make. But Conrad has to understand that on my very first vacation with Ingeborg, I can't ignore her and devote myself body and soul to the variant. Despite everything, I haven't given up hope of having it finished by the time we return to Germany.

In the afternoon something odd happened. I was sitting in the room when suddenly I heard the sound of a horn. I can't be one hundred percent certain, but then again, I know the difference between the sound of a horn and other sounds. The odd thing is that I was thinking (though in a vague way, I must admit) about Sepp Dietrich, who from time to time made mention of the horn call of peril. Anyway, I'm sure I didn't imagine it. Sepp claimed to have heard it twice, and both times the mysterious notes helped him to overcome tremendous physical exhaustion, first in Russia and then in Normandy. The horn, according to Sepp, who rose to the command of an army after starting out as a messenger boy and driver, is the warning cry of the ancestors, the call of the blood that alerts one to danger. As I say, I was sitting lost in thought when suddenly I seemed to hear it. I got up and went out on the balcony. Outside all that could be heard was the usual afternoon din; even the sound of the sea was drowned out. In the hallway, on the other hand, there reigned a pregnant silence. Did the horn sound in my head then? Did it sound because I was thinking about Sepp Dietrich or in order to warn me of a threat? If I look back on it, I was also thinking about Hausser and Bittrich and Meindl . . . Then did it sound for me? And if so, what threat did it mean to warn me of?

When I told Ingeborg about it, she suggested that I spend less time in the room. According to her we should sign up for some jogging sessions or exercise classes run by the hotel. Poor Ingeborg, she just doesn't get it. I promised I would talk to Frau Else. Ten years ago the hotel offered no classes of any kind. Ingeborg said that she would sign us up, that I didn't need to speak to Frau Else about something that could be taken care of with the receptionist. I said all right, she should do what she thought best.

Before I got in bed I did two things, namely:

1. Set up the armored corps for the lightning attack on France.
2. Went out on the balcony and searched for some light on the beach that might indicate the presence of El Quemado, but all was dark.

I'm following Ingeborg's instructions. Today I spent more time than usual at the beach. The result is that my shoulders are red from the sun and this afternoon I had to go buy a cream to take away the sting. Of course we were next to the pedal boats and since there was nothing else to do I spent the time talking to El Quemado. The day brought a few bits of news. The first is that yesterday Charly got outrageously drunk with the Wolf and the Lamb. Hanna, weepy, told Ingeborg that she didn't know what to do: leave him or not? She can't stop thinking about going back to Germany alone. She misses her son; she's fed up and tired. Her only consolation is her perfect tan. Ingeborg says that it all depends on whether she really loves Charly or not. Hanna doesn't know what to answer. The other news is that the manager of the Costa Brava has asked them to leave the hotel. It seems that last night Charly and the Spaniards tried to beat up the night watchman. Ingeborg, despite the signs I was making to her, suggested that they move to the Del Mar. Luckily Hanna is determined that the manager change his mind or at least return their deposit. I expect that everything will be resolved with a few explanations and apologies. In response to Ingeborg's question about where she was when all this took place, Hanna answers that she was in their room, sleeping. Charly didn't show up on the beach until noon, looking the worse for wear and dragging his board. Hanna, when she saw him, whispered in Ingeborg's ear:

"He's killing himself."

Charly's version is completely different. He couldn't care less about the manager and his threats. He says, with his eyes half closed and looking as sleepy as if he'd just stepped out of bed:

"We can move to the Wolf's house. Cheaper and more authentic. That way you'll get to know the real Spain." And he winks at me.

He's only half joking. The Wolf's mother rents rooms in the summer, with board or without, at modest prices. For a moment it seems that Hanna is about to cry. Ingeborg steps in and calms her down. In the same joking tone she asks Charly whether the Wolf and the Lamb aren't falling in love with him. But the question is serious. Charly laughs and says no. Then, recovered, Hanna says that she's the one the Wolf and the Lamb want to get into bed.

"The other night they kept touching me," she says, at once mortified and coquettish.

"Because you're pretty," explains Charly, unperturbed. "I'd try it too if I didn't already know you, wouldn't I?"

The conversation swings all of a sudden to places as far-flung as Oberhausen's Discotheque 33 and the Telephone Company. Hanna and Charly begin to wax sentimental and remember all of the places with romantic significance for them. But after a while, Hanna insists:

"You're killing yourself."

Charly puts an end to the reproaches by grabbing his board and heading into the water.

At first my conversation with El Quemado centered on topics like whether anyone had ever stolen a pedal boat from him, whether the work was hard, whether he didn't get bored spending so many hours on the beach under that merciless sun, whether he had time to eat, whether he could say who among the foreigners were his best customers, etc. His answers, invariably succinct, were as follows: twice someone had stolen a pedal boat, or rather, left it abandoned at the other end of the beach; the work wasn't hard; sometimes he got bored but not often; he ate sandwiches, as I suspected; he had no idea which country's natives rented the most pedal boats. I contented myself with his answers, and I endured the intervals of silence that followed. Clearly he wasn't used to conversation, and, as I noted by his evasive gaze, he was rather mistrustful. A few steps away, the bodies of Ingeborg and Hanna shone, soaking in the sun's rays. Then, suddenly, I said that I'd rather be back at the hotel. He glanced at me without curiosity and continued to watch the horizon, where his pedal boats were nearly indistinguishable from the pedal boats belonging to other stands. Far away I spotted a windsurfer who kept falling again and again. From the color of the sail I realized it wasn't Charly. I said that mountains were my thing, not the sea. I liked the sea, but I liked mountains better. El Quemado made no comment.

We were silent for a while again. The sun was scorching my shoulders but I didn't move or do anything to protect myself. In profile, El Quemado looked like a different person. I don't mean that he was less disfigured (actually, the side facing me was the more disfigured) but simply that he looked like someone else. More remote. Like a bust of pumice stone fringed with coarse, dark hairs.

I can't remember what made me confess that I wanted to be a writer. El Quemado turned around and, after hesitating, said that it was an interesting profession. I made him repeat what he'd said because at first I thought I'd misheard him.

"But not of novels or plays," I explained.

El Quemado's lips parted and he said something I couldn't hear.

"What?"

"Poet?"

Under his scars I seemed to glimpse a kind of monstrous smile. I thought the sun must be addling me.

"No, no, definitely not a poet."

I explained, now that I had paved the way for it, that I in no way scorned poetry; I could have recited from memory lines by Klopstock or Schiller. But to write poetry in this day and age, unless it was for the love object, was a bit pointless, didn't he agree?

"Or grotesque," said the poor wretch, nodding.

How can someone so deformed say that something is grotesque without taking it personally? Strange. In any case, my sense that El Quemado was secretly smiling grew stronger. Maybe it was his eyes that conveyed the hint of a smile. He hardly ever looked at me, but when he did I caught in his gaze a spark of jubilation and strength.

"Specialized writer," I said. "Creative essayist."

On the spot, I sketched in broad strokes a picture of the world of war games, with all its magazines, competitions, local clubs, etc. In Barcelona, I explained, there were a few associations in operation, for example, and although as far as I knew no federation existed, Spanish players were beginning to be quite active in the field of European competitions. In Paris I had met a few.

"It's a sport on the rise," I said.

El Quemado mulled over my words, then he got up to retrieve a pedal boat that was coming in to shore; with no sign of effort he pulled it back into the roped-off area.

"I did read something about people who play with little lead soldiers," he said. "It wasn't too long ago, I think, at the beginning of the summer . . ."

"Yes, it's essentially the same thing. Like rugby and American football. But I'm not very interested in lead soldiers, although they're all right . . . they look a little bit fussy." I laughed. "I prefer board games."

"What do you write about?"

"Anything. Give me any war or campaign and I'll tell you how it can be won or lost, the flaws of the game, where the designer got it right or wrong, the correct scale, the original order of battle . . ."

El Quemado watches the horizon. With his big toe he digs a little hole in the sand. Behind us Hanna has fallen asleep and Ingeborg is reading the last few pages of the Florian Linden novel; when our eyes meet she smiles and blows me a kiss.

For a moment I wonder whether El Quemado has a girlfriend. Or whether he's ever had one.

What girl could kiss that terrible mask? But there's someone for everyone, I know.

After a while:

"You must have lots of fun," he said.

I heard his voice as if it were coming from far away. The light bounced off the surface of the sea, making a kind of wall that grew until it touched the clouds, which—fat, heavy, the color of dirty milk—were drifting almost imperceptibly toward the cliffs to the north. Under the clouds a parachute came in toward the beach, pulled by a speedboat. I said I felt a little sick. It must be the work waiting for me, I said, I'm a wreck until I finish what I've started. I did my best to explain that being a specialized writer required a complicated and cumbersome setup. (This was the main argument that the players of computerized war games could make in their favor: the savings of space and time.) I confessed that for days a huge game had been spread out in my hotel room and that I should really be working on it.

"I promised to turn in an essay at the beginning of September, and here I am, lazing around."

El Quemado didn't say anything. I added that the essay was for an American magazine.

"It's an unheard-of variant. No one's ever come up with anything like it."

Maybe it was the sun that was making me ramble on. In my defense I should say that since I'd left Stuttgart I hadn't had the chance to talk to anyone about war games. My fellow gamers will know what I mean. For us it's fun to talk about games. But clearly I'd chosen the strangest conversation partner I could possibly have found.

El Quemado seemed to understand that I had to play in order to write.

"But that way you must always win," he said, showing his ruined teeth.

"Not at all. If you play yourself there's no way to cheat with strategies or maneuvers. All the cards are on the table. If my variant works, it's because it's mathematically guaranteed to work. As it happens, I've already tested it a few times, and both times I won, but it needs to be polished and that's why I play alone."

"You must write very slowly," he said.

"No," I said, laughing, "I write like lightning. I play slowly but I write fast. People say I'm high-strung but it isn't true; they say it because of the way I write. Without stopping!"

"I write fast too," murmured El Quemado.

"I guessed as much," I said.

My own words surprised me. Actually, I hadn't even imagined that El Quemado *could* write. But when he spoke, or maybe sooner, when I said that I wrote fast, I guessed that he must be a scribbler too. We stared at each other without saying anything for a few seconds. It was hard to look him in the face for too long, although little by little I was getting used to it. El Quemado's secret smile still lurked there, maybe mocking me and our newly discovered shared trait. I kept feeling sicker. I was sweating. I didn't understand how El Quemado could take so much sun. His craggy face, full of charred folds, sometimes glinted blue like cooking gas or took on a yellowish-black hue like something about to explode. And yet he could just sit there on the sand, with his hands on his knees and his eyes fixed on the sea, showing no signs of discomfort. In a departure from his usual behavior, which was so reserved, he asked whether I would help him bring in a pedal boat that had just arrived. Groggily, I nodded. The Italian couple on the boat couldn't steer to shore. We got in the water and pushed gently. From their seats, the Italians kidded around and pretended to fall in. They jumped out before we got to shore. I was happy to see them head away, skirting bodies and holding hands, toward the Paseo Marítimo. After we pulled the pedal boat in, El Quemado said that I should swim for a while.

"Why?"

"You'll fry your circuits in the sun," he said.

I laughed and asked whether he wanted to come in with me.

We swam for a while, intent only on getting past the first line of bathers. Then we turned around to face the beach: from that vantage point, next to El Quemado, the beach and the people crowded on it seemed different.

When we returned he advised me, in a strange voice, to rub myself down with coconut oil.

"Coconut oil and a dark room," he murmured.

With deliberate abruptness I woke Ingeborg and we left.

This afternoon I had a fever. I told Ingeborg. She didn't believe me. When I showed her my shoulders, she told me to put a wet towel over them or to take a cold shower. Hanna was waiting and she seemed to be in a hurry to be rid of me.

For a while I stared at the game with no energy for anything; the light hurt my eyes and the hum of the hotel was lulling me to sleep. With no little effort I managed to go out in search of a pharmacy. Under the terrible sun I wandered the old streets in the center of town. I don't remember seeing tourists. Actually, I don't remember seeing anyone. A couple of sleeping dogs; the girl who waited on me at the pharmacy; an old man sitting in the shadow of a doorway. Meanwhile, the Paseo Marítimo was so crowded that it was impossible to walk without elbowing and pushing. Near the port a little amusement park had been built and that's where everyone was, hypnotized. It was insanity. There were all kinds of tiny stalls that the human torrent threatened to crush at any moment. As best I could, I lost myself again in the streets of the old town and returned to the hotel the long way around.

I got undressed, closed the shutters, and smeared my body with salve. I was burning up.

Lying in bed, in the dark but with my eyes open, I tried to think about the events of the last few days before I fell asleep. Then I dreamed that I didn't have a fever anymore and I was with Ingeborg in this same room, in bed, each of us reading a book, but at the same time there was something very intimate about it. I mean, each of us felt close to the other even though we were absorbed in our respective books; each of us felt love for the other. Then someone *scratched* at the door and after a while we heard a voice on the other side saying: "It's Florian Linden, get out now, your life is in great danger." Immediately, Ingeborg let go of her book (the book dropped splayed on the rug) and fixed her eyes on the door. I hardly moved. Frankly, I was so comfortable there, my skin so cool, that I thought it wasn't worth being frightened. "Your life is in danger," repeated Florian Linden's voice, farther and farther away, as if from the end of the hallway. And in fact, just then we heard the sound of the elevator, the doors opening with a metallic click and then closing, carrying Florian Linden down to the ground floor. "He's gone to the beach or the amusement park," said Ingeborg, dressing quickly. "I have to find him. Wait here, I have to talk to him." I didn't object, of course. But left alone, I couldn't keep reading. "How can anyone be in danger in this room?" I asked aloud. "What's he scheming, that third-rate detective?" Getting more and more worked up, I went over to the window and looked out at the beach, expecting to see Ingeborg and Florian Linden. The sun was setting and only El Quemado was there, arranging his pedal boats under red clouds and a moon the color of a plate of boiling lentils, dressed only in shorts and remote from everything around him, that is, from the sea and the beach, the sea wall of the Paseo, and the shadows of the hotels. For a moment I was overcome by fear; I knew that danger and death lay out there. I woke up sweating. The fever was gone.

This morning, after I planned and wrote out the two first turns, obliterating essays by Benjamin Clark (*Waterloo*, #14) and Jack Corso (*The General*, #3, vol. 17) in which each advises against the creation of more than one front in the first year, I went down to the hotel in excellent spirits, bursting with the desire to read, write, swim, drink, laugh—all the visible signs of health and animal happiness. In the morning the bar usually isn't very full, so I brought along a novel and a folder of photocopies of the articles I need for my work. The novel was *Wally, die Zweiflerin*, by K. G., but perhaps due to my inner exultation, to the thrill of a productive morning, it was impossible for me to concentrate on reading or on studying the articles, which—it must be said—I plan to refute. So I settled down to watch the people shuttling between the restaurant and the terrace, and to enjoy my beer. Just as I was getting ready to go back to the room, where with a little luck I'd be able to sketch out the third turn (spring of '40, unquestionably of crucial importance), Frau Else appeared. When she saw me, she smiled. It was a strange smile. Then she stepped away from a few guests—leaving them in midsentence, or so it seemed—and came to sit at my table.

She looked tired, though her expression was as composed as ever and her gaze as luminous.

"I've never read him," she said, examining the book. "I don't even know who he is. Modern?"

I shook my head with a smile. He was an author from the previous century, I said. A dead man. For a second we stared at each other without looking away or muting the effect with words.

"What's it about? Tell me." She pointed at the novel by G.

"If you like, I'll lend it to you."

"I don't have time to read. Not in the summer. But you can tell me what happens." Her voice, while still soft, began to take on a commanding tone.

"It's the diary of a girl. Wally. At the end she kills herself."

"That's all? It sounds awful."

I laughed:

"You asked me to tell you what it was about. Take it, you can give it back later."

She took the book with a thoughtful expression.

"Girls like to write in their diaries . . . I hate that kind of drama . . . No, I won't read it. Don't you have anything a little more cheerful?" She opened the folder and glanced at the photocopied articles.

"That's something else," I hastened to explain. "Nothing worth looking at!"

"I see. You read English?"

"Yes."

She nodded as if in approval. Then she closed the folder and for a while we sat there in silence. The situation was rather embarrassing, at least for me. The most incredible thing was that she didn't seem to be in a hurry to leave. I searched mentally for a topic of conversation but I couldn't come up with anything.

Suddenly I remembered a scene from ten or eleven years ago: in the middle of a party, the occasion of which I can't recall, Frau Else left everyone, crossing the Paseo Marítimo and vanishing onto the beach. Back then there were no streetlights on the Paseo and you didn't have to go far in order to step into complete darkness. I can't remember whether anyone else noticed her flight. I don't think so. The party was noisy and everyone was drinking and dancing on the terrace, even people who had just been walking by and had no connection to the hotel. The point is, I don't think anyone missed her except me. I don't know how long it was before she turned up again; I suppose it was quite a while. When she did, she wasn't alone. Walking hand in hand with her was a tall man, very thin, with a white shirt that fluttered in the breeze as if it hung on nothing but bones, or rather, *a single bone*, as long as a flagpole. When they crossed the Paseo I recognized him. It was the owner of the hotel, Frau Else's husband. When Frau Else passed me, she said hello to me in German. I'd never seen such a sad smile.

Now, ten years later, she was smiling in the same way.

Without thinking twice, I told her I thought she was a very beautiful woman.

Frau Else looked at me as if she didn't quite understand what I'd said and then she laughed, but so softly that someone at the next table could barely have heard it.

"It's the truth," I said. The fear I generally felt when I was with her of making a fool of myself had disappeared.

Suddenly serious, perhaps realizing that I was serious myself, she said:

"You're not the only one who thinks so, Udo. I guess you must be right."

"You always have been," I said, unable to stop now, "although I wasn't just talking about your physical beauty, which is certainly undeniable, but about your . . . aura, the indefinable air that emanates from your most insignificant actions . . . Your silences . . ."

Frau Else laughed, this time openly, as if she'd just been told a joke.

"I'm sorry," she said. "I'm not laughing at you."

"Just at what I'm saying," I said, laughing too, as if I weren't offended at all. (Although the truth is I was offended.)

This response seemed to please Frau Else. I thought that without intending to I had grazed a hidden wound. I imagined Frau Else courted by a Spaniard, perhaps involved in a secret love affair. Her husband, of course, suspects and suffers agonies; she can neither give up her lover nor find the strength to leave her husband. She is trapped by her conflicting loyalties; her own beauty is the source of her tribulations. I envisioned Frau Else as a flame, the flame that sheds light but in the process consumes itself and dies, etc.; or like a wine that, upon mixing with the blood, ceases to exist as what it once was. Beautiful and distant. And *exiled* . . . This was her most mysterious quality.

Her voice woke me from my reflections:

"You seem very far away from here."

"I was thinking about you."

"For God's sake, Udo, you'll make me blush."

"I was thinking about the person you were ten years ago. You haven't changed at all."

"What was I like ten years ago?"

"The same as you are now. Magnetic. Active."

"Active, of course, what choice do I have? But magnetic?" Her hearty laugh echoed through the restaurant once more.

"Yes, magnetic. Do you remember that party on the terrace, when you went off to the beach? . . . It was pitch-black there, though the terrace was brightly lit. I was the only one who saw you leave and I waited until you came back. There, on those steps. After a while you returned, but now you were with your husband. When you passed me, you smiled. You were very beautiful. I don't remember having seen your husband go after you, so he must have been on the beach already. That's the kind of magnetism I'm talking about. You attract people."

"My dear Udo, I haven't the slightest memory of that party; there've been so many, and it was such a long time ago. Anyway, based on your story it seems that I'm the one attracted by others. Attracted by my own husband, no less. If you say that you didn't see him leave, then clearly he was already on the beach, but if the beach was dark, as you so rightly claim, I couldn't have known that he was there, so when I left it must have been been because I was drawn by *his* magnetism, wouldn't you say?"

I chose not to answer. Much as Frau Else tried to destroy it, a current of understanding had been established between the two of us that released us from the need for explanations.

"How old were you then? It's only natural that a fifteen-year-old should be attracted to a slightly older woman. The truth is that

I hardly remember you, Udo. My . . . interests lay elsewhere. I was a wild thing, I think, wild like all girls, and insecure. I didn't like it at the hotel. As you can imagine, I suffered a lot. Well, all foreigners suffer a lot at first."

"For me it was something . . . lovely."

"Don't look like that."

"Like what?"

"Like a clubbed seal, Udo."

"That's what Ingeborg always says."

"Really? I don't believe it."

"She puts it differently. But it amounts to the same thing."

"She's a very pretty girl."

"Yes, she is."

All of a sudden we were silent again. The fingers of her left hand began to drum on the plastic tabletop. I would have liked to ask about her husband, whom I still hadn't seen even from afar and who I sensed had something important to do with the nameless essence that radiated from Frau Else, but I didn't have the chance.

"Why don't we change the subject? Let's talk about literature. Or rather, you talk about literature and I'll listen. When it comes to books, I know nothing, but believe me, I do like to read."

I had the feeling that she was making fun of me. I shook my head in rejection. Frau Else's eyes seemed to rake my skin. I'd even say that her eyes sought mine as if by scrutinizing them she could read my innermost thoughts. And yet her intentions were kind.

"Then let's talk about the movies. Do you like the movies?" I shrugged. "Tonight there's a Judy Garland film on TV. I love Judy Garland. Do you like her?"

"I don't know. I've never seen her in anything."

"You haven't seen *The Wizard of Oz*?"

"Yes, but it was a cartoon, the way I remember it."

She gave me a disappointed look. From some corner of the restaurant came very soft music. We were both perspiring.

"No, that's something else entirely," said Frau Else. "Although I suppose that at night you and your girlfriend must have better things to do than come down to the hotel lobby to watch TV."

"Not much better. We go out to clubs. It's mostly boring."

"Are you a good dancer? Yes, I think you must be. One of those serious dancers, the kind who never gets tired."

"No, that's not me."

"What's your style, then?"

"I have two left feet." .

Frau Else nodded in an enigmatic way that indicated she understood. The restaurant was filling up with people coming back from the beach; we hadn't noticed. In the next room guests were already seated, ready to eat. I thought Ingeborg would be in soon.

"These days I don't do it as often; when I first came to Spain I went out dancing with my husband almost every night. Always at the same place, because back then there weren't as many clubs and also because this one was the best, the newest. No, it wasn't here, it was in X . . . It was the only club my husband liked. Maybe precisely because it was out of town. It doesn't exist anymore. It closed years ago."

I seized the opportunity to tell her what had happened on our last visit to a club. Frau Else listened unperturbed as I gave a detailed account of the dispute between the waiter and the man with the stick that had ended in a general brawl. She seemed more interested in the part of the story involving our Spanish companions, the Wolf and the Lamb. I thought she must know them, or know who they were, and I said so. No, she didn't know them, but they couldn't be the most appropriate company for a young couple on their first trip together, practically a honeymoon. But what harm could they do? A worried look crossed Frau Else's face. Did she perhaps know something that I didn't? I told her that the Wolf and the Lamb were more friends of Charly and Hanna's than mine, and that in Stuttgart I was acquainted with much shadier characters. I was lying, of course. Finally I promised that the Spaniards interested me only as conversation partners with whom I could practice my Spanish.

"You should think about your girlfriend," she said. "You should be considerate of her."

On her face was an expression akin to disgust.

"Don't worry, we'll be fine. I'm cautious by nature and I know how to keep my distance, depending on the person. Anyway, Ingeborg likes spending time with them. I guess she's not used to that kind of people. Of course, neither of us takes them seriously."

"But they are real."

I was about to tell her that everything seemed unreal to me just then: the Wolf and the Lamb, the hotel and the summer, El Quemado (whom I hadn't mentioned) and the tourists, everyone except for Frau Else herself, lonely and alluring; but luckily I kept my mouth shut.

We sat there for a while longer without speaking, although in the midst of our silence I felt closer to her than ever. Then, with a visible effort, she got up, *shook my hand*, and left.

As I was on my way up to the room, in the elevator, a stranger remarked in English that the boss was sick. "Too bad the boss is sick, Lucy," were his words. I knew, without a shadow of a doubt, that he was referring to Frau Else's husband.

When I got to the room, I surprised myself by repeating: He's sick, he's sick, he's sick . . . So it was true. On the map, the game pieces seemed to melt. The light fell at a slant on the table, and the counters that represented German armored units sparkled as if they were alive.

For lunch today we had chicken and french fries and salad, chocolate ice cream and coffee. A rather sad meal. (Yesterday it was cutlets and salad, chocolate ice cream and coffee.) Ingeborg told me that she'd been with Hanna at the Municipal Garden behind the port, between two cliffs that plunge straight into the sea. They took lots of pictures, bought postcards, and decided to walk back to town. A full morning. I hardly said a thing. The noise of the dining room gave me a slight but nagging headache. Just after we finished eating, Hanna came in, wearing only a bikini and a yellow T-shirt. When she sat down she looked at me with a somewhat forced smile, as if she were apologizing for something, or as if she felt ashamed. Of what, I have no idea. The truth is that I wasn't at all happy to see her, although I was careful not to show it. Finally the three of us went up to the room, where Ingeborg put on her bathing suit and then the two of them went to the beach.

Hanna asked: "Why does Udo spend so much time up here?" And after a pause: "What is that game board with all those counters there on the table?" Ingeborg was slow to find an answer. At a loss, she looked at me as if I were the one responsible for her friend's stupid curiosity. Hanna stood there waiting. In a calm and cold voice that disconcerted even me, I explained that since my shoulders were so burned I'd rather sit in the shade and read on the balcony. It's relaxing, I said, you should try it. It helps you think. Hanna laughed, not sure what I meant. Then I added:

"That game board, as you can see, is a map of Europe. It's a game. It's also a challenge. And it's part of my work."

Flustered, Hanna stammered that she'd heard that I worked for the electric company in Stuttgart, so I had to explain that even though nearly all of my income came from the electric company, neither my true passion nor much of my time was devoted to it. What's more, games like the one on the table brought in an extra bit of money. I don't know whether it was the mention of money or the gleam of the board and the counters, but Hanna came over and began to question me in earnest about the map. It was the ideal moment to introduce her to the gaming world . . . Just then Ingeborg said they should go. From the balcony I watched them cross the Paseo Marítimo and spread their towels a few yards from El Quemado's pedal boats. The way they moved, so delicately and in such an intensely feminine way, was strangely painful to me. For a few moments I felt sick, unable to do anything but lie on the bed, facedown, sweating. Absurd, agonizing images passed through my head. I thought about suggesting to Ingeborg that we head south, to Andalusia, or that we travel to Portugal, or that we lose ourselves on the back roads of Spain, or cross over to Morocco . . . Then I remembered that she had to be back at work on September 3 and that my own holiday ended on September 5, and that we didn't actually have the time . . . Finally I got up, showered, and found myself in the game.

(General aspects of the spring turn, 1940. France defends the classic front along the line of Hex 24s, and a second line of defense along the hex 23s. Of the fourteen infantry corps that by this point should be present in the European theater, at least twelve should cover hexes Q24, P24, O24, N24, M24, L24, Q23, O23, and M23. The two remaining corps should be placed in hexes O22 and P22. Of the three armored corps, one should probably be in Hex O22, another in Hex T20, and the last in Hex O23. The replacement units will be in hexes Q22, T21, U20, and V20; the air units in hexes P21 and Q20, on air bases. The British Expeditionary Force, which in the *best* of cases will consist of three infantry corps and an armored corps—of course, if the English attacked France in greater force, the variant to use would be the direct strike against Great Britain and to that end the German airborne corps should be in Hex K28—would be deployed in Hex N23 [two infantry corps] and Hex P23 [one infantry corps and one armored corps]. As a possible defensive variant, the English forces could be moved from Hex P23 to Hex O23, and the French forces [an armored corps and an infantry corps] from O23 to P23. In any deployment the strongest hex will be the one where the English armored corps is located, whether P23 or O23, and it will determine the focus of the German attack. This attack will be carried out with very few units. If the English armored corps is in P23, the German attack will be launched from O24; if, on the contrary, the English armored corps is in O23, the attack must be launched from N24, through the south of Belgium. To assure a breakthrough, the airborne corps must be launched from Hex O23 if the English armored corps is in P23, or from N23 if it's in O23. The initial strike will be made by two armored corps and the follow-through will be carried out by two or three different armored corps that must arrive at Hex O23 or N22, depending on the location of the English armored corps, and proceed to an immediate exploitation of Hex O22 [Paris]. To prevent a counterattack at a ratio greater than 1:2, some air factors must be left in reserve, etc.).

That afternoon we had drinks in the tourist district and then we went to play miniature golf. Charly was calmer than he had been for the last few days, his face relaxed and peaceful, as if a tranquillity thus far unsuspected had settled over him. Appearances are misleading. Soon he began to ramble on in the usual way, and he told us a story that was a good illustration of how stupid he is or how stupid he thinks we are, or both. Briefly: All day he had been windsurfing and at a certain point he got so far out that he lost sight of the coastline. The joke was that upon returning to the beach he confused our town with the next one; the buildings, the hotels, even the curve of the beach, made him suspect something, but he ignored his doubts. Disoriented, he asked a German bather to direct him to the Costa Brava hotel. Unhesitatingly, the German sent him to a hotel that was in fact called the Costa Brava but that looked nothing like the Costa Brava where Charly was staying. Still, Charly went in and asked for his room key. Since he wasn't registered, the receptionist of course wouldn't give it to him, despite Charly's threats. Strong words finally gave way to conversation, and since things were slow at the reception desk, they had some beers at the hotel bar, where, to the surprise of all those listening, everything was explained and Charly made a friend and won general admiration.

"What did you do then?" asked Hanna, though clearly she already knew the answer.

"Picked up my board and headed back. By sea, naturally!"

Charly is a serious braggart, or a serious idiot.

Why am I so afraid sometimes? And why, when I'm most afraid, does my spirit seem to surge, rise up, and observe the whole planet from above? (I see Frau Else from above and I'm afraid. I see Ingeborg from above and I know that she sees me too and I'm afraid and I want to cry.) Tears of love? Do I really want to escape with her not just from this town and the heat but from what the future holds for us, from mediocrity and absurdity? Others find peace in sex or the passage of time. Charly is satisfied with Hanna's legs and tits. He's happy. But I, when faced with Ingeborg's beauty, am forced to see clearly at last and am thrown into turmoil. I'm a nervous wreck. I feel like weeping and throwing punches when I think about Conrad, who has no holidays or spends his holidays in Stuttgart without even a trip to the pool. But my face remains unchanged. And my pulse is steady. I scarcely move a muscle, though inside I'm falling apart.

As we got ready for bed, Ingeborg remarked how well Charly looked. We'd been at a club called Adam's until three in the morning. Now Ingeborg is asleep and I'm writing and chain-smoking with the balcony door open. Hanna looked good too. She even danced a couple of slow songs with me. Our conversation: trivial as always. What can Hanna and Ingeborg have to talk about? Is it possible that they're truly becoming friends? Charly treated us to dinner at the restaurant at the Costa Brava. Paella, salad, wine, ice cream, and coffee. Then we left in my car for the club. Charly didn't feel like driving, nor did he feel like walking; maybe I'm exaggerating but I got the impression that he didn't even feel like being seen in public. Hanna kept leaning over and kissing him. I imagine she kisses her son in Oberhausen the same way. As we were on our way back I spotted El Quemado on the terrace of the Andalusia Lodge. The terrace was empty and the waiters were clearing the tables. A group of local kids were leaning on the railing, talking. El Quemado, a few yards away, seemed to be listening to them. When I remarked to Charly, half jokingly, that his friend was there, his reply was irritable: what do I care, keep going. I think he thought I was talking about the Wolf or the Lamb. In the darkness it's hard to tell people apart. Keep going, keep going, said Ingeborg and Hanna.

Today, for the first time, we woke up to gray skies. From our window, the beach looked majestic and empty. A few children were playing in the sand but soon it began to rain and one by one they disappeared. At the restaurant, during breakfast, the atmosphere was different; banished from the terrace because of the rain, people gathered at the indoor tables and the breakfast hour stretched on, encouraging the quick formation of new friendships. Everyone talked. The men started to drink early. The women were constantly going back up to their rooms in search of warmer clothes that most of the time they were unable to find. Jokes were made. A general air of frustration soon manifested itself. But since there was no point spending the whole day at the hotel, expeditions were organized; groups of five or six, huddled under a couple of umbrellas, went out to visit the shops and then a café or some video arcade. The rainswept streets seemed removed from the daily bustle, immersed in a different kind of ordinariness.

Charly and Hanna arrived partway through breakfast. They had decided to go to Barcelona and Ingeborg was going with them. I said I wouldn't go. Today will be all mine. After they left I sat watching people come and go. Despite what I expected, there was no sign of Frau Else. But at least it was a quiet and comfortable spot. I put my brain to work reviewing the beginnings of matches, opening moves and exploratory moves . . . A general lethargy had fallen over everything. Suddenly the only truly happy people were the waiters. They had twice as much work as on an ordinary day but they were kidding around and laughing. An old man sitting near me said that they were laughing at us.

"You're wrong," I said. "They're laughing because they can feel summer coming to an end, and work too."

"So they should be sad. They'll be out of a job, the lazy bastards!"

I left the hotel at noon.

I got in the car and drove slowly to the Andalusia Lodge. I would've gotten there faster by walking but I didn't feel like walking.

From the outside it looked like all the other bars with terraces: chairs upended and water dripping from the fringes of the umbrellas. The fun was inside. As if the rain had broken the ice, tourists and locals—mingling in a way somehow tinged with catastrophe—were enmeshed in an endless and unintelligible exchange of gestures. In the back, near the TV, I spotted the Lamb. He waved me over. I waited until I'd been served a coffee, and then I went to sit at his table. At first we just made small talk. The Lamb was sorry it was raining, though not on *his* account but on *mine*, because I had come in search of sunny days and beach, etc. I didn't bother to tell him that actually I was delighted it was raining. After a while he asked about Charly. I told him he was in Barcelona. With who? he wanted to know. The question took me by surprise; I would have liked to say that it was none of his business. After hesitating, I decided that it wasn't worth the trouble.

"With Ingeborg and Hanna, of course. Who did you think he was with?"

The poor guy seemed taken aback. Nobody, he said, smiling. On the fogged-up window someone had drawn a heart bisected by a hypodermic needle. Out the window, the Paseo Marítimo and some gray planks could be glimpsed. The few tables at the back of the bar were occupied by young people and they were the only ones who kept a certain distance from the tourists. The bar was tacitly divided between the people up front (families and older men) and those in the back. Suddenly the Lamb began to tell me a strange and meaningless story. He spoke rapidly, confidentially, leaning over the table. I hardly understood him. The story was about Charly and the Wolf, but the way he told it was like something out of a dream: an argument, a blonde (Hanna?), knives, the all-conquering power of friendship . . . "The Wolf is a good person, I know him, he's got a heart of gold. Charly too. But when they get drunk they'd drive anybody crazy." I nodded. I couldn't care less. Near us a girl stared into the empty fireplace, now a giant ashtray. Outside the rain came down harder. The Lamb bought me a cognac. Just then the owner came in and put on a video. To do so he had to get up on a chair. From his perch he announced: "I'm putting on a video for you kids." No one paid any attention. "You're a bunch of bums," he said on his way out. The movie was about postnuclear bikers. "I've seen it," said the Lamb when he returned with two drinks. It was good cognac. The girl near the fireplace started to cry. I don't know how to explain it but she was the only one in the whole bar who didn't seem to be there. I asked the Lamb why she was crying. I can hardly see her face, he replied, how do you know she's crying? I shrugged. On the TV a couple of bikers were riding through the desert; one of them was missing an eye; on the horizon sprawled the remains of a city: a gas station in ruins, a supermarket, a bank, a movie theater, a hotel . . . "Mutants," said the Lamb, turning sideways so he could see better.

Next to the girl by the fireplace was another girl, and a boy who might have been thirteen or eighteen. Both of them watched her cry and from time to time patted her on the back. The boy had a pimply face. He whispered into the girl's ear, more as if he were trying to convince her of something than as if he were consoling her, and out of the corner of his eye he made sure not to miss any of the most violent scenes in the movie, which, as it happened, followed constantly one after the other. In fact, the faces of all the kids (except the one who was crying) lifted automatically toward the TV at the sound of fighting or at the music that preceded the climactic moments of the fights. Either the rest of the movie didn't interest them or they'd seen it already.

Outside the rain was still coming down.

I thought about El Quemado. Where was he? Could he possibly be spending the day on the beach, buried under the pedal boats? For a second, as if I were gasping for air, I felt like running out to check.

Little by little the idea of visiting him began to take shape. What attracted me most was seeing for myself what I'd already imagined: part child's hideout, part third-world shack. But what did I really expect to find under the pedal boats? In my mind's eye I could see El Quemado sitting like a caveman beside a kerosene lantern; when I come in, he looks up and we gaze at each other. But how do I get in? Down a hole, like a rabbit burrow? Maybe. And there, at the end of the tunnel, is El Quemado, reading the paper and looking like a rabbit. A giant rabbit, scared to death. Of course, I didn't want to frighten him. I should announce myself first. Hello, it's me, Udo, are you there, the way I imagined? . . . And if no one answered, what to do? I imagined myself pacing around the pedal boats searching for the way in. A tiny crack. Sliding on my belly, creeping in with great difficulty . . . Inside everything is dark. Why?

"Do you want me to tell you how the movie ends?" asked the Lamb.

The girl by the fireplace wasn't crying anymore. On the TV a kind of executioner was digging a hole big enough to bury the body of a man and his bike. When it was over, the kids laughed, though there was something indefinable about the scene, something more tragic than comic.

I nodded. How did it end?

"So the good guy escapes the radioactive zone with the treasure. I can't remember whether it's a formula to make synthetic gasoline or water or what. Anyway, it's just another movie, right?"

"Right," I said.

I wanted to pay but the Lamb refused to let me. "You can pay tonight," he said, smiling. The idea was completely unappealing to me. But no one could make me go out with them, after all, though I was afraid that idiot Charly had already made plans. And if Charly went out, Hanna would go; and if Hanna did, Ingeborg probably would too. As I got up, I asked casually where El Quemado might be.

"No idea," said the Lamb. "That guy's kind of a nut job. Do you want to see him? Are you looking for him? I'll go with you, if you want. He might be at Pepe's bar. I doubt he'll be working in this rain."

I thanked him; I said it wasn't necessary. I wasn't looking for him.

"He's a weird guy," said the Lamb.

"Why? Because of his burns? Do you know how he got them?"

"No, that's not why, I don't know anything about that. He just seems strange to me. Or not strange, exactly, but a little off, you know what I mean."

"No, what do you mean?"

"He's got his hang-ups, like everybody. Maybe he's a little bitter. I don't know. We all have something, don't we? Take Charly, for example, all he cares about is the bottle and his fucking board."

"Come on, man, there are other things he likes too."

"Chicks?" said the Lamb with a malicious smile. "You have to admit Hanna's hot, right?"

"Yes," I said. "She's not bad."

"And she has a son, doesn't she?"

"I think so," I said.

"She showed me a picture. He's a good-looking kid, blond and everything, he looks like her."

"I don't know. I haven't seen any pictures."

Before I could explain that he knew Hanna practically as well as I did, I left. In some ways he probably knew her better, but there was no point saying so.

Outside it was still raining, though not as hard. On the wide sidewalks of the Paseo Marítimo a few tourists walked by in brightly colored windbreakers. I got in the car and lit a cigarette. From where I was I could see the fortress of pedal boats and the curtain of mist and foam raised by the wind. Through one of the bar's big windows the fireplace girl was also staring out at the beach. I started the car and drove off. For half an hour I circled around town. In the old part of the city the traffic was impossible. Water bubbled out of the drains and a warm and putrid scent crept into the car along with exhaust fumes, the blare of horns, children's shouts. At last I managed to escape. I was hungry, ravenously hungry, but rather than look for a place to eat, I left town.

I drove aimlessly, not knowing where I was going. From time to time I passed the cars and campers of tourists; the weather signaled the end of summer. The fields to each side of the highway were covered in plastic and dark grooves; against the horizon stood small, bare hills toward which the clouds sped. In a grove, under the trees, I saw a group of black workers sheltering from the rain.

Suddenly I came upon a pottery shop. So this was the road that led to the nameless club. I parked the car in the lot and got out. From a hut an old man stared at me in silence. Everything was different: there were no spotlights or dogs, no otherworldly glow emanating from the plaster statues on which the rain pattered.

I picked out a few pots and went over to the old man's lair.

"Eight hundred pesetas," he said without emerging.

I felt for the money and handed it to him.

"Bad weather," I said as I waited for the change and the rain fell on my face.

"Yes," said the old man.

I put the pots in the trunk and left.

I ate at a chapel on top of a mountain with a view of the whole bay. Centuries ago a stone fortress stood here as a defense against pirates. Maybe the town didn't exist yet when the fortress was built. I don't know. In any case, all that's left of the fortress are a few stones scrawled with names, hearts, obscene drawings. Next to the ruins rises the chapel, of more recent construction. The view is incredible: the port, the yacht club, the old town, the new town, the campgrounds, the beachfront hotels. In good weather it's possible to make out some of the other towns along the coast and, peeking over the skeleton of the fortress, a web of back roads and an infinity of small towns and hamlets inland. In a building adjoining the chapel there's a kind of restaurant. I don't know whether the people who run it belong to a religious order or whether they got the license in the usual way. They're good cooks, which is what matters. The locals, especially couples, are in the habit of driving up to the chapel, though not exactly to admire the landscape. When I got here I found several cars parked under the trees. Some drivers remained inside their vehicles. Others were sitting at tables in the restaurant. The silence was almost total. I took a stroll around a kind of lookout point with a guardrail; at both ends there were telescopes, the coin-operated kind. I went up to one and put in fifty pesetas. I couldn't see anything. Utter darkness. I whacked it a few times and then gave up. At the restaurant I ordered rabbit and a bottle of wine.

What else did I see?

1. A tree dangling over the precipice. Its crazed-looking roots were snarled around the stones and in the air. (But this isn't a sight unique to Spain; I've seen trees like it in Germany.)

2. An adolescent vomiting by the side of the road. His parents, in a car with British license plates, waited with the radio turned all the way up.

3. A dark-eyed girl in the kitchen at the chapel restaurant. We made eye contact for only a second but something about me made her smile.

4. The bronze bust of a bald man in a small, out-of-the-way square. On the pedestal, a poem written in Spanish of which I could make out only the words: "land," "man," "death."

5. A group of young people shrimping on the rocks north of town. For no apparent reason, they erupted every so often in cheers and vivas. Their shouts echoed off the rocks like the clamor of drums.

6. A dark red cloud—the color of dirty blood—taking shape in the east, which, among the dark clouds that covered the sky, was like the promise of an end to the rain.

After eating, I went back to the hotel. I showered, changed clothes, and went out again. There was a letter for me at the reception desk. It was from Conrad. For a moment I vacillated between reading it immediately or putting off the pleasure for later. I decided that I'd save it until after I saw El Quemado. So I put the letter in my pocket and headed for the pedal boats.

The sand was wet though it wasn't raining anymore; here and there on the beach one could make out the vague shapes of people walking along the shore, gazing down as if they were searching for bottles with messages inside or jewels washed up by the sea. Twice I almost went back to the hotel. And yet the sense that I was making a fool of myself was less powerful than my curiosity.

Long before I reached the pedal boats I heard the sound made by the tarp as it slapped against the floaters. Some rope must have come undone. With cautious steps I circled the pedal boats. In fact, there was a loose rope, and the tarp flapped ever more violently in the wind. I remember that the rope seethed like a snake. A river snake. The tarp was wet and heavy from the rain. Without thinking, I grabbed the rope and tied it as best I could.

"What are you doing?" asked El Quemado from the pedal boats.

I jumped backward. As I did, the knot came undone and the tarp made a sound like a plant ripped out by the roots, like something wet and alive.

"Nothing," I said.

Immediately it occurred to me that I should have added: "Where are you?" Now El Quemado would be able to deduce that I knew his secret, since I wasn't surprised to hear his voice, which clearly came from within. Too late.

"What do you mean, nothing?"

"Nothing," I shouted. "I was taking a walk and I saw that the wind was about to rip the tarp off. Didn't you notice?"

Silence.

I took a step forward and decisively retied the confounded rope.

"There you go," I said. "The pedal boats are protected. Now you just need the sun to come out!"

An unintelligible grunt came from inside.

"Can I come in?"

El Quemado didn't answer. For an instant I was afraid that he would come out and curse at me in the middle of the beach, demanding to know what the hell I wanted. I wouldn't have known what to say. (Was I killing time? Confirming a suspicion? Conducting a small behavioral study?)

"Can you hear me?" I shouted. "Can I come in or not?"

"Yes." El Quemado's voice was barely audible.

Politely, I sought the entrance; of course there was no hole dug in the sand. The pedal boats, propped against each other in an unlikely fashion, seemed to leave no gap through which a person could fit. I looked up: between the tarp and a floater there was a space through which a body could slip. I climbed up carefully.

"Through here?" I asked.

El Quemado grunted something that I took as a yes. From up above, the hole looked bigger. I closed my eyes and let myself drop.

A smell of rotting wood and salt assaulted my senses. At last I was inside the fortress.

El Quemado was sitting on a tarp like the one that covered the pedal boats. Next to him was a bag almost as big as a suitcase. On a sheet of newspaper he had some bread and a can of tuna. Despite what I had expected, there was enough light to see by, especially considering that it was a cloudy day. Along with the light, air came in through any number of openings. The sand was dry, or so it seemed, but it was cold in there. I said: It's cold. El Quemado took a bottle out of a bag and handed it to me. I took a swig. It was wine.

"Thanks," I said.

El Quemado took the bottle and drank in turn; then he cut a chunk of bread, split it open, stuffed it with some shreds of tuna, drenched it in olive oil, and proceeded to eat it. The space under the pedal boats was six feet long and just over three feet high. Soon I discovered other objects: a towel of indeterminate color, the rope-soled shoes (El Quemado was barefoot), another can of tuna (empty), a plastic bag printed with a supermarket logo . . . In general, order reigned in the fortress.

"Aren't you surprised that I knew where you were?"

"No," said El Quemado.

"Sometimes I help Ingeborg solve mysteries . . . When she reads crime novels . . . I can figure out who the killers are before Florian Linden . . ." My voice had dwindled to almost a whisper.

After gulping down the bread, he scrupulously deposited both cans in the plastic bag. His huge hands moved swiftly and silently. The hands of a criminal, I thought. In a second there was no trace of food left, only the bottle of wine between us.

"The rain . . . Did it bother you? . . . But you're fine in here, I see . . . You must be happy to see it rain every once in a while: today you're just another tourist, like everybody else."

El Quemado stared at me in silence. In the jumble of his features I thought I detected a sarcastic expression. Are you taking time off too? he asked. I'm alone today, I explained, Ingeborg, Hanna, and Charly went to Barcelona. What was he trying to insinuate by asking me whether I was taking time off too? That I would never finish my article? That I wasn't hunkered down at the hotel?

"How did you decide on the idea of living out here?"

El Quemado shrugged his shoulders and sighed.

"I can understand that it must be beautiful to sleep under the stars, out in the open, though from here I doubt you see many stars." I smiled and slapped myself on the forehead, an unusual gesture for me. "No matter what, you sleep closer to the water than any tourist. Some people would pay to be in your place!"

El Quemado dug for something in the sand. His toes burrowed slowly up and down; they were disproportionately large and surprisingly (though there was no reason to expect otherwise) unmarred by a single burn, smooth, the skin intact, without even a callus, which daily contact with the sea must have endeavored to smooth away.

"I'd like to know how you decided to set up house here, how it occurred to you to arrange the pedal boats like this for shelter. It's a good idea, but why? Was it so you wouldn't have to pay rent? Is it really so expensive to rent a place? I apologize if it's none of my business. I'm just curious, you know? Shall we go get coffee?"

77

El Quemado picked up the bottle, and after raising it to his lips he handed it to me.

"It's cheap. It's free," he murmured when I set the bottle back down between us.

"But is it legal? Besides me, does anyone know you sleep here? Say, the owner of the pedal boats, does he know you spend the nights here?"

"I'm the owner," said El Quemado.

A strip of light fell directly on his forehead: the charred flesh, in the light, seemed to grow paler, stir.

"They're not worth much," he added. "Any pedal boat in town is newer than mine. But they still float and people like them."

"I think they're wonderful," I said in a burst of enthusiasm. "I would never get on a pedal boat built to look like a swan or a Viking ship. They're hideous. *Yours*, on the other hand, seem . . . I don't know, more classic. More trustworthy."

I felt stupid.

"That's where you're wrong. The new pedal boats are faster."

In a scattered way, he explained that with all the speedboat, ferry, and windsurfing traffic, the beach could sometimes be as busy as a highway. So the speed that the pedal boats were able to attain in order to avoid other craft became an important consideration. He had no accidents to complain of yet, just a few bumps to swimmers' heads, but even in this regard the new pedal boats were better: a collision with the floater of one of his old pedal boats could crack someone's head open.

"They're heavy," he said.

"Yes, like tanks."

El Quemado smiled for the first time that afternoon.

"You've got a single-track mind," he said.

"True."

Still smiling, he traced a picture in the sand that he immediately erased. Even his infrequent gestures were enigmatic.

"How is your game going?"

"Perfect. Full sail ahead. I'll destroy all the schemes."

"All the schemes?"

"That's right. All the old ways of playing. Under my system, the game will have to be reinvented."

When we emerged, the sky was a metallic gray, auguring new showers. I told El Quemado that a few hours ago I had spotted a red cloud in the east; I thought that was a sign of good weather. At the bar, reading the sports news at the same table where I'd left him, was the Lamb. When he saw us he beckoned us over to sit with him. The conversation then proceeded into territory that Charly would have loved but that frankly bored me. Bayern Münich, Schuster, Hamburg, Rummenigge, were the subjects. Naturally, the Lamb knew more about the teams and personalities than I did. To my surprise, El Quemado took part in the conversation (which was in my honor, since there was no talk about Spanish sports stars, only German ones, which I did fully appreciate and which at the same time made me uncomfortable) and he revealed an acceptable knowledge of German soccer. For example, the Lamb asked: Who's your favorite player? and after my response (Schumacher, for the sake of saying something) and the Lamb's (Klaus Allofs), El Quemado said "Uwe Seeler," whom neither the Lamb nor I had heard of. Seeler and Tilkowski are the names El Quemado holds in highest esteem. The Lamb and I didn't know what he was talking about. When we asked him to tell us more, he said that as a boy he saw both of them on the soccer field. Just as I thought that El Quemado was about to reflect on his childhood, he suddenly fell silent. The hours passed and despite the grayness of the day, night was long in coming. At eight I said good-bye and returned to the hotel. Sitting in an armchair on the first floor, next to a window through which I could see the Paseo Marítimo and a slice of the parking lot, I settled down to read Conrad's letter. This is what it said:

Dear Udo:

I got your postcard. I hope swimming and Ingeborg are leaving you enough time to finish the article as planned. Yesterday we finished a round of *Third Reich* at Wolfgang's house. Walter and Wolfgang (Axis) against Franz (Allies) and me (Russia). It was a three-way game, and the final result was: W & W, 4 Objective hexes; Franz, 18; me, 19, including Berlin and Stockholm (you can imagine the condition in which W & W left the Kriegsmarine!). Surprises in the diplomatic module: in autumn of '41 Spain goes over to the Axis. Turkey wooed away from the Allies thanks to the DP that Franz and I spent prodigally. Alexandria and Suez, untouchable; Malta pounded but still standing. W & W did their *best* to test parts of your Mediterranean Strategy. And Rex Douglas's Mediterranean Strategy. But it was too much for them. Down they went. David Hablanian's Spanish Gambit might work one time out of twenty. Franz lost France in the summer of '40 and weathered an invasion of England in spring '41! Almost all of his army corps were in the Mediterranean and W & W couldn't resist the temptation. We applied the Beyma variant. In '41 I was saved by the *snow* and by W & W's insistence on *opening fronts*, at a huge cost of BRP; they were always bankrupt by the last turn of the year. Regarding your strategy: Franz says it isn't much different from Anchors's. I told him that *you* were *corresponding* with Anchors and that his strategy had nothing to do with yours. W & W are ready to mount a giant TR as soon as you get back. First they suggested the GDW Europe series, but I convinced them otherwise. I *doubt* you'd want to play for more than a *month* straight. We've agreed that W & W and Franz and Otto Wolf will take the Allies and the Russians, respectively, and that you and I will take Germany, what do you say? We also talked about the Paris conference, December 23–28. It's confirmed that Rex Douglas will be there in person. I know he'd like to meet you. A picture of you came out in *Waterloo*: it's the one where you're playing Randy Wilson, and there's an article about our Stuttgart group. I got a letter from *Mars*, do you remember *them*? They want an article from you (there'll be another by Mathias Müller, can you believe it?) for a special issue about players who specialize in WWII. Most of the participants are French and Swiss. And there's more news, which I'd rather wait to give you when you get back from vacation. So what do you think the Objective hexes were that stymied W & W? Leipzig, Oslo, *Genoa*, and *Milan*. Franz wanted to *hit* me. In fact, he *chased* me around the table. We've set up a Case White. We'll get started tomorrow night. The kids at *Fire and Steel* have discovered *Boots & Saddles* and *Bundeswehr*, from the Assault Series. Now they plan to sell their old *Squad Leaders* and they're talking about putting out a fanzine and calling it *Assault* or *Radioactive Combat* or something like that. They make me *laugh*. Get lots of sun. Say hello to Ingeborg.

Fondly,
Conrad

After the rain, evening at the Del Mar is tinted a dark blue shot through with gold. For a long time all I do is sit in the restaurant watching people come back to the hotel looking tired and hungry. Frau Else is nowhere to be seen. I discover that I'm cold: I'm in shirtsleeves. Also, Conrad's letter leaves me with a trace of sadness. Wolfgang is an idiot: I can picture his slowness, his hesitation at each move, his lack of imagination. If you can't control Turkey with DP, invade it, you moron. Nicky Palmer has said so a thousand times. I've said so a thousand times. Suddenly, for no apparent reason, I felt alone. Conrad and Rex Douglas (whom I know solely through letters) are my only friends. The rest is emptiness and darkness. Unanswered calls. Snubs. "Alone in a ravaged land," I remembered. In an amnesiac Europe, with no sense of the epic or heroic. (It doesn't surprise me that adolescents spend their time playing Dungeons & Dragons and other role-playing games.)

How did El Quemado buy his pedal boats? Yes, he told me how. With what he had saved from picking grapes. But how could he buy the whole lot, six or seven at once, with the money from just one harvest season? That was the down payment. The rest he paid little by little. The former owner was old and tired. It's hard enough to make money in the summer, and if on top of that you have to pay an employee salary . . . so he decided to sell them and El Quemado bought them. Did he have any experience renting out pedal boats? No. It isn't hard to learn, said the Lamb, mockingly. Could I do it? (Silly question.) Of course, said the Lamb and El Quemado in unison. Anyone could. Really, it was a job that required nothing but patience and a sharp eye for runaway pedal boats. You didn't even have to know how to swim.

El Quemado came to the hotel. We went upstairs without being seen by anyone. I showed him the game. The questions he asked were intelligent. Suddenly the street filled with the noise of sirens. El Quemado went out on the balcony and said the accident was in the tourist district. How stupid to die on vacation, I remarked. El Quemado shrugged. He was wearing a clean white T-shirt. From where he stood he could keep an eye on the shapeless mass of his pedal boats. I came over and asked what he was looking at. The beach, he said. I think he'd be a quick study.

The hours go by and there's no sign of Ingeborg. I waited until nine in the room, jotting down moves.

Dinner at the hotel restaurant: cream of asparagus soup, cannelloni, coffee, and ice cream. Lingering at the table after dinner, I once more failed to spot Frau Else. (She certainly is nowhere to be found today.) I shared the table with a Dutch couple in their fifties. The subject of conversation at my table and across the restaurant was the bad weather. The diners expressed a number of different views on the subject, which the waiters—invested with a presumed meteorological wisdom, and locals, after all—took it upon themselves to arbitrate. In the end the faction that forecast good weather for the following day won.

At eleven I took a stroll through the various rooms on the main floor. There was no sign of Frau Else and I headed on foot to the Andalusia Lodge. The Lamb wasn't there but half an hour later he showed up. I asked him where the Wolf was. The Lamb hadn't seen him all day.

"I don't suppose he's in Barcelona," I said.

The Lamb gave me a horrified look. Of course he wasn't, today he worked late, the idea. How could I imagine the poor Wolf had gone to Barcelona? We drank cognac and for a while we watched a game show on TV. The Lamb was stuttering, by which I deduced that he was nervous. I can't remember why the subject came up, but at some point, unprompted, he told me that El Quemado wasn't from Spain. We might have been talking about hardship and life and accidents. (The game show featured hundreds of small accidents, apparently simulated and bloodless.) I might have been saying something about the Spanish character. After that we may have gone on to talk about fire and burns. I don't know. The point is that the Lamb said that El Quemado wasn't Spanish. Where was he from, then? South America; which country specifically, he didn't know.

The Lamb's revelation struck me like a blow. El Quemado wasn't Spanish. And he hadn't told me. This fact, in itself trivial, struck me as particularly disturbing and significant. What motives could El Quemado have for hiding his true nationality from me? I didn't feel deceived. I felt observed. (Not by El Quemado; actually, by nobody in particular: observed by a void, an absence.) After a while I paid for our drinks and left. I expected to find Ingeborg back at the hotel.

There was no one in the room. I went downstairs again: ghost-like on the terrace I made out some shadowy figures scarcely speaking a word. At the bar a single old man drank in silence. At the reception desk the night watchman told me that there hadn't been any calls for me.

"Do you know where I can find Frau Else?"

He doesn't know. At first he doesn't even understand who I'm talking about. Frau Else, I shout, the owner of this hotel. The watchman's eyes widen and he shakes his head again. He hasn't seen her.

I thank him and get a cognac at the bar. At one in the morning

I decide that I might as well head upstairs and go to bed. There's no one on the terrace anymore, although a few recently arrived guests have come into the bar and are joking with the waiters.

I can't sleep; I'm not tired.

At last, at four in the morning, Ingeborg appears. A phone call from the watchman informs me that a young lady wants to see me. I hurry downstairs. At the reception desk I find Ingeborg, Hanna, and the watchman embroiled in something that, from the stairs, resembles a secret council. When I come up to them the first thing I notice is Hanna's face: a violet and pinkish bruise covers her left cheek and part of her eye; there are bruises on her right cheek and upper lip too, though not as bad. Also, she can't stop crying. When I inquire how she came to be in such a state, Ingeborg abruptly shuts me up. Her nerves are frayed; she keeps repeating that something like this could happen only in Spain. Wearily, the watchman suggests calling an ambulance. Ingeborg and I discuss it, but it's Hanna who categorically refuses. (She says things like: "It's my body," "I'm the one who's hurt," etc.) The discussion continues and Hanna cries harder. Up until now I had forgotten about Charly. Where is he? When I mention him, Ingeborg, unable to contain herself, spits out a string of curses. For an instant I have the sense that Charly has been *lost forever.* Unexpectedly I feel we share a common bond. It's something I can't define, something that painfully unites us. As the clerk goes in search of a first aid kit—a compromise solution that we've reached with Hanna—Ingeborg fills me in on the latest developments, which, as it happens, I've already guessed.

The excursion couldn't have gone worse. After an apparently normal and quiet day—even too quiet—during which they walked around the Barri Gòtic and La Rambla, taking pictures and buying souvenirs, the calm was shattered. According to Ingeborg, everything began after dessert. Charly, without any provocation whatsoever, underwent a notable change, as if something in the food had poisoned him. At first it all took the form of hostility toward Hanna and jokes in poor taste. Words were exchanged, but that was all. The explosion—the first warning—came later, after Hanna and Ingeborg reluctantly agreed to stop at a bar near the port; they were going to have a last beer before they left the city. According to Ingeborg, Charly was nervous and irritable, but not belligerent. The incident might not have occurred if in the course of the conversation Hanna hadn't reproached Charly for something that had happened in Oberhausen, something that Ingeborg knew nothing about. Hanna's words were vague and cryptic. At first, Charly listened to her recriminations in silence. "He was as white as a sheet and he looked scared," said Ingeborg. Then he got up, took Hanna by the arm, and disappeared with her into the bathroom. After a few minutes, worried, Ingeborg decided to knock on the door, not sure what was going on. The two of them were locked in the women's bathroom but they made no protest when they heard Ingeborg's voice. When they came out, both were crying. Hanna didn't say a word. Charly paid the bill and they left Barcelona. After half an hour's drive they stopped on the outskirts of one of the many towns along the coastal highway. The bar they went into was called Mar Salada. This time Charly didn't even try to talk them into it. He just ignored them and started to drink. After five or six beers he burst into tears. Then Ingeborg, who had planned to have dinner with me, asked for a menu and persuaded Charly to eat something. For a moment everything seemed to return to normal. The three of them had dinner and—with some difficulty—maintained the simulacrum of a civilized conversation. When it was time to leave, the trouble started up again. Charly was determined to stay and Ingeborg and Hanna were determined to get the keys so they could drive home. According to Ingeborg, the argument was pointless, and Charly was enjoying it. Finally he got up and pretended to be about to give them the keys or drive them back. Ingeborg and Hanna followed him. Once they were through the door Charly turned around abruptly and hit Hanna in the face. Hanna's response was to run toward the beach. Charly sprinted after her and in a few seconds Ingeborg heard Hanna's cries, muffled and plaintive as those of a child. When she reached them, Charly wasn't hitting Hanna anymore, although every so often he kicked her or spat on her. Ingeborg's first impulse was to get between them, but when she saw her friend on the ground with blood on her face she lost the little composure she had left and began to shout for help. Of course, no one came. The drama ended with Charly leaving in the car, Hanna bloodied and with only enough strength to refuse to call the police or an ambulance, and Ingeborg alone in a strange place and responsible for getting her friend home. Luckily the owner of the bar came to their aid, helped clean Hanna up without asking questions, and then called a taxi that brought them back. Now the problem was what Hanna should do. Where would she sleep? At her hotel or ours? If she slept at her hotel, what were the chances that Charly would hit her again? Should she go to the hospital? Was it possible that she had been more seriously injured than we thought? The watchman settled both questions: according to him there was no damage to the cheek-bone; the wound looked worse than it was. Regarding sleeping at the hotel, tomorrow there would surely be vacancies, but tonight, unfortunately, there were none. Hanna looked relieved when she realized she had no options. "It's my fault," she whispered. "Charly is on edge and I pushed him too far, that's just the way he is, the bastard, and he's not about to change." I think Ingeborg and I felt better when we heard this; it was for the best. We thanked the clerk for his help and went to leave Hanna at her hotel. It was a beautiful night. Not only the buildings but also the air had been rinsed clean by the rain. There was a cool breeze and everything was absolutely still. We walked her to the door of the Costa Brava and waited in the middle of the street. In a moment Hanna came out on the balcony to tell us that Charly hadn't returned. "Go to sleep and try not to think about anything," shouted Ingeborg before we headed back to the Del Mar. Back in our room, we talked about Charly and Hanna (critically, I would say) and we made love. Then Ingeborg picked up her Florian Linden novel and soon she was asleep. I went out on the balcony to smoke a cigarette and see if I could spot Charly's car.

At dawn the beach is full of seagulls. Along with the seagulls, there are pigeons. The seagulls and pigeons stand at the water's edge, *staring* out to sea, motionless except for the occasional short flight. There are two kinds of seagulls: big and small. From the distance the pigeons look like seagulls too. Seagulls of a third kind, only smaller. From the mouth of the port, boats set out, leaving behind them a dark wake on the smooth surface of the sea. Last night I didn't sleep at all. The sky is a pale and liquid blue. The edge of the horizon is white; the sand of the beach is brown, dotted with little mounds of debris. From the terrace—the waiters haven't arrived yet to set the tables—it promises to be a clear and calm day. One could say that the seagulls lined up along the beach watch imperturbably as the boats dwindle until they're nearly lost from sight. At this time of day the hotel corridors are warm and deserted. At the restaurant, a half-asleep waiter brusquely pulls back the curtains, but the light that bathes everything is pleasant and cold, a faint, contained light. The coffee machine has yet to be turned on. From the waiter's attitude I surmise that it will be a while. In the room Ingeborg is asleep with the Florian Linden novel tangled in the sheets. Softly I set it on the night table, though not before a sentence catches my eye. Florian Linden (I imagine) says: "You say you've committed the same crime several times. No, you're not crazy. That happens to be the very nature of evil." Carefully I replaced the bookmark and closed the book. On the way out I was struck by the strange notion that no one in the Del Mar planned to get up. But the streets weren't completely empty anymore. In front of the newsstand, on the border between the old town and the tourist quarter, at the bus stop, bundles of magazines and newspapers were being unloaded from a truck. I bought two German papers before heading down narrow streets toward the port, in search of an open bar.

In the doorway, silhouetted, stood Charly and the Wolf. Neither of them looked surprised to see me. Charly came straight over to my table while the Wolf ordered breakfast for two at the bar. I was afraid to say a word; outwardly, Charly and the Spaniard seemed calm, but behind their apparent calm they were on their guard.

"We followed you," said Charly. "We saw you leaving the hotel . . . You seemed very tired so we decided to *let you* walk for a while."

I realized that my left hand was trembling, just a little—they didn't notice—but I immediately hid it under the table. I began to prepare myself for the worst.

"You haven't slept either, have you?" said Charly.

I shrugged.

"I couldn't sleep," said Charly. "I suppose you'll have heard the whole story by now. I don't care; I mean, one day of sleep more or less doesn't matter to me. I feel a little bit bad about having woken up the Wolf. It's my fault he hasn't slept either, isn't that right, Wolf?"

The Wolf smiled uncomprehendingly. For an instant I had the crazy idea of translating what Charly had just said, but I didn't. Something obscure warned me that I'd better not.

"Friends are there to help in times of need," said Charly. "At least that's how I see it. Did you know that the Wolf is a true friend, Udo? For him, friendship is sacred. For example, right now he should be on his way to work, but I *know* he won't go until he leaves me at the hotel or some other safe place. He might lose his job, but he doesn't care. And why is that? It's because he understands that friendship is sacred. You don't mess around with friendship!"

Charly's eyes were bright; I thought he was about to cry. He gave his croissant a scowl of disgust and pushed it away. The Wolf made a motion as if to say that if Charly didn't want it he would eat it. Yes, take it, said Charly.

"I stopped by his house at four in the morning. Do you think I could do that with a stranger? Everyone is a stranger, of course, in the end we're all scum, and yet the Wolf's mother, who was the one who let me in, thought I'd been in an accident, and the first thing she did was offer me some cognac, which of course I accepted even though I was blotto. What a wonderful person. When the Wolf got up he found me sitting in one of his armchairs drinking cognac. What else could I do!"

"Nothing you say is making any sense to me," I said. "I think you're still drunk."

"No, I swear . . . It's simple: I knocked at the Wolf's door at four in the morning; his mother welcomed me like a prince; the Wolf and I tried to talk; we went out for a drive; we stopped at a few bars; we bought two bottles; then we went to the beach, to drink with El Quemado . . ."

"With El Quemado? On the beach?"

"The guy sleeps on the beach sometimes so that no one steals his disgusting pedal boats. So we decided to share our booze with him. Listen, Udo, here's something strange: from the beach we could see your balcony and I swear you had the light on all night. Yes or no? Oh, I know I'm right, it was your balcony and your windows and your goddamn light. What were you doing? Were you playing your war games or were you doing the nasty with Ingeborg? Ah ah! Don't look at me like that, it's a joke, what do I care. It really was your room, I realized that right away, and El Quemado realized it too. Anyway, busy night, seems like none of us got much sleep, did we?"

Beyond the embarrassment and rage I felt at learning that Charly was well aware of my love of games and that it must have been Ingeborg who informed him or malinformed him of it—I could even imagine the three of them on the beach laughing at their own clever riffs on the subject: "Udo may be the champ, but what a loser"; "This is how the General Staff spend their vacations, shut up indoors"; "Udo is convinced he's the reincarnation of von Manstein"; "What will you give him for his birthday, a water pistol?")—beyond, as I say, my embarrassment and rage at Charly, at Ingeborg, and at Hanna, I was visited by a quiet, creeping feeling of terror upon hearing that El Quemado too knew which was my balcony.

"Don't you think you'd better ask me about Hanna?" I said, trying to sound as normal as possible.

"What for? I'm sure she's fine. Hanna's always fine."

"What are you going to do now?"

"About Hanna? I don't know. Pretty soon I think I'll drop the Wolf off at work and then I'll head for the hotel. I hope Hanna will be at the beach by then because I want to get some serious sleep . . . It was a happening night, Udo. Even on the beach! Believe it or not, nobody here stops for a second, Udo, nobody. From the pedal boats, we heard a noise. That's something you don't expect, hearing noises on the beach at that time of night. The Wolf and I went to see what was going on and what do you think we found? A couple screwing. Two Germans, of course, because when I told them to have fun they answered in German. I didn't get a good look at the guy, but the girl was pretty, dressed in a white party dress like Inge's, lying there on the beach with her dress wrinkled and all that poetic crap."

"Inge? Are you talking about Ingeborg?" My hand started to shake again; I could literally smell the violence surrounding us.

"Not her, man, her white dress; she has a white dress, doesn't she? That's all I'm talking about. Do you know what the Wolf said then? That we should get in line. That we should get in line so we could take our turns when the guy was done. My God, I laughed so hard! He thought we could fuck her after that poor jerk! A bona fide rape! So funny. All I felt like was drinking and staring up at the stars. Yesterday it rained, remember? Anyway, there were a couple of stars in the sky, maybe three. And I was feeling good. If things had been different, Udo, maybe I would have gone along with the Wolf. Maybe the girl would have liked it. Maybe not. When we got back to the pedal boats I think the Wolf tried to convince El Quemado to go with him. El Quemado didn't want to go either. But I'm not sure, you know my Spanish isn't so good."

"Your Spanish is nonexistent," I said.

Charly laughed without much conviction.

"Do you want me to ask him and then you'll know for sure?" I added.

"No. It's none of my business . . . Anyway, believe me, I can communicate with my friends and the Wolf is my friend and we communicate just fine."

"I'm sure you do."

"That's right . . . It was a gorgeous night, Udo . . . A quiet night, full of dangerous ideas but no bad behavior . . . A quiet night, let me try to explain, quiet and yet without a still moment, a single still moment . . . Even when the sun came up and it seemed as if everything might be over, you came out of the hotel . . . At first I thought you'd seen me from the balcony and were coming to join the party. When you went off toward the port I woke up the Wolf and we followed you . . . Taking our time, as you saw. Like we were just out for a stroll."

"Hanna's not all right. You should go see her."

"Inge's not all right either, Udo. Neither am I. Neither is my pal the Wolf. Neither are you, if you don't mind me saying so. Only the Wolf's mother is all right. And Hanna's little boy, in Oberhausen. They're the only one's who're . . . well, not exactly all right, but compared to everybody else, more or less all right. Yes: all right."

There was something obscene about hearing him call Ingeborg Inge. Unfortunately, her friends, a few work colleagues, called her that too. It was no big deal and yet I'd never thought of this: I didn't know any of Ingeborg's friends. A shiver ran through me.

I ordered another coffee. The Wolf had one with a shot of rum (if he had to go to work, he didn't seem very worried about it). Charly didn't want anything. He only felt like smoking, which he did without stopping, one cigarette after another. But he promised he would pick up the bill.

"What happened in Barcelona?" I was about to say "You've changed," but it seemed ridiculous: I hardly knew him.

"Nothing. We walked around. We shopped for souvenirs. It's a pretty town. Too crowded, though. For a while I was a fan of FC Barcelona, when Lattek was coach and Schuster and Simonsen were playing. Not anymore. I've lost interest in the club but I still like the city. Have you been to the Sagrada Família? Did you like it? Yeah, it's pretty. And we went out drinking at some really old bar, full of posters of bullfighters and Gypsies. Hanna and Ingeborg thought it was cool. And it was cheap, much cheaper than the bars here."

"If you'd seen Hanna's face you wouldn't be sitting here like this. Ingeborg thought about reporting you to the police. If it had happened in Germany, I'm sure she would have."

"You're exaggerating . . . In Germany, in Germany . . ." He made a face, as if to say there was nothing to be done. "I don't know, maybe things there don't stand still for a second either. Shit. I don't care. Anyway, I don't believe you, I don't think it ever crossed Ingeborg's mind to call the police."

I shrugged, offended. Maybe Charly was right, maybe he knew Ingeborg's heart better than I did.

"What would you have done?" There was an evil gleam in Charly's eye.

"In your place?"

"No, in Inge's."

"I don't know. Beaten you up. Knocked you around."

Charly closed his eyes. To my surprise, my answer hurt him.

"Not me." He grasped in the air as if something very important were escaping him. "In Inge's place, I wouldn't have done that."

"Of course not."

"And I didn't want to rape the German girl on the beach, either. I could have done it, but I didn't. See what I mean? I could have wrecked Hanna's face, really wrecked it, and I didn't. I could have thrown a stone and broken your window or kicked your ass after you bought those filthy newspapers. I didn't do any of it. All I do is talk and smoke."

"Why would you want to break my window or hit me? That's idiotic."

"I don't know. It was just an idea. Fast, quick, with a stone the size of a fist." His voice broke as if suddenly he were remembering a nightmare. "It was El Quemado. When he looked up at the light in your window, just a way to get attention, I guess . . ."

"It was El Quemado's idea to break my window?"

"No, Udo, no. You don't understand anything, man. El Quemado was drinking with us, none of us saying a word, just listening to the sea, that's all, and drinking, but wide-awake, you know? and El Quemado and I were looking up at your window. I mean, when I spotted your window El Quemado was already staring up at it, and I realized it, and he realized that I had him. But he didn't say anything about throwing stones. That was my idea. I planned to *warn you* . . . Do you know what I mean?"

"No."

Charly gave me a look of disgust. He picked up the newspapers and flipped through them at incredible speed, as if before he was a mechanic he'd been a bank teller; I'm sure he didn't read a single full sentence. Then, with a sigh, he put them aside; by this he seemed to say that the news was for me, not for him. For a few seconds we were both silent. Outside, the street slowly resumed its daily rhythm; we were no longer alone in the bar.

"Deep down, I love Hanna."

"You should go see her right now."

"She's a good girl, she really is. And there's been a lot of good in her life even though she doesn't think so."

"You should go back to the hotel, Charly . . ."

"First let's drop the Wolf off at work, all right?"

"Fine, let's go right now."

When he got up from the table he was white, as if there was no blood left in his body. Without stumbling once, by which I deduced that he wasn't as drunk as I'd thought he was, he went up to the bar and paid, and we left. Charly's car was parked near the water. On the roof rack I saw the windsurfing board. Had he taken it with him to Barcelona? No, he must have put it there when he came back, which meant that he'd already been to the hotel. Slowly we covered the distance that separated us from the supermarket where the Wolf worked. Before the Wolf got out Charly told him that if he got fired he should come see him at the hotel, that he'd find some way to fix things. I translated. The Wolf smiled and said they wouldn't dare. Charly nodded gravely, and when we'd left the supermarket behind he said it was true, that with the Wolf any altercation could get complicated, not to say dangerous. Then he talked about dogs. In the summer it was common to see abandoned dogs starving in the streets. "Especially here," he said.

"Yesterday, on my way to the Wolf's house, I hit one."

He waited for me to say something, and he continued:

"A little black dog, one I'd seen on the Paseo Marítimo . . . Looking for his rotten owners or scraps of food . . . I don't know . . . Do you know the story of the dog who died of hunger next to his owner's body?"

"Yes."

"I thought about that. At first the poor animals don't know where to go, all they do is wait. That's loyalty, isn't it, Udo? If they make it through that stage they go roaming around and looking for food in trash cans. Yesterday, I got the feeling that the little black dog was still waiting. What does that say to you, Udo?"

"How are you so sure that you'd seen it before or that it was a stray dog?"

"Because I got out of the car and took a good look at it. It was the same one."

The light inside the car was beginning to put me to sleep.

For an instant I thought I saw tears in Charly's eyes.

"We're both tired," I said to myself.

At the door to his hotel I advised him to take a shower, go to bed, and wait to talk to Hanna until after he got up. Some guests were beginning to file toward the beach. Charly smiled and vanished down the corridor. I went back to the Del Mar, feeling uneasy.

I found Frau Else on the roof, after blithely ignoring the signs that indicated which areas were for guests and which were reserved for the hotel staff. And yet I must confess that I wasn't looking for her. It just so happened that Ingeborg was still asleep, the bar made me feel claustrophobic, I didn't feel like going out again, and I wasn't sleepy. Frau Else was reading, lying on a sky-blue lounge chair with a glass of juice beside her. She wasn't surprised to see me. In fact, in her usual calm voice she congratulated me on discovering the entrance to the roof. "The advantages of sleepwalking," I answered, cocking my head to get a look at the book she was holding. It was a guide to the south of Spain. Then she asked me whether I wanted something to drink. At my inquiring gaze she explained that even on the roof she had a bell to call the staff. Out of curiosity, I accepted. After a while I asked what she'd been up to the day before. I added that I'd been searching for her all over the hotel, to no avail. "You vanish with the rain," I said.

Frau Else's face darkened. In a gesture that seemed studied (but I know this is just the way she is, just another part of her spontaneity and verve), she took off her sunglasses and fixed her eyes on me before answering: yesterday she spent all day in her husband's room. Was he ill, perhaps? The bad weather, the clouds charged with electricity, bothered him; he had terrible headaches that affected his sight and his nerves; a few times he'd been afflicted with temporary blindness. Brain fever, said Frau Else's perfect lips. (As far as I know, there is no such illness.) Immediately, with the hint of a smile, she made me promise that I wouldn't come looking for her anymore. We'll see each other only when fate ordains. And if I refuse? I'll have to make you promise, whispered Frau Else. At that moment a maid appeared with a glass of juice just like the one in Frau Else's hand. For a few seconds, dazzled by the sun, the poor girl blinked and didn't know where to turn, then she set the glass on the table and left.

"I promise," I said, walking away toward the edge of the roof.

The day was yellow and from everywhere there came a glow of human flesh that made me sick.

I turned toward her and confessed that I hadn't slept all night. "No need to swear to it," she answered without lifting her gaze from the book again in her hands. I told her that Charly had hit Hanna. "Some men do that," was her reply. I laughed. "Clearly you're no feminist!" Frau Else turned the page without answering me. I told her then what Charly had explained to me about dogs, the dogs that people abandon before or during their vacations. I noticed that Frau Else was listening with interest. When I finished my story I saw a look of alarm in her eye; I was afraid that she was about to get up and come over to me. I was afraid that she would speak the words that at that moment I least wanted to hear. But she made no comment, and shortly afterward I considered it most prudent to retire.

Tonight everything was back to normal. At a club near the campgrounds, Hanna, Charly, Ingeborg, the Wolf, the Lamb, and I all raised our glasses to friendship, wine, beer, Spain, Germany, Real Madrid (the Wolf and the Lamb aren't Barcelona fans, as Charly assumed, but Real Madrid fans), pretty women, vacations, etc. Peace restored. Hanna and Charly, of course, had made up. Charly was back to being more or less the same ordinary boor we met on August 21, and Hanna had put on her flashiest and lowest-cut dress to celebrate it. Even her bruised cheek gave her a kind of erotic and roguish charm. (While she was sober she hid it under sunglasses, but in the clamor of the club she flaunted it cheerfully, as if she'd rediscovered herself and her raison d'être.) Ingeborg officially forgave Charly, who, in everyone's presence, kneeled at her feet and praised her virtues, to the delight of all those who could hear and understand German. The Wolf and the Lamb were no laggards in this show of goodwill; we owe to them the discovery of the most authentically Spanish restaurant we've been to thus far. A restaurant where, in addition to eating well and cheaply and to drinking even more abundantly and more cheaply, we got to hear a flamenco singer (that is, a singer of typical songs) who turned out to be a transvestite called Andromeda, a close acquaintance of our Spanish friends. After dinner, we spent a long time telling stories, singing, and dancing. Andromeda, sitting with us, showed the women how to clap their hands and then danced a dance called a *sevillana* with Charly; soon everybody was getting up to join them, even people from other tables, except for me; I refused categorically and a bit brusquely. I would have made a fool of myself. My brusqueness, however, seemed to please the transvestite, who read my palm once the dance was over. I'll have money, power, love; a full life; a gay son (or grandson) . . . Andromeda read the future and interpreted it. At first her voice was almost inaudible, a whisper, then gradually it rose, and by the end she was speaking so loudly that everyone could hear and laugh at her witty remarks. Anyone who volunteers for these games becomes the butt of the other patrons' jokes, but she had nothing unpleasant to say and before we left she gave us each a carnation and invited us to return. Charly left a thousand-peseta tip and swore in the name of his parents that he would. We all agreed that it was a place "worth seeing"; praise was showered on the Wolf and the Lamb. At the club the atmosphere was different, there were more young people and the setting was artificial, but it didn't take us long to get into the groove. Resignation. There I did dance and I kissed Ingeborg and Hanna and I went looking for the bathroom and I vomited and combed my hair and returned to the dance floor. At one point I grabbed Charly by the lapels and asked: Everything all right? Everything's amazing, he answered. From behind, Hanna threw her arms around him and pulled him away from me. Charly was trying to tell me something but all I could see were his lips moving and finally just his smile. Ingeborg had also gone back to being the Ingeborg of the night of August 21, the same old Ingeborg. She kissed me, hugged me, begged me to make love to her. So when we got back to our room, at five in the morning, we made love. Ingeborg came quickly; I held out and possessed her for many long minutes afterward. We were both tired. Naked on the sheets, Ingeborg said everything was simple. "Even your miniatures." She insisted on this term before falling asleep. "Miniatures." "Everything is simple." For a long time I lay staring at my game and *thinking*.

Today's events are still confused, but I'll try to set them down in
orderly fashion so that I can perhaps discover in them something
that has thus far eluded me, a difficult and possibly useless task,
since there's no remedy for what's happened and little point in nur-
turing false hopes. But I have to do something to pass the time.

I'll start with breakfast on the hotel terrace, in our bathing
suits, on a cloudless morning tempered by a pleasant breeze blowing from the sea. My original plan was to go back to the room after
it had been tidied and spend a few hours immersed in the game,
but Ingeborg did her best to change my mind: the morning was too
splendid not to leave the hotel. On the beach we found Hanna and
Charly lying on a giant mat; they were asleep. The mat, brand-new,
still had the price tag in one corner. I remember it with the sharp-
ness of a tattoo: 700 pesetas. It occurred to me then, or maybe it
occurs to me now, that the scene was familiar. The same thing
often happens when I stay up too late: insignificant details are
magnified and linger in my mind. I mean, it was nothing out of
the ordinary. And yet it struck me as disturbing. Or it strikes me
that way now, in the dark of night.

We spent the morning wrapped up in the same vain activities
as ever: swimming, talking, reading magazines, plastering our
bodies with lotions and tanning oils. We ate early, at a restaurant
packed with tourists who, like us, were in bathing suits and smelled

of sunscreen (not a pleasant scent at mealtime). Afterward I managed to escape; Ingeborg, Hanna, and Charly went back to the beach and I returned to the hotel. What did I do? Not much. I stared at my game, unable to concentrate, then I took a nap plagued with nightmares until six. When I saw from the balcony that the bathers were beating a mass retreat toward the hotels and campgrounds, I went down to the beach. It's a sad time of day, and the bathers are sad: tired, sated with sun, they turn their gazes toward the line of buildings like soldiers already sure of defeat. With tired steps they cross the beach and the Paseo Marítimo, prudent but with a hint of scorn, of arrogance in the face of a remote danger, their peculiar way of turning down side streets where they immediately seek out the shade leading them directly—they're a tribute—toward the void.

The day, viewed in retrospect, seems devoid of people and of omens. No Frau Else, no Wolf, no Lamb, no letter from Germany, no phone call, nothing significant. Only Hanna and Charly, Ingeborg and me, the four of us in peaceful coexistence, and El Quemado, but in the distance, busy with his pedal boats (there weren't many takers anymore), though Hanna, I don't know why, went over to talk to him, just for a bit, less than a minute, to be polite, she said afterward. Overall, a quiet day, a day of sunbathing and that was all.

I remember that when I went down to the beach for the second time, the sky suddenly filled with an infinity of clouds, tiny clouds that began to scurry toward the east or the northeast, and that Ingeborg and Hanna were swimming and when they saw me they came out, first Ingeborg, who kissed me, and then Hanna. Charly was lying facedown in the sun, which was no longer so strong, and he seemed to be asleep. To our left, El Quemado was patiently building his nightly fortress, removed from everything, at the time of day when surely his monstrous appearance was plainly revealed to him. I remember the ashen yellow color of the late afternoon, our insubstantial conversation (I couldn't tell you for sure what we talked about), the girls' wet hair, Charly's voice telling the absurd story of a boy learning to ride a bike. Everything indicated that this was a pleasant evening like any other and that soon we would return to our hotels to shower, preparing to cap off the night in some club.

Then Charly leaped up, grabbed his windsurfing board, and headed for the water. Until that instant I hadn't noticed the board was there, that it had been there all the time.

"Don't be long," shouted Hanna.

I don't think he heard her.

The first few yards he swam dragging the board after him; then he got up, raised the sail, waved to us, and headed out to sea on a favorable gust of wind. It must have been seven o'clock, not much later. He wasn't the only windsurfer. Of that I'm sure.

After an hour, tired of waiting, we went for a drink on the terrace of the Costa Brava, with a view of the whole beach and of the place where it seemed logical that Charly would appear. We felt dirty and thirsty. I remember that El Quemado, whom I saw every time I turned around in search of Charly's sail, never once stopped moving around his pedal boats, a kind of hardworking golem, until suddenly he simply disappeared (into his hut, I infer), but so unexpectedly, so dryly, that the beach telegraphed a double absence: Charly was missing and now El Quemado was missing. I think it was then that I began to worry that something was wrong.

At nine o'clock, though it still wasn't dark, we decided to ask the advice of the receptionist at the Costa Brava. He sent us to the Red Cross of the Sea, whose offices are on the Paseo Marítimo, just outside of the old town. There, after getting a detailed account from us, they radioed a rescue Zodiac. After half an hour the Zodiac called back, advising that we alert the police and the port's maritime authorities. Night was falling fast; I remember that I looked out the window and for a second I glimpsed the Zodiac we'd been speaking to. The clerk explained that the best thing for us to do was to return to the hotel and call Navy Headquarters, the police, and the Civil Protection offices; the manager of the hotel could advise us on everything. We said that's what we would do and we left. Half of the way home we were silent and the other half we spent arguing. According to Ingeborg they were all incompetents.

Hanna wasn't so sure, but she insisted that the manager of the Costa Brava hated Charly. There was also the possibility that Charly had ended up in a nearby town, the way he had once before, did we remember? I gave her my opinion: that she should do exactly what we'd been told to do. Hanna said yes, I was right, and she broke down in sobs.

At the hotel, the receptionist and later the manager explained to Hanna that windsurfing accidents were frequent around this time of year but that everything usually turned out all right. In the worst of cases the windsurfer might spend forty-eight hours adrift, but he was always rescued, etc. Upon hearing this Hanna stopped crying and seemed a little calmer. The manager offered to drive us to Navy Headquarters. There they took a statement from Hanna, got in touch with the port authority, and again with the Red Cross of the Sea. Shortly afterward two policemen arrived. They needed a detailed description of the board; a helicopter search was about to be launched. When asked whether the board was equipped with survival gear, we all declared ourselves absolutely ignorant of the existence of such a thing. One of the policemen said: "That's because it's a Spanish invention." The other policeman added: "Then everything will depend on how tired he is; if he falls asleep he'll be in trouble." It bothered me that they would talk like that in front of us, especially when they knew I could understand Spanish. Naturally, I didn't translate everything they said for Hanna. The manager, meanwhile, didn't seem worried at all, and on our way back to the hotel he actually joked about what was happening. "Are you enjoying this?" I asked. "Sure, everything's fine," he said. "Your friend will turn up soon enough. We're all working together on this. There's no way things can go wrong."

We had dinner at the Costa Brava. As might be expected, it wasn't a lively meal. Chicken with mashed potatoes and fried eggs, salad, coffee, and ice cream, which the waiters, who were aware of what was going on (in fact every eye was upon us), served with unusual friendliness. Our appetites hadn't suffered. As it happens, we were eating dessert when I saw the Wolf's face pressed to the glass wall between the dining room and the terrace. He was signaling to me. When I said that he was outside, Hanna turned red and lowered her eyes. In a tiny voice she asked me to get rid of them, let them come tomorrow, whatever I thought best. I shrugged and went out. The Wolf and the Lamb were waiting on the terrace. Briefly I explained what had happened; both were affected by the news (I think I saw tears in the Wolf's eyes, but I couldn't swear to it). Then I explained that Hanna was very upset and that we were waiting for news from the police. I couldn't think of any reason to object when they proposed coming back in an hour. I waited on the terrace until they left. One of them smelled like cologne, and within the bounds of their slovenly style they were dressed with care. When they got to the sidewalk they began to argue; when they turned the corner they were still gesticulating.

What happened next must, I presume, be standard routine in cases like this, though it was also annoying and unnecessary. First, one policeman arrived, then another one in a different uniform, accompanied by a civilian who spoke German and a navy seaman (in full garb!). Luckily they weren't here long (the sailor, according to the manager, was about to join the search in a speedboat equipped with spotlights). When they left they promised to let us know what they discovered, no matter the hour. In their faces I could see that the likelihood of finding Charly was growing increasingly slim. The last person to appear was a member—the secretary, I think—of the town's Windsurfing Club, who had come to promise us the material and moral support of the club's members. They had also sent out a rescue boat in cooperation with Navy Headquarters and Civil Protection the moment they heard news of the shipwreck. That's what the club secretary called it: a shipwreck. Upon this latest show of solidarity, Hanna, who during dinner had put on a brave face, once more fell into tears that soon turned into an attack of hysteria.

With the assistance of a waiter, we brought her up to her room and put her to bed. Ingeborg asked whether she had any sedatives. Sobbing, Hanna said no, the doctor had forbidden them. Finally we decided that it would be best if Ingeborg spent the night there.

Before returning to the Del Mar, I looked in at the Andalusia

Lodge. I hoped to find the Wolf and the Lamb, or El Quemado, but I didn't see anybody. The owner, sitting at the table closest to the television, was watching a Western, as usual. I left immediately. He didn't even turn around. From the Del Mar I called Ingeborg. No news. They were in bed although neither of them could sleep. Stupidly I said, "Try to console her." Ingeborg didn't answer. For a moment I thought the connection had been lost.

"I'm here," said Ingeborg. "I'm thinking."

"Yes," I said. "I'm thinking too."

Then we said good night and hung up.

For a while I lay on the bed with the lights off, wondering what could have happened to Charly. In my head I could come up with only random images: the new mat with the price tag still attached, the midday meal impregnated with repulsive scents, the water, the clouds, Charly's voice . . . I thought it was strange that no one had asked Hanna about her bruised cheek; I thought about what drowned people looked like; I thought that our vacation was essentially shot. This final thought made me jump up and get to work with uncommon energy.

At four in the morning I finished the Spring '41 turn. My eyes were closing with exhaustion but I was satisfied.

At ten in the morning Ingeborg called me to say that we had an appointment at Navy Headquarters. I waited for Ingeborg and Hanna in the car in front of the Costa Brava and we set off. Hanna was more animated than the night before. Her eyes and lips were made up, and when she saw me she smiled. Ingeborg's face, meanwhile, presaged nothing good. The Navy Headquarters is a few yards from the marina, on a narrow street in the old town. To get to the offices you have to cross an inner courtyard paved in dirty tiles, with a dry fountain in the middle. There, propped on the fountain, we discovered Charly's board. We knew that was what it was before anyone told us, and for an instant we were unable to speak or to keep walking. "Come on up, please, come on up," said a young man (I later recognized him as being from the Red Cross) from a second-story window. After the initial shock we went up; waiting on the landing were the head of Civil Protection and the secretary of the Windsurfing Club, who greeted us with warmth and sympathy. They asked us to come in: in the office were two other civilians, the kid from the Red Cross, and two policemen. One of the civilians asked us whether we recognized the board in the courtyard. Hanna, her tanned skin paling, shrugged. They asked me. I said I couldn't be sure; Ingeborg said the same thing. The secretary of the Windsurfing Club looked out the window. The policemen seemed fed up. I got the impression that no one dared to speak. It was hot. It was Hanna who broke the silence.

"Have you found him?" she asked in such a shrill voice that we all jumped. The German speaker rushed to answer no, we've only found the board and boom, which as you'll realize is quite significant . . . Hanna shrugged again. "Probably he knew he would fall asleep and he decided to tie himself on" . . . "Or he guessed that his strength wouldn't hold, the sea, the fear, the darkness, you know" . . . "In any case, he did the right thing: he let the sail go and tied himself to the board" . . . "These are guesses, of course" . . . "No effort has been spared: the search has been lengthy and we've taken every risk" . . . "This morning a boat belonging to the Fishermen's Guild found the board and the boom" . . . "Now we'll have to get in touch with the German consulate" . . . "Naturally we'll keep combing the area" . . . Hanna had her eyes closed. Then I realized that she was crying. We all exchanged somber glances. The kid from the Red Cross bragged: "I've been up all night." He seemed excited. His next move was to pull out some papers for Hanna to sign; I don't know what they were. We went to have sodas at a bar in town. We talked about the weather and the Spanish officials, well-intentioned people with few resources. The place was jammed with a dirty sort of day-tripper and it smelled strongly of sweat and tobacco. It was past twelve when we left. Ingeborg decided to stay with Hanna and I went up to the room. I could hardly keep my eyes open, and soon I was asleep.

I dreamed that someone was knocking at the door. It was nighttime, and when I opened the door I saw someone slipping down the hall. I followed. Unexpectedly we came to a huge dark room filled with the outlines of heavy old furniture. The smell of mildew and dampness was strong. On a bed a shadowy figure was twisting and turning. At first I thought it was an animal. Then I recognized Frau Else's husband. At last!

When Ingeborg woke me, the room was full of light and I was sweating. The first thing I noticed was her face, which was definitely changed: irritation was etched on her forehead and eyelids, and for a few instants we stared at each other blankly, as if we had both just woken up. Then she turned her back on me and gazed at the closets and the ceiling. She'd wasted half an hour trying to call me from the Costa Brava, she said, and there had been no answer. In her voice I heard anger and sadness; my attempt at conciliation only disgusted her. Finally, after a long silence during which I took a shower, she admitted: "You were asleep but I thought you'd left."

"Why didn't you come upstairs to see for yourself?"

Ingeborg reddened.

"There was no need . . . Anyway, this hotel scares me. The whole town scares me."

For some obscure reason I thought that she was right, but I didn't say so.

"That's silly . . ."

"Hanna loaned me some clothes, they fit just right, we're almost the same size." Ingeborg is talking quickly and for the first time she looks me in the eye.

In fact, the clothes she's wearing aren't hers. All of a sudden I'm aware of Hanna's taste, Hanna's aspirations, Hanna's steely determination to enjoy her vacation, and it's disconcerting.

"Any word of Charly?"

"Nothing. Some reporters were at the hotel."

"Then he's dead."

"Maybe. Better not to say anything to Hanna."

"No, of course not, that would be absurd."

When I got out of the shower, Ingeborg, who was sitting next to my game lost in thought, struck me as the image of perfection. I suggested that we make love. Without turning, she rejected me with a slight shake of the head.

"I don't know what appeals to you about this," she said, gesturing at the map.

"The clarity of it," I answered as I dressed.

"I think I hate it."

"Because you don't know how to play. If you knew how, you'd like it."

"Are women interested in this kind of game? Have you ever played with one?"

"I haven't. But they do exist. Not many of them, true; it isn't a game that particularly attracts girls."

Ingeborg gave me a bleak look.

"Everyone in the world has handled Hanna," she said suddenly.

"What?"

"Everyone's handled her." She made a terrible face. "Just because. I don't understand it, Udo."

"What do you mean? That everyone has slept with her? And who is everyone? The Wolf and the Lamb?" How or why I can't say, but I started to shake. First my knees and then my hands. It was impossible to hide.

After hesitating for a moment, Ingeborg jumped up, put her bikini and a towel in a straw bag, and literally fled the room. From the door, which she didn't bother to close, she said:

"Everyone's touched her and here you were in this room with your war."

"So what?" I shouted. "Does that have anything to do with it? Is it my fault?"

I spent the rest of the afternoon writing postcards and drinking beer. Charly's disappearance hadn't affected me the way one might expect it should. Every time I thought about him—which was often, I admit—I felt a kind of emptiness, and nothing more. At seven I went over to the Costa Brava to check things out. I found Ingeborg and Hanna in the TV room, a long narrow room with green walls and a window that looked out onto an inner courtyard full of dying plants. The place was depressing, and I said so. Poor Hanna gave me a sympathetic look. She had put on dark glasses and she smiled when she said that this meant no one ever came in, the guests usually watched TV in the hotel bar; the manager had promised that this was a quiet place. And are the two of you all right here? I asked stupidly, even stuttering. Yes, we're all right, answered Hanna for both of them. Ingeborg didn't even look at me: she kept her eyes glued to the screen, faking interest in an American series dubbed in Spanish of which obviously she didn't understand a word. Near them, in a kind of toy armchair, an old woman was dozing. I nodded toward her inquiringly. Someone's mother, said Hanna, and she laughed. They made no objection when I offered to buy them a drink, but they refused to leave the hotel; according to Hanna, news could come when we least expected it. So we were there until eleven, talking among ourselves and to the waiters. Hanna has evidently become the hotel celebrity; everyone knows about her misfortune and at least superficially she's the object of admiration. Her bruised cheek contributes to people's vague sense of a tragic tale. It's as if she herself has escaped from some shipwreck.

Life in Oberhausen, of course, was evoked. In an uninterrupted murmur, Hanna recalled the basic traits of a man and a girl, a woman and an old woman, two old women, a boy and a woman—all disastrous pairs whose ties to Charly were scarcely explained. The truth is that Hanna had met only half of them. Alongside all of these masks, Charly's face shone with virtue: he had a heart of gold, he was always seeking adventure and the truth (what *truth* and what *adventure* I chose not to inquire), he knew how to make a woman laugh, he didn't have stupid prejudices, he was reasonably brave, and he loved children. When I asked what she meant when she said that he didn't have stupid prejudices, Hanna answered: "He knew how to ask for forgiveness."

"Do you realize that you've started to talk about him in the past tense?"

For an instant Hanna seemed to ponder my words. Then, with her head bowed, she started to cry. Fortunately this time there were no hysterics.

"I don't think Charly is dead," she said at last, "though I'm sure I'll never see him again."

Seeing that we were incredulous, Hanna said she believed it was all one of Charly's jokes. She couldn't imagine that he'd died for the simple reason that he was such a good swimmer. Then why hadn't he turned up? What reason did he have to hide? Hanna believed it had something to do with madness and the loss of love. An American novel told a similar story, except that in it the motive was hatred. Charly didn't hate anyone. Charly was crazy. Also: he had stopped loving her (this final certainty seemed to give Hanna strength).

After dinner we went out to talk on the terrace of the Costa Brava. Actually, it was Hanna who talked and we who followed the erratic twists of her conversation as if we were taking turns caring for an invalid. Hanna has a soft voice, and despite the silly things she rattled off it was soothing to listen to her. She described the telephone conversation she'd had with an official at the German consulate as if it were a romantic encounter; she pontificated on the "voice of the heart" and the "voice of nature"; she told stories about her son and wondered whom he would look like when he grew up: at present he looked just like her. In short, she had grown resigned to the horror or, perhaps more astutely, she had exchanged the horror for rupture. When we said our good nights there was no one left on the terrace and the hotel restaurant was dark.

According to Ingeborg, Hanna hardly knows anything about Charly:

"When she talked to the official from the consulate she couldn't give a single address of near or distant relatives to contact about his disappearance. She could only give the name of the company where they both worked. The truth is, she knows nothing about Charly's past life. On the bedside table in her room she had Charly's ID booklet open, with his picture surveying everything. Next to the booklet there was a little pile of money and Hanna was very explicit: it's *his* money."

Ingeborg was afraid to look at the suitcase where Hanna had put Charly's things.

Departure date: the hotel is paid up through September 1, that is, tomorrow noon. She'll have to decide whether to go or stay. I suppose she'll stay, although she starts work on September 3. Charly would've started work on September 3 too. Which reminds me that Ingeborg and I have to be back on the 5th.

At noon Hanna left for Germany in Charly's car. As soon as the manager of the Costa Brava heard the news, he said it was a grave mistake. The only reason Hanna gave was that she couldn't stand the stress anymore. Now, in a dark and inescapable way, we're alone, which until recently was something that I desired, though certainly not in the way it came about. Everything seems the same as yesterday, although sadness has already begun to roll over the landscape. Before leaving, Hanna begged me to take care of Ingeborg. Of course I will, I reassured her, but who will take care of me? You're stronger than she is, she said from inside the car. This surprised me, since most people who know both of us think Ingeborg is stronger. Behind Hanna's dark glasses there was a troubled look in her eyes. Nothing bad will happen to Ingeborg, I promised. Beside us, Ingeborg snorted sarcastically. I believe you, said Hanna, squeezing my hand. Later the manager of the Costa Brava began to pester us by phone, as if he blamed us for Hanna's departure. The first call arrived while we were eating. A waiter came to get me at the table and I thought, against all logic, that it was Hanna calling from Oberhausen to let us know that she had arrived safely. It was the manager; he was so upset that he couldn't speak clearly. He had called to confirm that Hanna had just left. I said yes and then he told me that by "fleeing" Hanna had just flouted every principle of Spanish law. Her situation now was very precarious. I ventured to suggest that Hanna might not have known she was breaking a law. Not one law, said the manager, several! And ignorance, young man, is never an excuse. No, the hotel bill was paid. The problem was Charly, because when his body appeared, which no doubt it would, someone had to be present to identify it. Of course, the Spanish police could wire the German police the information that Charly had given when he registered at the hotel; the Germans would do the rest with their computers. It's utterly irresponsible of her, he said before he hung up. The second call, a few minutes later, was to inform us in astonishment that Hanna had taken Charly's car, which could be considered a criminal act. This time it was Ingeborg who talked to him, saying that Hanna was no thief and that she needed the car to get back to Germany. Why else would she want it? What she did afterward with the damn car was her business and nobody else's. The manager insisted that it was a theft and the conversation ended a bit abruptly. The third call, conciliatory, was to ask us whether, as friends, we could represent the "party in question" (by this I suppose he meant poor Charly) in the search efforts. We accepted. Despite the sound of it, representing the affected party didn't mean much. True, the rescue efforts continued, though no one had any hopes now of finding Charly alive. All of a sudden we understood Hanna's decision. The situation was unbearable.

Nothing has changed. That's what surprises me. This morning it was impossible to navigate the hotel corridors because of all the people leaving, but this afternoon, on the terrace, I've already spotted the pale and enthusiastic faces of a new influx. The temperature has gone up, as if we were back in July, and the evening breeze that cooled the sweltering town streets has vanished. A sticky sweat makes clothes cling to the body, and going out for a walk is torture. I saw the Wolf and the Lamb about three hours after Hanna left, at the Andalusia Lodge. At first they pretended not to see me; then they came over, looking stricken, and proceeded to ask me the obligatory questions. I answered that there was nothing new to tell and that Hanna was on her way back to Germany. With this last bit of news, their expressions and demeanor changed notably. They grew more relaxed and friendlier; after a few minutes I realized that I wasn't about to get rid of them anytime soon: the conversation continued along the usual lines, in the same code that they had used with Charly, except that instead of Charly, there I was, and instead of Hanna, there was Ingeborg!

Later I asked Ingeborg what she'd meant when she said that everybody handled Hanna. Her answer put an end to my speculations, at least in part. It was a generalization, Hanna as the victim of men, an unlucky woman, in perpetual search of balance and happiness, etc. . . . The possibility of a Hanna raped by the Spaniards was absurd; in fact, Ingeborg hardly gave them a second thought: she spoke of them as if they were invisible. Two average kids, not very hardworking, to judge by their schedules, who liked to have a good time; she liked to go clubbing too and even do crazy things once in a while. Crazy like what? I wondered. Staying out late, drinking too much, singing in the street. Craziness—Ingeborg's—of the mildest variety. Healthy crazy, she explained. So there was no reason to avoid the Spaniards or be angry at them, beyond the obvious reasons. This was how things stood when, at ten o'clock, the Wolf and the Lamb appeared once more on the scene. The conversation, really a spurned invitation to go out, proceeded in highly tasteless fashion, with us sitting on the hotel terrace (all the tables were full and crowded with ice cream dishes and empty glasses) and the two of them standing on the sidewalk, separated from us by the iron railing, the boundary between the terrace and the mass of passersby who at that time of night, suffocated by the heat, were strolling along the Paseo Marítimo. At first neither of them made anything but the tamest of remarks. The one who talked (and gestured) more was the Lamb, and what he said managed to draw a smile or two from Ingeborg, even before I translated. The Wolf's contributions, meanwhile, were careful and deliberate, as if he were feeling out the territory, expressing himself in an English superior to his education, the manifestation of a steely will, a desire to poke his nose into a world whose outline he could only imagine. Never had the Wolf's nickname so truly suited him; Ingeborg's face—bright, fresh, tanned—attracted his gaze as the moon attracts werewolves in old horror movies. Seeing that we were reluctant to go, he insisted, and his voice grew hoarse. He promised clubs worthy of the trip, he assured us that our weariness would vanish the minute we stepped into one of his famous dives . . . All for nothing. Our refusal was irrevocable and issued two feet over their heads, because the sidewalk is lower than the terrace. The Spaniards didn't insist. Imperceptibly, as a prelude to their farewell, they began to reminisce about Charly. The capital-F Friend. Anyone would think they really did miss him. Then they shook hands with us and walked off toward the old town. Their figures, soon lost in the crowd, struck me as unbearably sad, and I said so to Ingeborg. She stared at me for a few seconds and said she didn't understand me:

"A minute ago you thought they'd raped Hanna. Now you feel sorry for them. The truth is, those morons are nothing but a couple of pathetic Latin lovers."

Neither of us could stop laughing until Ingeborg suggested that for once we go to bed early. I agreed.

After making love, I sat down to write in the room while Ingeborg immersed herself in the Florian Linden novel. She still hasn't figured out who the killer is, and from the way she reads one would think she doesn't care. She seems tired; these last few days haven't been pleasant. I don't know why, but I found myself thinking about Hanna in the car, before she left, giving me advice in her broken voice . . .

"Do you think Hanna's gotten to Oberhausen yet?"

"I don't know. She'll call tomorrow," says Ingeborg.

"What if she doesn't?"

"You mean what if she forgets about us?"

No, of course, she wouldn't forget Ingeborg. Or me. Suddenly I was afraid. Afraid and a little excited. But what was I afraid of? I remembered Conrad's words: "Play on your own turf and you'll always win." But what is my turf? I asked. Conrad laughed in a peculiar way, without taking his eyes off me. The side that calls to your blood. I answered that playing like that was no guarantee of winning; for example, if in *Destruction of the Central Army Group* I chose the Germans, the most I could hope for was to win one time out of every three. Unless I was playing a complete idiot. You don't understand, said Conrad. You have to use the Grand Strategy. You have to be more cunning than a fox. Was this a dream? The truth is I've never heard of a game called *Destruction of the Central Army Group*!

Otherwise, it's been a boring and unproductive day. I spent a while lying patiently on the beach in the sun, trying unsuccessfully to think clearly and rationally. Images from a decade ago drifted through my mind: my parents playing cards on the hotel balcony, my brother floating twenty yards offshore with his arms outstretched, Spanish boys (Gypsies?) roaming the beach armed with sticks, the staff dorm room, smelly and full of bunk beds, a strip of nightclubs, one after the other, running down to the sea, a black sand beach fronting a sea of black water where the only note of color, suddenly, was El Quemado's fortress of pedal boats . . . My article awaits. The books I pledged to read await. And yet the hours and days speed by, as if time were running downhill. But that's impossible.

The police . . . I told Frau Else that we were leaving tomorrow. Unexpectedly, the news surprised her; her face betrayed a faint hint of regret that she hurried to hide under a professional cheeriness. The day had begun badly: my head hurt and I was sweating copiously despite the three aspirins and the cold shower I'd taken. Frau Else asked me whether a satisfactory conclusion had been reached. To what? Our vacation. I shrugged, and she took my arm and led me to a little office tucked behind the reception desk. She wanted to know everything about Charly's disappearance. In a monotone, I gave her a summary of what had happened. It came out pretty well. In proper chronological order.

"I spoke today to Mr. Pere, the manager of the Costa Brava. He thinks you're an idiot."

"Me? What do I have to do with anything?"

"Nothing, I suppose. But it would be a good idea to prepare yourself . . . The police want to question you."

I turned white. Me! Frau Else's hand patted me on the knee.

"There's nothing to worry about. They just want to know why the girl went back to Germany. It was a rather odd thing to do, don't you think?"

"What girl?"

"The girlfriend of the dead man."

"I just told you. She was tired of all the chaos; she has personal problems; there were plenty of reasons."

"All right, but it was her boyfriend. The least she could do was wait until they had finished the search."

"Tell that to her, not me . . . So I have to stay here until the police turn up?"

"No, do whatever you want. If I were you I'd go to the beach. When they get here I'll send a staff person to find you."

"Does Ingeborg have to be here too?"

"No, one of you is enough."

I did as Frau Else suggested, and we were at the beach until six when a messenger came to get us. The messenger, a boy of about twelve, was dressed like a beggar and it was hard to see how he had been hired to work at a hotel. Ingeborg insisted on coming with me. The beach was a deep golden color and it seemed frozen in time; really, I would've been happy to stay there. The policemen were in uniform and they were at the bar, talking to a waiter. Frau Else pointed them out to us from the reception desk, though there was no need. I remember that, as we approached them, I thought they would never turn around to face us and I would have to tap one on the back the way a person knocks at the door. But they must have sensed that we'd come in by the glance of the waiter or some other sign I didn't notice, and before we got to them they stood up and saluted us, which had an unsettling effect on me. We sat at a secluded table and they got straight to the point: did Hanna know what she was doing when she left Spain? (we didn't know whether Hanna knew), what ties bound her to Charly? (friendship), why had she left? (we didn't know), what was her address in Germany? (we didn't know—a lie, Ingeborg has it written down—but they could get it from the German consulate in Barcelona, where Hanna had, we presumed, left all her personal information), did Hanna think or did we think that Charly had committed suicide? (we certainly didn't think so; who knew what Hanna thought), and so on, more pointless questions until the interview was over. The policemen were nothing but polite, and when they left they gave us another military salute. Ingeborg smiled at them although when we were alone she said that she couldn't wait to be in Stuttgart, far away from this sad, corrupt town. When I asked her what she meant by "corrupt," she got up and left me alone in the dining room. Just as she was leaving, Frau Else came out from behind the reception desk and headed toward us. Neither of the two of them stopped, but Frau Else smiled as she passed Ingeborg; Ingeborg, I'm sure, didn't smile back. In any case, Frau Else gave no sign that she'd noticed. When she reached me she wanted to know how the interrogation had gone. I admitted that Hanna had made things worse by leaving. According to Frau Else, the Spanish police were charming. I didn't argue. For a moment neither of us spoke, though the silence was charged. Then Frau Else took me by the arm as she'd done before and led me down a series of corridors; the entire way she opened her mouth only to say, "You shouldn't let this get you down"; I think I nodded. We stopped at a room near the kitchen. It seemed to serve as the hotel's laundry. Through a window was a cement-paved inner courtyard full of wooden baskets and covered by a huge green tarp through which the evening light barely filtered. In the un-air-conditioned kitchen a girl and an old man were still washing the lunch dishes. Then, without warning, Frau Else kissed me. The truth is, it didn't take me by surprise. I wanted it and I was hoping for it. But to be honest, I didn't think it was likely. Naturally, her kiss got the passionate response called for under the circumstances. Though we didn't do anything untoward. From the kitchen the dishwashers could have seen us. After five minutes we pulled apart; we were both shaken and we returned to the dining room without saying a word. There Frau Else shook my hand and left me. I can still hardly believe it happened.

The rest of the afternoon I spent with El Quemado. First I went up to the room, but Ingeborg wasn't there. I supposed she had gone out shopping. The beach was half deserted and El Quemado didn't have much work. I found him sitting next to the pedal boats, for once lined up and facing the sea, with his gaze fixed on the only pedal boat that had been rented, which seemed to be very far from shore. I sat down next to him as if he were an old friend and soon I was drawing a map in the sand of the Battle of the Ardennes (one of my specialties), or the Battle of the Bulge, as the Americans call it, and I gave a detailed explanation of battle plans, the order in which units would appear, highways to use, river crossings, the demolition and construction of bridges, the offensive activation of the Fifteenth Army, real and simulated advances of Battle Group Peiper, etc. Then I erased the map with my foot, smoothed the sand, and drew a map of the area around Smolensk. There, I pointed out, Guderian's panzer group had fought an important battle in '41, a crucial battle. I had always won it. For the Germans, of course. I erased the map again, smoothed the sand, drew a face. Only then did El Quemado smile, without diverting his attention for long from the pedal boat still lost in the distance. A slight shiver ran through me. The flesh of his cheek, two or three poorly healed scars, bristled, and for a second I was afraid that with this optical effect—there was nothing else it could be—he could hypnotize me and ruin my life forever. I was rescued by El Quemado's own voice. As if speaking from an insurmountable distance, he said: do you think we get along well? I nodded several times, happy to be able to escape the spell cast by his deformed cheek. The face that I had drawn was still there, barely a sketch (though I should say that I'm not bad at drawing), until suddenly I realized with horror that it was a portrait of Charly. The realization left me speechless. It was as if someone had guided my hand. I hurried to erase it and immediately I drew a map of Europe, North Africa, and the Middle East, and with the aid of many arrows and circles I illustrated my decisive strategy to win at *Third Reich*. I'm afraid El Quemado didn't understand a thing.

The big news of the night is that Hanna called. She had telephoned twice before, but neither Ingeborg nor I was at the hotel. When I arrived, the receptionist gave me the message and I wasn't happy to get it. I didn't want to talk to Hanna and I prayed that Ingeborg would show up before the third call came. My mood thus altered, I went up to wait in the room. When Ingeborg got back we decided to change our plan, which had been to eat at a restaurant near the port, and to stay and wait at the Del Mar. It was the right choice. Hanna called just as we were about to dig into our frugal dinner: toasted ham and cheese sandwiches and french fries. I remember that a waiter came to find us and as we got up from the table Ingeborg said it wasn't necessary for both of us to go. I said it didn't matter, the food wouldn't get cold anyway. Frau Else was at the reception desk. She was wearing a different dress from the one she'd been wearing that afternoon and she seemed to have just stepped out of the shower. We smiled and tried to carry on a conversation as Ingeborg, with her back to us, as far away as she could get, whispered things like "Why?" "I can't believe it," "Disgusting," "For God's sake," "The pigs," and "Why didn't you tell me before?" which I couldn't help hearing and that wore on my nerves. I also noticed that with each exclamation Ingeborg hunched over a little more until she looked like a snail. I felt sorry for her; she was scared. Meanwhile, Frau Else, with her elbows firmly planted on the counter and her face aglow, began to resemble a Greek statue: only her lips moved when she spoke plainly about what had happened hours before in the laundry room. (I think she asked me not to harbor false hopes; I can't say for sure.) As Frau Else talked, I smiled, but all of my senses were focused on what Ingeborg was saying. The phone cord seemed about to wind itself around her neck.

The conversation with Hanna was interminable. After she hung up, Ingeborg said:

"Good thing we're leaving tomorrow."

We went back to the dining room but we didn't touch our plates. Cruelly, Ingeborg remarked that Frau Else, without makeup, reminded her of a witch. Then she said that Hanna was crazy, that she didn't understand her at all. She avoided my eyes and tapped the table with her fork. From a distance, I thought, a stranger would have taken her for no more than sixteen. An overwhelming tenderness for her rose from the pit of my stomach. Then her voice rose to a scream: How could this happen, how could this happen? Startled, I feared that she would make a scene in front of the people left in the dining room, but Ingeborg, as if reading my mind, suddenly smiled and said she'd never see Hanna again. I asked her what Hanna had said. Anticipating her response, I said that it was logical that Hanna should still be a little off balance. Ingeborg shook her head. I was wrong. Hanna was much smarter than I thought. Her voice was icy. In silence we finished our dessert and went up to the room.

I accompanied Ingeborg to the station; for half an hour we sat on a bench waiting for the arrival of the train to Cerbère. We hardly said a thing. Wandering around on the platform were crowds of tourists whose vacations were almost over and who still fought for a place in the sun. Only the elderly sat on benches in the shade. Between those who were leaving and me an abyss yawned. Ingeborg, however, didn't strike me as out of place on that crowded train. We wasted our last few minutes giving directions: many people didn't know where to go and the station employees hardly offered much guidance. People are like sheep. After showing one or two the exact spot to catch the train (not difficult to figure out, after all: there are only four tracks), we were accosted by German and English tourists wanting to check their information with us. From the train window Ingeborg asked whether she'd see me soon in Stuttgart. Very soon, I said. The face that Ingeborg made, a slight pursing of the lips and a quiver of the tip of the nose, suggested she didn't believe me. I don't care!

Until the last moment I thought she'd stay. No, that's not true, I always knew that nothing could stop her. Her work and her independence come first, not to mention that after Hanna's call all she could think about was leaving. So it wasn't a happy farewell. And it surprised more than one person, Frau Else first among them, though maybe what surprised Frau Else was my decision to stay. To be perfectly honest, Ingeborg herself was the first to be surprised.

What was the exact moment when I knew she would leave?

Yesterday, as she was talking to Hanna, everything fell into place. Everything became clear and irrevocable. (But we didn't discuss it at all.)

This morning I paid her bill, hers alone, and carried down her suitcases. I didn't want to make a scene or have it look as if she were running away. I was an idiot. I suppose the receptionist hurried off to give the news to Frau Else. It was still early when I ate lunch at the chapel. From the lookout point, the beach appeared to be deserted. Deserted compared to previous days, I mean. Again I ate rabbit stew and drank a bottle of Rioja. I think I didn't want to go back to the hotel. The restaurant was almost empty, except for some businessmen who were celebrating something at two tables pushed together in the middle of the room. They were from Gerona and they were telling jokes in Catalan that their wives hardly bothered to acknowledge. As Conrad says: meetings are no place for girl-friends. The atmosphere was deadly; they all seemed as dazed as me. I took a nap in the car, at a cove near town that I thought I remembered from vacations with my parents. I woke up sweating and not the least bit drunk.

In the afternoon I visited the manager of the Costa Brava, Mr. Pere, and assured him that he could find me at the Del Mar if he needed me for anything. We exchanged pleasantries and I left. Then I was at Navy Headquarters, where no one could give me any information about Charly. The woman I saw first didn't even know what I was talking about. Luckily there was an official there who was familiar with the case and everything was cleared up. No news. Efforts were continuing. Patience. In the courtyard a small crowd gathered. A boy from the Red Cross of the Sea said they were the relatives of a new drowning victim. For a while I stayed there, sitting on the stairs, until I decided to go back to the hotel. I had a massive headache. At the Del Mar I searched in vain for Frau Else. No one could tell me where she was. The door to the hallway that leads to the laundry room was locked. I know there's another way to get there, but I couldn't find it.

The room was a wreck: the bed was unmade and my clothes were scattered all over the floor. Several *Third Reich* counters had fallen too. It would've made the most sense if I had packed my bags and left. But I called down to the reception desk and asked them to tidy the room. Soon the girl I'd met before appeared, the same one who'd tried to find a table for me. A good omen. I sat down in a corner and told her to clean everything up. In a minute the room was neat and bright (easy enough to achieve the latter: all it required was opening the curtains). When she'd finished she gave me an angelic smile. Satisfied, I found one thousand pesetas for her. She's a smart girl: the fallen counters were lined up beside the board. Not a single one was missing.

The rest of the afternoon, until it got dark, I spent on the beach with El Quemado, talking about my games.

SEPTEMBER 4

I bought sandwiches at a bar called Lolita and beers at a supermarket. When El Quemado arrived I told him to sit beside the bed and I took a seat to the right of the table, with one hand resting in a relaxed fashion on the edge of the game board. I had a wide-angle view: to one side El Quemado, with the bed and the bedside table (the Florian Linden book still on it!) behind him, and to the other side, to the left, the open balcony, the white chairs, the Paseo Marítimo, the beach, the pedal boat fortress. I planned to let him speak first, but words didn't come easily to El Quemado, so I talked. I began by giving him a brief account of Ingeborg's departure: the train trip, her job, full stop. I don't know whether he was convinced. I went on to talk about the nature of the game, saying who knows how many stupid things, among them that the urge to play is simply a kind of song and that the players are singers performing an infinite range of compositions, dream compositions, deep-bore compositions, wish compositions, against the backdrop of a constantly shifting geography; decomposing food, that was what the maps and their constituent parts—the rules, the throws of the dice, the final victory or defeat—were like. Rotting food. I think that was when I brought out the sandwiches and beers, and as El Quemado began to eat I sprang over his legs and grabbed the Florian Linden book as if it were a treasure about to vanish into thin air. Among its pages I found no letter, no note, not the tiniest sign of

124

hope. Just random words, police interrogations and confessions. Outside, night gradually crept over the beach and created the illusion of movement, of small dunes and fissures in the sand. Without moving from where he was, in a corner that grew darker and darker, El Quemado ate with the slowness of a ruminant, his lowered gaze fixed on the floor or on the tips of his huge fingers, emitting at regular intervals moans that were almost inaudible. I must confess that I experienced something like revulsion, a feeling of suffocation and heat. El Quemado's moans each time he swallowed a mouthful of bread and cheese, or bread and ham, depending on which of the two sandwiches he was eating, constricted my chest until it felt as if it would burst. Overcome by weakness, I stepped over to the switch and turned on the light. Immediately I felt better, although there was still a hum in my temples, a hum that didn't prevent me from picking up where I'd left off. Instead of sitting down again, I paced back and forth from the table to the bathroom door (I turned the bathroom light on too) and talked about the distribution of the army corps, about the dilemmas that two or more fronts could pose for the German player possessed of a limited number of forces, about the difficulties involved in transferring vast masses of infantry and armored units from west to east, from the north of Europe to the north of Africa, and about the common fate of average players: a fatal insufficiency of units to cover everything. These reflections caused El Quemado, with his mouth full, to pose a question that I didn't bother to answer; I didn't even understand it. I suppose I was carried away by my own momentum and inside I didn't feel very well. So instead of responding I told him to come over to the map and take a look for himself. Meekly El Quemado approached and agreed that I was right: anyone could see that the black counters wouldn't win. But wait! With my strategy, the situation changed. As an example, I described a match played in Stuttgart not long ago, although in my heart I gradually realized that this wasn't what I wanted to say. What did I want to say? I don't know. But it was important. Then: complete silence. El Quemado sat down next to the bed again, holding a little piece of sandwich between two fingers like an engagement ring, and I went out on the balcony walking as if in slow motion and I looked up at the stars and down at the tourists passing below. If only I hadn't. Sitting on the edge of the Paseo Marítimo, the Wolf and the Lamb were watching my room. When they saw me they waved and shouted. Although at first I thought they were shouting insults, their cries were friendly. They wanted us to come down and have a drink with them (how they knew that El Quemado was there is a mystery to me) and beckoned more and more urgently; it wasn't long before I saw passersby raising their eyes to search for the balcony that was the source of all the commotion. I had two options: either to retreat and close the balcony door without a word or to get rid of them with a promise that I had no intention of keeping. Both possibilities were unpleasant; red faced (a detail that the Wolf and the Lamb couldn't see, considering the distance), I promised that I'd meet them in a while at the Andalusia Lodge. I stood on the balcony until they were lost from sight. In the room El Quemado was studying the counters deployed on the Eastern front. Engrossed, he seemed to understand how and why the units were deployed along particular lines, though obviously that was impossible. I dropped into a chair and said I was tired. El Quemado scarcely blinked. Then I asked why that pair of morons couldn't leave me alone. What do they want? To play? asked El Quemado. I noticed an attempt at clumsy irony on his lips. No, I answered, they want to go out drinking, have fun, anything that makes them feel less mummified.

"A monotonous life, isn't it?" he croaked.

"Even worse, a monotonous holiday."

"Well, *they're* not on holiday."

"It doesn't make any difference, they live off of other people's holidays, they attach themselves to other people's holidays and leisure and make tourists' lives miserable. They're parasites."

El Quemado stared at me incredulously. Evidently the Wolf and the Lamb were his friends despite the apparent divide between them. In any case, I didn't regret what I'd said. I remembered—or rather saw—Ingeborg's face, fresh and rosy, and the certainty of happiness I felt when I was with her. All wrecked. The force of the injustice quickened my movements: I picked up tweezers and with the speed of a cashier counting out bills I placed the counters in the force pools, the units in the proper squares, and, trying not to sound dramatic, I invited him to play one or two turns, though my intention was to play a full game, through the Great Destruction. El Quemado hunched his shoulders and smiled several times, still undecided. This made him look almost uglier than I could bear, so as he considered his response I stared at a random point on the map, as is done in matches when the opponents are two players who have never met before, each avoiding the physical presence of the other until the first turn begins. When I looked up I met El Quemado's innocent eyes, and I could see that he accepted. We pulled our chairs over to the table and deployed our forces. The armies of Poland, France, and the USSR were left with an unpropitious opening gambit, though it wasn't as bad as it could have been, considering that El Quemado was such a beginner. The English Army, meanwhile, occupied decent positions, its fleet evenly distributed—with support in the Mediterranean from the French fleet—and the few army corps covering hexes of strategic importance. El Quemado turned out to be a fast learner. The global situation on the map to some degree resembled the historic situation, which doesn't often happen when it's veterans playing each other. They would never deploy the Polish Army along the border, or the French Army on *all* the hexes of the Maginot Line, since it makes most sense for the Poles to defend Warsaw in a ring, and for the French to cover just one hex of the Maginot Line. I took the first turn, explaining as I went, so that El Quemado was able to understand and appreciate the elegance with which my armored units broke through the Polish defenses (air superiority and mechanized exploitation), the massing of forces on the border with France, Belgium, and Holland, Italy's declaration of war, and the advance (toward Tunis!) of the bulk of the troops stationed in Libya (the conventional wisdom is that Italy should enter the war no sooner than the winter of '39, or if possible the spring of '40, a strategy to which I obviously don't subscribe), the entry of two German armored corps into Genoa, the trampoline hex (Essen) where I based my paratrooper corps, etc., all this with a minimal expenditure of BRP. El Quemado's response could only be tentative: on the Eastern front he invaded the Baltic states and the adjoining section of Poland, but he forgot to occupy Bessarabia; on the Western front he opted for the Attrition Option and disembarked the British Expeditionary Force (two infantry corps) in France; in the Mediterranean he sent reinforcements to Tunis and Bizerte. I still had the initiative. In the Winter '39 turn I launched an all-out attack in the West; I conquered Holland, Belgium, Luxembourg, Denmark; through the south of France I reached Marseilles, and through the north I reached Sedan and Hex N24. I restructured my Army Group East. I disembarked an armored corps in Tripoli during the SR. The Option in the Mediterranean was Attrition and I got no results, but the threat is now tangible: Tunis and Bizerte are under siege and the First Italian Expeditionary Corps has penetrated Algeria, which was completely undefended. On the border with Egypt, the forces are balanced. The problem for the Allies lies in knowing exactly where to throw their weight. El Quemado's response can't be as vigorous as the situation requires; on the Western front and in the Mediterranean he chooses the Attrition Option and he throws everything he can into the attack, but he's playing with short stacks and, to make things worse, the dice don't go his way. In the East he occupies Bessarabia and stakes out a line from the Romanian border to East Prussia. The next turn will be decisive, but by now it's late and we have to put it off. We leave the hotel. At the Andalusia Lodge we run into the Wolf and the Lamb with three Dutch girls. The girls seem thrilled to meet me and they're amazed that I'm German. At first I thought they were pulling my leg; in fact, they were surprised that a German would have anything to do with such eccentric characters. At three in the morning I returned to the Del Mar feeling content for the first time in days. Could it be that I was convinced at last that it hadn't been pointless to stay? Maybe. At some point during the night, from the depths of his defeat (were we discussing my Offensive in the West?), El Quemado asked how long I planned to stay in Spain. I sensed fear in his voice.

"Until Charly's body turns up," I said.

After breakfast I headed to the Costa Brava. The manager was at the reception desk. When he saw me he finished up a few things and motioned for me to follow him into his office. I don't know how he knew that Ingeborg had left, but he did. With a few rather inappropriate insinuations, he made it clear that he understood my situation. Then, without giving me a chance to respond, he proceeded to sum up the current state of the search: no progress, many of the searchers had given up, and the operations, if one could dignify with such a name the efforts of one or two police Zodiacs, seemed headed for bureaucratic deadlock. I told him I planned to demand a personal report from Navy Headquarters and if necessary I was prepared to twist the requisite arms. Mr. Pere shook his head paternally. Not necessary; there was no need to get all worked up. As far as the paperwork was concerned, the German consulate had taken care of everything. Really, I was free to leave whenever I liked. Of course, they understood that Charly was my friend, the bonds of friendship, it goes without saying, but . . . Even the Spanish police, usually so skeptical, were about to close the case. All that remained was for the body to appear. Mr. Pere seemed much more relaxed than he had during our previous encounter. Now, somehow, he saw the case as if he and I were the sole, dutiful mourners of an inexplicable but natural death. (So is death always natural? Is it always a part of the essential order of things? Even if it involves windsurfing?) I'm sure it was an accident, he said, the kind we see every summer. I hinted at the possibility of suicide, but Mr. Pere shook his head and smiled. He'd been in the hotel business all his life and he thought he knew the *souls* of tourists; Charly, poor bastard, wasn't the suicidal type. In any case, when you really thought about it, it was always a bitter paradox to die on vacation. Mr. Pere had been witness to many similar cases in his long career: old women who suffered heart attacks in August, children who drowned in the pool under everyone's eyes, families wiped out on the highway (in the middle of their holidays!) . . . Such is life, he concluded, I'm sure your friend never imagined that he would die far from his homeland. Death and Homeland, he whispered, two tragedies. At eleven in the morning, there was something crepuscular about Mr. Pere. Here's a happy man, I said to myself. It was pleasant to be there, talking to him, while at the reception desk tourists argued with the receptionist, and their voices, inoffensive and remote from matters of real concern, filtered into the office. As we talked I saw myself sitting comfortably there at the hotel, and I saw Mr. Pere and the people in the corridors and rooms, faces that were attracted to each other or pretended to be attracted to each other in the midst of empty or tense exchanges, couples sunbathing with linked hands, single men who worked alone, and friendly men who worked with others, all happy, or if not, at least at peace with themselves. Unfulfilled! But still convinced they were at the center of the universe. What did it matter whether Charly was alive or not, whether I was alive or not? Everything would roll on, downhill, toward each individual death. Everyone was the center of the universe! The bunch of morons! Nothing was beyond their sway! Even in their sleep they controlled everything! With their indifference! Then I thought about El Quemado. He was outside. I saw him as if from underwater: the enemy.

I tried to spend the rest of the day being productive, but it was impossible. I was incapable of putting on my bathing suit and going down to the beach, so I settled at the hotel bar to write postcards. I planned to send one to my parents, but in the end I wrote only to Conrad. I spent a long time sitting there just watching the tourists and the waiters making the rounds carrying trays loaded with drinks. I don't know why, but I had the thought that this would be one of the last hot days. Who cared? For the sake of doing something, I had a salad and tomato juice. I think the food made me sick, because I started to sweat and feel queasy, so I went up to the room and took a cold shower. Then I went out again, this time without the car, heading toward Navy Headquarters, but when I got there I decided it wasn't worth enduring another string of excuses and I walked on.

The town was sunk in a kind of crystal ball; everyone seemed to be asleep (transcendentally asleep!) no matter if they were walking or sitting outside. Around five the sky clouded over and at six it began to rain. The streets cleared all at once. I had the thought that it was as if autumn had unsheathed a claw and scratched: everything was coming apart. The tourists running on the sidewalks in search of shelter, the shopkeepers pulling tarps over the merchandise displayed in the street, the increasing number of shop windows closed until next summer. Whether I felt pity or scorn when I saw this, I don't know. Detached from any external stimulus, the only thing I could see or feel with any clarity was myself. Everything else had been bombarded by something dark; movie sets consigned to dust and oblivion, as if for good.

The question, then, was what I was doing in the middle of such gloom.

The rest of the afternoon I spent lying in bed waiting for El Quemado to return to the hotel.

On my way up to the room I asked whether I had received any calls from Germany. The answer was no; there were no messages for me.

From the balcony I watched as El Quemado left the beach and crossed the Paseo Marítimo toward the hotel. I hurried downstairs so that when he arrived I would be at the door, waiting for him; I suppose I was afraid that they wouldn't let him in if he wasn't with me. As I was passing the reception desk, Frau Else's voice brought me up short. It was hardly louder than a whisper, but it took me by surprise, echoing in my head like a trumpet blast.

"Udo, you're still here," she said as if she hadn't known.

I stood there in the main hall, in an embarrassing position, to say the least. At the other end of the hall, behind the glass doors, El Quemado was waiting. For a moment I saw him as part of a film projected on the door: El Quemado and the deep blue horizon punctuated by a car parked across the street, the heads of people walking by, and the fuzzy images of the tables on the terrace. Only Frau Else was completely real, beautiful and solitary behind the counter.

"Yes, of course . . . As you well know." When I addressed her with the informal *du*, Frau Else blushed. I think I had seen her like that only once, with her defenses down. I wasn't sure whether I liked it or not.

"I hadn't . . . seen you. That's all. I don't keep track of all your movements," she said in a low voice.

"I'll be here until the body of my *friend* turns up. I hope you don't have any problem with that."

With a scowl of distaste she looked away. I was afraid she would see El Quemado and use him as a pretext for changing the subject.

"My husband is sick and he needs me. These last few days I've spent with him, unable to do anything else. *You* wouldn't understand that, would you?"

"I'm sorry."

"Well, that's enough. I didn't mean to bother you. Good-bye."

But neither she nor I moved.

El Quemado was watching me from the other side of the door. And I have to imagine that he was being watched by the hotel guests sitting on the terrace or by the people walking by on the sidewalk. At any minute someone would come up to him and ask him to leave; then El Quemado would strangle him, using only his right arm, and all would be lost.

"Is your . . . husband better? I sincerely hope so. I'm afraid I've been an idiot. Forgive me."

Frau Else bowed her head and said:

"Yes . . . Thank you . . ."

"I'd like to talk to you tonight . . . to see you alone . . . But I don't want to force you to do something that might cause trouble for you later . . ."

Frau Else's lips took an eternity to move into a smile. I don't know why, but I was shaking.

"Someone's waiting for you now, yes?"

Yes, a comrade in arms, I thought, but I didn't say anything and I nodded in a way that expressed the inevitability of the engagement. A comrade in arms? An enemy in arms!

"Remember that even though you're a friend of the owner, you should respect the hotel rules."

"What rules?"

"Among many others, the rule that prohibits certain visitors in the guest rooms." Her voice was back to normal, sounding part ironic and part authoritarian. Clearly, this was Frau Else's realm.

I tried to protest, but her raised hand commanded silence.

"This is not to suggest anything, or say anything. I'm not making any accusations. I feel sorry for that poor boy too." She meant El Quemado. "But I have to look out for the Del Mar and its guests. And I have to look out for you. I don't want anything bad to happen to you."

"What could possibly happen to me? We're just playing."

"What?"

"You know very well what."

"Ah, the game at which you're champion." When she smiled her teeth gleamed dangerously. "A winter sport; at this time of year you'd do better to swim or play tennis."

"If you want to laugh at me, go ahead. I deserve it."

"All right, we'll meet tonight, at one, at the church on the square. Do you know how to get there?"

"Yes."

Frau Else's smile vanished. I tried to come closer but I realized it wasn't the right moment. We said good-bye and I went out. On the terrace everything was normal; two steps down from El Quemado a couple of girls were discussing the weather as they waited for their dates. Just as on every other night, people laughed and made plans.

I exchanged a few words with El Quemado and we went back in.

As we passed the reception desk I didn't see anyone behind the counter, although it occurred to me that Frau Else could be hiding. With an effort I repressed the urge to go over and look.

I think I didn't do it because I would have had to explain everything to El Quemado.

Our match continued along predictable lines: in the spring of '40 I launched an Offensive Option in the Mediterranean and conquered Tunis and Algeria; on the Western front I spent twenty-five BRP, which bought me the conquest of France; during the SR I placed four armored corps with infantry and air support on the Spanish border (!). On the Eastern front I consolidated my forces.

El Quemado's response was purely defensive. He made the fewest moves he could; he strengthened some defenses; most of all, he asked questions. His plays still reveal what a novice he is. He doesn't know how to stack the counters, he plays sloppily, he has either no grand strategy or the one he has is too schematic, he trusts in luck, he makes mistakes in his calculations of BRP, he confuses the Creation of Units phase with the SR.

Still, he tries and it seems that he's beginning to get into the spirit of the game. I can tell by the way he keeps his eyes glued to the board and by the way the charred planes of his face twist in an effort to calculate retreats and costs.

It inspires sympathy and pity. A dense kind of pity, I should note, leached of color, cuadriculated.

The church square was lonely and poorly lit. I parked the car on a side street and settled down to wait on a stone bench. I felt good, although when Frau Else appeared—she literally materialized from the formless mass of shadows under the only tree in the plaza—I couldn't help jumping in surprise and alarm.

I suggested leaving town, maybe parking the car in the woods or somewhere with a view of the sea, but she refused.

She talked. She talked freely and without pause, as if she'd been silent for days. In conclusion, she gave a vague, allusive explanation of her husband's illness. Only after that did she allow me to kiss her. And yet from the very start our hands had met, our fingers naturally interlacing.

There we stayed, holding hands, until two thirty in the morning. When we got tired of sitting, we took a walk around the square; then we returned to the bench and kept talking.

I talked a lot too, I suppose.

The silence of the square was interrupted only by a brief series of distant cries (of happiness or desperation?) and then the roar of motorcycles.

I think we kissed five times.

On our way back I suggested parking the car far from the hotel; I had her reputation in mind. Laughing, she refused; she isn't afraid of gossip. (The truth is she isn't afraid of *anything*.)

The church square is rather sad, small and dark and silent. In the center rises a medieval stone fountain with two jets of water. Before we left we drank from it.

"When you die, Udo, you'll be able to say, 'I'm returning to where I came from: Nothingness.'"

"When a person's dying, he'll say anything," I answered.

After this exchange, Frau Else's face shone as if I'd just kissed her. And that was exactly what I did then—I kissed her. But when I tried to slip my tongue between her lips she pulled away.

I don't know whether the Wolf has lost his job or the Lamb has, or both of them have. They grumble and complain but I hardly hear them. I do, however, register their low-frequency fear and rage. The owner of the Andalusia Lodge makes merciless fun of them and their misfortunes. He calls them "bums," "dirty bastards," "AIDS scum," "beach faggots," "deadbeats"; then he takes me aside, laughing, and tells me a story that I can't follow but that's about a rape in which they're somehow implicated. Showing no curiosity whatsoever—though the owner is talking loud enough for everyone to hear—the Wolf and the Lamb are mesmerized by some TV sports show. This is the generation of kids that were going to put their shoulder to the wheel! This troop of zombies was going to bring glory to Spain, I shit on the Holy Virgin! the owner ends his speech. There's nothing left for me to do but nod and return to the table with the Spaniards and order another beer. Later, through the half-open bathroom door, I see the Lamb pulling down his pants.

After I ate I headed to the Costa Brava. I was received by Mr. Pere as if it had been years since our last meeting. Our conversation—trivial—this time took place at the hotel bar, where I got to know more than a few of the manager's circle of friends. They all radiated an air of distinction and boredom, and, naturally, they were all over forty; when I was introduced to them, they treated me with great tact. It was as if they had been presented with a celebrity or, rather, a young man of *promise*. Clearly Mr. Pere and I were charmed by each other.

Later, at Navy Headquarters (my visits to the Costa Brava inevitably lead there), I was told there was no news about Charly. Not intending to cause trouble, I decided to venture some suppositions. Wasn't it strange that his body hadn't turned up yet? Was it possible that he was still alive, suffering from amnesia and wandering around some town on the coast? I think even the two bored secretaries gave me looks of pity.

I took a leisurely walk back to the Del Mar and was able to confirm what I'd already sensed: the town is beginning to empty, there are fewer and fewer tourists, the natives' movements are infused with a cyclical weariness. And yet the air and the sky and the sea shine clear and pure. Breathing is a delight. And anyone out for a stroll can stand and stare at whatever catches his eye without the risk of being shoved or mistaken for a drunk.

When the owner of the Andalusia Lodge disappeared into the back, I brought up the subject of the rape.

The Wolf and the Lamb guffawed and said it was all in the old man's head. I got the sense that they were making fun of me.

When I left I paid only for what I'd had to drink. The Spaniards' faces turned stony. Significantly, our good-byes made reference to the date of my departure. (It's as if everyone is eager for me to leave.) At the last minute, they tried to patch things up by offering to go with me to Navy Headquarters, but I refused.

Summer 1940. The match has heated up. Against expectations, El Quemado was able to transfer enough troops to the Mediterranean to cushion against my strikes. Even more important: he guessed that it wasn't Alexandria but Malta that was under threat, and he fortified the island with infantry, air, and naval forces. On the Western front the situation remains unchanged (after the conquest of France a turn is necessary for the Western armies to regroup and receive replacements and reinforcements); my troops there have trained their sights on England—the invasion of which would demand a considerable logistical effort, but El Quemado doesn't know that—and on Spain, an unnecessary conquest but one that clears the way to Gibraltar, without which English control of the Mediterranean is almost nonexistent. (This play, recommended by Terry Butcher in *The General*, involves moving the Italian fleet into the Atlantic.) In any case, El Quemado doesn't expect an attack on Gibraltar by land; on the contrary, my movements in the East and the Balkans (after the classic play: the obliteration of Yugoslavia and Greece) make him fear an impending invasion of the Soviet Union—I think my friend sympathizes with the Reds— and neglect other fronts. My position, needless to say, is enviable. Operation Black Beard, perhaps with a Turkish strategic variant, promises to be exciting. El Quemado's spirits never flag. He isn't a brilliant player or an impulsive one: his movements are calm and methodical. The hours have gone by in silence; we've spoken only when strictly necessary, questions about the rules receiving clear and honest answers, our play unfolding in enviable harmony. I'm writing this as El Quemado takes his turn. It's interesting: the game relaxes him, I see it in the muscles of his arms and chest, as if at last he's able to look at himself and not see *anything*. Or as if he sees only the tortured Europe of the game board and the grand maneuvers and countermaneuvers.

The session took place as if in a fog. On our way out of the room, in the hallway, we ran into a maid who upon seeing us stifled a scream and went running. I glanced at El Quemado, unable to say a thing; embarrassment for him stung me until we got on the elevator. Then I thought that perhaps it wasn't El Quemado's face that had given the maid a fright. My sense that I was treading on uncertain ground grew sharper.

We parted on the hotel terrace. A quick handshake, a smile, and finally El Quemado disappeared, ambling off along the Paseo Marítimo.

The terrace was empty. In the restaurant, which was livelier, I spotted Frau Else. She was sitting at a table near the bar with two men in suits and ties. I was struck by the idea that one of them was her husband, though he looked nothing like the way I remembered him. Their conversation had every appearance of being a business meeting and I didn't want to intrude. Nor did I want to seem timid, and with that in mind I went up to the bar and ordered a beer. The waiter took more than five minutes to bring it to me. He wasn't slow because the bar was so busy, since it was hardly busy at all; he just chose to dawdle until I had run out of patience. Only then did he bring the beer, and I could sense the defiance and hostility in his attitude, as if he were waiting for the slightest complaint from me to start a fight. But that was unthinkable with Frau Else right there, so I tossed a few coins on the bar and waited. No reaction. The miserable waiter shrank against the shelves of bottles and stared at the floor. He seemed to be angry at the whole world, starting with himself.

I drank my beer in peace. Frau Else, regrettably, continued to be immersed in conversation with her tablemates and she chose to pretend she didn't see me. I supposed she had her reasons, and I decided to leave.

In the room I was surprised by the smell of tobacco and stale air. The lamp had been left on, and for an instant I thought that Ingeborg had come back. But the smell, in an almost tangible way, ruled out the possibility of a woman. (Strange: I had never stopped to think about smells.) All of this depressed me, and I resolved to go for a drive.

I circled slowly through the empty streets of the town. A warm breeze swept the sidewalks, scattering paper wrappings and advertising leaflets.

Only every so often did the figures of drunk tourists emerge from the shadows, stumbling blindly toward their hotels.

I don't know what made me stop on the Paseo Marítimo. But I did, and inevitably I found myself on the dark beach, heading toward the abode of El Quemado.

What did I expect to find there?

The voices stopped me by the time I could see the fortress of pedal boats rising from the sand.

El Quemado had visitors.

With extreme caution, almost crawling, I approached; whoever was there preferred to talk outside. Soon I could make out two shapes: El Quemado and his guest were sitting in the sand with their backs to me, gazing out to sea.

It was the other man who was leading the conversation: a quick series of grunts of which I could catch only stray words like "necessity" and "courage."

I didn't dare go any closer.

Then, after a long silence, the wind stopped blowing and a kind of weight of warm stone fell over the beach.

Someone—which of the two I don't know—was talking in a vague and lighthearted way about some "bet," something "forgotten and done with." Then he laughed . . . Then he got up and walked toward the water's edge . . . . Then he turned around and said something I couldn't hear.

For an instant—a mad instant that made my hair stand on end—I thought it was Charly: his profile, his way of letting his head slump as if he had a broken neck, his sudden silences. Good old Charly, escaped from the dirty waters of the Mediterranean in order to . . . give sibylline advice to El Quemado. A kind of stiffness migrated from my arms to the rest of my body as my sense of logic fought to regain control. All I wanted was to get out of there. Then, as if the rest of the conversation was simply reinforcing the madness, I heard the kind of advice that El Quemado's visitor was giving him. "How to stop the strikes?" "Don't worry about the strikes; worry about breaks in the line." "How to avoid them?" "Reinforce the front line; annihilate any advances of the armored units; always keep an operative reserve."

Advice on how to beat me in *Third Reich*!

More concretely, El Quemado was receiving instructions on how to counter what he saw as imminent: the invasion of Russia!

I closed my eyes and tried to pray. I couldn't. I thought that I'd never get the madness out of my head. I was sweating and the sand stuck to my face. My whole body itched and I was afraid (if I can call it that) that suddenly I'd see Charly's shining face looming above me. The filthy traitor. The thought jolted my eyes open; there was no one next to the pedal boat shack. They must both be inside, I thought. I was wrong: the shadowy figures were still standing at the water's edge with the waves licking their ankles. They had their backs to me. In the sky the clouds parted for a moment and the moon shone weakly. El Quemado and his visitor were talking now—as if it were the most pleasant of subjects—about a rape. With some effort I rose to my knees and grew a little calmer. It wasn't Charly, I told myself a few times. Elementary: El Quemado and his visitor were speaking in Spanish and Charly couldn't even order a beer in Spanish.

With a feeling of relief, but still numb and trembling, I rose to my feet and left the beach.

At the Del Mar, Frau Else was sitting in a wicker armchair at the end of the hallway that led to the elevator. The lights of the restaurant were all out except for a faint one that illuminated only the shelves of bottles and a section of the bar where a waiter was still laboring away at something I couldn't make out. When I'd passed the reception desk I'd seen the night watchman with his nose in a sports paper. Not everyone in the hotel was asleep.

I sat down next to Frau Else.

She made some remark about my face. Haggard!

"I'm sure you hardly sleep, and you don't sleep well. Not a good advertisement for the hotel. I'm worried about your health."

I nodded. She nodded too. I asked for whom she was waiting. Frau Else shrugged; she smiled; she said: For you. She was lying, of course. I asked her what time it was. Four in the morning.

"You should go back to Germany, Udo," she said.

I invited her up to my room. She refused. She said: No, I *can't*. She gazed into my eyes as she said it. How beautiful she was!

We were quiet for a long time. I would have to liked to say: Don't worry about me, really, don't worry. But it was ridiculous, of course. At the end of the hallway, I saw the watchman peer around the corner and then disappear. I concluded that Frau Else's staff adore her.

I pretended to be tired and stood up. I didn't want to be there when the person Frau Else was waiting for appeared.

Without rising from the chair, she offered me her hand and we said good night.

I walked to the elevator. Luckily it was stopped at the ground floor and I didn't have to wait. Once I was inside I went through the farewell ritual again. I said a silent good-bye, only my lips moving. Frau Else held my gaze and my smile until the doors closed with a pneumatic wheeze and I began to rise.

I felt something heavy rolling around in my head.

After taking a hot shower, I got in bed. My hair was wet, and in any case sleep wouldn't come.

Why, I don't know, maybe because it was the nearest thing to me, I picked up the Florian Linden book and opened it at random.

"The killer is the owner of the hotel."

"Are you sure?"

I closed the book.

I dreamed that I was woken by a phone call. It was Mr. Pere, who wanted me to come—he offered to take me—to the Guardia Civil headquarters. They had a body there and they were hoping that I could identify it. So I showered and went out without breakfast. The hotel corridors were achingly bleak; it must have been just after dawn. Mr. Pere's car was waiting at the front entrance. During the ride to the Guardia Civil headquarters, located on the edge of town, at a crossroads plastered with signs that pointed toward various borders, Mr. Pere unburdened himself by talking about the mutations that the natives underwent when the summer—or rather, the summer season—was over. General depression! Deep down we can't live without tourists! We get used to them! A pale young Guardia Civil officer led us to a garage where there were several tables set up in rows and, hanging on the walls, a collection of car parts. On a white-veined black slab, next to the metal door where the van that would remove the body was already waiting, there lay a lifeless form in what seemed to me to be a state close to putrefaction. Behind me, Mr. Pere raised a hand to his nose. It wasn't Charly. He was probably about the same age and he might have been German, but it wasn't Charly. I said I didn't know him and we left. As we were going, the Guardia Civil stood to attention. We headed back to town laughing and making plans for next season. The Del Mar still looked like a slumbering thing, but this time I spotted Frau Else through the glass, at the reception desk. I asked Mr. Pere how long it had been since he'd seen Frau Else's husband.

"It's been a long time since I had the pleasure," said Mr. Pere.

"It seems he's sick."

"So it seems," said Mr. Pere, his face darkened by an expression that could have meant anything.

After that, the dream advanced (or so I remember it) in leaps. I had a breakfast of fried eggs and tomato juice on the terrace. I went upstairs; some English children were coming downstairs and we almost collided. From the balcony I watched El Quemado, out in front of his pedal boats, musing on his poverty and the end of summer. I wrote letters with intentional and studied slowness. Finally I got in bed and fell asleep. Another phone call, this time real, dragged me from sleep. I checked my watch: it was two in the afternoon. It was Conrad, and his voice repeated my name as if he thought I would never answer.

Despite what I might have expected, maybe because Conrad was shy and I was still half-asleep, the conversation proceeded coldly, in a way that horrifies me now. The questions, the answers, the inflections of voice, the poorly hidden desire to get off the phone and save a few cents, the familiar expressions of irony all seemed cloaked in a supreme lack of interest. No confidences were shared, except one stupid one at the end; instead, fixed images of the town, the hotel, and my room superimposed themselves tenaciously on the scene sketched by my friend as if they were trying to warn me of the new order in which I was immersed and within which the coordinates transmitted to me over the phone line had little value. What are you doing? Why don't you come back? What's keeping you? At your office they don't know what to think, Mr. X asks about you every day and it's no use when everyone assures him that you'll soon be back among us, he's filled with foreboding and predicts disaster. What kind of disaster? What do I care? All of this followed by information about the club, work, games, magazines, recounted ceaselessly and relentlessly.

"Have you seen Ingeborg?" I asked.

"No, of course not."

We were silent for a brief instant, after which there came a new avalanche of questions and appeals: at my office they were *more than a little* upset; the group wondered whether I still planned to go to Paris to meet Rex Douglas in December. Would I be fired? Would I get into trouble with the police? Everyone wanted to know what mysterious and inexplicable thing was keeping me in Spain. A woman? Loyalty to a dead man? To what dead man? And incidentally, how was my article going, the one that was going to lay the foundations for a new strategy? It was as if Conrad were mocking me. For a second I imagined him taping the conversation, his lips curved in a wicked smile. The champion in exile! Out of circulation!

"Listen, Conrad, I'm going to give you Ingeborg's address. I want you to go see her and then call me."

"Yes, all right, whatever you say."

"Perfect. Do it today. And then call me."

"Fine, fine, but I have no idea what's going on and I'd like to be as useful as I can. Do you follow me, Udo? Can you hear me?"

"Yes. Tell me you'll do as I say."

"Yes, of course."

"Good. Did you get a letter from me? I think I explained everything in it. You probably haven't gotten it yet."

"All I've gotten are two postcards, Udo. One of hotels on the beach and another of a mountain."

"A mountain?"

"Yes."

"A mountain by the sea?"

"I don't know! All you can see is the mountain and a kind of monastery in ruins."

"Anyway, you'll get it. The postal system is terrible here."

Suddenly I realized that I hadn't written any letter to Conrad. I didn't really care.

"Are you having good weather there, at least? It's raining here."

Instead of answering his question, as if taking dictation, I said:

"I'm playing . . ."

Maybe I thought it was important for Conrad to know. In the future it could be useful to me. From the other end of the line I heard a kind of amplified sigh.

"*Third Reich*?"

"Yes . . ."

"Really? Tell me how it's going. You're incredible, Udo, only you would think to play at a time like this."

"Of course, I know what you mean, with Ingeborg far away and everything hanging by a thread," I said, yawning.

"That's not what I meant. I was talking about the risks. About that strange drive of yours. You're one of a kind, kid, the king of fandom!"

"It's not such a big deal, don't shout, you're hurting my ears."

"So who are you playing? A German? Do I know him?"

Poor Conrad. He took it for granted that in a small town on the Costa Brava it was possible to run into another war games player who also happened to be German. It was clear he never went on vacation and God only knows what his idea of a summer on the Mediterranean, or wherever, was.

"Well, my opponent is a little strange," I said, and I went on to give him a general description of El Quemado.

After a silence, Conrad said:

"I don't like the sound of that. It doesn't make sense. How do you communicate?"

"In Spanish."

"And how did he read the rules?"

"He didn't. I explained them to him. In a single afternoon. You'd be amazed how sharp he is. You don't need to tell him anything twice."

"How is he as a player?"

"His defense of England is acceptable. He couldn't prevent the fall of France, but who can? He's not bad. You're better, of course, and so is Franz, but he's a decent sparring partner."

"The way you describe him . . . it makes my hair stand on end. I've never played with someone like that, the kind of person who might scare me if he showed up all of a sudden . . . In a multiplayer match, all right, but alone . . . And you say he lives on the beach?"

"That's right."

"What if he's the devil?"

"Are you serious?"

"Yes. The devil, Satan, Belial, Mephistopheles, Beelzebub, Lucifer, the Prince of Darkness . . ."

"The Prince of Darkness . . . No, he's more like an ox . . . Strong and brooding, the typical ruminant. Melancholic. Oh, and he's not Spanish."

"How do you know that?"

"Some Spanish guys told me. At first, of course, I thought he was Spanish, but he isn't."

"Where is he from?"

"I don't know."

From Stuttgart Conrad protested weakly:

"You should find out. It's crucial, for your own safety . . ."

I thought he was exaggerating, but I promised that I would ask. Soon afterward we hung up, and after I showered I went out for a walk before returning to the hotel to eat. I felt good, as if the passage of time had no effect on me, and my body was wholly surrendered to the pleasure of being precisely where I was, and nowhere else.

Autumn 1940. I play the Offensive Option on the Eastern front. My armored corps break through the flank of the central Russian sector, advancing deep into Russian territory and sealing off a vast swath one hex west of Smolensk. Behind me, between Brest Litovsk and Riga, ten Russian armies are trapped. My losses are minimal. On the Mediterranean front I spend BRP for another Offensive Option and I invade Spain. El Quemado is taken completely by surprise. His eyebrows shoot up, he sits up straighter, his scars vibrate. It's as if he hears my armored divisions advancing along the Paseo Marítimo, and his confusion doesn't help him to mount a good defense (he chooses—unconsciously, of course—a variant of

147

David Hablanian's Border Defense, undoubtedly the worst possible response to an attack from the Pyrenees). And so with only two armored corps and four infantry corps plus air support I conquer Madrid, and Spain surrenders. During the Strategic Redeployment phase I place three infantry corps in Seville, Cádiz, and Granada, and an armored corps in Córdoba. In Madrid I station two German air fleets and one Italian fleet. Now El Quemado can see what I'm up to . . . and he smiles. He congratulates me! He says: "That never would have occurred to me." He's such a good loser it's hard to even comprehend Conrad's suspicions and fears. Bent over the map during his turn, El Quemado talks and tries to repair the irreparable. In the USSR he moves troops from the south—where there's been almost no fighting—to the north and center, but his capacity for movement is minimal. In the Mediterranean he keeps his hold on Egypt and he reinforces Gibraltar, though not very convincingly, as if he didn't believe in his own efforts. Muscular and charred, his torso looms over Europe like a nightmare. And he talks—without looking at me—about his work, the scarcity of tourists, the fickle weather, the retirees who flock en masse to certain hotels. Prying while feigning a lack of interest—I'm actually writing as I ask him questions—I learn that he knows Frau Else, who's called "the German lady" around the neighborhood. Forced to give his opinion, he concedes that she's pretty. Then I inquire about her husband. El Quemado answers: he's sick.

"How do you know?" I say, leaving my notes aside.

"Everyone knows it. He's been sick for a long time, years. He's sick but he's not dying."

"He feeds it!" I say with a smile.

"Never," says El Quemado, returning to the tangle of the game, his whole logistical network in ruins.

In the end our farewell follows the usual ritual: we drink the last cans of beer that I've bought for the occasion and that I keep in the sink full of cold water, we discuss the match (El Quemado outdoes himself with compliments but he still won't acknowledge defeat), we take the elevator down together, we say good night at the door to the hotel . . .

Just then, as El Quemado disappears along the Paseo Marítimo, a voice beside me makes me jump in alarm.

It's Frau Else, sitting in the shadows, in a corner of the empty terrace scarcely reached by the lights from the hotel and the street.

I admit that as I walked toward her I was angry (at myself, mostly) because of the fright I'd just gotten. When I sat down across from her, I saw that she was crying. Her face, usually full of color and life, glowed with a ghostly pallor that was heightened by the effect of glimpsing her half-hidden under the giant shade of an umbrella that swayed rhythmically in the night breeze. Without hesitating, I took her hands and asked what was wrong. As if by magic a smile appeared on Frau Else's face. You, always so considerate, she said, forgetting in the heat of the moment to use the informal *du*. I protested. The speed with which Frau Else's mood changed was surprising: in less than a minute she went from ghostly mourner to concerned older sister. She wanted to know what I was doing—"but tell me the truth, now"—in my room with El Quemado. She wanted me to promise that I would return soon to Germany, or at least that I would call my bosses at work and Ingeborg. She wanted me to go to bed earlier and spend the mornings lying in the sun—"the little we have left"—on the beach. You're pasty, it must be months since you took a look in the mirror, she whispered. And she wanted me to swim and eat well, which was an exhortation that went against her best interests, since I ate at her hotel. At this point she started to cry again, but more softly, as if all the advice she had given was a bath that cleansed her of her own suffering, and little by little she grew calmer and more relaxed.

This was the perfect situation, everything I could have asked for, and I hardly noticed the time passing. I think we might have sat across from each other like that all night, our eyes scarcely meeting and her hand clasped in mine, but everything comes to an end, and this time the end arrived in the form of the night watchman, who, after searching for me all over the hotel, appeared on the terrace with the message that I had a long-distance phone call.

Frau Else got up wearily and followed me down the empty corridor to the reception desk. She ordered the watchman to take out the last bags of garbage from the kitchen and we were left alone. The immediate sensation was of being on an island, just the two of us, except for the receiver lying there off the hook, like a cancerous appendage that I would happily have ripped out and handed to the clerk like another piece of garbage.

It was Conrad. When I heard his voice my disappointment was great, but then I remembered that I'd asked him to call me.

Frau Else sat on the other side of the counter and tried to read a magazine that I suppose the clerk had left behind. She couldn't. Nor was there much to read because it was almost all photographs. With a mechanical gesture she dropped it on the edge of the desk, where it rested precariously, and pinned her gaze on me. Her blue eyes were the shade of a child's colored pencil, a cheap and beloved Faber.

I felt like hanging up and making love to her right there. I imagined myself—or maybe I'm imagining it now, which makes it worse—dragging her to her private office, lifting her up on the desk, ripping off her clothes and kissing her, climbing on top of her and kissing her, turning off all the lights again and kissing her . . .

"Ingeborg is fine. She's working. She doesn't plan to call you, but she says that when you get back she wants to talk to you. She asked me to say hello to you," said Conrad.

"Fine. Thanks. That's what I wanted to know."

With her legs crossed, Frau Else was gazing at the tips of her shoes now and seemed immersed in labored and complicated thoughts.

"Listen, your letter never came. It was Ingeborg, this afternoon, who explained everything to me. As far as I can see you're under no obligation to stay there."

"Well, when you get my letter, you'll understand. I can't explain anything to you now."

"How's the match going?"

"I'm screwing him three ways from Thursday," I said, though maybe the expression was "He's shafted" or "I'm tearing him a new one" or "He's getting a good hosing," I honestly can't remember now.

Maybe I said: I'm roasting him alive.

Frau Else gave me a soft look that I'd never seen a woman give and smiled at me.

I felt a kind of shiver.

"You haven't bet anything?"

I heard voices, maybe in German, I couldn't say for sure, unintelligible conversations and computer sounds, far, very far away.

"Nothing."

"I'm glad. All afternoon I was worried that you'd bet something. Do you remember our last conversation?"

"Yes, you suggested he was the devil. I'm not senile yet."

"Don't get all worked up. I only have your best interests at heart, you know."

"Of course."

"I'm glad you haven't bet anything."

"What did you think was on the table? My soul?"

I laughed. Frau Else had one tanned and perfect arm raised in the air, ending in a hand with long, slender fingers that closed around the night clerk's magazine. Only then did I realize that it was pornography. She opened a drawer and put it away.

"The Faust of war games." Conrad laughed like an echo of my own laugh bouncing back from Stuttgart.

I felt a cold rage rise up my spine from my heels to my neck and shoot into every corner of the room.

"It's not funny," I said, but Conrad didn't hear me. I hadn't been able to muster more than the faintest of voices.

"What? What?"

Frau Else got up and came over, so close that I thought that she could hear Conrad's cackling. She put a hand on my head, and immediately she could feel the rage boiling inside me. Poor Udo, she whispered. Then, with a velvety gesture, as if in slow motion, she pointed to the clock indicating that she had to leave. But she didn't go. Maybe it was the desperation she saw in my face that stopped her.

"Conrad, I don't feel like kidding around, I'm not in the mood, it's late. You should be in bed, not up worrying about me."

"You're my friend."

"Listen, at some point the sea will puke up whatever's left of Charly. Then I'll pack my bags and come back. To kill time while I'm waiting, just to kill time and get examples for my article, I'm playing *Third Reich*; you'd do the same, wouldn't you? Anyway, the only thing I'm jeopardizing is my job, and you know that's crap. I could find something better in less than a month. Yes? Or I could devote myself exclusively to writing essays. I might even come out ahead. It might be fate. In fact, being fired might be the best thing that could happen to me."

"But they don't want to fire you. And I know you care about the office, or at least the people you work with. When I was there they showed me a postcard you'd sent them."

"You're wrong, I don't give a shit about them."

Conrad choked back a groan, or at least that's what I thought I heard.

"It's not true," he parried, very sure of himself.

"What do you want? Honestly, Conrad, sometimes you're a fucking pain in the ass."

"I want you to come back to your senses."

Frau Else brushed my cheek with her lips and said: It's late, I have to go. I felt her warm breath on my ears and neck, a spider's embrace, light and disturbing. Out of the corner of my eye I saw the watchman at the end of the hallway, docile, waiting.

"I have to hang up," I said.

"Should I call you tomorrow?"

"No, don't waste your money."

"My husband is waiting for me," said Frau Else.

"It doesn't matter."

"Yes, it does."

"He can't fall sleep until I'm there," said Frau Else.

"How is the match going? Did you say it's autumn of '40? Have you invaded the USSR?"

"Yes! Blitzkrieg on all fronts! He's no match for me! For Christ's sake, am I the champ or aren't I?"

"Of course, of course . . . And I hope with all my heart that you win . . . How are the English doing?"

"Let go of my hand," said Frau Else.

"I have to go, Conrad. The English are in trouble, as always."

"And your article? Going well, I suppose. Remember that it would be ideal if it's published before Rex Douglas gets here."

"If nothing else, it'll be written. Rex is going to love it."

Frau Else tried to pull her hand away.

"Don't be childish, Udo. What if my husband comes in?"

I covered the receiver so that Conrad couldn't hear and I said:

"Your husband is in bed. I suspect that's his favorite place. And if he isn't in bed he's probably at the beach. That's another one of his favorite places, especially after dark. Not to mention the guest rooms. In fact, your husband manages to be everywhere at once. I wouldn't be surprised if he were spying on us right now, hiding behind the watchman. The watchman's shoulders aren't broad, but your husband, I believe, is thin."

Frau Else's gaze turned instantly toward the end of the corridor. The watchman was waiting, leaning against the wall. In Frau Else's eyes I caught a glimmer of hope.

"You're crazy," she said when she had determined that no one was watching, before I pulled her to me and kissed her.

I don't know how long we kissed, first urgently and then lazily. I know that we could have gone on forever but I remembered that Conrad was on the phone and that time was ticking away and eating a hole in his pocket. When I lifted the receiver to my ear I heard the chattering of thousands of crossed lines and then emptiness. Conrad had hung up.

"He's gone," I said, and I tried to drag Frau Else with me toward the elevator.

"No, Udo, good night," she said, rejecting me with a forced smile.

I insisted that she come with me, though frankly without much conviction. With a motion of her hand that at the time I didn't understand, a dry, authoritarian gesture, Frau Else had the watchman step between us. Then, in a new tone of voice, she said good night to me again and disappeared . . . toward the kitchen!

"What a woman," said the night watchman.

The watchman went behind the desk and searched for his magazine in the drawers. I watched him in silence until he had it in his hands and had gone to sit on the leather armchair in the reception area. I sighed, with my elbows on the desk, and asked whether there were many tourists left at the Del Mar. Lots, he answered without looking at me. Above the shelf of keys there was a big, long mirror in a heavy golden frame that looked like something out of an antiques shop. Reflected in it were the lights of the corridor and, lower down, the back of the watchman's head. I felt a kind of queasiness upon realizing, however, that my own reflection wasn't visible. Slowly and somewhat fearfully, I slid to the left along the desk. The watchman looked at me, and after a moment of hesitation he asked why I had said "those things" to Frau Else.

"None of your business," I said.

"You're right," he said with a smile, "but I don't like to see her suffer, she's so good to us."

"What makes you think she's suffering?" I said, still sliding toward the left. My palms were sweating.

"I don't know . . . The way you treat her . . ."

"I care for her deeply and have the greatest respect for her," I assured him, as gradually my image began to appear in the mirror, and although what I saw was rather unpleasant (wrinkled clothes, flushed cheeks, tousled hair), it was still me, alive and tangible. A stupid fear, I realize.

The watchman shrugged and turned as if he were about to go back to his magazine. I felt relief and a deep weariness.

"This thing . . . is it a trick mirror?"

"What do you mean?"

"The mirror. A minute ago I was directly in front of it and I couldn't see myself. It's only now, off to the side, that I'm reflected. And you're sitting beneath it but I can see you in it."

The watchman turned his head without getting up and looked at himself in the mirror. He made a face: he could see himself and he didn't like his looks and that struck him as funny.

"It's a little bit tilted, but it's not a trick mirror; look, there's a wall here, see?" Smiling, he lifted the mirror and touched the wall as if he were stroking a body.

For a while I reflected on the matter in silence. Then, after vacillating, I said:

"Let's see. Stand here." I pointed to the exact place where I hadn't been reflected before.

The watchman got up and stood where I told him to.

"I can't see myself," he acknowledged, "but that's because I'm not in front of the mirror."

"Yes you are, damn it," I said, getting behind him and turning him to face the mirror.

Over his shoulder I had a vision that made my pulse quicken: I heard our voices but I couldn't see our bodies. The objects in the corridor—an armchair, a big jar, the spotlights that shone from the juncture of the ceiling and the walls—looked brighter in the mirror than they did in the real corridor behind me. The watchman let out a compulsive giggle.

"Let go of me, let go, I'll prove it to you."

Without intending to, I had him immobilized in a kind of wrestling hold. He looked feeble and afraid. I let him go. In a leap the watchman was behind the counter and he pointed at the wall where the mirror hung.

"It's slanted. Slanted. It's not straight. Come over here and see for yourself."

When I stepped through the gap in the counter my equanimity and caution spun like the blades of a crazed windmill; I think I was ready to wring the poor watchman's neck. Then, as if I were suddenly waking up to a new reality, Frau Else's scent enveloped me. Everything was different back there—outside the laws of nature, I'd venture to say—and it smelled like her even though the rectangle behind the reception desk wasn't physically separated from the broad and—by day—heavily trafficked hall. The mark of Frau Else's serene passage lingered and that was enough to calm me.

After a cursory examination I could see that the watchman was right. The wall on which the mirror hung didn't run parallel to the counter.

I sighed and let myself fall into the leather armchair.

"So white," said the watchman, surely referring to my pallor, and he began to fan me calmly with the pornography magazine.

"Thanks," I said.

After a few interminable minutes I rose and went up to the room.

I was cold, so I put on a sweater and then I opened the windows. From the balcony I could see the lights of the port. A soothing spectacle. The port and I tremble in unison. There are no stars. The beach looks like a black hole. I'm tired and I don't know how I'll get to sleep.

SEPTEMBER 8

Winter 1940. The First Russian Winter Gambit should be played when the German Army has penetrated deep into the Soviet Union so that the German position, together with the adverse weather, favors a decisive counterattack able to destabilize the front and create pincer movements and pockets. In short: a counterattack that makes it necessary for the German Army to retreat. For this to happen, however, it's essential that the Soviet Army have enough reserves (not necessarily armored reserves) to launch such a counterattack. In other words, where the Soviet Army is concerned, in order to use the First Russian Winter Gambit with any likelihood of success one must have maintained at least twelve factors along the border during the Autumn Unit Construction phase. Where the German Army is concerned, playing the First Russian Winter with a high degree of confidence implies something crucial about the war in the East, something that annihilates any Russian defenses: the destruction, in each and every previous turn, of the maximum number of factors of Soviet force. Thus the First Russian Winter is rendered innocuous, which, in the worst of cases, only slows the German Army's advance into Russia, and, where the Soviets are concerned, means an instant reordering of priorities: instead of seeking to fight, it must retreat, leaving large swaths of land to the enemy army in a desperate attempt to remake its borders.

In any case, El Quemado doesn't know how to play FRW (because I didn't explain it to him, of course), and the best that can be said about his movements is that they're confused: in the north he counterattacks (he scarcely grazes my units) and in the south he retreats. At the end of the turn I'm able to establish the front along the most advantageous line possible, through hexes E42, F41, H42, Vitebsk, Smolensk, K43, Briansk, Orel, Kursk, M45, N45, O45, P44, Q44, Rostov, and the approaches to the Crimea.

On the Mediterranean front the English disaster is absolute. With the fall of Gibraltar (without too many losses on my part), the English Army in Egypt is caught in a trap. There's no need even to attack it: the lack of supplies, or rather the length of supply lines, which must be routed English port–South Africa–Gulf of Suez, guarantees its inefficacy. In fact, the Mediterranean, except for the Egyptian Army and an infantry corps stationed in Malta, is all mine. Now the Italian fleet has free passage into the Atlantic, where it will join the German war fleet. With it and with the few infantry corps stationed in France, I can now begin to think about invading Great Britain.

Plans simmer at the General Staff Command: invade Turkey, penetrate the Caucasus from the south (if it has yet to be conquered), and attack the Russians from the rear in order to secure Maikop and Grozny. Short-range plans: in the Strategic Redeployment phase, transfer the maximum number of air factors deployed in Russia to support the invasion of Great Britain. And long-range plans: for example, calculate the line that the German Army will hold in Russia by the spring of '42.

It's annihilation, a victory of arms for me. Thus far, I'd hardly spoken. The next turn could be devastating, I said.

"Could be," answers El Quemado.

His smile indicates that he believes otherwise. The way he circles the table, moving in and out of the light, is gorillalike: calm, confident. Whom does he expect to save him from defeat? The Americans? By the time they enter the war, Europe will probably be entirely controlled by Germany. Perhaps the remnants of the Red Army will still be fighting on the Eastern front, in the Urals; there'll be no significant resistance, in any case.

Does El Quemado plan to play to the bitter end? I'm afraid so. He's what we call a mule. I once faced a specimen of the genus. The game was *NATO: The Next War in Europe* and my opponent was playing the part of the Warsaw Pact troops. He was winning at first, but I brought him to a halt just before he reached the Ruhr Valley. From that point on, my air force and the Federal Army clobbered him and it was clear that he had no chance of winning. Even when his friends begged him to give up, he kept going. The match was completely emotionless. In the end, when I had won, I asked why he wouldn't give up when even to him (a complete dolt) his defeat was obvious. Coldly, he confessed that he expected that I, worn down by his persistence, would finish him off with a nuclear attack, and there would thus be a fifty percent chance that the initiator of the atomic holocaust would lose the game.

He hoped in vain. I'm not the champ for nothing. I know how to wait and be patient.

Is that what El Quemado is waiting for before he surrenders? There are no atomic weapons in *Third Reich*. What is he waiting for, then? What is his secret weapon?

SEPTEMBER 9

With Frau Else in the dining room:

"What were you doing yesterday?"

"Nothing."

"What do you mean, nothing? I looked everywhere for you and I didn't see you all day. Where were you?"

"In my room."

"I went looking for you there too."

"What time?"

"I don't remember. At five and then later, at eight or nine."

"That's odd. I think I was back by then."

"Don't lie to me."

"All right, it was a bit later. I went out for a drive; I ate in the next town, at a place out in the woods. I needed to be alone, to think. You have very good restaurants around here."

"And then?"

"I got in the car and drove back. Slowly."

"That's all?"

"What do you mean?"

"It's a question. It means did you do anything other than drive around and eat?"

"No. I came back to the hotel and went up to my room."

"The watchman says he didn't see you come in. I'm worried about you. I feel responsible, I think. I'm afraid that something bad will happen to you."

"I know how to take care of myself. Anyway, what could happen to me?"

"Something bad . . . Sometimes I have presentiments . . . A nightmare . . ."

"You mean I could end up like Charly? First I'd have to be into windsurfing. Which, between us, is a sport for morons. Poor Charly. Deep down I'm grateful to him. If he hadn't died in such an idiotic way, I'd be gone by now."

"If I were you I'd go back to Stuttgart and make up with that . . . child, your girlfriend. Right now! Immediately!"

"But you want me to stay, I can tell."

"You scare me. You act like an irresponsible boy. I'm not sure whether you can see it or you're blind to it. But don't listen to me, I'm nervous. It's the end of the summer. I'm usually a very level-headed person."

"I know. And very beautiful."

"Don't say that."

"Yesterday I would rather have stayed here with you, but I couldn't find you either. The hotel was full of retirees and I was suffocating. I needed to think."

"And then you were with El Quemado."

"Yesterday. Yes."

"He came up to your room. I saw the game. It was all set up."

"He came up with me. I always wait for him at the front entrance. To be safe."

"And that was all? He went up with you and didn't come out again until past midnight?"

"More or less. A bit later, maybe."

"What did you do all that time? Don't tell me you were playing."

"Actually, we were."

"I find that hard to believe."

"If you were really in my room you must have seen the game board. It was right there."

"I saw it. A strange map. I don't like it. It smells bad."

"The map or the room?"

"The map. And the pieces. Actually, everything in your room

smells bad. Doesn't anyone dare to go in and clean? No. Maybe it's your friend's fault. Maybe it's his burns that stink."

"Don't be ridiculous. The bad smell comes from outside. Your sewers aren't made for the summer season. Ingeborg said so herself: after seven at night the streets reek. The smell comes from the clogged drains!"

"From the Municipal Sewage Treatment Plant. Yes, it's possible. In any case, I don't like it when you go up to your room with El Quemado. Do you know what people would say about my hotel if some tourist saw you scurrying along the hallways with that hunk of charred flesh? I don't care what the staff whispers. The guests are a different story. I have to be more careful there. I can't jeopardize the reputation of the hotel just because you're bored."

"I'm not bored. Quite the contrary, in fact. If you'd rather, I can bring the board downstairs and set it up in the restaurant. Of course then everyone would see El Quemado and that would be bad for business. And I'd have a hard time concentrating. I don't like to play in front of too many people."

"Are you afraid they'd think you were crazy?"

"Well, they spend all afternoon playing cards. My game is more complicated, of course. You've got to be a risk taker, you need somebody with a cool and calculating mind. It's a hard game to master. Every few months new rules and variants are added. People write about it. You wouldn't understand. I mean, you wouldn't understand the *dedication*."

"Does El Quemado fit the mold?"

"I think he does. He's coolheaded and not afraid to take risks. Though he's no strategist."

"I suspected as much. On the inside he must be a lot like you, I suppose."

"I don't think so. I'm a happier person."

"I don't see anything happy about shutting yourself up in a room for hours when you could be out at a club or reading on the terrace or watching TV. The idea of you and El Quemado roaming around my hotel sets me on edge. I can't imagine you sitting still in your room. You're always moving!"

"We move the counters. And we make mathematical calculations . . ."

"Meanwhile, the family reputation of my hotel rots like your friend's body."

"Whose body?"

"The drowned man, Charly's."

"Oh, Charly. What does your husband think of all this?"

"My husband is sick, and if he found out he'd kick you out of the hotel."

"I think he already knows. In fact, I'm sure he does; he's no fool, your husband."

"It would kill him."

"What's wrong with him exactly? He's quite a bit older than you, isn't he? And he's tall and thin. And he doesn't have much hair, does he?"

"I don't like it when you talk that way."

"The thing is, I think I've seen him."

"Your parents were very fond of him, I remember."

"No, I'm talking about this season. A little while ago. When he was supposedly in bed, down with a fever, among other things."

"At night?"

"Yes."

"In his pajamas?"

"Wearing a bathrobe, I'd say."

"Impossible. What color was the bathrobe?"

"Black. Or dark red."

"Sometimes he gets up and takes a walk around the hotel. Through the kitchen and the service areas. He's always concerned about quality and making sure that everything is clean."

"I didn't see him in the hotel."

"Then you didn't see my husband."

"Does he know that you and I . . . ?"

"Of course. We tell each other everything . . . What's happened between us is only a game, Udo, and I think it's about time to wrap it up. It could end up becoming as obsessive as this thing you're playing with El Quemado. By the way, what's it called?"

"El Quemado?"

"No, the game."

"*Third Reich.*"

"What a horrible name."

"Perhaps . . ."

"So who's winning? You?"

"Germany."

"What country are you? Germany, of course."

"Yes, Germany, of course, silly."

Spring 1941. I don't know El Quemado's name. And I don't care. Just as I don't care what country he's from. Wherever it is, it doesn't matter. He knows Frau Else's husband and that does matter; it gives El Quemado a previously unsuspected range of movement. Not only does he fraternize with the Wolf and the Lamb, he also has a taste for the more complex (one supposes) conversation of Frau Else's husband. And yet why do they talk on the beach, in the middle of the night, like two conspirators, rather than meeting at the hotel? The setting seems better suited to plotting than to leisurely conversation. And what do they talk about? The subject of their encounters—I haven't the slightest doubt—is me. Thus, Frau Else's husband has news of me from two sources: El Quemado tells him about the match and his wife tells him about our flirtation. I'm the one at a disadvantage; I don't know anything about him, except that he's sick. But I can guess a few things. He wants me to leave; he wants me to lose the match; he doesn't want me to sleep with his wife. The Eastern offensive continues. The armored wedge (four corps) meets and pierces the Russian front in Smolensk, then goes on to take Moscow, which falls in an Exploitation move. In the south I conquer Sevastopol after a bloody battle, and from Rostov–Kharkov I advance toward the Elista–Don line. The Red Army counterattacks all along the Kalinin–Moscow–Tula line, but I manage to fend it off. The defeat of Moscow entails a gain of ten BRP for the Germans—this according to the Beyma variant. Under the old rules I would have raked in fifteen and left El Quemado not on the verge of collapse but utterly routed. In any case, the Russian losses are heavy: in addition to the BRP cost of the Offensive Option to try to retake Moscow, there are the troops defeated in the effort, their quick replacement hampered by a lack of BRP. In sum, on the Central front alone, El Quemado has lost more than fifty BRP. The situation around Leningrad is unchanged; the line holds firm in Tallinn and in hexes G42, G43, and G44. (Questions that I don't ask El Quemado, though I'd like to: Does Frau Else's husband visit him every night? What does he know about war games? Has Frau Else's husband used the hotel master key to come into my bedroom and poke around? Note to self: scatter talcum powder—I don't have any—around the door, anything to detect intrusions. Is Frau Else's husband, by chance, a fellow gamer? And what the hell is wrong with him? Does he have AIDS?) On the Western front, Operation Sea Lion is carried out successfully. The second phase— invasion and conquest of the island—will take place in the summer. For now, the hardest work is done: a beachhead has been established in England, protected by a powerful air fleet stationed in Normandy. As expected, the English fleet managed to intercept me in the channel. After a long battle in which I gambled the whole German fleet, part of the Italian fleet, and more than half of my airborne units, I managed to disembark in Hex L21. Perhaps too cautiously, I kept my parachute corps in reserve, which means that the beachhead isn't quite as liquid as I'd like (impossible to route my Strategic Redeployment in that direction), but even so, it's a favorable position. At the end of the turn, the hexes occupied by the British Army are the following: the Fifth and the Twelfth Infantry in London; the Thirteenth Armored Corps in Southampton– Portsmouth; the Second Infantry in Birmingham; five air factors in Manchester–Sheffield. And replacement units in Rosyth, J25, L23, and Plymouth. The poor English troops can see my units (the Fourth and the Tenth Infantry) from their hex-dunes and their hex-trenches, and they're frozen in place. The long-anticipated day has come. Paralysis extends through the playing pieces to El Quemado's fingers: the Seventh Army disembarking in England! I try not to laugh, but I can't help myself. El Quemado doesn't take it amiss. Very well planned! he acknowledges, though in his tone I note a hint of mockery. Honestly, I must say that as an opponent he never loses his cool. Completely absorbed in the game, he plays as if overcome by the sadness of real war. And finally, something odd to ponder: before El Quemado left I went out on the balcony to get some fresh air, and whom did I see on the Paseo Marítimo talking to the Wolf and the Lamb, though admittedly escorted by the hotel watchman? Frau Else.

SEPTEMBER 10

Today, at ten in the morning, I was woken by a phone call giving me the news. They had found Charly's body and wanted me to come to the police station to identify it. Shortly afterward, as I was having breakfast, the manager of the Costa Brava appeared, exuberant and brimming with excitement.

"At last! We have to go as soon as possible; the body leaves today for Germany. I just talked to the German consulate. They're efficient people, I must say."

At twelve we were at a building on the edge of town—nothing like the one in the dream I'd had a few days ago—where a young man from the Red Cross was waiting for us with the representative from Navy Headquarters, whom I already knew. Inside, in a dirty, smelly waiting room, the German official was reading the Spanish papers.

"Udo Berger, friend of the deceased," the manager of the Costa Brava introduced me.

The official got up, shook my hand, and asked me if we could proceed to the identification.

"We have to wait for the police," explained Mr. Pere.

"But aren't we at the police station?" asked the official.

Mr. Pere nodded and shrugged. The official sat down again. Soon afterward the rest of us—talking all at once and in whispers—followed his lead.

Half an hour later, the policemen arrived. There were three of them and they didn't seem to have any idea why we were waiting. Again, it was the manager of the Costa Brava who took it upon himself to explain, after which they had us follow them up and down corridors and stairs until we came to a rectangular white room—underground, or so I thought—where Charly's body lay.

"Is this him?"

"Yes, it's him," I said, Mr. Pere said, everyone said.

With Frau Else on the roof:

"Is this your hideaway? The view is nice. You can pretend you're queen of the town."

"I don't play pretend."

"Actually it's nicer now than in August. Less stark. If the place were mine, I think I'd bring up some potted plants, a touch of green. It would be cozier that way."

"I don't want to be cozy. I like it the way it is. Anyway, it's not my hideaway."

"Oh, I know, it's the only place where you can be alone."

"Not even that."

"Well, I followed you because I need to talk to you."

"But I don't want to talk to you, Udo. Not now. Later, if you like, I'll come down to your room."

"And will we make love?"

"Who knows?"

"You and I have never done it, you realize. We kiss and kiss and we still can't make up our minds to go to bed together. We're behaving like children!"

"Don't worry. It'll happen when the conditions are right."

"What conditions do you mean?"

"Attraction, friendship, the urge to escape the unescapable. Everything has to be spontaneous."

"I'd do it this minute. Time flies, don't you know?"

"I want to be alone now, Udo. Also, I'm a little afraid of becoming emotionally dependent on a person like you. Sometimes I think you have no sense at all and other times I think the opposite. I see you as a tragic soul. Deep down you must be quite unbalanced."

"You think I'm still a child . . ."

"You idiot, I don't even remember you as a boy. Were you ever one?"

"You really don't remember?"

"Of course not. I have a vague recollection of your parents and that's all. The way you remember tourists is different from the way you remember normal people. It's like snippets of film, no, not film, photographs, snapshots, thousands of snapshots, and all of them blank."

"I don't know whether the silly things you say make me feel better or terrify me . . . Last night, as I was playing with El Quemado, I saw you. You were with the Wolf and the Lamb. Would you say that they're normal people, the kind you'll remember in the normal way, not as blanks?"

"They were asking about you. I told them to leave."

"I'm glad to hear it. Why did it take you so long?"

"We were talking about other things."

"What things? About me? About what I was doing?"

"We talked about things that are none of your business. Nothing to do with you."

"I don't know whether to believe you or not, but thanks anyway. I wouldn't have liked it if they'd come up to bother me."

"What are you? Just a war games player?"

"Of course not. I'm a young person who's trying to have a good time . . . a healthy good time. And I'm a German."

"And what does it mean to be a German?"

"I don't know exactly. Something difficult, that's for sure. Something that we've gradually forgotten."

"Me too?"

"All of us. Though in your case, maybe a little less so."

"I should take that as a compliment, I suppose."

I spent the afternoon at the Andalusia Lodge. Now that the tourists are gone the bar is gradually returning to its true sinister self. The floor is dirty, sticky, covered with cigarette butts and napkins, and there are plates, cups, bottles, and the remains of sandwiches stacked on the bar, everything jumbled together in a strangely desolate and peaceful tableau. The Spanish kids are still glued to the VCR, and sitting at a table near them the owner reads the sports page. Of course everyone knows that Charly's body has been found, and although for the first few minutes they keep a certain respectful distance, soon the owner comes over to offer me his condolences: "Life is short," he says without further ado as he serves me my coffee and sits down next to me. Surprised, I muttered something vague. "Now you'll go home and everything will start over again." I nodded. Everyone else began to pretend they were watching the movie but they were really listening to what I had to say. Leaning up against the other side of the bar, with her forehead in her hand, an older woman was staring at me. "Your girlfriend must be waiting for you. Life goes on and you have to live it as best you can." I asked who the woman was. The owner smiled. "That's my mother. The poor thing is lost. She doesn't like it when the summer ends." I pointed out that she was quite young. "Yes, she had me when she was fifteen. I'm the oldest of ten. The poor thing is worn-out." I said she didn't look her age. "She works in the kitchen. All day she makes sandwiches, beans with sausage, paella, fried eggs and potatoes, pizza." I'll have to come and try the paella, I said. The owner blinked. His eyes were wet. Next summer, I added. "It isn't what it used to be," he said gloomily. "Not half as good as it was before." Before what? "Back in the old days." Oh, I said, that's normal, maybe you've had it too often and you can't appreciate it anymore. "Maybe." The woman, still in the same position, pouted in a way that might have been for my sake but might just as easily have been a commentary on life and time. Behind her sad and wrinkled smile I thought I glimpsed a kind of fierce excitement. The owner seemed to meditate for an instant and then, with obvious effort, he got up and offered me a drink, "on the house," which I turned down since I hadn't finished my coffee yet. As he passed the bar he turned and, with his eyes on me, kissed his mother on the forehead. He came back with a cognac in his hand, looking noticeably more animated. I asked what had happened to the Wolf and the Lamb. They were looking for jobs. Doing what, he didn't know, anything, construction or whatever. The subject wasn't to his liking. I hope they find something they like, I said. He doubted they would. He had hired the Wolf a few seasons ago and he couldn't remember a worse waiter. He lasted only a month. "Anyway, it's better to be out looking for work, even if no one has any intention of giving it to you, than to bore yourself like a pig." It was better, I agreed. At least it showed a more positive attitude. "Now that you're leaving, the one who'll be bored as a dog is El Quemado." (Why "dog" and not "pig"? The owner knew how to call things by their names.) We're good friends, I said, but I doubt it'll matter that much to him. "I didn't mean that," said the owner, his eyes glinting. "I meant the game." I looked at him without saying anything, the bastard had his hands under the table and was making motions like someone masturbating. Whatever he was talking about, it amused him. "Your game, El Quemado is excited about it. I've never seen him so interested in anything." I cleared my throat and said yes. The truth is that I was surprised that El Quemado had gone around talking about our match. The movie-watching kids were giving us side-long glances, hardly bothering to hide it anymore. I had the feeling that they were waiting, menacingly, for something to happen. "El Quemado is a smart kid, though he keeps to himself, because of the burns, of course." The owner's voice had dropped to a barely au-dible murmur. At the other end of the bar, his mother or whoever she was me gave me a fierce smile. It's only natural, I said. "Your game is a kind of chess, a sport, isn't it?" Something like that. "And it has to do with war, with World War II, doesn't it?" Yes, that's right. "And El Quemado is losing, or at least that's what you think, isn't it? Because it's all very confusing." Yes, in fact. "Well, the match will never be finished, which is all for the best." I asked why he thought it was better for the match to remain unfinished. "For the sake of humanity!" The owner gave a start and then smiled reassuringly. "If I were you I wouldn't get him upset." I chose to sit expectantly, in silence. "I don't think he likes Germans." Charly liked El Quemado, I remembered, and he claimed it was mutual.

Or maybe it was Hanna who said that. Suddenly I was depressed and I felt like going back to the Del Mar, packing my bags, and leaving immediately. "The burns, you know, were inflicted on purpose, it was no accident." Had it been Germans? Was that why he didn't like Germans? The owner, hunched over so that his chin almost grazed the red plastic surface of the table, said, "The German side," and I realized that he was talking about the game, *Third Reich*. El Quemado must be crazy, I exclaimed. In response I felt myself pierced by the resentful gazes of the movie watchers. It was just a game, that's all, and the man was talking as if Gestapo counters (ha-ha) were about to stomp on the face of the Allied player. "I don't like to see him suffer." He's not suffering, I said, he's having fun. And he's using his brain! "That's the worst of it, the kid thinks too much." The woman behind the bar shook her head and then dug in her ear. I thought about Ingeborg. Had we really had drinks here and talked about our love in this dirty, smelly place? It's no surprise that she got tired of me. My poor, faraway Ingeborg. Every corner of the bar was steeped in misfortune, the inescapable. The owner screwed up the left side of his face: he drew his cheek up until it hid his eye. I didn't remark at his dexterity. The owner didn't seem offended; beneath it all, he was in a good mood. "The Nazis," he said. "The real Nazi soldiers on the loose around the world." Uh-huh, I said. I lit a cigarette. Little by little, this was all beginning to seem otherworldly. Then was it Nazis who were responsible for his burns, was that the story? And where had this happened, and when and why? The owner gave me a superior look before replying that El Quemado, in some hazy distant past, had been a soldier, "the kind of soldier who has to fight tooth and nail." Infantry, I deduced. Immediately, with a smile on my lips, I asked whether El Quemado was Jewish or Russian, but such subtleties were beyond the owner. He said: "No one crosses him, the very thought of it petrifies them" (he must be talking about the louts at the Andalusia Lodge). "You, for example, have you ever felt his arms?" No, not me. "I have," said the owner in a sepulchral voice. And then he added: "He spent last summer working here, in the kitchen, it was his own idea, so I wouldn't lose customers, you know, tourists don't want to see a face like that, especially when they're drinking." I said that it wasn't that simple; tastes differ, as everyone knows. The owner shook his head. His eyes shone with a malicious light. I'll never set foot in this dive again, I thought. "I would have liked him to stay on here, I have a lot of respect for him, that's why I'm happy that the game will end in a draw, I'd hate to see him get in trouble." What kind of trouble was he talking about? I asked. The owner, as if admiring the scenery, stared for a long time at his mother, the bar, the shelves of dusty bottles, the soccer club posters. "The real problem is when a person can't keep a promise," he said thoughtfully. What kind of promise? The light in the owner's eyes suddenly dimmed. I admit that for an instant I was afraid he would cry. I was wrong. The stubborn bastard laughed and waited, like an old cat, fat and evil. Is this something to do with my dead friend? I ventured carefully. With my dead friend's girlfriend? With one hand on his stomach, the owner exclaimed: "Oh, I don't know, I really don't know, but it's cracking me up." I didn't understand what he meant and I was quiet. Soon I would have to meet El Quemado at the entrance to the hotel, and for the first time the prospect made me somewhat uneasy. The counter, dimly lit by some yellow hanging lamps, was empty; the woman had gone. You know El Quemado, tell me something about him. "Impossible, impossible," murmured the owner. Through the partially closed windows, the night and the damp began to creep in. Outside, on the terrace, only shadowy figures remained, swept occasionally by the headlights of cars turning off the Paseo toward the center of town. Glumly, I imagined myself searching for the well-hidden road to France, far from this town and vacation days. "Impossible, impossible," he again murmured sadly, hunching in on himself as if he were suddenly very cold. At least tell me where El Quemado is from, for Christ's sake. One of the movie-watching kids glanced over his shoulder at our table and said he's a ghost. The owner gazed at the boy with pity. "Now he'll feel empty, but he'll be in peace." Where is he from? I asked again. The movie-watching kid stared at me with an obscene smile. From here.

Summer 1941. Situation of the German Army in England: satisfactory. Army corps: Fourth Infantry in Portsmouth, reinforced in the Strategic Redeployment phase by the Forty-eighth Armored. The Tenth is still at the beachhead, reinforced by the Twentieth and Twenty-ninth Infantry. The British are gathering their forces in London and reserving their airborne units in case of air-to-air attacks. (Should I have marched straight on London? I don't think so.) Situation of the German Army in Russia: optimal. Siege of Leningrad; the Finnish and German units meet in Hex C46; from Yaroslavl I begin to press toward Vologda; from Moscow toward Gorki; in the hexes between I49 and L48 the front remains stable; in the south I advance toward Stalingrad. El Quemado digs in now on the other side of the Volga and between Astrakhan and Maikop. Units engaged in the north of Russia: five infantry corps, two armored corps, four Finnish infantry corps. Units engaged in the central region: seven infantry corps, four armored corps. Units engaged in the south: six infantry corps, three armored corps, one Italian infantry corps, four Romanian infantry corps, and three Hungarian infantry corps. Situation of the Axis armies in the Mediterranean: unchanged; Attrition Option.

Surprise: when I got up—it couldn't have been twelve yet—the first thing I saw when I opened the balcony doors was El Quemado. He was walking along the beach with his hands behind his back, his eyes on the ground like someone searching for something in the sand, his tanned and scorched skin so shiny that he nearly left a wake on the golden beach.

Today is a holiday. The last reserves of retirees and Surinamese have gone out after lunch, leaving the hotel at just quarter capacity. At the same time, half the staff have taken the day off. The hallways echoed softly and sadly when I headed to breakfast. (The sound of broken plumbing or something tinkled on the stairs but no one seemed to notice.)

In the sky a Cessna prop plane strove to trace letters that the strong wind erased before I could make out entire words. I was gripped then by a vast melancholy that seized my belly, my spine, my bottom ribs, until I doubled over under the sunshade!

I realized in a vague way, as if I were dreaming, that the morning of September 11 was unfolding above the hotel, at the height of the Cessna's ailerons, and that those of us who were down below that morning, the retirees leaving the hotel, the waiters sitting on the terrace watching the little plane's maneuvers, Frau Else hard at work, and El Quemado loafing on the beach, were in some way condemned to walk in darkness.

Was this true of Ingeborg too, protected by the orderliness of a sensible city and a sensible job? Was it true of my bosses and office mates, who understood, suspected, and waited? Was it true of Conrad, who was loyal and guileless and the best friend anybody could ask for? Was everyone down in the depths?

As I ate breakfast, the tentacles of a huge sun crept over the Paseo Marítimo and all the terraces without managing to actually warm anything. Not even the plastic chairs. I caught a glimpse of Frau Else at the reception desk and though we didn't speak I thought I detected a trace of affection in her gaze. I asked my waiter what the hell the plane up there was trying to write. It's commemorating September 11, he said. But what is there to commemorate? Today is Catalonia Day, he said. El Quemado, on the beach, kept pacing back and forth. I waved; he didn't see me.

What went almost unnoticed in the hotel and campground zone was glaringly evident in the old town. The streets were decorated and flags hung from windows and balconies. Most of the businesses were closed, and the crowded bars made it clear that it was a holiday. In front of a movie theater some adolescents had set up a couple of tables where they were selling books, pamphlets, and little flags. When I asked what kind of literature it was, a skinny kid, no older than fifteen, said, "Patriotic books." What did he mean by that? One of his friends, laughing, shouted something that I didn't catch. They're Catalan books! said the skinny kid. I bought one and walked away. In the church square—just a few old ladies whispering on a bench—I glanced through it and then tossed it in a trash can.

I returned to the hotel, taking the long way around.

That afternoon I called Ingeborg. First I tidied the room: papers on the night table, dirty clothes under the bed, all the windows open so that I could watch the sky and the sea, and the balcony doors open so that I could see the beach all the way to the port. The conversation was chillier than I had expected. On the beach people were swimming and there was no trace of the little plane. I said that Charly had turned up. After an embarrassing silence, Ingeborg replied that sooner or later it was bound to happen. Call

Hanna, let her know, I said. Not necessary, according to Ingeborg. The German consulate would inform Charly's parents, and Hanna would find out from them. After a while I realized that we didn't have anything to say to each other. And yet I wasn't the one who ended the conversation. I described the weather, what it was like at the hotel and the beach, how things were at the clubs, though since she left I haven't set foot in a single one. I didn't say that, of course. At last, as if we were afraid of waking someone asleep nearby, we hung up. Then I called Conrad and more or less repeated the same thing. Then I decided not to make any more calls.

Reassessment of August 31. Ingeborg says what she thinks, and what she thought that day was that I'd left. Of course I was dumb enough not to ask her where she thought I would go. To Stuttgart? Did she have any reason to think I might have gone to Stuttgart? Furthermore: when I woke up and our eyes met, we didn't recognize each other. I realized it and she realized it too and turned away. She didn't want me to look at her! That I, who had just woken, shouldn't have recognized her is normal; what's unacceptable is that the bafflement was mutual. Was that when our love ended? It could be. In any case, *something* ended then. I don't know what, though I sense its importance. She said to me: I'm scared, the Del Mar scares me, the town scares me. Had she sensed the thing—the one thing—that I was overlooking?

Seven in the evening. On the terrace with Frau Else.

"Where's your husband?"

"In his room."

"And where is that room?"

"On the first floor, above the kitchen. In a little corner where guests never set foot. Completely off-limits."

"Does he feel well today?"

"Not very. Do you want to visit him? No, of course you don't."

"I'd like to get to know him."

"Well, you don't have time now. I would've liked the two of you to meet too, but not in the state he's in at the moment. You understand, don't you? On equal terms, both of you in good form."

"Why do you think I don't have time? Because I'm leaving for Stuttgart?"

"That's right, because you're going back."

"Well, you're wrong, I still haven't made up my mind to leave, so if your husband gets better and you're able to bring him to the dining room—after dinner, say—I'd like to have the pleasure of meeting him and talking to him. Especially talking to him. On equal terms."

"So you aren't leaving . . ."

"Why should I? You can't think I've been staying at your hotel just waiting for Charly's body to turn up. In terrible shape too. The body, I mean. You wouldn't have liked it if you'd had to go and identify it."

"Are you staying for me? Because we haven't slept together?"

"His face was ravaged. From the ears to the chin, all eaten away by fish. His eyes were gone, and his skin—the skin of his face and neck—had turned nearly gray. Sometimes I think the poor bastard wasn't Charly. He might have been, and he might not have been. I'm told that the body of an Englishman who drowned around the same time still hasn't been found. Who knows. I didn't want to say anything to the man from the consulate so he wouldn't think I was crazy. But that's what passed through my mind. How can you sleep above the kitchen?"

"It's the biggest room in the hotel. It's very nice. Everything a girl could ask for. And it's the place where tradition says the owners should sleep. Before us, my husband's parents slept there. A tradition in its infancy, really, because my in-laws built the hotel. Do you realize how disappointed everyone will be that you're not leaving?"

"Who is everyone?"

"Oh, three or four people, my dear, please don't be upset."

"Your husband?"

"No, not him especially."

"Then who?"

"The manager at the Costa Brava; my night watchman, who's very touchy lately; Clarita, the maid . . ."

"Which maid? The young skinny one?"

"That's right."

"She's terrified of me. I suppose she thinks I might rape her at any moment."

"I don't know, I don't know. You don't understand women."

"Who else wants me to leave?"

"Nobody else."

"What reason can Mr. Pere have for wanting me to leave?"

"I don't know, maybe for him it's like putting the case to rest."

"Charly's case?"

"Yes."

"How idiotic. And your night watchman? Why does he care?"

"He's sick of you. Tired of seeing you wandering around at night like a sleepwalker. I think you make him nervous."

"Like a sleepwalker?"

"Those were his words."

"But I've only spoken to him a few times!"

"That's not the point. He talks to all kinds of people, especially drunks. He likes to make conversation. But with you, he watches you come in and go out at night . . . with El Quemado. And he knows that the last light on in the hotel is the light in your window."

"I thought he liked me."

"Our watchman doesn't like any of the guests. Especially not one he's seen kissing his boss."

"A very peculiar individual. Where is he now?"

"I forbid you to talk to him. I don't want this to get any more complicated, is that clear? He must be asleep now."

"When I tell you the things I tell you, do you believe me?"

"Mmm . . . yes."

"When I tell you that I've seen your husband at night on the beach with El Quemado, do you believe me?"

"It seems so unfair to mix him up in this, so disloyal of me."

"But he mixed himself up in it!"

"..."

"When I tell you that the body the police showed me might not be Charly's, do you believe me?"

"Yes."

"I'm not saying that they know it's not, I'm saying we're all wrong."

"Yes. It wouldn't be the first time."

"Do you believe me, then?"

"Yes."

"And if I tell you that I feel something intangible, strange, circling around me in a threatening way, do you believe me? A higher force keeping watch over me. I rule out your night watchman, of course, though unconsciously he's aware of it too, which is why he doesn't like me. Working at night heightens some of the senses."

"Now you've gone too far. Don't ask me to be an accomplice to your madness."

"It's too bad, because you're the only one who's any help to me, the only one I can trust."

"You should go back to Germany."

"With my tail between my legs."

"No, with your mind at ease, ready to reflect on what you've experienced."

"Slip away unnoticed, the way El Quemado wishes he could."

"Poor boy. He lives in a perpetual prison."

"Forgetting that at a certain point everything has had the ring of hell to it, musically speaking."

"What is it you're so afraid of?"

"I'm not afraid of anything. Soon you'll see for yourself."

We climbed slowly to the top of the hill. From the lookout point, some hundred people, adults and children, watched the lights of the town, holding their breath and pointing toward a spot on the horizon between the sky and the sea, as if a miracle were about to occur and the sun were about to rise out of turn. It's Catalonia Day, a voice whispered in my ear. I know, I said. What's supposed to happen now? Frau Else smiled and her index finger, so long it was almost transparent, pointed toward where everyone was looking. Suddenly, from one, two, or more fishing boats that no one could see or at least that I couldn't see, preceded by a sound like chalk on a blackboard, there appeared various bursts of fireworks that together made up, according to Frau Else, the Catalonian flag. When all that was left were tentacles of smoke, everyone went back to their cars and drove down to the town, where the late summer night awaited them.

Autumn 1941. Battles in England. The German Army is unable to take London, but the British Army can't manage to push me back to the sea either. Copious losses. The British fighting strength grows. In the Soviet Union, the Attrition Option. El Quemado is waiting for 1942. Meanwhile, he holds on.

My generals:

"In Great Britain: Reichenau, Salmuth, and Hoth."

"In the Soviet Union: Guderian, Kleist, Busch, Kluge, von Weichs, Küchler, Manstein, Model, Rommel, Heinrici, and Geyr."

"In Africa: Reinhardt and Hoeppner."

My BRP: low, which means it's impossible to choose the Offensive Option in the East, West, or Mediterranean. Sufficient only to rebuild units. (Hasn't El Quemado noticed? What's he waiting for?)

A cloudy day. It's been raining since four in the morning and the forecast calls for more rain. Still, it's not cold, and from the balcony one can watch children in their bathing suits jumping waves on the beach, if not for long. The atmosphere in the dining room, invaded by card-playing guests who stare gloomily at the fogged-up windows, is charged with electricity and suspicion. When I sit down and order breakfast I'm observed by the disapproving faces of people who can hardly grasp that there are those who rise after noon. At the entrance to the hotel, a bus has been waiting for hours (the driver is gone now) to take a group of tourists to Barcelona. The bus is a pearl gray color, like the horizon upon which there appear the faint silhouettes (but this must be an optical illusion) of milky whirlwinds, like explosions or fissures of light under the roof of the storm. After breakfast I went out on the terrace: immediately I felt the cold rain on my face and I retreated. Miserable weather, said an old German in shorts sitting in the TV room smoking a cigar. The bus was waiting for him, among others, but he didn't seem to be in a hurry. From my balcony I could see that the only pedal boats left on the beach, forlorn, looking more like a tumbledown shack than ever, were El Quemado's; for everyone else the summer season was over. I closed the balcony doors and went out again. At the reception desk I was told that Frau Else had left the hotel first thing in the morning and wouldn't be back until that night. I asked whether she'd gone out alone. No, with her husband.

I covered the distance between the Costa Brava and the Del Mar by car. When I got out I was sweating. At the Costa Brava I found Mr. Pere reading the paper. "Friend Udo, how delightful to see you!" He really did seem to be happy, so I let down my guard. For a while we exchanged banalities about the weather. Then Mr. Pere said that he would send me to his doctor. Alarmed, I refused. "Take a few little pills, if nothing else!" I asked for a cognac and drank it in a single gulp. Then I asked for another. When I tried to pay, Mr. Pere said it was on the hotel. "The anxiety of the wait is already cost enough!" I thanked him and after a bit I got up. Mr. Pere followed me to the door. Before we parted I told him that I was keeping a diary. A diary? A diary of my vacation, of my life, basically. Oh, I see, said Mr. Pere. In my day that was for girls . . . and poets. I detected the mockery: smooth, weary, deeply malicious. Before us the sea seemed about to leap onto the Paseo Marítimo. I'm not a poet, I said, smiling. I'm interested in daily life, even the unpleasant parts; for example, I'd like to write something in my diary about the rape. Mr. Pere looked pale. What rape? The one that happened just before my friend drowned. (At that instant, maybe because I'd referred to Charly as a friend, I was seized by a wave of nausea so severe it gave me the shivers.) You're wrong, spluttered Mr. Pere. There was no rape here, though of course in the past we haven't been able to completely avoid such embarrassing incidents, generally attributable to outside elements, since today, as you know, our main problem is the decline in the quality of our tourists, etc. Then I must be wrong, I said. No doubt, no doubt. We shook hands and I ran to the car to escape the downpour.

Winter 1941. I want to talk to Frau Else, or see her for a while, but El Quemado turns up before she does. For a moment, from the balcony, I consider the possibility of not receiving him. All I have to do is not show up at the entrance to the hotel, since if I don't go to meet him, El Quemado won't come any farther. But he must have spotted me from the beach when I was on the balcony, and now I wonder whether I didn't stand there precisely so El Quemado would see me, or to prove to myself that I wasn't afraid of being seen. An easy target: I exhibit myself behind the wet glass in order to be spotted by El Quemado, the Wolf, and the Lamb.

It's still raining. During the afternoon the hotel has gradually been emptying of tourists, picked up by Dutch buses. What can Frau Else be doing? Now that everyone has gone, is she sitting in a doctor's waiting room? Is she strolling on her husband's arm along the streets of the Barri Gòtic? Are they on their way to a little movie theater almost hidden in the trees? Unexpectedly, El Quemado launches an offensive in England. It fails. Because of my lack of BRP, my response is limited. On the other fronts there are no changes, though the Soviet line is reinforced. The truth is that I stop paying attention to the game (not so El Quemado, who spends the night circling the table and making calculations in a notebook, which he brought today for the first time!). The rain, persistent thoughts of Frau Else, a vague and languid nostalgia, make me lie on the bed smoking and leafing through the photocopies that I brought with me from Stuttgart and that I suspect will be left here, in some trash can. How many columnists really think through what they write? How many have a passion for it? I *could* work for *The General*; even in my sleep—sleepwalking, as Frau Else's watchman says—I could demolish them. How many have looked into the abyss? Only Rex Douglas knows anything about it! (Beyma, perhaps, is historically rigorous, and Michael Anchors is original and full with enthusiasm, a kind of American Conrad.) The rest: deadly boring and inconsistent. When I tell El Quemado that the papers I'm reading are plans for beating him, all moves and countermoves foreseen, all expenses foreseen, all possible strategies invariably noted, a hideous smile crosses his face (against his will, I have to believe), and that is his only answer. As a coda: a few little steps, back hunched, tweezers in hand, troop movements. I don't watch him. I know he won't cheat. His BRP have also dropped to a minimum, just enough to keep his armies alive. Has the rain put an end to his business? Surprisingly, El Quemado says no, that the sun will come out again. And meanwhile, what? Will you keep living under the pedal boats? With his back to me, moving counters, he responds mechanically that it's no problem for him. Sleeping on the wet sand isn't a problem? El Quemado whistles a song.

El Quemado arrives earlier than usual today. And he comes up alone, without waiting for me to meet him. When I open the door, he looks like a figure rubbed out with an eraser. (Like a suitor who, instead of flowers, carries photocopies clutched to his chest.) Soon I realize what's behind this transformation. The initiative is now his. The offensive mounted by the Soviet Army unfolds in the zone between Lake Onega and Yaroslavl; his armored units breach my front in Hex E48 and move north, toward Karelia, leaving four German infantry corps and a German armored corps cut off at the gates of Vologda. With this move, the eastern flank of the armies pressing toward Kuibyshev and Kazan is left totally exposed. The only immediate solution is to bring in units during the Strategic Redeployment phase, units from Army Group South deployed on the Volga and Caucasus lines, thereby lessening the pressure on Batum and Astrakhan. El Quemado knows this and seizes his advantage. Though his face remains unchanged, sunk in God knows what hells, I can still sense—in the creases of his cheeks!—the relish with which he executes his ever more agile movements. The offensive, calculated down to the last detail, has been set up a turn in advance. (For example, the only usable air base within the zone of the offensive is in the city of Vologda; Kirov, the next closest, is too far; to solve the problem, and since a greater concentration of air support was required, in the Winter '41 turn he moved an air base counter to Hex C51 . . .) He's not improvising, not at all. In the

West the only substantial change is the entry into the war of the United States; a soft entry due to the limitations of Initial Deployment, which means that the British Army must wait to act until it has achieved the necessary conditions for a war of matériel (the BRP expenditures of the Western allies are mostly earmarked for the support of the USSR). Ultimately, the situation of the American Army in Great Britain is as follows: Fifth and Tenth Infantry in Rosyth, five air factors in Liverpool, and nine naval factors in Belfast. The option that he chooses for the West is Attrition, and he has no luck with the dice. My option is also Attrition and I manage to occupy a hex in the southwest of England, vital for my plans in the next turn. In the summer of '42 I'll take London, defeat the British, and the Americans will have their Dunkirk. Meanwhile I amuse myself with El Quemado's photocopies, copies that only eventually does he acknowledge are for me. A gift. They make for surprising reading. But I'd rather not show too much vulnerability, so I choose to see the funny side and ask where he got them. El Quemado's answers—and my questions gradually begin to adjust themselves to the same rhythm—are slow, bristling, as if they've just learned to stand upright and walk. They're for you, he says. I got them from a book. A book of his, a book he keeps under the pedal boats? No. A book borrowed from the Catalonia Pension Fund Library. He shows me his membership card. Incredible. He goes rummaging around in the library of a *bank* and finds this shit to fling in my face, no less. Now El Quemado gives me a sidelong glance, waiting for the fear to blossom in the room; his shadow falls on the wall near the door, indefinable and quivering. I refuse to give him satisfaction. Coolly and carefully, I set the copies on the night table. Later, when I walk him to the door of the hotel, I ask him to stop with me for a moment at the reception desk. The watchman is reading a magazine. Our intrusion into his domain irritates him, but fear prevails. I ask for pushpins. Pushpins? His wary gaze flits from El Quemado to me as if he expects a bad joke and doesn't want to be caught off guard. Yes, you idiot, check the drawers and get me a few, I shout. (I've discovered that the watchman is the cowardly, shrinking type who requires a firm hand.) As he rummages through the desk drawers, I catch a glimpse of a few porn magazines. Finally, wavering between triumph and hesitance, he holds up a little clear plastic jar of pushpins. Do you want all of them? he whispers, as if he's about to put an end to this nightmare. Shrugging, I ask El Quemado how many photocopies there are. Four, he says, uncomfortable and staring at the floor. He doesn't like my lessons in the use of force. Four pushpins, I repeat, and hold out my hand, into which the clerk carefully deposits two green and two red pins. Then, without a backward glance, I walk El Quemado to the door and we say our good-byes. The Paseo Marítimo is deserted and poorly lit (someone has smashed one of the streetlights), but I stand behind the glass until I'm satisfied that El Quemado has hopped down to the beach and vanished in the direction of the pedal boats; only then do I go back to my room. There I calmly choose a wall (the one against which my bed stands) and tack up the photocopies. Then I wash my hands and carefully pore over the game. El Quemado is a quick study, but the next turn will be mine.

It was two in the afternoon when I got up. My body ached and an inner voice told me that I should try to spend as little time as possible at the hotel. I went out without even showering. After coffee at a nearby bar and a glance at some of the German papers, I returned to the Del Mar and inquired after Frau Else. Not back yet from Barcelona. Nor is her husband, obviously. The atmosphere at the reception desk is hostile. Same at the bar. Dirty looks from the waiters, that kind of thing. Nothing serious. The sun was shining, though there were still some black clouds on the horizon, heavy with rain, so I put on my bathing trunks and went to keep El Quemado company. The pedal boats were unstacked, but El Quemado was nowhere to be seen. I decided to wait for him and I lay down in the sand. I hadn't brought a book, so the only thing I could do was stare at the sky, which was a deep blue, and remember happy things to pass the time. At some point, of course, I fell asleep; the beach—warm and nearly empty, the clamor of August now remote—was conducive to sleep. I dreamed then about Florian Linden. Ingeborg and I were at the hotel in a room like ours, and someone was knocking at the door. Ingeborg didn't want me to see who it was. Don't, she said, if you love me, don't do it. As she spoke, her lips trembled. It might be something urgent, I said resolutely, but when I tried to move toward the door Ingeborg clung to me with both hands so that I couldn't move at all. Let me go, I shouted, let me go, as the pounding grew louder and louder, until I thought that maybe Ingeborg was right and it was best to stay where we were. In the struggle, Ingeborg fell to the floor. I gazed down at her from far above. She was in some kind of swoon, with her legs flung wide. Anyone could rape you now, I said, and then she opened one eye, just one, the left one, I think, huge and ultrablue, and didn't take it off me; wherever I moved it followed me. Its expression, I'd say, though I can't be sure, wasn't vigilant or accusatory but curious, attentive to something new, and terrified. Then I couldn't stand it any longer and I pressed my ear to the door. The person outside wasn't knocking, he was *scratching* at the door from the other side! Who is it? I asked. Florian Linden, private detective, answered a tiny voice. Do you want to come in? No, for the love of God, don't open the door! Florian Linden's voice insisted, more vigorously, though not much. It was clear that he was hurt. For a while we were both silent, trying to listen, but the truth is that there was nothing to be heard. It was as if the hotel were underwater. Even the temperature was different. It was colder now, and since we were wearing summer clothes, that made it worse. Soon it became unbearable and I had to get up and get blankets out of the closet to wrap around Ingeborg and me. But it was no good. Ingeborg began to sob: she said she couldn't feel her legs anymore and we were going to freeze to death. You'll die only if you fall asleep, I promised, trying not to look at her. On the other side of the door sound could be heard at last. Steps: someone was approaching, as if on tiptoe, and then retreating. The same progression three times. Is that you, Florian? Yes, it's me, but now I have to leave, answered Florian Linden. What's going on? Shady business, I don't have time to explain. You're safe for now, though you'd better go home tomorrow morning. Home? The detective's voice creaked and crackled as he spoke. They're vaporizing him! I thought. Then I tried to go open the door and I couldn't get up. I had no feeling in my feet or hands. I was frozen. In terror, I realized that there was no way out and we were going to die at the hotel. Ingeborg had stopped moving; she was sprawled at my feet, and all that could be seen of her under the blanket was her long blond hair on the black tile floor. I would have liked to hug her and weep, I felt so forlorn; but just then, without any help from me, the door opened. Where Florian Linden should have been there was no one, but there was a huge shadow at the end of the corridor. Then I opened my eyes, trembling, and I saw the cloud, giant and dark, looming over the town and lumbering like an aircraft carrier toward the hills. I was cold. Everyone had left the beach and El Quemado wasn't going to come. I don't know how long I lay there on the sand, looking up at the sky. I was in no hurry. I might have been there for hours and hours. When at last I decided to get up, instead of returning to the hotel I headed for the sea. The water was warm and dirty. I swam for a bit. The dark cloud kept moving overhead. Then I stopped stroking and sank down until I touched the bottom. I'm not sure whether I made it; while I was underwater I think I kept my eyes wide open, but I didn't see anything. I was being swept out to sea. When I emerged I saw that I hadn't drifted as far from the shore as I thought. I returned to the pedal boats, picked up my towel, and dried myself carefully. It was the first time that El Quemado hadn't shown up for work. Suddenly shivers ran through me. I did some exercises: push-ups, sit-ups, a brief jog. When I was dry I tied the towel around my waist and walked off to the Andalusia Lodge. There I asked for a cognac and told the owner that I would come by later to pay. Then I asked after El Quemado. No one had seen him.

The afternoon dragged on. Frau Else never turned up at the hotel, nor did El Quemado appear on the beach, though at six the sun came out, and near the point by the campgrounds I spotted a pedal boat, beach umbrellas, and people playing in the waves. My stretch of beach wasn't as lively. The hotel guests had signed up en masse for an excursion—to a vineyard or a famous monastery, I seem to remember—and the only people left on the terrace were a few old men and the waiters. By the time it started to get dark I knew what I wanted to do, and soon afterward I asked the reception desk to put through a call to Germany. Before the call went through I had reviewed the state of my finances and discovered that I had only enough to pay the bill, spend one more night at the Del Mar, and put a little gasoline in the car. On the fifth or sixth attempt I managed to reach Conrad. His voice sounded sleepy. And there were other voices in the background. I got straight to the point. I said I needed money. I said I planned to stay a few more days.

"How many days?"

"I don't know, it depends."

"Why are you staying?"

"That's my business. I'll return the money as soon as I get back."

"The way you're acting, a person might think you plan never to come back."

"What an absurd idea. What could I do here for the rest of my life?"

"Nothing, I know. But do *you* know it?"

"Actually, there are things I could do here: I could work as a tour guide, start my own business. This place is full of tourists, and a person who can speak three languages will always be able to find work."

"Your place is here. Your career is here."

"What career are you talking about? The office?"

"I'm talking about writing, Udo, the articles for Rex Douglas, the novels, yes, listen to me, the novels you could write if you weren't such a mess. I'm talking about the plans we've made together . . . The cathedrals . . . do you remember?"

"Thank you, Conrad, yes, you're probably right . . ."

"Come back as soon as you can. I'll send the money tomorrow. Your friend's body must already be in Germany. End of story. What more is there for you to do there?"

"Who told you that they'd found Charly? . . . Ingeborg?"

"Of course. She's worried about you. We see each other almost every day. And we talk. I tell her things about you. From before you met. The day before yesterday I took her to your apartment. She wanted to see it."

"My apartment? Shit! And did she go in?"

"Obviously. She had her key but she didn't want to go alone.

Between the two of us we cleaned it up. The floor needed sweeping. And she took some things of hers, a sweater, some records . . . I don't think she'll be happy to hear that you've borrowed money in order to stay longer. She's a good girl, but there's a limit to her patience."

"What else did she do there?"

"Nothing. I told you: she swept, threw out the spoiled things in the refrigerator . . ."

"She didn't go through my files?"

"Of course not."

"What about you? What did you do?"

"For God's sake, Udo, the same things."

"All right . . . Thanks . . . So you see each other often?"

"Every day. I think it's because she doesn't have anyone to talk to about you. She wanted to call your parents, but I convinced her not to. I don't think it's a good idea to worry them."

"My parents wouldn't worry. They know the town . . . and the hotel."

"I don't know. I hardly know your parents, I don't know how they'd react."

"You hardly know Ingeborg either."

"True. You're our connection. Though it seems to me that we've gotten to be friends, in a way. These last few days I've gotten to know her better and I really like her. She's not just beautiful, she's smart and practical too."

"I know. The same thing always happens. She's . . ."

"What, she's seduced me?"

"No, 'seduced' isn't the right word; she's like ice. She has a calming effect on you. On you and everybody else. Being with her is like being alone, focused exclusively on your own pursuits, in a state of total relaxation."

"Don't talk like that. Ingeborg loves you. Tomorrow I promise I'll send you the money. Are you coming back?"

"Not yet."

"I don't understand what's keeping you there. Is there something you haven't told me? I'm your best friend . . ."

"I want to stay a few days longer, that's all. There's no mystery.

I want to think, write, enjoy the place, now that there's hardly anybody here."

"That's it? Nothing to do with Ingeborg?"

"Don't be silly, of course not."

"I'm happy to hear it. How is your match going?"

"Summer of '42. I'm winning."

"I figured as much. Do you remember that match against Mathias Müller? The one we played a year ago at the Chess Club?"

"Which match?"

"A *Third Reich*. Franz, you, and me against the group from *Forced Marches*."

"Yes, and what happened?"

"Don't you remember? We won and Mathias was so angry—he's a bad loser, you know—that he swung a chair at little Bernd Rahn and broke it."

"The chair?"

"That's right. The members of the Chess Club kicked him out and he hasn't shown his face there since. Remember how we laughed that night?"

"Sure, of course, my memory is still good. It's just that some things don't seem so funny to me anymore. But I remember everything."

"Of course."

"Ask me a question, anything, and you'll see . . ."

"I believe you, I do . . ."

"Ask me. Ask if I remember which parachute divisions were at Anzio."

"I'm sure you do . . ."

"Ask me . . ."

"All right, which . . ."

"The First Division: First, Third, and Fourth Regiments; the Second Division: Second, Fifth, and Sixth Regiments; and the Fourth Division: Tenth, Eleventh, and Twelfth Regiments."

"Very good . . ."

"Now ask me about the SS Panzer Divisions in *Fortress Europa*."

"All right, what are they?"

"The First Leibstandarte Adolf Hitler, the Second Das Reich, the Ninth Hohenstaufen, the Tenth Frundsberg, and the Twelfth Hitlerjugend."

"Perfect. Your memory is in perfect working order."

"What about yours? Do you remember who led the 352nd, Heimito Gerhardt's Infantry Division?"

"All right, that's enough."

"Tell me, do you remember or not?"

"No . . ."

"It's very simple, you can check it tonight in *Omaha Beachhead* or in any book of military history. General Dietrich Kraiss was the division commander and Colonel Meyer was the head of Heimito's regiment, the 915th."

"All right, I'll look it up. Is that all?"

"I've been thinking about Heimito. He really knows everything. He can recite from memory the complete setup for *The Longest Day*, down to battalion level."

"Of course, since that's when he was taken prisoner."

"Don't mock him, Heimito is one of a kind. I wonder how he's doing now?"

"Fine, why wouldn't he be?"

"Because he's old and everything changes; because people abandon you, Conrad. I'm surprised you don't know that."

"He's a tough, happy old man. And he isn't alone. He went to Spain in July with his wife on vacation. He sent me a postcard from Seville."

"Yes, I got one too. The truth is I couldn't read his handwriting. I should have asked to take my vacation in July."

"So you could travel with Heimito?"

"Maybe."

"We can still do it in December. For the Paris convention. I got the program a little while ago, it'll be quite the affair."

"It's not the same. I wasn't talking about that."

"We'll be able to present our paper. You'll get to meet Rex Douglas *in person*. We'll play *World in Flames* with real natives. Try to muster a little enthusiasm. It will be fantastic . . ."

"What do you mean, 'World in Flames with real natives'?"

"A team of Germans will play Germany, a team of Brits will play Great Britain, a team of Frenchmen will play France, each group under its own flag."

"I had no idea. Who will play the Soviet Union?"

"That's a good question. The French, I think, though you never know, there might be some surprises."

"And Japan? Will the Japanese come?"

"I don't know, maybe. If Rex Douglas comes, why not the Japanese . . . Though maybe we'll have to play Japan ourselves, or the Belgian delegation can. I'm sure the French organizers have it all worked out."

"The Belgians will be ridiculous as the Japanese."

"Let's not get ahead of ourselves."

"This all sounds ridiculous. I can't believe it's true. So the main event of the convention will be *World in Flames*? Whose idea was that?"

"Not exactly the main event. It's just in the program and people are excited about it."

"I thought *Third Reich* would be given a place of honor."

"And it will, Udo, during the presentation of papers."

"Right, while I'm droning on about multiple strategies everyone will be watching *World in Flames*."

"Not true. Our talk is on the 21st in the afternoon and the match takes place after the lectures each day, from the 20th to the 23rd. And the game was chosen because several teams could play, not for any other reason."

"Now I don't feel like going . . . Of course the French want to play the Soviet Union because they know we'll wipe them out on the first afternoon . . . Why don't they play Japan? . . . Out of loyalty to the old alliances, of course . . . They'll probably monopolize Rex Douglas the minute he lands . . ."

"You shouldn't speculate like this, it's pointless."

"And the Cologne gang will be there, of course . . ."

"That's right."

"All right. Enough. Say hello to Ingeborg."

"Come back soon."

"I will."

"Don't be depressed."

"I'm not depressed. I'm fine here. Happy."

"Call me. Remember that Conrad is your best friend."

"I know. Conrad is my best friend. Good-bye . . ."

Summer 1942. El Quemado shows up at eleven. I hear his shouts as I'm lying in bed reading the Florian Linden novel. Udo, Udo Berger, his voice echoes on the empty Paseo Marítimo. My first impulse is to lie still and wait. El Quemado's call is hoarse and raw as if fire had also scorched his throat. When I open the balcony doors I see him on the sidewalk across the street, sitting on the seawall of the Paseo, waiting for me as if he has all the time in the world, with a big plastic bag at his feet. There's a familiar air of terror to our greeting, to the way we acknowledge each other, essentially encapsulated in the abruptly silent and absolute manner in which we raise our arms. Between the two of us a stern and mute awareness is established, to galvanizing effect. But this state is brief and lasts only until El Quemado, in the room now, opens the bag to reveal an abundance of beers and sandwiches. Pathetic but sincere cornucopia! (Earlier, when I passed the reception desk, I asked for Frau Else again. She isn't back yet, said the watchman, avoiding my gaze. Next to him, sitting in a huge white armchair, an old man with a German paper on his knees watches me with a scarcely concealed smile on his fleshless lips. Judging by his appearance one would say he has no more than a year left to live. And yet from beneath that extreme thinness, the cheekbones and temples especially prominent, the old man stares at me with a strange intensity, as if he knows me. How goes the war? asks the watchman, and then the old man's smile grows more marked. If only I could stretch over the counter and grab the watchman by the shirt and shake him, but the watchman senses something and backs a little farther away. I'm an admirer of Rommel, he explains. The old man nods in agreement. No, you're a miserable loser, I shoot back. The old man forms a tiny

o with his lips and nods again. Maybe, says the watchman. The
looks of hatred that we shoot each other are naked and full of real
aggression. And you're scum, I add, wanting to put him over the
edge or at least get him to come a few inches closer to the counter.
Well, that's that, then, murmurs the old man in German, and he
gets up. He's very tall, and his arms, like a caveman's, dangle down
almost to his knees. Actually, that's a false impression, caused by
the old man's stoop. Still, his height is notable: standing upright he
must be (or must once have been) well over six feet tall. But it's in
his voice, the voice of a stubborn dying man, that his authority lies.
Almost immediately, as if all he'd intended was for me to see him
in his full grandeur, he drops back into the armchair and asks: Any
further difficulties? No, of course not, the watchman hastens to say.
No, none, I say. Perfect, says the old man, infusing the word with
malice and virulence—*per-fect*—and he closes his eyes.

El Quemado and I eat sitting on the bed, staring at the wall
where I've pinned up the photocopies. Without needing to put it
into words, he understands the degree of defiance in me. The degree of acceptance. Regardless, we eat wrapped in a silence interrupted only by banal observations that are really silences, added by
us to the great silence that for something like an hour has fallen
over the hotel and the town.

Finally we wash our hands so that we don't stain the tokens
with oil, and we start to play.

Later I'll take London and lose it immediately. I'll counterattack in the East and be forced to retreat.

ANZIO. FORTRESS EUROPA. OMAHA
BEACHHEAD. SUMMER 1942.

I walked the beach when all was Dark, reciting the names of the forgotten, names languishing on dusty shelves, until the sun came out again. But are they forgotten names or only names in waiting? I remembered the player as viewed by Someone from above, just the head, the shoulders, and the backs of the hands, and the board game and counters like a stage set where thousands of beginnings and endings eternally unfold, a kaleidoscopic theater, the only bridge between the player and his memory, a memory that is desire and gaze. How many infantry divisions was it—depleted, untrained— that held the Western front? Which ones halted the advance in Italy, despite treachery? Which armored divisions pierced the French defenses in '40 and the Russian defenses in '41 and '42? And with what key division did Marshal Manstein retake Kharkov and exorcise the disaster? What infantry divisions fought to clear the way for tanks in '44, in the Ardennes? And how many countless combat groups sacrificed themselves to stall the enemy on all fronts? No one can agree. Only the player's memory knows. Roaming the beach or curled up in my room, I invoke the names and they come in soothing waves. My favorite counters: the First Parachute in *Anzio*, the Lehr Panzer and the First SS LAH in *Fortress Europa*, the eleven counters of the Third Parachute in *Omaha Beachhead*, the Seventh Armored Division in *France '40*, the Third Armored Division in *Panzerkrieg*, the First SS Armored Corps in *Russian Cam-*

paign, the Fortieth Armored Corps in *Russian Front*, the First SS LAH in *Cobra*, the Grossdeutschland Armored Corps in *Third Reich*, the Twenty-first Armored Division in *The Longest Day*, the 104th Infantry Regiment in *Panzer Armee Afrika* . . . Not even reading Sven Hassel aloud at the top of my lungs could be more invigorating . . . (Oh, who was it who read nothing but Sven Hassel? Everyone will say it was M.M.—it sounds like him, it suits him—but it was someone else, someone who resembled his own shadow, someone Conrad and I liked to mock. This kid organized a Role-Playing Festival in Stuttgart in '85. With the whole city as stage he set up a macrogame about the last days of Berlin, using the re-worked rules of *Judge Dredd*. Describing it now, I can see the interest it sparks in El Quemado, interest that could well be faked to distract me from the match, a legitimate but vain strategy, since I can move my corps with my eyes closed. What the game—dubbed *Berlin Bunker*—was about, what its objectives were, how victory was achieved, and who achieved it was never quite clear. Twelve people played the ring of soldiers defending Berlin. Six people played the Nation and the Party, and could move only inside the ring. Three people played the Leadership, and their task was to manage the other eighteen so that they weren't left outside the perimeter when it shrank, as it generally did, and especially to prevent the perimeter from being breached, which was inevitable. There was a final player whose role was murky and secret; he could (and should) move all over the besieged city, but he was the only one who never knew the coordinates of the defensive ring; he could (and did) move all over the city but he was the only one who didn't know any of the other players; he had the capacity to unseat a member of the Leadership and replace him with a member of the Nation, for example, but he did this blindly, leaving written orders and receiving reports in an agreed-upon spot. His power was as great as his blindness—his innocence, according to Sven Hassel—and his freedom was as great as his constant exposure to danger. He was watched over by a kind of invisible and careful guardian, because his fate determined the ultimate destiny of all. The game, as might have been predicted, ended disastrously, with players lost in the suburbs, cheating, plotting, protesting, sectors of the ring abandoned at nightfall, players who throughout the entire match saw only the referee, etc. Naturally neither Conrad nor I took part, though Conrad went to the trouble of following events from the gymnasium of the School of Industrial Arts where the festival was held and was later able to explain to me the initial dismay and then the moral collapse of Sven Hassel when faced with the evidence of his failure. A few months later Hassel left Stuttgart, and now, according to Conrad, who knows everything, he lives in Paris and has taken up painting. I wouldn't be surprised to run into him at the convention . . .)

After midnight, the photocopies tacked to the wall take on a funereal air, little doors to the void.

"It's starting to get chilly," I say.

El Quemado is wearing a leather jacket, too small, doubtless the gift of some charitable soul. The jacket is old but well made. When he comes over to the game board after eating, he takes it off and sets it on the bed, folding it carefully. His abstracted courtesy is touching. He has a notebook (or maybe a diary, like mine?) in which he jots down the strategic or economic shifts in his alliance, a notebook that he never lets out of his sight . . . It's as if he's found, in *Third Reich*, a satisfactory mode of communication. Here, alongside the map and the Force Pool, he isn't a monster but rather a thinking being who expresses himself through hundreds of counters . . . He's a dictator and a creator . . . And he's having fun . . . If it weren't for the photocopies, I'd say that I've done him a favor. But these are like a clear warning, the first signal that I should watch my step.

"Quemado," I ask him, "do you like the game?"

"Yes, I do."

"And do you think that because you've brought me to a standstill you're going to win?"

"I don't know, it's still too early to tell."

As I open the balcony doors to let the night air clear the smoke from the room, El Quemado, like a dog, his head tilted, snuffles with difficulty and says:

"Tell me which counters are your favorite. Which divisions you think are the most beautiful (yes, literally!) and which battles the most difficult. Talk to me about the games . . ."

WITH THE WOLF AND THE LAMB

The Wolf and the Lamb show up at my room. The absence of Frau Else has relaxed the apparently strict rules of the hotel and now anyone is allowed in. As the hot days come to an end, anarchy is quietly settling in at every level. It's as if people knew how to work only when they were drenched in sweat, or when they saw us, the tourists, drenched in sweat. This might be a good moment to leave without paying, an ignoble act that I would contemplate only if some genie could guarantee that afterward I would see the look on Frau Else's face, her surprise, her astonishment. Maybe when summer ends and many of the seasonal workers also reach the end of their contracts, discipline grows lax and the inevitable occurs: thefts, poor service, untidiness. Today, for example, no one came up to make the bed. I had to do it myself. And I need clean sheets. When I call the reception desk, no one can give me a convincing explanation. As it happens, the Wolf and the Lamb arrive while I'm waiting for someone from the laundry room to bring up clean sheets.

"We just had a little free time and we decided to come and see you. We didn't want you to leave without saying good-bye."

I reassured them that I still hadn't decided when to go.

"Then we should go out for a few drinks to celebrate."

"Maybe you'll stay here to live," says the Lamb.

"Maybe you've found something worth staying for," says the

Wolf, winking an eye. Is he referring to Frau Else or something else?

"What did El Quemado find?"

"Work," answer the two of them, as if it were the most obvious thing in the world. Both are dressed as laborers in overalls stained with paint and cement.

"The good life is over," says the Lamb.

Meanwhile, the Wolf's nervous pacing carries him to the other end of the room, where he stares curiously at the game board and the Force Pool, at this point in the match a chaos of counters hard for a neophyte to understand.

"This is the famous game?"

I nod in assent. I'd like to know *who* made it famous. It's probably all my fault.

"And is it very difficult?"

"El Quemado learned to play," I answer.

"But El Quemado is a special case," says the Lamb, without poking around the game; in fact, he hasn't even glanced at it, as if he fears leaving his fingerprints near the scene of the crime. Florian Linden?

"If El Quemado learned how, I could too," says the Wolf.

"Do you speak English? Could you read the rules in English?"

The Lamb is addressing the Wolf but he looks at me with a smile, complicit and sympathetic.

"A little bit, from when I was a waiter, not enough to read, but . . ."

"But nothing. If you can't read the *Sporting World* in Spanish, how are you going to be able to read a set of rules in English? Don't be an idiot."

For the first time, at least in front of me, the little Lamb has taken the upper hand with the Wolf. The Wolf, still mesmerized by the game, points to the hexes where the Battle of Britain is unfolding (though he never touches the map or the piles of counters!) and says that as he understands it, "here, for example"—he means the southeast of London—"there's been a battle or there's about to be one." When I tell him he's right, the Wolf gestures at the Lamb in a way that I imagine is obscene, but that I've never seen before, and says, "See, it's not so hard."

"Don't kid yourself, man," answers the Lamb, stubbornly refusing to look at the table.

"All right, I guessed it by sheer luck, are you happy?"

The Wolf's attention wanders now, cautiously, from the map to the photocopies. With his hands on his hips he examines them, skipping from one to the next without lingering long enough to read any of them. One might say that he's looking at them like paintings.

Part of the rules? Of course not.

"Statement of the Meeting of the Council of Ministers, November 12, 1938," reads the Wolf. "Fuck, this is the beginning of the war!"

"No, the war starts later. In the autumn of the following year. The photocopies just help us . . . to set the scene. This kind of game creates a pretty interesting documentary urge. It's as if we want to know exactly how everything was done in order to change what was done wrong."

"I get it," says the Wolf, understanding nothing, of course.

"It's because if you just repeated the whole thing it wouldn't be fun. It wouldn't be a game," whispers the Lamb, sitting down on the rug and blocking the path to the bathroom.

"Something like that. Though it depends on your motive . . . on your point of view . . ."

"How many books do you have to read to play well?"

"All of them and none of them. To play a simple match you just have to know the rules."

"The rules, the rules, where are the rules?" The Wolf, sitting on my bed, picks up the *Third Reich* box from the floor and takes out the rules in English. He weighs them in one hand and shakes his head admiringly. "I can't figure it out . . ."

"What?"

"How El Quemado could read this thing, with all the work he has."

"What work? The pedal boats aren't bringing in any money now," said the Lamb.

"Maybe the money's not there, but it's hard work, for sure. I've spent time with him, helping him, in the sun, and I know what it's like."

"You were just trying to hook up with some foreign chick, don't pretend you weren't . . ."

"Man, that too . . ."

The superiority, the ascendance, of the Lamb over the Wolf was undeniable. I imagined that something extraordinary had happened to the latter that reversed, even if only for now, the hierarchy between the two of them.

"He didn't read anything. I explained the rules to El Quemado little by little, very patiently!" I said.

"But then he read them. He photocopied the rules and at night, at the bar, he went over them underlining the parts that he thought were most interesting. I thought he was studying to get his driver's license; he said no, it was the rules of your game."

"Photocopied?"

The Wolf and the Lamb nodded.

I was surprised, because I knew I hadn't lent the rules to anyone. There were two possibilities: either they were wrong and they had misunderstood El Quemado or El Quemado had told them the first thing that came into his head to get rid of them, or they were right and El Quemado, without my permission, had taken the original to photocopy it, putting it back the next day. As the Wolf and the Lamb moved on to a discussion of other matters (how nice the room was, how comfortable, how much it cost per night, the *things* they would do in a place like this instead of wasting time on "a puzzle," etc.), I pondered how likely it really was that El Quemado had taken the rules and, the next day, having photocopied them, returned them to the box. It was impossible. Except for last night, he was always wearing a T-shirt, usually a ragged one, and shorts or long pants that left no room to hide a booklet even half the size of the *Third Reich* manual. In addition, he was always escorted in and out by me, and if it was naturally difficult to ascribe ulterior motives to El Quemado, it was even harder for me to believe that I would have overlooked a change, no matter how small—a telltale bulge!—in El Quemado's appearance between his arrival and his departure.

The logical conclusion exonerated him; it was materially impossible. At this point I was promptly confronted with a third explanation, at once simple and disturbing: another person, a person from the hotel, using the master key, had been in my room. I could think of only one possible suspect: Frau Else's husband.

(Just imagining him, on tiptoe, among my things, made my stomach turn. I imagined him, tall and skeletal and faceless or with his face wreathed in a kind of dark and shifting cloud, going through my papers and my clothes, alert to footsteps in the hallway, the sound of the elevator, the bastard, as if he'd been waiting for me for ten years, just waiting and biding his time, so that once the moment came he could toss me to his fire-scarred dog and destroy me . . .)

A sound that at first struck me as bizarre and later came to seem like a portent managed to return me to reality.

Someone was knocking at the door.

I opened the door. It was the maid with the clean sheets. Somewhat brusquely, since her arrival couldn't have been more inopportune, I let her in. All I wanted just then was for her to finish her job quickly so I could tip her and be left alone for a while longer with the Spaniards, in order to subject them to a series of questions that I was convinced couldn't wait.

"Go ahead and put them on," I said. "I turned in the other ones this morning."

"Hey there, Clarita, how's it going?" The Wolf lounged on the bed as if to emphasize his position as a guest and gave her a lazy, familiar wave.

The maid, the same one who according to Frau Else wanted me to leave the hotel, hesitated for an instant as if she'd gotten the wrong room, an instant in which her eyes, deceptively dull, discovered the Lamb, still sitting on the rug and waving to her, and immediately the shyness or distrust (or terror!) that had blossomed in her the minute she crossed the threshhold of my room vanished. She responded to the greetings with a smile and set about putting on the clean sheets—or, that is, she took possession of a strategic spot next to the bed.

"Get off of there," she ordered the Wolf. The Wolf leaned up against the wall and started to make faces and clown around. I watched him curiously. The faces he was making, at first just idiotic, began to take on a *color*, gradually darkening until they traced a black mask barely softened by some red and yellow creases.

Clarita spread the sheets. Though she didn't look it, I realized she was nervous.

"Careful, don't knock the counters," I warned.

"What counters?"

"The ones on the table, the game pieces," said the Lamb. "You could cause an earthquake, Clarita."

Hesitating between finishing her task and leaving, she chose to stand motionless. It was hard to believe that this girl was the same maid who had such a poor opinion of me, the girl who more than once had received my tips in silence, the girl who never opened her mouth in my presence. Now she was giggling, finally laughing at jokes, and saying things like "You'll never learn," "Look at the mess you've made," "You're such slobs," as if the room belonged to the Wolf and the Lamb, not to me.

"I'd never live in a room like this," said Clarita.

"I don't live here, I'm just passing through," I explained.

"It doesn't matter," said Clarita. "This is a bottomless pit."

Later I realized that she was referring to her work, to the infinite labor of cleaning a hotel room, but at the time I took it for a personal judgment and it made me sad that even an adolescent should feel the right to express a critical view of my situation.

"I need to talk to you about something important." The Wolf, no longer making faces, came around the bed and grabbed the maid by the arm. She jumped as if she'd been bitten by a snake.

"Later," she said, looking at me and not at him, a tense smile creeping onto her lips, seeking my approval, but approval of what?

"Now, Clarita, we have to talk now."

"That's right, now." The Lamb got up from the floor and cast an approving glance at the fingers gripping the maid's arm.

Little sadist, I thought, he doesn't dare knock her around himself but he likes to watch and goad the Wolf on. Then my full attention was seized again by Clarita's gaze, a gaze that had already piqued my interest during the unfortunate incident of the table, but which on that occasion, maybe because it had to compete with another gaze, Frau Else's, faded into the background, into the limbo of gazes, in order to reemerge now, as rich and quiet as a landscape: Mediterranean? African?

"Man, Clarita, you act like you're the one who deserves an apology. That's funny."

"You owe us an explanation, at least."

"What you did wasn't right, was it?"

"Javi is a mess and you don't even care."

"Nobody wants to have anything to do with you anymore."

"Nothing."

With a sharp movement, the maid pulled away from the Wolf—Let me work!—and fixed the sheets, tucked them under the mattress, changed the pillowcase, pulled up the cream-colored coverlet and smoothed it. Once everything was done, the flurry of movement having left the Wolf and the Lamb with nothing more to say and no desire to continue, she didn't leave but rather folded her arms on the opposite side of the room, separated from us by the immaculate bed, and asked what else anybody had to say to her. For an instant I thought she was talking to me. Her defiant attitude, starkly contrasting with her size, seemed charged with meaning that only I could read.

"I don't have anything against you. Javi is an asshole." The Wolf sat on a corner of the bed and started to roll a joint. A single, distinct wrinkle spread until it reached the far edge of the coverlet, the precipice.

"A fucking idiot," said the Lamb.

I smiled and shook my head several times as if to inform Clarita that I was taking charge of the situation. I didn't want to say anything, but deep down it bothered me that they would take the liberty of smoking in my room without asking my permission. What would Frau Else think if she showed up all of a sudden? What would the hotel guests and staff say if they heard about it? Who, when it came down to it, could promise that Clarita wouldn't blab?

"Want some?" The Wolf dragged on the joint a few times and passed it to me. For appearances' sake, out of timidity, I inhaled deeply just once, relieved that it wasn't damp, and handed the joint to Clarita. Inevitably our fingers brushed, maybe for longer than was strictly necessary, and it seemed to me that her cheeks turned red. Resignedly, and as if assuming that her mysterious business with the Spaniards was settled, the maid sat down by the table with her back to the balcony and blew a steady stream of smoke over the map. What a complicated game! she said in a loud voice, adding, in a whisper: For brains only!

The Wolf and the Lamb exchanged glances, whether troubled or uncertain, I can't say, and then they too sought my approval, but I had eyes only for Clarita, and especially for the smoke, the immense cloud of smoke hanging over Europe, blue and pearly, augmented by the dark lips of the girl, who painstakingly, like a builder, exhaled long, fine tubes of smoke that flattened out over France, Germany, the vast expanses of the East.

"Man, Clarita, pass it back," complained the Lamb.

As if we were wrenching her from a beautiful and heroic dream, the maid looked at us and without getting up reached out her arm with the joint between her fingers; she had thin arms dotted with small circles lighter than the rest of her skin. I said that maybe she felt sick, maybe she wasn't used to smoking, maybe it would be better if everyone got back to what they were doing, this last suggestion meant to include the Wolf and the Lamb.

"Nah, she loves it," said the Wolf, passing me the joint, which this time was soggy and which I smoked with my lips curled inward.

"What do I love?"

"Smoking, cunt," spat the Lamb.

"It's not true," said Clarita, jumping up in a way that was more theatrical than spontaneous.

"Cool it, Clarita, cool it," said the Wolf in a suddenly honeyed, velvety, even faggotty voice, as he grabbed her by the shoulder and with his other hand tapped her in the ribs. "Don't knock over the playing pieces, what would our German friend think? That you're an idiot, right? And you're no idiot."

The Lamb winked at me and sat on the bed, behind the maid, miming sex in a way that was doubly silent because even his ear-to-ear smile was turned not toward me or Clarita's back but toward . . . a kind of realm of stone . . . a silent zone (with raw staring eyes) that had surreptitiously established itself in the middle of my room . . . say, from the bed to the wall where the photocopies were tacked.

The Wolf's hand, which only then did I notice was balled into a fist—so the taps *could* have hurt—opened and closed around one of the maid's breasts. Clarita's body seemed to surrender completely, melted by the confidence with which the Wolf explored it. Without getting up from the bed, his torso unnaturally stiff and his arms moving like a mechanical doll's, the Lamb grabbed the girl's buttocks with both hands and whispered an obscenity. He said "slut," or "bitch," or "cunt." I thought I was going to witness a rape and I remembered the words of Mr. Pere at the Costa Brava about the town's rape statistics. Whether rape was their aim or not, they weren't in a hurry: for an instant the three of them composed a living tableau in which the only jarring element was the voice of Clarita, who every so often said no, each time with different emphasis, as if she wasn't sure of the most appropriate tone in which to refuse.

"Should we make her more comfortable?" The question was directed at me.

"Yeah, man, that would be better," said the Lamb.

I nodded, but none of the three moved: the Wolf standing and gripping Clarita by the waist, her muscles and bones seemingly turned to jelly, and the Lamb on the edge of the bed massaging the girl's ass in a circular, rhythmic motion as if he were shuffling dominoes. Such a lack of dynamism led me to act without thinking. I wondered whether it wasn't all a performance, a trick to make me look ridiculous, a strange in-joke. I reasoned that if this was the case, the hallway wouldn't be empty. Since I was the one closest to the door, it was easy to reach out and open it, thus clearing up any doubts. With unnecessary swiftness, that's what I did. There was no one there. Nevertheless, I left the door open. As if they'd been dashed with a bucket of cold water, the Wolf and the Lamb interrupted their gropings with a leap; the maid, meanwhile, gave me a warm look that I fully appreciated and understood. I ordered her to leave. This instant, no arguments! Obediently, Clarita said goodbye to the Spaniards and went off down the corridor with the weary step of all hotel maids. Seen from behind she looked vulnerable and not very attractive. Which probably she wasn't.

When we were left alone, and before the Spaniards had recovered from the surprise, I asked in a tone that admitted of no rejoinders or subterfuge whether Charly had *raped* anyone. In the moment, I was convinced that my words were divinely inspired. The Wolf and the Lamb exchanged a glance that was equal parts blank and wary. They had no idea what was about to hit them!

"Rape a girl? Poor Charly, may he rest in peace?"

"Yes, Charly, that bastard," I said.

I think I was prepared to get the truth out of them even if it came to blows. The only one who would make a worthy opponent was the Wolf; the Lamb wasn't much over five feet tall and he was the scrawny type who could be dropped with a single punch. Though it didn't pay to trust them, nor was there reason for me to be overly cautious. Strategically, I was ideally situated: I controlled the only exit, which I could block if it seemed convenient or use as a means of escape if things went badly. And I counted on the surprise factor. On the terror of unexpected confessions. On the Wolf's and the Lamb's predictable lack of mental agility. To be completely candid, none of this had been planned; it simply happened, like in those thrillers where you see an image over and over again before you realize that it's the key to the crime.

"Let's respect the dead, especially since he was a friend, man," said the Lamb.

"Bullshit," I yelled.

Both of them were pale and I realized that they weren't going to fight, they just wanted to get out of the room as quickly as possible.

"Who do you think he raped?"

"That's what I want to know. Hanna?" I asked.

The Wolf looked at me the way you look at a crazy person or a child:

"Hanna was his girlfriend, how could he have raped her?"

"Did he or didn't he?"

"No, man, of course not, how can you think such a thing?" said the Lamb.

"Charly didn't rape anybody," said the Wolf. "He had a heart of gold."

"Charly, a heart of gold?"

"I can't believe that you were his friend and you didn't realize it."

"He wasn't my friend."

The Wolf laughed a brief, deep, heartfelt laugh and said he had realized that by now, believe it or not, he was no idiot. Then he repeated that Charly was a good person, incapable of forcing anyone, and that if anybody had come close to being fucked, it was Charly himself, on the night when he left Ingeborg and Hanna abandoned on the highway. When he returned to town he got drunk with some strangers; according to the Wolf they must have been foreigners, possibly Germans. From the bar, a group of men—it wasn't clear how many—headed to the beach. Charly remembered the taunts, not all of them directed at him, the shoves (which might have been poor attempts at humor), and an attempt to pull down his pants.

"He was raped, then?"

"No. He fought off the guy who was harassing him and got out of there. There weren't many of them and Charly was strong. But he was pretty upset and he wanted revenge. He came to my place looking for me. When we got back to the beach, no one was there."

I believed them: the silence of the room, the muffled noise from the Paseo Marítimo, even the sun behind the clouds and the sea veiled by the balcony curtains—everything seemed to stand witness for that pair of deadbeats.

"You think Charly committed suicide, don't you? Well, he didn't, Charly never would've killed himself. It was an accident."

The three of us abandoned our aggressive and defensive stances and segued directly into attitudes of sadness (though the description is excessive and imprecise), sitting down on the bed or the floor, the three of us enveloped in a warm mantle of solidarity, as if we really were friends or as if we had just fucked the maid, gravely delivering short speeches that the others celebrated with mono-syllables, and enduring the extra presence that throbbed with its powerful back to us at the far end of the room.

Luckily the Lamb relit the joint and we passed it around until it was gone. There wasn't another. With a puff, the Wolf scattered the ash that had fallen on the rug.

We went out for beers at the Andalusia Lodge.

The bar was empty and we sang a song.

An hour later I couldn't stand them any longer and I left.

MY FAVORITE GENERALS

I don't look for perfection in them. Perfection on a game board:
what does it mean but death, the void? In the names, the brilliant
careers, in the stuff of memory, I search for the image of their sure-
fingered white hands, I search for their eyes watching battles
(though there are only a few photographs that show them thus engaged): imperfect and singular, delicate, distant, gruff, daring,
prudent—in all of them one can find courage and love. In Manstein, Guderian, Rommel. My Favorite Generals. And in Rund-
stedt, von Bock, von Leeb. In neither them nor others do I demand
perfection; I content myself with their faces, open or impassive,
with their dispatches, with just a name and a tiny deed sometimes.
I even forget whether General X started the war at the head of a
division or a corps, whether he showed more skill at commanding
tanks or infantry; I mix up the scenes and the operations. Not for
that do they shine less bright. They fade against the larger picture,
depending on how one looks at it, but the picture always contains
them. No exploit, no weakness, no resistance, however brief or prolonged, is lost. If El Quemado had the slightest knowledge or appre-
ciation of twentieth-century German literature (and it's likely that
he does!) I'd tell him that Manstein is like . . . Celan. And Paulus is
like Trakl, and his predecessor, Reichenau, is like Heinrich Mann.
Guderian is the equivalent of Jünger, and Kluge of Böll. He wouldn't
understand. Or at least he wouldn't understand yet. I, however, find

it easy to assign these generals occupations, nicknames, hobbies, types of house, seasons of the year, etc. Or to spend hours comparing and compiling statistics from their respective service records. Arranging and rearranging them: by game, by decorations, by victories, by defeats, by years lived, by books published. They're not saints or anything like it, but sometimes I see them in the sky, like in the movies, their faces superimposed on the clouds, smiling at us, gazing into the distance, rehearsing salutes, some nodding as if clearing up unspoken doubts. They share clouds and sky with generals like Frederick the Great, as if the two eras and all games had merged in a single jet of steam. (Sometimes I imagine that Conrad is sick, in the hospital, with no visitors—except maybe me, standing by the door—and in his suffering he discovers, reflected on the wall, the maps and counters that he'll never touch again! The era of Frederick and all the other generals escaped from the laws of the afterlife! The void knocking fists with my poor Conrad!) Sympathetic figures, despite everything. Like Model the Titan, Schörner the Ogre, Rendulio the Bastard, Arnim the Obedient, Witzleben the Squirrel, Blaskowitz the Upright, Knobelsdorff the Paladin, Balck the Fist, Manteuffel the Intrepid, Student the Fang, Hausser the Black, Dietrich the Autodidact, Henrici the Rock, Busch the Nervous, Hoth the Thin, Kleist the Astronomer, Paulus the Sad, Breith the Silent, Vietinghoff the Obstinate, Bayerlein the Studious, Hoeppner the Blind, Salmuth the Academic, Geyr the Inconstant, List the Luminous, Reinhardt the Silent, Meindl the Warthog, Dietl the Skater, Wöhler the Stubborn, Chevallerie the Absentminded, Bittrich the Nightmare, Falkenhorst the Leaper, Wenck the Carpenter, Nehring the Enthusiast, Weichs the Clever, Eberbach the Depressive, Dollman the Cardiac, Halder the Butler, Sodenstern the Swift, Kesselring the Mountain, Küchler the Preoccupied, Hube the Inexhaustible, Zangen the Dark, Weiss the Transparent, Friessner the Lame, Stumme the Ashen, Mackensen the Invisible, Lindemann the Engineer, Westphal the Calligrapher, Marcks the Bitter, Stulpnagel the Elegant, von Thoma the Garrulous . . . Firmly ensconced in heaven . . . On the same cloud as Ferdinand, Brunswick, Schwerin, Lehwaldt, Ziethen, Dohna,

Kleist, Wedell, Frederick's generals . . . On the same cloud as Blücher's triumphant army at Waterloo: Bülow, Ziethen, Pirch, Thielman, Hiller, Losthin, Schwerin, Schulenburg, Watzdorf, Jagow, Tippelskirchen, etc. Symbolic figures with the ability to storm into your dreams to the cry of Eureka! Eureka! Awake! and make you open your eyes, if you're able to hear their call without fear, and at the foot of the bed you find the Favorite Situations that were and the Favorite Situations that might have been. Among the former I would single out Rommel's ride with the Seventh Armored in '40, Student falling upon Crete, Kleist's advance through the Caucasus with the First Panzer Army, Manteuffel's offensive in the Ardennes with the Fifth Panzer Army, Manstein's campaign in the Crimea with the Eleventh Army, the Dora gun itself, the Mt. Elbrus flag itself, Hube's resistance in Russia and Sicily, Reichenau's Tenth Army breaking the necks of the Poles. From among the Favorite Situations that never were, I have a special fondness for the capture of Moscow by Kluge's troops, the conquest of Stalingrad by Reichenau (rather than Paulus), the disembarking of the Ninth and Sixteenth Armies in Great Britain (parachute drop included), the securing of the Astrakhan–Arkhangel'sk line, the triumphs in Kursk and Mortain, the orderly retreat to the far side of the Seine, the reconquest of Budapest, the reconquest of Antwerp, the sustained resistance in Courland and Königsberg, the holding of the line along the Oder, the Alpine Redoubt, the death of Zarina and the switching of alliances . . . . Silliness, idiocy, useless feats, as Conrad says, in order to avoid witnessing the generals' last farewell; happy in victory, good losers in defeat. Even in utter defeat. They wink an eye, rehearse military salutes, stare off into the distance, or nod. What have they to do with this hotel that's falling apart? Nothing, but they help, they comfort. Their farewells stretch on for an eternity and remind me of old matches, afternoons, nights, of which all that remains is not victory or defeat but a movement, a feint, a clash, and friends' claps on the back.

AUTUMN 1942. WINTER 1942

"I thought you'd gone," says El Quemado.

"Where?"

"Back home, to Germany."

"Why would I leave, Quemado? Do you think I'm scared?"

El Quemado says no no no, very slowly, almost without moving his lips, avoiding my eyes. He only stares at the game board; nothing else holds his attention for more than a few seconds. Nervous, he shifts from wall to wall, like a prisoner, but he avoids the balcony area as if he doesn't want to be seen from the street. He's wearing a short-sleeved shirt, and on his arm, on the burns, there's a very faint gloss of mossy green, possibly the residue of some lotion. And yet it wasn't sunny at all today, and as far as I can remember I never saw him applying lotion even on the most scorching days. Should I deduce that this is a growth? Is what looks to me like moss actually new skin, regenerated? Is this his body's way of replacing dead skin? Whatever it is, it's disgusting. By the way he moves I'd say that something is bothering him, though with his kind it's impossible to say for sure. Suddenly his luck with the dice is overwhelming. Everything goes his way, even the most lopsided attacks. Whether his movements are part of an overarching strategy or the result of chance, of random strikes here and there, I can't say, but it's undeniable that beginner's luck is with him. In Russia, after a series of attacks and counterattacks, I'm forced to retreat to the Leningrad–Kalinin–Tula–Stalingrad–Elista line, at the same time as a new Red threat, double-pronged, looms far to the south in the Caucasus, poised to attack Maikop, which is almost undefended, and Elista. In England I manage to hold on to at least one hex—Portsmouth—after a massive Anglo-American offensive that, despite everything, fails to achieve its goal of running me off the island. With Portsmouth still in my grasp, London remains under threat. In Morocco, El Quemado disembarks two corps of American infantry—his only simpleminded play—with seemingly no purpose other than to annoy and to divert German forces from other fronts. The bulk of my army is in Russia, and for now I don't think I can pull out even a replacement unit.

"So why did you come if you thought I was gone?"

"Because we had an agreement."

"Do you and I have an agreement, Quemado?"

"Yes. We play nights, that's the agreement. Even if you're gone, I'll come until the game is over."

"One of these days they won't let you in or they'll kick you out."

"Maybe."

"One of these days too I will decide to leave, and since it's not always easy to find you I might not be able to say good-bye. I could leave you a note on the pedal boats, true, if they're still on the beach. But one of these days I'll get up and go and everything will be over before '45."

El Quemado smiles fiercely (and his ferocity reveals glimpses of a precise and insane geometry) with the certainty that his pedal boats will remain on the beach even when every pedal boat in town has retired to winter quarters. The fortress will still stand, he'll still wait for me or for the shadow even when there are no tourists or the rains come. His stubbornness is a kind of prison.

"The truth is there's nothing between us, Quemado. By 'agreement' do you mean 'obligation'?"

"No, I see it as a pact."

"Well, we don't have any kind of pact, we're just playing a game, that's all."

El Quemado smiles, says yes, he understands, that's all it is, and in the heat of combat, with the dice going his way, he pulls new photocopies folded into quarters out of his pocket and offers them to me. Some paragraphs are underlined and there are spots of grease and beer on the paper that speak of likely study at a bar table. As with the first offering, an inner voice dictates my reactions. Thus, instead of reproaching him for a gift that might well hide an insult or a provocation—though it might also be the innocent device (involving politics rather than military history!) by which El Quemado engages in discussion with me—I proceed to calmly pin them up next to the first photocopies, in such a way that at the end of the operation the wall behind the head of the bed looks completely different from usual. For a moment I feel as if I'm in someone else's room: the room of a foreign correspondent in a hot and war-torn country? Also: the room seems smaller. Where do the photocopies come from? From *two* books, one by X and the other by Y. I've never heard of them. What kind of strategic lessons do they have to teach us? El Quemado averts his gaze, then smiles innocently and says that he's not ready to reveal his plans. This is an attempt to make me laugh; out of politeness, I do.

The next day El Quemado comes back even stronger, if possible. He attacks in the East and I have to retreat again, he masses forces in Great Britain, and he begins to advance from Morocco and Egypt, though very slowly for the time being. The patch on his arm has disappeared. All that's left is the burn, smooth and flat. His movements around the room are confident, even graceful, and they no longer reveal the nervousness of the day before. Still, he doesn't talk much. His preferred topic is the game, the world of games, the clubs, magazines, championships, matches by correspondence, conventions, etc., and all my attempts to steer the conversation in a different direction—for example, toward the person who gave him photocopies of the *Third Reich* rules—are in vain. When he's told something he doesn't want to hear, he sits there like a rock or a mule. He simply acts as if he hasn't heard. It's likely that my tactics are too subtle. I'm cautious, and ultimately I try not to hurt his feelings. El Quemado may be my enemy, but he's a good enemy and those are hard to come by. What would happen if I were honest with him, if I told him what the Wolf and the Lamb have told me and asked him for an explanation? In the end, I'd probably have to choose between taking his word or theirs. Which I'd rather not have to do. So we talk about games and gamers, a subject of seemingly endless appeal to El Quemado. I think if I took him with me to Stuttgart—no, Paris!—he would be the star of the matches: the sense of the ridiculous that I sometimes feel—stupid, I know, but it's true—when I get to a club and from a distance I see older people trying their hardest to solve military problems that to the rest of the world are old news would vanish solely with his presence. His charred face lends dignity to the act of gaming. When I ask him whether he'd like to come with me to Paris, his eyes light up, but then he shakes his head. Have you ever been to Paris, Quemado? No, never. Would you like to go? He'd like to, but he can't. He'd like to play other people, lots of matches, "one after the other," but he can't. All he's got is me, and that's enough for him. Well, there are worse fates; I am the champion, after all. That makes him feel better. But he'd still like to play other people, though he doesn't plan to buy the game (or at least he doesn't say so), and in the middle of his speech, I have the impression that we're talking about different things. I'm documenting myself, he says. After an effort I realize that he's talking about the photocopies. I can't help laughing.

"Are you still going to the library, Quemado?"

"Yes."

"And you only borrow books about the war?"

"Now I do, but before I didn't."

"Before what?"

"Before I started playing with you."

"So what kind of books did you borrow before, Quemado?"

"Poetry."

"Books of poetry? How nice. What kind of poetry?"

El Quemado looks at me as if I'm a bumpkin:

"Vallejo, Neruda, Lorca . . . Do you know them?"

"No. Did you learn the poems by heart?"

"My memory is no good."

"But you remember something? Can you recite something to give me an idea?"

"No, I only remember feelings."

"What kind of feelings? Tell me one."

"Despair . . ."

"Nothing else? That's all?"

"Despair, heights, the sea, things that aren't closed, things that are partway open, like something bursting in the chest."

"Yes, I see. And when did you stop reading poetry, Quemado? When we started *Third Reich*? If I'd known, I wouldn't have played. I like poetry too."

"Which poets?"

"Goethe."

And so on until it's time to leave.

I left the hotel at five in the afternoon, after talking on the phone to Conrad, dreaming about El Quemado, and making love with Clarita. My head was buzzing, which I attributed to a lack of nourishment, so I headed to the old town planning to eat at a restaurant that I'd noticed earlier. Unfortunately it was closed and suddenly I found myself walking down alleys where I'd never set foot, in a neighborhood of narrow but clean streets behind the shopping district and the port, increasingly sunk in thought, surrendered to the simple pleasure of my surroundings, no longer hungry, and in the mood to keep walking until night fell. That's the state of mind I was in when I heard someone calling me by name. Mr. Berger. When I turned, I saw that it was a boy whose face I didn't recognize, though he looked vaguely familiar. His greeting was effusive. It occurred to me that it might be one of the town friends my brother and I had made ten years before. The simple prospect made me happy. A ray of sunlight fell directly on his face, so that he couldn't stop blinking. The words came tumbling out of his mouth and I could understand barely a quarter of what he said. His two outstretched hands grabbed me by the elbows as if to make sure I wouldn't slip away. The situation seemed likely to stretch on indefinitely. At last, exasperated, I confessed that I couldn't remember who he was. I work at the Red Cross, I'm the one who helped you with your friend's paperwork. So those were the sad circumstances of our meeting! Resolutely, he pulled a wrinkled card out of his pocket that identified him as a member of the Red Cross of the Sea. The matter solved, we both sighed in relief and laughed. Immediately he suggested that we get a beer, and I was happy to agree. With no little surprise I realized that we weren't going to a bar but to the rescue worker's house, not far from here, on the same street, on a dark and dusty third floor.

My room at the Del Mar was bigger than the whole apartment, but my host's good intentions compensated for any material deficiencies. His name was Alfons and he said he was studying at night school: the springboard for a future move to Barcelona. His goal: to become a designer or painter, mission impossible, judging by his clothes, the posters that covered every bit of wall space, the clutter of furniture, all in the worst possible taste. And yet there was something uncanny about the rescue worker. We hadn't exchanged more than two words, me sitting in an old armchair covered with an Indian-print blanket and him in a chair that he'd probably built himself, when he suddenly asked whether I was an artist "too." I answered vaguely that I wrote articles. Where do they come out? In Stuttgart, Cologne, sometimes Milan, New York . . . I knew it, said the rescue worker. How could you know it? By your face. I read faces like books. Something in his tone or maybe in the words he used put me on my guard. I tried to change the subject, but all he wanted to talk about was art and I let him.

Alfons was a bore, but after a while I realized that it was nice to be there, drinking in silence, and protected from what was going on in the town—that is, from what was being plotted in the minds of El Quemado, the Wolf, the Lamb, Frau Else's husband— protected by the aura of brotherhood that the rescue worker had implicitly spun around us. Beneath the skin we were brothers-in-arms, and, as the poet says, we had recognized each other in the dark—in this case, he had recognized me with his special gift— and we had fallen into each other's embrace.

Lulled by the stories he couldn't stop telling, to which I paid not the slightest attention, I revisited the notable incidents of the day. In the first place, in chronological order, the phone conversation with Conrad—brief, since it was he who had called—which basically revolved around the disciplinary measures that my office planned to take if I didn't show up in the next forty-eight hours. In the second place, Clarita, who after straightening my room agreed without much protest to make love with me. She was so small that if by means of some kind of astral projection I could have looked down on the bed from the ceiling, I'm sure that all I would have seen was my back and maybe the tips of her toes. And finally the nightmare, for which the maid was partly responsible, since once our session was over and even before she got dressed and returned to her labors, I fell into a strange doze, as if I were drugged, and I had the following dream. I was walking along the Paseo Marítimo at midnight, aware that Ingeborg was waiting for me in my room. The street, the buildings, the beach, the very sea, if such a thing is possible, were much larger than in reality, as if the town had been turned into a destination for giants. And yet the stars, though they were as numerous as usual on summer nights, were noticeably smaller, pinpoints that cast no more than a sickly glow over the vault of night. I was walking quickly, but the Del Mar still failed to appear on the horizon. Then, just as I was losing hope, El Quemado came walking wearily down the beach with a cardboard box under his arm. He didn't wave, but sat down on the wall and pointed out to sea, into the darkness. Even though I kept a cautious distance of some thirty feet, the lettering and orange color of the box were perfectly visible and familiar: it was *Third Reich*, my *Third Reich*. What was El Quemado doing out so late with my game? Had he gone to the hotel and had Ingeborg given it to him, out of spite? Had he stolen it? I decided to wait and not ask any questions yet, because I sensed that in the darkness between the sea and the Paseo there was another person, and I thought that El Quemado and I would still have time to resolve our business in private. So I stood quietly and waited. El Quemado opened the box and began to set up the game on the wall. He's going to ruin the counters, I thought, but still I said nothing. The game board shifted a few times in the night breeze. I can't remember when exactly El Quemado arranged the units in positions that I had never seen before. Germany was in bad shape. You'll play Germany, said El Quemado. I took a seat on the wall facing him and studied the situation. Yes, a bad business, all the fronts about to collapse and the economy sunk, with no air force, no navy, and a land army outmatched by such great foes. A little red light went on in my head. What are we playing for? I asked. Are we playing for the championship of Germany, or of Spain? El Quemado shook his head and pointed again out to where the waves were breaking, toward where the pedal boat fortress rose, huge and forbidding. What are we playing for? I insisted, with my eyes full of tears. I had the horrible sense that the sea was approaching the Paseo, slowly and without pause, ineluctably. We're playing for the only thing that matters, answered El Quemado, avoiding looking at me. The situation of my armies didn't offer much hope, but I made an effort to play as precisely as possible and I rebuilt the fronts. I didn't plan to surrender without a fight.

"What's the only thing that matters?" I asked, watching the movement of the sea.

"Life." El Quemado's armies began to methodically demolish my lines.

Does the loser lose his life? I must be crazy, I thought, as the tide continued to rise, higher than anything I had seen before in Spain or anywhere else.

"The loser forfeits his life to the winner." El Quemado broke through my front in four different places and invaded Germany through Budapest.

"I don't want your life, Quemado, let's not get carried away," I said, transferring my only reserves to Vienna. By now the sea was licking at the edge of the wall. I began to feel tremors all over my body. The shadows of the buildings were swallowing up the scarce light that still shone on the Paseo.

"And this game is set up to make Germany lose!"

The water rose up the stairs from the beach and spilled over the sidewalk. Consider your next play very carefully, warned El Quemado, and he began to splash away toward the Del Mar; there was no other sound to be heard. Like a whirlwind in my head, there spun images of Ingeborg alone in the room, of Frau Else alone in a hallway between the laundry and the kitchen, of poor Clarita leaving work through the service entrance, tired and thin as a broomstick. The water was black and now it came up to my ankles. A kind of paralysis so thoroughly prevented me from moving my arms and legs that I couldn't rearrange my counters on the map or set off running after El Quemado. The die, white as the moon, sat with the 1 faceup. I could move my neck and I could talk (or at least whisper), but that was all. Soon the water swept the board off the wall, and it began to float away from me, along with the force pool and the counters. Where would they go? Toward the hotel or the old town? Would someone find them someday? And if they did, would they be able to see that it was a map of the battles of *Third Reich*, and that the counters were *Third Reich* armored corps and infantry corps, the air force, the navy? Of course not. The pieces, more than five hundred of them, would float together for the first few minutes, then inevitably they would drift apart, until they were lost in the depths of the sea; the map and force pool, since they were bigger, would last longer and there was even the chance that the waves would wash them onto the rocks where they could rot in peace. With the water up to my neck, I thought that after all they were just pieces of cardboard. I can't say that I was distressed. Calmly, and with no hope of saving myself, I waited for the instant when the water would cover me. Then, emerging from under the streetlights, came El Quemado's pedal boats. Falling into a wedge-shaped formation (one pedal boat at the head, six two-by-two behind, and three bringing up the rear), they glided noiselessly along, synchronized and gallant in their way, as if the flood were the perfect moment for a military parade. They took turn after turn around what had once been the beach, with my dumbstruck gaze fixed on them; if anyone was pedaling and steering, it must have been ghosts, because I couldn't see a soul. Finally they moved out to sea, though not far, and they changed formation. Now they were lined up in Indian file and somehow, mysteriously, they didn't advance or retreat, didn't even move in that madman's sea illuminated by a lightning storm in the distance. From my position all I could see was the nose of the first one, so perfect was their new alignment. Suspecting nothing, I watched the blades cleave the water and the boats begin to move again. They were coming straight for me! Not very fast, but as relentlessly and ponderously as the old dreadnoughts of Jutland. Just before the floater of the first one, surely followed by the remaining nine, was about to smash into my head, I woke up.

Conrad was right, not in insisting that I should come back but in painting my situation as the result of some nervous disorder. But that's a bit of an exaggeration. I've always had nightmares; I was the only one to blame—and possibly that idiot Charly for drowning. Conrad, however, saw instability in the fact that for the first time I was losing at *Third Reich*. I'm losing, true, but I haven't resorted to playing dirty. To illustrate this, I laughed out loud a few times. (Germany, according to Conrad, lost because it played fair; the proof is that it didn't use poison gas, not even against the Russians, ha-ha-ha.)

Before I left, the rescue worker asked me where Charly was buried. I told him I had no idea. We could go visit his grave some afternoon, he suggested. I can find out at Navy Headquarters. The idea that Charly might be buried in town lodged in my head like a time bomb. Don't do it, I said. The rescue worker, I realized then, was drunk and overexcited. We *must*—he stressed the word—pay our friend our last respects. He wasn't your friend, I muttered. It doesn't matter, he could have been, we artists are brothers no matter where we are, dead or alive, beyond the limits of age or time. The likeliest thing is that they shipped him to Germany, I said. The rescue worker's face flushed and then he snorted so violently with laughter that he almost fell over backward. That's a rotten lie! You ship potatoes, not dead bodies, and definitely not during the *summer*. Our friend is here, he said, pointing at the floor in a way that admitted no response. I had to take him by the shoulders and order him to bed. He insisted on walking me out, with the excuse that the main door might be locked. And tomorrow I'll find out where they've buried our brother. He wasn't our brother, I repeated wearily, though I realized that at that precise instant, due to who knows what outrageous distortion, his world was made up almost exclusively of us three, the only individuals on a vast and uncharted sea. In this new light the rescue worker took on the guise of a hero or a madman. Standing in the doorway with him, I looked him in the face, and his glassy stare expressed gratitude for my look without entirely understanding it. We were like two trees, until the rescue worker began to take swipes at me. Like Charly. Then I decided to push him, to see what would happen, and as might have been expected, he fell and didn't get up again, his legs drawn up and his face half covered by an arm, a white arm, untouched by the sun, like mine. Then I went coolly down the stairs and returned to the hotel with time enough to shower and have dinner.

Spring 1943. El Quemado makes his entrance a little later than usual. In fact, as the days go by, his arrival time keeps getting pushed back. If we go on like this, the final turn will start at six in the morning. Is there any significance to this? In the West I lose my last hex in England. El Quemado continues to have luck with the dice. In the East the front runs through Tallin–Vitebsk–Smolensk–Bryansk–Kharkov–Rostov–Maikop. In the Mediterranean I plot an American attack on Oran but I can't take the offensive; in Egypt no change: the front holds in LL26 and MM26, the hexes along the Qattara Depression.

SEPTEMBER 18

Like a ray of lightning, Frau Else appears at the end of the hallway. I've just gotten up and I'm on my way to breakfast, but I'm frozen in place by the surprise.

"I've been looking for you," she says, coming toward me.

"Where the hell have you been?"

"I was in Barcelona, with my family. My husband is sick, as you know, but you aren't well either and you're going to listen to what I have to say."

I let her into my room. It smells bad, like tobacco and stale air. When I open the curtains the sun makes me blink in pain. Frau Else stares at El Quemado's photocopies pinned to the wall; I imagine she'll scold me for breaking the hotel rules.

"This is obscene," she says, and I don't know whether she's talking about the content of the pages or my decision to display them.

"They're El Quemado's edicts."

Frau Else turns. She's even more beautiful than she was a week ago, if possible.

"Was he the one who put them up here?"

"No, it was me. El Quemado gave them to me and . . . I decided it was better not to hide them. For him the copies are like a backdrop to our game."

"What kind of horrible game are you talking about? The game of atonement? It's all so tasteless."

Frau Else's cheekbones may have gotten slightly sharper during her absence.

"You're right, it's tasteless, though the truth is it's my fault, I was the first to bring out photocopies; of course, mine were articles on the game. Anyway, coming from El Quemado it's to be expected, we all have to do things our own way."

"Statement of the Meeting of the Council of Ministers, November 12, 1938," she read in her sweet and melodious voice. "Doesn't it make your stomach turn, Udo?"

"Sometimes," I said equivocally. Frau Else seemed increasingly upset. "History in general is a bloody thing, you have to admit."

"I wasn't talking about history but about your comings and goings. I don't care about history. What I do care about is the hotel, and you are a disruptive element here." With great care she began to take down the photocopies.

I suspected that it wasn't just the watchman who had come to her telling tales. Clarita too?

"I'm taking them," she said with her back to me, gathering up the copies. "I don't want you to suffer."

I asked whether that was all she had to say to me. Frau Else was slow to answer. She shook her head, came over to me, and planted a kiss on my forehead.

"You remind me of my mother," I said.

With her eyes open, Frau Else kissed me hard on the mouth. How about now? Without knowing very well what I was doing I took her in my arms and deposited her on the bed. Frau Else started to laugh. You've had nightmares, she said, thinking probably of the terrible mess the room was in. Her laughter, though it may have verged on the hysterical, was like a girl's. With one hand she stroked my hair, murmuring unintelligible words, and when I lay down beside her I felt on my cheek the contrast between the cold linen of her blouse and her warm skin, soft to the touch. For an instant I thought she was going to surrender at last, but when I slid my hand under her skirt and tried to pull down her underpants, it was all over.

"It's early," she said, sitting up on the bed as if propelled by a spring of unpredictable force.

"Yes," I admitted. "I just got up, but what does it matter?"

Frau Else got all the way up and changed the subject as her perfect—and quick!—hands straightened her clothes, moving like entities completely separate from the rest of her body. Cleverly she managed to turn my words against me. I'd just gotten up? Did I have any idea what time it was? Did I think it was decent get up so late? Didn't I realize how confusing it was for the cleaning staff? As she delivered this speech, she kicked every so often at the clothes scattered on the floor and put the photocopies in her pocket.

Basically, it became clear that we weren't about to make love, and my only consolation was the discovery that she had yet to find out about the incident with Clarita.

As we said good-bye, in the elevator, we agreed to meet that evening in the church square.

With Frau Else at Playamar, a restaurant about three miles inland, nine p.m.

"My husband has cancer."

"Is it serious?" I ask, aware that this is a ridiculous question.

"Terminal." Frau Else looks at me as if we're separated by bulletproof glass.

"How much time does he have left?"

"Not much. He might not live through the summer."

"The summer's almost over . . . Though it looks as if the good weather will last until October," I stammer.

Under the table, Frau Else's hand squeezes my hand. Her gaze, however, is lost in the distance. Only now does the news begin to take shape in my head: her husband is dying; this is the explanation, or the catalyst, for many of the things that have been happening in the hotel and outside of it. Frau Else's strange mix of seductiveness and rejection. El Quemado's mysterious adviser. The intrusions into my room and the vigilant presence that I sense in the hotel. Considered from this perspective, was the dream about Florian Linden a warning from my subconscious that I should watch out for Frau Else's husband? The truth is that it would be disappointing if it all boiled down to a question of jealousy.

"What's going on between your husband and El Quemado?" I ask after a lapse occupied only by our fingers secretly interlacing. The Playamar is a busy place and in a short time Frau Else has greeted several people.

"Nothing."

Then I try to tell her that she's wrong, that between the two of them they're planning to crush me, that her husband stole the rules from my room so that El Quemado could hone his game, that the strategy the Allies are following can't be the fruit of a single mind, that her husband has spent hours in my room studying the game. I can't. Instead I promise her that I won't leave until her situation (that is, the disappearance of her husband) is cleared up, that I'll stand by her, that she can count on me for anything she needs, that I understand if she doesn't want to make love, that I'll help her to be strong.

Frau Else's way of thanking me for my words is to squeeze my hand in a crushing grip.

"What's the matter?" I ask, pulling away as surreptitiously as possible.

"You should go back to Germany. You need to take care of yourself, not me."

Upon declaring this, her eyes fill with tears.

"You are Germany," I say.

Frau Else lets out a laugh—strong, ringing, irresistible—that draws the gaze of everyone in the restaurant. I also choose to laugh heartily: I'm a hopeless romantic. A hopeless sentimentalist, she corrects me. Fine, then.

On our way back I stop the car at a kind of inn. Down a gravel path there's a pine grove with stone tables, benches, and garbage cans scattered about at random. When we roll down the window we hear distant music that Frau Else identifies as coming from a club in town. How can that be when the town is so far away? We get out of the car and Frau Else leads me by the hand to a cement balustrade. The inn is at the top of a hill, and from up here we can see the lights of the hotels and the neon signs in the shopping district. I try to kiss her but Frau Else refuses me her lips. Paradoxically, back in the car, it's she who takes the lead. For an hour we kiss and listen to music on the radio. The cool breeze that comes in through the half-open windows smells like flowers and fragrant herbs, and the spot is ideal for making love, but I thought it best not to steer things in that direction.

Before I realized, it was after midnight, though Frau Else, her cheeks flushed from so much kissing, seemed in no hurry to get back.

On the steps leading up to the hotel we found El Quemado. I parked on the Paseo Marítimo and Frau Else and I got out of the car together. El Quemado didn't see us until we were almost on top of him. His head was bowed and he was staring distractedly at the ground; despite his broad back, from the distance he looked like a child, hopelessly lost. Hello, I said, trying to radiate happiness, though from the instant when Frau Else and I got out of the car a vague and insistent sadness settled over me. El Quemado raised his sheeplike eyes and said good evening. For the first time, if only briefly, Frau Else remained standing by my side, as if we were a couple, with shared interests. Have you been here a long time? El Quemado looked at us and shrugged his shoulders. How is business? asked Frau Else. Decent. Frau Else laughed her best crystalline laugh, which sweetened the night:

"You're the last of the season to leave. Do you have work for the winter?"

"Not yet."

"If we paint the bar I'll call you."

"All right."

I felt a twinge of envy: Frau Else obviously knew how to talk to El Quemado.

"It's late and I have to get up early tomorrow. Good night."

From the stairs we watched as Frau Else stopped for a moment at the reception desk, where presumably she spoke to someone, and then moved on down the dark corridor, waited for the elevator, vanished . . .

"What do we do now?" El Quemado's voice startled me.

"Nothing. Sleep. We'll play another day," I said harshly.

It took an instant for El Quemado to digest what I'd said. I'll be back tomorrow, he said in a tone in which I caught a hint of resentment. He rose in a leap, like a gymnast. For an instant we eyed each other like bitter enemies.

"Tomorrow, perhaps," I said, trying to control the sudden trembling of my legs and my desire to lunge at his neck.

In a fair fight, the two sides are equally matched. He's heavier and shorter, I'm nimbler and taller; we both have long arms; he's accustomed to physical exercise; my determination is my best weapon. The decisive factor might be the spot chosen for the fight. The beach? It seems like the right place, the beach at night, but there, I fear, El Quemado will have the advantage. Where, then?

"If I'm not busy," I added dismissively.

In reponse El Quemado was silent, and then he left. As he was crossing the Paseo Marítimo, he looked back as if to check that I was still on the stairs. If only at that moment a car had appeared out of the darkness, going one hundred and fifty miles an hour!

From the balcony, not even the faintest glow can be seen from the pedal boat fortress. I've turned out my lights too, of course, except the one in the bathroom. The bulb over the mirror sheds an aquatic radiance that barely illuminates a wedge of carpet through the half-open door.

Later, after closing the curtains, I turn the lights back on and study one by one the various elements of my situation. I'm losing the war. I've almost certainly lost my job. Every day that goes by distances me a little further from an improbable reconciliation with Ingeborg. As he lies dying, Frau Else's husband amuses himself by hating me, assaulting me with all the subtlety of the terminally ill. Conrad has sent me only a little money. The article that I originally planned to write at the Del Mar is set aside and forgotten . . . not an encouraging panorama.

At three in the morning, I got in bed without undressing and picked up the Florian Linden book where I'd left off.

I awoke a little before five, feeling suffocated. I didn't know where I was and it took me a few seconds to realize that I was still in the town.

As summer fades (or as the visible signs of it fade), noises begin to be heard at the Del Mar that we never suspected before: the pipes now seem *empty* and *bigger*. The regular muted sound of the elevator has been replaced by scratching and races behind the plaster of the walls. The wind that every night shakes the window frame and hinges is more powerful. The faucets of the sink squeak and shudder before releasing water. Even the smell of the hallways, perfumed with artificial lavender, breaks down more quickly and turns into a pestilent stink that causes terrible coughing fits late at night.

One can't help noticing those coughing fits! One can't help noticing those footsteps in the night that the rugs never manage to muffle!

But if you go out into the hallway overcome by curiosity, what do you see? Nothing.

I wake up to find Clarita in the room. She's at the foot of the bed in her maid's uniform, looking at me. I don't know why her presence makes me happy. I smile and ask her to get in bed with me, though without realizing it, I ask in German. How Clarita manages to understand me is a mystery, but first I prudently lock the door and then she curls up beside me, taking off nothing but her shoes. As during our previous encounter, her breath smells of black tobacco, which happens to be very attractive in a woman-child like her. According to tradition, her lips should taste of sausage and garlic, or mint gum. I'm glad that's not the case. When I climb on top of her, her skirt rides up to her waist and if her knees weren't desperately gripping my thighs I'd say she feels nothing. Not a moan, not a sigh. Clarita makes love with perfect discretion. When we're done, just like the first time, I ask her if she enjoyed herself. She nods her head, and immediately she jumps out of bed, straightens her skirt, puts on her underpants and shoes, and as I head to the bathroom to wash, she begins to tidy the room in workmanlike fashion, careful not to knock any counters on the floor.

"Are you a Nazi?" I hear her voice as I'm wiping my penis with toilet paper.

"What did you say?"

"I asked whether you're a Nazi."

"No. No, I'm not. In fact, I'm more like an anti-Nazi. What

makes you think that, the game?" On the *Third Reich* box there are some images of swastikas.

"The Wolf told me you were a Nazi."

"The Wolf is wrong." I made her come into the bathroom so I could keep talking to her as I showered. Clarita is so ignorant that I think if I told her the Nazis were in power, say, in Switzerland, she would believe it.

"Doesn't anybody wonder why it takes you so long to clean a room? Doesn't anyone miss you?"

Clarita is sitting on the toilet with her back hunched as if getting out of bed brought on a fresh bout of some undisclosed illness. A contagious illness? The rooms are usually cleaned in the morning, she tells me. (I'm a special case.) No one misses her and no one keeps tabs on her. It's bad enough having to work so hard and earn so little money, without also having to endure constant supervision. Even Frau Else's?

"Frau Else is different," says Clarita.

"Why is she different? She lets you do whatever you want? She doesn't get mixed up in your business? She protects you?"

"My business is *my* business, isn't it? What does Frau Else have to do with my business?"

"I meant does she overlook your hookups, your little adventures."

"Frau Else understands people." Her sulky voice can scarcely be heard over the noise of the shower.

"Does that make her different?"

Clarita doesn't answer. But she makes no move to leave either. Separated by the ugly white plastic curtain with yellow polka dots, both of us quiet, both of us waiting, I felt great pity for her and the desire to help her. But how could I help her when I was unable to help myself?

"I'm harassing you, I'm sorry," I said when I got out of the shower.

My body, partly reflected in the mirror, and Clarita's body, huddled imperceptibly on the toilet as if it weren't that of a girl (how old must she be, sixteen?) but the cold body of an old woman, managed to move me to tears.

"You're crying." Clarita smiled stupidly. I toweled off my face and hair and exited the bathroom to get dressed. Clarita was left behind mopping up the wet tiles.

There was a five-thousand-peseta bill somewhere in my jeans but I couldn't find it. As best I could I scraped together three thousand in change and gave it to Clarita. She accepted the money without saying anything.

"Since you know everything, Clarita"—I circled her waist with my arms as if I were about to start groping her again—"do you know what room Frau Else's husband sleeps in?"

"The biggest room in the hotel. The dark room."

"Why dark? Doesn't it get any sun?"

"The curtains are always closed. He's very sick."

"Will he die, Clarita?"

"Yes . . . If you don't kill him first . . ."

For some reason I can't explain, Clarita brings out an instinctual cruelty in me. So far I've treated her well; I've never hurt her. But by her very presence she's capable of awakening slumbering images deep inside of me. Quick and terrible images like lightning, which I fear and flee. How to exorcise this power so suddenly unleashed inside of me? By forcing her down on her knees and making her suck my dick and tongue my ass?

"You're joking, of course."

"Yes, it's a joke," she says, looking down at the floor as a drop of sweat slides neatly down to the tip of her nose.

"Then tell me where your boss sleeps."

"On the second floor, at the end of the hallway, over the kitchen . . . You can't miss it . . ."

After lunch I call Conrad. Today I haven't left the hotel. I don't want to risk a chance encounter with the Wolf and the Lamb (how chance would it really be?), or the Red Cross worker, or Mr. Pere . . . For once, Conrad doesn't seem surprised by my call. I detect a hint of wariness in his voice, as if he were afraid to hear precisely what I plan to ask. Of course, he refuses me nothing. I need money and he agrees to send it. I ask for news of Stuttgart, Cologne, the preparations, and he gives a brief account, with none of the pointed and sarcastic commentary that I used to like so much. I don't know why, but I can't bring myself to ask about Ingeborg. When I finally work up the courage, the answer just depresses me. I have the dim suspicion that Conrad is lying. His lack of curiosity is a new symptom; he neither begs me to come back nor asks when I'm leaving. Don't worry, he says at some point, by which I gather that my end of the conversation hasn't been entirely reassuring, I'll wire the money tomorrow. I thank him. Our farewell is almost a murmur.

I run into Frau Else in one of the hotel corridors. We halt, shaken—in earnest or pretending, what does it matter?—some fifteen feet from each other, hands on hips, pale and sad, exchanging glances that reveal the despair beneath our flurry of activity. How is your husband? Frau Else points at the line of light under a door, or maybe the elevator, I don't know. All I know is that, carried away by a powerful and painful impulse (an impulse generated in my churning stomach), I stepped forward and drew her to me without fear of discovery, meeting little resistance, wanting only to lose myself in her for a few seconds or for life. Udo, are you mad? You almost crushed my ribs. I lowered my head and apologized. What's wrong with your lips? I don't know. Frau Else's finger on my lips is freezing cold, and I jump. They're bleeding, she says. After promising her that I'll clean up in my room, we agree to meet in ten minutes at the hotel restaurant. My treat, says Frau Else, apprised of my new financial straits. If you aren't there in ten minutes, I'll send a couple of the toughest waiters to get you. Oh, I'll be there.

Summer 1943. The English and Americans land in Dieppe and Calais. I didn't expect El Quemado to go on the offensive so soon. It's worth stressing that the beachheads he's won aren't very strong; he's got a foothold in France but it will still cost him something to establish a secure position and advance. In the East the situation is deteriorating; after a new strategic retreat, the front runs through Riga, Minsk, Kiev, and hexes Q39, R39, and S39. Dnepropetrovsk has gone over to the Reds. El Quemado has air superiority in Russia as well as in the West. In Africa and the Mediterranean the situation remains unchanged, though I suspect that things will look very different by the next turn. Curious detail: as we were playing I fell asleep. For how long, I don't know. El Quemado shook my shoulder a few times, saying wake up. Then I woke up and I couldn't get back to sleep again.

I left the room at seven. For hours I had been sitting on the balcony waiting for dawn. When the sun came up I shut the balcony doors, closed the curtains, and stood there in the dark desperately searching for something to do to pass the time. Taking a shower, changing clothes—these seemed like excellent morning activities, but I just stood there, frozen in place, my breathing agitated. Daylight began to filter through the blinds. I opened the balcony doors again and stared for a long time at the beach and the hazy outline of the pedal boat fortress. Happy are those who have nothing. Happy are those who by leading such a life earn themselves a rheumatic future and are lucky with the dice and resign themselves to living without women. Not a soul was out on the beach so early in the morning, but I heard voices from another balcony, an argument in French. Who but the French raise their voices before seven! I closed the curtains again and tried to undress so I could get in the shower. I couldn't. The light in the bathroom was like the glare of a torture chamber. With an effort I turned on the water and washed my hands. When I tried to splash my face I realized that my arms were stiff and I decided it would be best to leave it until later. I turned off the lights and went out. The hallway was deserted and lit only at each end by half-hidden bulbs that gave off a faint ocher glow. Without making any noise, I went down the stairs until I reached the first-floor landing. From there, reflected in the huge hallway mirror, I could see the the night watchman's head resting on the edge of the counter. He had to be asleep. I retraced my steps to the second floor, where I turned toward the back (northeast) with my ears pricked for the familiar sounds of the kitchen in case the cooks had arrived, which was highly unlikely. At the beginning of my journey down the hallway, the silence was complete, but as I walked along I was able to make out an asthmatic snore that, at brief intervals, interrupted the monotony of doors and walls. When I came to the end I stopped. Before me was a wooden door with a marble plaque in the middle, with a four-line poem (or so I imagined) inscribed on it in black, written in Catalan. Exhausted, I set my hand on the jamb and pushed. The door opened without the slightest impediment. There was the room, big and dark, as Clarita had described it. All I could see was the outline of a window, and the air was thick, though there was no smell of medicine. I was about to close the door that I had so boldly opened when I heard a voice that seemed to come from everywhere and nowhere at once. A voice of contradictory qualities: icy and warm, threatening and friendly:

"Come in." The voice spoke in German.

I took a few steps blindly, feeling my way along the wallpaper, after overcoming an instant of hesitation in which I was tempted to slam the door and flee.

"Who's there? Come in. Are you all right?" The voice seemed to issue from a tape recorder, though I knew that it was Frau Else's husband who was speaking, enthroned on his giant hidden bed.

"It's Udo Berger," I said, standing there in the dark. I was afraid that if I kept moving I would run into the bed or some other piece of furniture.

"Ah, the young German, Udo Berger, Udo Berger, are you all right?"

"Yes. I'm fine."

From an unfathomable corner of the room, some murmurs of assent. And then:

"Can you see me? What can I do for you? To what do I owe the honor of your visit?"

"I thought we should talk. Get to know each other, at least, exchange ideas in a civilized way," I said in a whisper.

"Excellent idea!"

"But I can't see you. I can't see anything . . . and it's hard to carry on a conversation like this . . ."

Then I heard the sound of a body sliding between starched sheets, followed by a groan and a curse, and finally, some ten feet from where I stood, the lamp on a night table came on. Lying on his side, in navy blue pajamas buttoned up to the neck, Frau Else's husband smiled: Are you an early riser or haven't you been to bed yet? I slept a few hours, I said. Nothing in that face matched my memories from ten years ago. He had aged rapidly and poorly.

"Did you want to talk to me about the game?"

"No, about your wife."

"My wife . . . My wife, as you can see, isn't here."

Suddenly I realized that Frau Else was, in fact, missing. Her husband pulled the sheets up to his chin while I scanned the rest of the room reflexively, fearing a practical joke or a trap.

"Where is she?"

"That, my dear young man, is something that neither you nor I needs concern himself about. What my wife does or doesn't do is nobody's business but her own."

Was Frau Else in someone else's arms? Did she have a secret lover about whom she'd said nothing? Probably someone from the town, another hotelier, the owner of a seafood restaurant? Someone younger than her husband but older than me? Or was it possible that at this time of night Frau Else was taking a therapeutic drive on the back roads, trying to forget her troubles?

"You've made a number of mistakes," said Frau Else's husband. "The main one was attacking the Soviet Union so soon."

My baleful stare seemed to disconcert him for a moment, but he recovered immediately.

"If one could avoid war against the USSR in this game," he continued, "I'd never attack; I'm speaking, of course, from the German perspective. Your other big mistake was to underestimate the resistance that England could put up; you lost time and money there. It would have been worth it to stake at least fifty percent of your forces in the attempt, but you couldn't because you were bogged down in the East."

"How many times have you been in my room without my knowledge?"

"Not many . . ."

"And aren't you ashamed to admit it? Do you think it's ethical for the owner of a hotel to snoop around in his guests' rooms?"

"It depends. Everything is relative. Do you think it's ethical to try to get my wife to sleep with you?" A smile, wicked and knowing, rose from under the sheets and settled on his cheeks. "More than once too, and with no success."

"That's different. I don't pretend to hide anything. I'm worried about your wife. Her health concerns me. I love her. I'm prepared to overcome any obstacles . . ." I saw that he had flushed red.

"Enough talk. I have my worries too. About the boy you're playing with."

"El Quemado?"

"Yes, El Quemado, El Quemado, El Quemado. You have no idea of the mess you've gotten yourself into. He's a viper!"

"El Quemado? Do you mean because of the Soviet offensives? I think much of the credit has to go to you. Really, who devised his strategy? Who advised him where to stand his ground and where to attack?"

"Me, me, me—but it wasn't all me. He's a sharp boy. Watch yourself! Keep an eye on Turkey! Retreat from Africa! Tighten your fronts, man!"

"That's what I'm doing. Do you think he plans to invade Turkey?"

"The Soviet Army tends only to grow in strength, and he can permit himself that luxury. Diversify operations! Personally I don't think it's necessary, but the advantage of holding Turkey is obvious: the control of the straits and the free movement of the Black Sea fleet into the Mediterranean. A Soviet landing in Greece followed by Anglo-American landings in Italy and Spain and you'll be forced to retreat behind your borders. Capitulation." From the bedside table he picked up the photocopies that Frau Else had taken from my room and waved them in the air. Two red spots appeared on his cheeks. I got the sense that he was threatening me.

"You've forgotten that I can take the offensive too."

"You're a man after my own heart! You never give up, do you?"

"Never."

"I suspected as much. That is, because of the way you've kept after my wife. In my day, if a woman gave me the brush-off, I would have nothing else to do with her, even if she was Rita Hayworth. Do you know what these papers mean? Yes, they're copied from war books, more or less, but I didn't suggest any of this to El Quemado. (I would have recommended Liddell Hart's *History of the Second World War*, a fair-minded and straightforward book, or Alexander Werth's *Russia at War*.) But this was on his own initiative. And the meaning of it is clear, I think, as my wife and I realized at once. Didn't you? I guessed as much. Well, I can tell you that young people have always sought my advice. And El Quemado has a special place among them, which is why my wife is holding me somewhat responsible—me, a sick man!—for what might happen to you."

"I don't understand anything you're saying. If we're talking about *Third Reich*, I must inform you that in Germany I'm the national champion of the sport."

"Sport! These days anything can be called a sport. That's no sport. And I can promise you that I'm not talking about *Third Reich* but about the plans that poor boy has in store for you. Not as part of the game (because that's what it is, that's all it is), but in real life!"

I shrugged. I wasn't about to argue with a sick man. I expressed my skepticism with a friendly laugh; after that I felt better.

"Of course I told my wife that there wasn't much I could do. At this point that boy only hears what he wants to hear, he's in this up to his neck and I don't think he'll back down."

"Frau Else worries too much about me. Though of course it's very kind of her."

Her husband's face took on a dreamy and absent expression.

"She's a good woman, yes sir, very good. Too good . . . My only regret is not having given her a couple of children."

The remark struck me as being in poor taste. I thanked the heavens for the probable sterility of that poor man. A pregnancy might have disturbed the classical harmony of Frau Else's body, the way she commanded a room even from a distance.

"And deep down, like any woman, she wants to be a mother. Well, I hope she'll have more luck with the next man." He winked at me and I could swear that beneath the sheets he made an obscene gesture. "Don't fool yourself, it won't be you. And the sooner you realize it the better, that way you won't suffer or make her suffer. Though she holds you in great esteem, there's no denying that. She told me that years ago you used to come to the Del Mar with your parents. What's your father's name?"

"Heinz Berger. I came with my parents and my older brother. Every summer."

"I don't remember."

I said it didn't matter. Frau Else's husband seemed to focus all his energies on the past. He looked unwell. I was alarmed.

"And you, do you remember me?"

"Yes."

"What was I like? What image do you have of me?"

"You were tall and very thin. You wore white shirts and Frau Else looked happy to be with you. Nothing much."

"Enough."

He sighed and his face relaxed. My legs were beginning to ache from standing for so long. I thought I'd better leave, sleep a little, or get in the car and go in search of a deserted cove where I could take a dip and then get some rest on the clean sand.

"Wait, I still have a warning to give you. Stay away from El Quemado. Starting now!"

"I will," I said wearily, "when I leave town."

"So what are you waiting for to go home? Don't you realize that . . . unhappiness and misfortune haunt this hotel?"

By this he meant Charly's death, I guessed. And yet, if trouble loomed over a hotel, it should be the Costa Brava, where Charly had stayed, not the Del Mar. My smile of understanding bothered Frau Else's husband.

"Do you have any idea what will happen the night that Berlin falls?"

Suddenly I realized that the misfortune to which he was alluding was the war.

"Don't underestimate me," I said, trying to get a glimpse of the inner courtyards that were surely visible through the curtains. Why hadn't they chosen a room with sea views?

Frau Else's husband telescoped his neck like a worm. He was pale and his skin was slick with fever.

"You fool, do you still think you can win?"

"I can try. I'm good at comebacks. I can mount offensives that keep the Russians at bay. I still have great strike potential . . ." I talked and talked, about Italy, Romania, my armored forces, the reorganization of my air force, my plans for wiping out the beachheads in France, even for the defense of Spain, and gradually I felt that the inside of my head was turning to ice and that the cold was trickling down into my mouth, my tongue, my throat, so that even the words that came out of my mouth grew foggy on their way toward the sick man's bed. I heard him say: Give up, pack your things, pay your bill—and go. I understood with horror that all he wanted was to help me. That in his own way—and because he'd been asked to do so—he was watching out for me.

"What time is your wife coming back?" Despite myself, my voice sounded desperate. From outside came birdsong and the muted sound of motors and doors. Frau Else's husband pretended not to hear me and said he was tired. As if to confirm this, his eyelids drooped.

I was afraid he really would fall asleep.

"What will happen after the fall of Berlin?"

"As I see it," he said in a drawl without opening his eyes, "he won't be satisfied with a handshake."

"What do you think he'll do?"

"The logical thing, Herr Udo Berger, the logical thing. Think, what does the winner do? What traits does he possess?"

I confessed my ignorance. Frau Else's husband turned on his side so that all I could see was his profile, haggard and angular. This was how I discovered that he looked like Don Quixote. A weakened Quixote, ordinary and terrible as Fate. The discovery disturbed me. Maybe that was what had attracted Frau Else.

"It's in all the history books"—his voice sounded weak and tired—"even the German ones. Let the trial of the war criminals begin."

I laughed in his face:

"The game ends with Decisive Victory, Tactical Victory, Marginal Victory, or Stalemate, not with trials or stupid things like that," I intoned.

"Ah, my friend, in that poor boy's nightmares the trial may be the most important part of the game, the only thing that makes it worthwhile to spend so many hours playing. A chance to hang the Nazis!"

I stretched the fingers of my right hand, waiting to hear each bone crack.

"It's a game of strategy," I whispered, "of high strategy. What kind of insanity is this?"

"I'm simply advising you to pack your suitcases and go. After all, Berlin—the one true Berlin—fell some time ago, didn't it?"

We both nodded our heads sadly. The sense that we were talking about different and even categorically opposed things was increasingly obvious.

"Who does he plan to put on trial? The little counters for the SS corps?" Frau Else's husband seemed amused by my outburst and he smiled in a nasty way, half sitting up in bed.

"I'm afraid you're the one who inspires his hatred." The sick man's body suddenly became a single throb, irregular, big, clear.

"Am I the one he's going to sit in the dock?" Though I was trying to keep my composure, my voice shook with indignation.

"Yes."

"And how does he plan to do that?"

"On the beach, like a man—like a man with balls." The nasty smile broadened and at the same time grew more pronounced.

"Will he rape me?"

"Don't be an idiot. If that's what you're expecting, you've got the wrong movie."

I admit that I was confused.

"What will he do to me, then?"

"What people usually do to Nazi pigs: beat their brains out. Bleed them to death in the sea! Send you to Valhalla with your friend, the windsurfer!"

"Charly wasn't a Nazi, as far as I know."

"And neither are you, but at this point in the war, El Quemado doesn't care. You've laid waste to the English Riviera and the wheat fields of the Ukraine, poetically speaking. You can't expect that now he'll handle you with kid gloves."

"Are you the one who came up with this diabolical plan?"

"No, certainly not. But it sounds like fun!"

"It's partly your fault; without your advice El Quemado would've had no chance."

"You're wrong! El Quemado has gone beyond my advice. In a way he reminds me of Atahualpa, the Inca prisoner of the Spaniards who learned to play chess in a single afternoon by watching how his captors moved the pieces."

"Is El Quemado from South America?"

"Warm, warm . . ."

"And the burns on his body . . . ?

"Jackpot!"

Giant drops of sweat bathed the sick man's face when I said good-bye. I would have liked to throw myself into Frau Else's arms and hear only words of reassurance for the rest of the day. Instead, when I found her, much later and with my spirits considerably lower, all I did was whisper abuse and recriminations. Where did you spend the night? Who were you with? Etc. Frau Else gave me a withering look (at the same time, she didn't seem surprised at all that I had talked to her husband), but I was numb to everything.

Fall 1943 and a new offensive for El Quemado. I lose Warsaw and Bessarabia. The west and the south of France fall to the Anglo-Americans. It's possible it's exhaustion that's impairing my ability to respond.

"You're going to win, Quemado," I say in a low voice.

"Yes, that's how it looks."

"And what will we do then?" But fear made me elaborate on the question in order to avoid a concrete response. "Where will we celebrate your initiation as a war games player? I'll be getting money soon from Germany and we can have a night out on the town, at a club, with girls, champagne, that kind of thing."

El Quemado, removed from anything but the progress of his two huge steamrollers, answered with a remark to which I later ascribed symbolic meaning: "Keep watch over what you've got in Spain."

Did he mean the three German infantry corps and the one Italian infantry corps that appear to be stranded in Spain and Portugal now that the Allies control the south of France? The truth is that if I *wanted* to I could evacuate them from the Mediterranean ports during the Strategic Redeployment phase, but I won't. In fact, maybe I'll bring in reinforcements to create a threat or a diversion on the enemy's flank; at least that will slow the Anglo-American march toward the Rhine. This is a strategic possibility that El Quemado must be aware of, if it's as good as it seems. Or did he mean something else? Something personal? What have I got in Spain? Myself!

SEPTEMBER 21

"You're falling asleep, Udo."

"The sea breeze does me good."

"You drink too much and you hardly sleep. That's not good."

"But you've never seen me drunk."

"Even worse: that means you drink alone. You're constantly eating and coughing up your own demons."

"Don't worry, I have a big big big stomach."

"There are terrible circles under your eyes and you just keep getting paler, as if you were gradually turning into the Invisible Man."

"It's my natural complexion."

"You look sickly. You don't listen to what anyone says, you don't see anyone, you seem resigned to staying here forever."

"Every day I stay costs me money. No one is making me a gift of anything."

"This isn't about money, it's about your health. If you gave me your parents' phone number, I would call them to come and get you."

"I can take care of myself."

"It doesn't seem that way. One minute you're in a state of rage, and the next you lapse into passivity. Yesterday you yelled at me and today you just smile like a moron, sitting at the same table all morning."

"I can't tell the mornings and the afternoons apart. I can breathe better here. The weather has changed; it's humid and oppressive now. This is the only comfortable spot."

"You should be in bed."

"If I doze off, don't worry. It's because of the sun. It comes and goes. Inside, my resolve is still strong."

"But you're talking in your sleep!"

"I'm not asleep, I only look it."

"I think I'll have to get a doctor to come and give you a checkup."

"A friend?"

"A fine German doctor."

"I don't want anyone to come. The truth is, I was sitting quietly, enjoying the sea breeze, and you come along to lecture me unintuited, out of the blue, just for kicks."

"You're not well, Udo."

"And you're a cock tease, all this kissing, all this fooling around, and no more. Half here and half somewhere else."

"Don't raise your voice."

"Now that I'm raising my voice, at least you can see I'm not asleep."

"We could try to talk like good friends."

"Go ahead, you know my patience and curiosity are boundless. Like my love."

"Do you want to know what the waiters call you? The freak. And you can see why: someone who spends all day on the terrace, huddled under a blanket like an old cripple, nodding off, and who at night turns into a lord of war and welcomes the lowest of the low—disfigured, to make it even more grotesque; it's not what you'd call ordinary. There are those who think you're a homosexual and others who say you're just eccentric."

"Eccentric! What idiocy. All freaks are eccentric. Did you hear that, or did you make it up just now? The waiters only make fun of things they don't understand."

"The waiters hate you. They think you bring bad luck to the hotel. When I hear them talk I think they wouldn't mind if you drowned like your friend Charly."

"Fortunately, I don't do a lot of swimming. The weather is getting worse and worse. In any case, lovely sentiments."

"It happens every summer. There's always a guest who rubs everyone the wrong way. But why you?"

"Because I'm losing the match and no one likes a loser."

"Maybe you haven't been polite to the staff. Don't fall asleep, Udo."

"My armies in the East are collapsing," I said to El Quemado. "Just the way it really happened, the Romanian flank is crumbling and there are no reserves to contain the wave of Russian tokens advancing on the Carpathians, the Balkans, the Hungarian plain, Austria. This is the end of the Seventeenth Army, the First Panzer Army, the Sixth Army, the Eighth Army."

"Next turn," whispers El Quemado, burning like a torch swollen with veins.

"Will I lose in the next turn?"

"Deep down, very deep down, I love you," says Frau Else.

"This is the coldest winter of the war and nothing could possibly go worse. I'm in a deep hole that I may not be able to dig myself out of. Confidence is a poor counselor," I hear myself say in a neutral voice.

"Where are the photocopies?" asks El Quemado.

"Frau Else gave them to your coach," I answer, knowing that El Quemado has no coach or anything of the kind. The closest thing might be me, since I taught him to play! But not even.

"I don't have a coach," says El Quemado, predictably.

In the afternoon, before the match, I lay down in bed, exhausted, and dreamed that I was a detective (Florian Linden?) who, following a clue, made my way into a temple like the one in *Indiana Jones and the Temple of Doom*. What was I doing there? I don't know. All I know is that I went up and down corridors and through halls with no sense of foreboding, almost with pleasure, and that the coldness inside reminded me of the cold weather of childhood and an imaginary winter when everything, though only for an instant, was white and infinitely still. In the middle of the temple, which must have been built into the hill that looms over the town, I found a man, lit by a cone of light, who was playing chess. Though no one told me who it was, I knew it was Atahualpa. When I approached, peering over the player's shoulder, I saw that the black pieces were charred. What had happened? The Indian chief turned to study me without much interest and said that someone had thrown the black pieces into the fire. Why? For spite? Instead of answering, Atahualpa moved the white queen to a square within reach of the black pieces. She'll be taken! I thought. Then I told myself that it didn't matter since Atahualpa was playing himself. In the next move the white queen was eliminated by a bishop. What's the point of playing yourself if you're going to cheat? I asked. This time the Indian didn't even turn around. Extending his arm, he pointed toward the back of the temple, a dark space suspended between the vaulted ceiling and the granite floor. I took a few steps, more or less in the direction he was pointing, and I saw a huge redbrick fireplace with cast-iron guards that still contained the embers of a fire that must have consumed hundreds of logs. Poking out here and there among the ashes were the twisted tips of different chess pieces. What was the meaning of this? My face burning with indignation and rage, I turned and challenged Atahualpa to play me. He didn't bother to look up from the game board. When I examined him more carefully, I realized that he wasn't as old as I had mistakenly thought at first; his gnarled fingers and the long dirty hair that fell over his face were misleading. Play me if you're a man, I shouted, wanting to escape from the dream. Behind me I felt the presence of the fireplace as a living organism: cold-hot, alien to me and alien to the Indian lost in thought. Why destroy a beautiful work of craftsmanship? I asked. The Indian laughed, but the laugh caught in his throat. When the game was over, he got up and went over to the fireplace, carrying the board and pieces on a tray. I realized that he was going to feed the fire, and I decided that it would be wisest to watch and wait. From the embers, flames sprang up again, swift tongues of fire that soon vanished, scarcely sated by such a meager offering. Atahualpa's eyes were now fixed on the temple vault. Who are you? he asked. From my mouth came an outlandish answer: I'm

Florian Linden and I'm looking for the murderer of Karl Schneider, otherwise known as Charly, a tourist here. The Indian gave me a scornful look and returned to the central circle of light, where, as if by magic, another board and more pieces were waiting for him. He grunted something unintelligible; I begged him to repeat it: That man was killed by the sea, by his own kindness and stupidity, the curt words in Spanish echoing off the walls of the cave. I understood that the dream wasn't making sense anymore or that it was coming to an end, and I hurried to ask a last few questions. Were the chess pieces offerings to a god? Why was he playing alone? When would it all be over? (I still don't know what I meant by this.) Who else knew of the existence of the temple and how to get out of it? The Indian made his first play and sighed. Where do you think we are? he asked in turn. I confessed that I didn't know for sure but I suspected that we were under the hill on which the town was built. You're wrong, he said. Where are we? My voice was growing more and more hysterical. I was scared, I admit, and I wanted out. Atahualpa's bright eyes observed me through the hair that fell over his face like a cascade of stagnant water. Haven't you realized? How did you get here? I don't know, I said, I was walking along the beach . . . Atahualpa laughed: we're under the pedal boats, he said. With luck El Quemado will gradually rent them out—though, considering the weather, it's hard to say for sure—and you'll be able to leave. My last memory is of me hurling myself at the Indian, yelling . . . I woke up just in time to go down to let in El Quemado but not in time to shower. My groin and inner thighs burned. In Poland and on the Western front I made two grave mistakes. In the Mediterranean, El Quemado has wiped out the few army corps left behind as a diversion in western Libya and Tunisia. In the next turn I'll lose Italy. And by the summer of '44 I'll probably have lost the game. Then what will happen?

This afternoon—or this morning, I can't say for sure, whenever it was that I got up for breakfast!—I ran into Frau Else, her husband, and a man I had never seen before sitting at a table off to one side in the restaurant, having tea and cakes. The stranger, tall, with blond hair and a deep tan, was the one leading the conversation, and every so often Frau Else and her husband laughed at his jokes or witticisms, leaning in toward each other until their heads touched and waving their hands as if in a plea to stop the avalanche of stories. After considering whether it was a good idea to join the group, I perched on a stool at the bar and ordered coffee. For once, the waiter hurried to bring it, which only backfired: the coffee spilled, the milk was too hot. As I was waiting I buried my face in my hands and tried to escape the nightmare. It didn't work, so as soon as I had paid I hurried back up to my room.

I slept for a while, and when I woke up I felt dizzy and sick to my stomach. I asked to have a call put through to Stuttgart. I needed to talk to someone, and who better than Conrad? Little by little I felt calmer, but no one picked up the phone at Conrad's house. I ended the call and paced around the room, glancing at the German line of defense every time I passed the table, going out on the balcony, pounding or rather slapping at the walls and the doors, fighting the octopus of nerves that squirmed in my stomach.

A little while later the phone rang. It was a call from downstairs, announcing a visitor. I said I didn't want to see anyone, but the clerk insisted. My visitor refused to leave without seeing me. It was Alfons. Alfons who? I was given a last name that meant nothing to me. I could hear voices arguing. The designer I had gotten drunk with! I gave strict instructions that I didn't want to see him, that they shouldn't let him up. Through the receiver I could now hear with utter clarity the voice of my visitor protesting the rudeness, the lack of manners, the inhospitality, etc. I hung up.

A minute or two later some agonized howls in the street drew me out onto the balcony. In the middle of the Paseo the designer was yelling up at the front of the hotel, shouting himself hoarse. The poor kid, I decided, was shortsighted and couldn't see me. It took me a while to realize that he was just saying "asshole," over and over. His hair was matted and he was wearing a mustard-colored blazer with huge shoulder pads. For an instant I was afraid he would be hit by a car, but luckily the Paseo Marítimo was almost deserted at that hour.

Unnerved, I went back to bed, but I couldn't sleep anymore. The insults had ceased a while ago, but the mysterious and hurtful words still echoed in my head. I asked myself who the long-winded stranger spotted with Frau Else could be. Her lover? A friend of the family? The doctor? No, doctors are quieter, more reserved. I asked myself whether Conrad had seen Ingeborg again. I imagined them holding hands and strolling down an autumn street. If only Conrad were less shy! The scene, full of possibilities as I saw it, brought tears of pain and happiness to my eyes. How I loved both of them, in my innermost being.

As I lay there thinking, I suddenly realized that the hotel was sunk in a wintry silence. I got nervous and began to pace the room again. With no hope of getting things straight, I studied the strategic situation: at best I could hold out for three turns or, with great luck, four. I coughed, I talked out loud, I searched through my notebooks for a postcard that I then wrote while listening to the sound of the pen as it moved across the stiff surface. I recited these lines by Goethe:

> And until you have possessed
> dying and rebirth,

you are but a sullen guest
on the gloomy earth.

[Und so lang du das nicht hast,
Dieses: Stirb und werde!
Bist du nu rein trüber Gast
Auf der dunklen Erde.]

All for nothing. I tried to assuage the loneliness, the sense of
forlornness, by calling Conrad, Ingeborg, Franz Grabowski, but no
one answered. For a moment I wondered whether there was a single soul left in Stuttgart. I began to make random calls, flipping
through my address book. It was fate that led me to dial the number
of Mathias Müller, the pompous kid from *Forced Marches*, one of
my sworn enemies. He was in. The surprise, I suppose, was mutual.

Müller's voice, phonily masculine, obeys his intent to show no
emotion. Coldly, then, he welcomes me home. Naturally, he thinks
I've returned. Naturally, too, he expects that I have some professional reason for calling, that perhaps I want to invite him to work
together to prepare our Paris lectures. I disabuse him of this notion. I'm still in Spain. I heard something of the kind, he lies. Immediately he turns defensive, as if calling from Spain in itself
constituted a trap or an insult. I'm just calling you at random, I
said. Silence. I'm in my room making calls at random, and you're
the lucky winner. I burst out laughing and Müller tried in vain to
imitate me. All he managed was a kind of squawk.

"I'm the lucky winner," he repeated.

"That's right. It could have been any other citizen of Stuttgart,
but it was you."

"It was me. So did you get the numbers from a phone book or
your address book?"

"My address book."

"Then I wasn't *so* lucky."

Suddenly Müller's voice changed markedly. It was as if I were
talking to a ten-year-old boy trying out bizarre ideas for size. Yesterday I saw Conrad, he said, at the club; he's changed a lot, did you

know? Conrad? How could I know when I've been in Spain for ages? This summer it looks like someone snagged him at last. Snagged him? Yes, dropped him, roped him, brought him down, took him out, put a bullet in him. He's in love, he concluded. Conrad in love? On the other end of the line there was an affirmative "uh-huh" and then the two of us retreated into an embarrassing silence as we realized that we'd said too much. At last, Müller said: The Elephant is dead. Who the hell is the Elephant? My dog, he said, and then he burst into a torrent of onomatopoeic sounds: *oink oink oink*. That was a pig! Did his dog bark like a pig? See you later, I said hurriedly, and I hung up.

When it got dark I called the reception desk asking for Clarita. The clerk said she wasn't there. I thought I caught a hint of disgust in her reply. To whom am I speaking? The suspicion that it was Frau Else disguising her voice again lodged in my breast like a horror movie with swimming pools full of blood. This is Nuria, the receptionist, said the voice. How are you, Nuria? I asked in German. Fine, thank you, and you? she answered, also in German. Fine, fine, very well. It wasn't Frau Else. Convulsing with happiness, I rolled to the edge of the bed and fell off, hurting myself. With my face buried in the rug, I let out all the tears that had built up over the course of the afternoon. Then I showered, shaved, and kept waiting.

Spring 1944. I lose Spain and Portugal, Italy (except for Trieste), the last bridgehead on the western side of the Rhine, Hungary, Königsberg, Danzig, Kraków, Breslau, Poznan, Lodz (east of the Oder, only Kolberg still stands), Belgrade, Sarajevo, Ragusa (in Yugoslavia, only Zagreb still stands), four armored corps, ten infantry corps, fourteen air factors . . .

SEPTEMBER 23

I'm woken by a noise from the street. When I sit up in bed I can't hear anything. And yet the feeling of having been called is strong and ineffable. I go out to the balcony in my undershorts: the sun isn't up yet or maybe it has set already, and parked in front of the hotel is an ambulance with all its lights on. Between the back of the ambulance and the stairs, three people are speaking in soft voices, though they gesture emphatically. Their voices reach the balconies reduced to an unintelligible murmur. The horizon glows dark blue with phosphorescent streaks, like the prelude to a storm. The Paseo Marítimo is empty except for a shadow that vanishes along the boardwalk toward the tourist district, which at this time of day (but what time of day is it?) resembles a milky gray cupola, a bulge in the curve of the beach. At the other end, the lights of the port have faded or simply gone out. The asphalt of the Paseo is wet, a clear sign that it has rained. Suddenly an order rouses the men who are waiting. The doors to the hotel and the ambulance open simultaneously and a stretcher comes down the stairs carried by a couple of medics. With them, lagging solicitously a few steps behind, near the head of the prone figure, come Frau Else dressed in a long red coat and the big talker with the heavy tan, followed by the receptionist, the night watchman, a waiter, the fat lady from the kitchen. On the stretcher, a blanket pulled up to his chin, is Frau Else's husband. The way they come down the stairs is ex-

tremely cautious, or so it seems to me. Everyone is watching the
sick man. Lying on his back and looking desolate, he murmurs
instructions for going down the stairs. No one pays any attention to
him. Just then our gazes meet in the transparent (and shuddering)
space between the balcony and the street.

Like this:

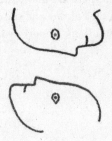

Then the doors close, the ambulance sets off with its siren blar-
ing, though there isn't a single car to be seen on the Paseo, the light
coming through the ground-floor windows goes out, silence de-
scends once again on the Del Mar.

Summer 1944. Like Krebs, Freytag-Loringhoven, Gerhard Boldt, I
record the stages of war despite knowing that it is lost. The storm
has broken and now the rain is beating down on the open balcony
like a long and bony hand, strangely maternal, as if trying to warn
me of the hazards of hubris. There's no one keeping watch over the
doors to the hotel, so El Quemado had no problem coming up to my
room on his own. The sea is rising. It whispers inside the bathroom
where I've brought El Quemado to towel off his hair. It's the perfect
moment to hit him, but I don't move a muscle. El Quemado's head,
wrapped in the towel, exerts a cold and bright fascination over me.
Under his feet a little puddle of water forms. Before we start playing I make him take off his wet T-shirt and put on one of mine. It's
a bit tight on him but at least it's dry. As if at this point it were only
natural for me to give him something, El Quemado puts it on
without a word. It's the end of summer and the end of the game.

The Oder front and the Rhine front collapse at the first onslaught. El Quemado moves around the table as if he's dancing. Which may be the case. My final circle of defense is Berlin–Stettin–Bremen–Berlin; everything else, including my armies in Bavaria and the north of Italy, is cut off from supply lines. Where will you sleep tonight, Quemado? I ask. At my place, answers El Quemado. The other questions, of which there are many, stick in my throat. After we parted, I went out on the balcony and stared into the rainy night. Big enough to swallow us all up. Tomorrow there is no doubt I'll be defeated.

SEPTEMBER 24

I woke up late and with no appetite. Which is all for the best because I don't have much money left. The rain hasn't let up. When I ask for Frau Else at the reception desk, I'm told that she's in Barcelona or Gerona, "at the Grand Hospital," with her husband. The verdict on his health is unequivocal: he's dying. My breakfast consisted of coffee and a croissant. At the restaurant only one waiter was left to wait on five elderly Surinamese and me. All of a sudden the Del Mar is empty.

In midafternoon, sitting on the balcony, I realized that my watch wasn't working anymore. I tried to wind it, I tapped at it, but nothing helped. How long has it been broken? Is this a sign? I hope so. Through the balcony railing I watched the few passersby who hurry along the Paseo Marítimo. Walking toward the port, I spotted the Wolf and the Lamb, in identical denim jackets. I raised a hand to wave, but of course they didn't see me. They looked like two puppies, jumping puddles, pushing each other and laughing.

A little while later I went down to the dining room. There once again were the elderly Surinamese, sitting around a big paella pot heaped with yellow rice and seafood. I took a seat at a table nearby and ordered a hamburger and a glass of water. The Surinamese were talking very fast, whether in Dutch or their native tongue I couldn't say, and the hum of their voices managed to soothe me for an instant. When the waiter appeared with the hamburger, I asked whether they were the only people left at the hotel. No, there are other guests who go on bus tours during the day. Retirees, he said. Retirees? How odd. And do they come in very late? Late and making a racket, said the waiter. After eating, I went back to my room, took a hot shower, and went to bed.

I woke up in time to pack my suitcases and to ask that a collect call be put through to Germany. The novels I'd brought to read on the beach (and that I hadn't even flipped through) I left on the night table for Frau Else to find when she got back. The only one I kept was the Florian Linden novel. After a while the receptionist came to inform me that I could talk now. Conrad had accepted the call. In a few brief words I told him that I was happy to talk to him and that with luck we would see each other soon. At first Conrad was a bit brusque and distant, but he soon realized the gravity of what was brewing. Is this our last good-bye? he asked in a rather affected way. I said no, though I was starting to sound less and less sure. Before we hung up we reminisced about our evenings at the club, the epic and unforgettable matches, and we had a good laugh when I told him about my phone conversation with Mathias Müller. Take good care of Ingeborg, I said by way of farewell. I will, Conrad promised solemnly.

I left the door ajar and waited. The sound of the elevator preceded the arrival of El Quemado. The room clearly looked different than it had on previous nights—the suitcases were next to the bed, in a very visible spot—but El Quemado didn't even give them a glance. We sat down, I on the bed and he near the table, and for an instant nothing happened, as if we had been granted the ability to exit and enter the inside of an iceberg at will. (Now, as I think about it, I see El Quemado with a face floured lunar white, though beneath the thin layer of paint his scars are visible.) The initiative was his, and with no need to draw up sums—he hadn't brought his notebook, but all the BRP in the world were his—he unleashed the Russian Army on Berlin and conquered it. With the British and American armies he made sure to destroy the units that I might have been able to send to retake the city. Victory was that simple. When my turn came, I tried to move my armored reserves out of the Bremen area and came up against a wall of Allies. Actually, it was a symbolic move. Immediately thereafter I acknowledged defeat and surrendered. And now what? I asked. El Quemado exhaled a giant's sigh and went out on the balcony, gesturing for me to follow. The rain and the wind grew stronger, bowing the palm trees of the Paseo. El Quemado's finger pointed ahead of us, over the seawall. On the beach, where the fortress of pedal boats rose, I saw a light, flickering and unearthly as St. Elmo's fire. A light inside the pedal boats? El Quemado roared like the rain. I'm not ashamed to confess that I thought of Charly, a ghostly Charly returned from beyond the grave to mourn my ruin. Clearly I wasn't in my right mind. El Quemado said: "Come on, there's no turning back now," and I followed him. We went down the steps of the hotel, passing through the bright and empty reception hall, until we were in the middle of the Paseo. The rain that struck my face worked on me like a stimulant. I stopped and shouted: Who's there? El Quemado didn't answer and kept heading down to the beach. Without thinking I went running after him. Suddenly the mass of stacked pedal boats rose up before me. I don't know whether it was because of the rain or the bigger and bigger waves, but it looked to me as if the pedal boats were sinking in the sand. Were we all sinking? I remembered the night when I slipped stealthily out this way to hear the war counsels of the stranger whom I later took to be Frau Else's husband. I remembered how hot it was back then and I compared it to the heat that I now felt coursing through my body. The light we'd seen from the balcony sputtered furiously inside the hut. I leaned heavily on a floater in a stance that communicated both determination and exhaustion, and through the cracks I tried to make out who could be in there by the light; it was useless. Pushing with all my might, I tried to topple the structure and managed only to scratch my hands on wood and rusting metal. The fortress was like granite. I had taken my eyes off of El Quemado for a few seconds, and now he was standing with his back to the pedal boats, absorbed in contemplation of the storm. Who's there? Please answer, I shouted. Without waiting for a response that might never come, I tried to scale the hut but took a wrong step and fell flat on the sand.

As I was getting up, El Quemado appeared beside me. I understood that there was nothing left to do. El Quemado's hand grabbed me by the scruff of the neck and yanked me up. I flailed a little, without hope, and tried to kick him, but my limbs were limp. Though I don't think El Quemado heard me, I whispered that I was no Nazi, that none of it was my fault. Beyond that, there was nothing I could do; the strength and determination of El Quemado, spurred on by the storm and surf, were boundless. After this my memories are vague and fragmented. I was lifted up like a rag doll and instead of what I expected (death by water), I was dragged toward the opening of the pedal boat hut. I put up no resistance, I made no further pleas, I didn't close my eyes except when—grabbed by the neck and the crotch—I commenced my trip inside. Then I did close my eyes and I saw myself inhabiting another day, less black but still not bright, the "sullen guest on the gloomy earth," and I saw El Quemado leaving town and country down a winding path of cartoons and nightmares (but what country? Spain? the European Union?) like the eternal mourner. I opened my eyes when I felt myself beached in the sand, a few inches from a kerosene lamp. It wasn't long before I realized, as I twisted like a worm, that I was alone and that there never had been anyone beside the lamp; it had been lighted in the storm precisely so that I would see it from the hotel balcony. Outside, walking in circles around the fortress, El Quemado laughed. I could hear his footsteps in the sand and his clear, happy laugh, like that of a child. How long was I there, on my knees among El Quemado's sparse belongings? I don't know. When I came out it wasn't raining anymore and dawn was beginning to appear on the horizon. I put out the lamp and hoisted myself out of the hole. El Quemado was sitting cross-legged, gazing toward the east, away from his pedal boats. He might easily have been dead and still propped up there on the sand. I came closer, but not much, and said good-bye.

SEPTEMBER 25. BAR CASANOVA. LA JONQUERA

With the first light of day I left the Del Mar; in my car, I rolled slowly along the Paseo Marítimo, careful not to make too much noise and disturb anyone. When I reached the Costa Brava I turned and parked in the lot where at the start of our vacation Charly had shown us his windsurfing board. On my way to the pedal boats I saw no one on the beach except for a couple of runners in track suits who vanished in the direction of the campgrounds. The rain had stopped some time ago; by the purity of the air one could sense that it would be a sunny day. The sand, however, was still wet. When I reached the pedal boats, I listened for any sound that might betray the presence of El Quemado and I thought I caught a very soft snore coming from inside, but I can't be sure. In a plastic bag I was carrying *Third Reich*. Carefully I set it on the tarp that covered the pedal boats and returned to the car. It was nine in the morning when I left town. The streets were half-deserted, which made me think it must be some local holiday. Everyone seemed to be in bed. On the highway the traffic picked up, cars with French and German license plates headed in the same direction as me.

Now I'm in La Jonquera . . .

SEPTEMBER 30

For three days I saw no one. Yesterday, at last, I dropped by the club, secretly convinced that seeing my old friends wasn't a good idea, at least not yet. Conrad was sitting at a table in the corner. His hair was longer and he had dark circles under his eyes that I didn't remember. For a while I watched him without saying anything as the others came up to greet me. Hello, champ. With what warmth and sincerity I was welcomed, and yet all I felt was bitterness! When he saw me in the midst of the commotion, Conrad sauntered over and shook my hand. It was a less effusive welcome than that of the others but more genuine, which was balm to my soul; I felt at home. Soon everyone went back to their tables and new battles were begun. Conrad got someone to take his place and asked whether I wanted to talk at the club or outside. I said I'd like to walk. We ended up at my house, drinking coffee and talking about everything except what really mattered, until after midnight, when I offered to drive him home. We spent the whole ride in silence. I chose not to come in. I'm tired, I explained. When we parted, Conrad said that if I needed money I shouldn't hesitate to ask him for it. I probably will need a little money. Again we shook hands, longer and more earnestly than before.

INGEBORG

Neither of us had any intention of making love and yet we ended up in bed. This was due in part to the seductive arrangement of the furniture, rugs, and various objects with which Ingeborg has re-decorated her large room, and to the music of an American singer whose name I can't recall, and also to the rare peace of the indigo Sunday afternoon. This doesn't mean that we've resumed our rela-tionship; the decision to remain friends is firm on both sides and surely will lead to better things than our old bond. To be honest, nothing much has changed. Of course I had to tell her some of the things that happened in Spain after she left. Basically I talked about Clarita and the discovery of Charly's body. Both stories made a strong impression on her. In return, she revealed something that I'm not sure whether to consider pathetic or funny. While I was away, Conrad tried to woo her. Always, it goes without saying, in the most respectful fashion. And what happened? I asked, sur-prised. Nothing. Did he kiss you? He tried, but I slapped him. Inge-borg and I laughed, but later I felt bad about it.

HANNA

I spoke to Hanna on the phone. She told me that Charly had arrived in Oberhausen in a twenty-inch plastic bag—like an extra-large trash bag, more or less—according to Charly's older brother, who was the one who dealt with receiving the remains and handling the red tape. Hanna's son is fine. Hanna is happy, or so she says, and she plans to vacation in Spain again someday. "Charly would have liked that, don't you think?" I said yes, maybe. So what really happened to you? asks Hanna. Poor Ingeborg believed the whole story, but I've been around longer, haven't I? Nothing happened to me, I said. What happened to you? After a moment (voices in the background, Hanna isn't alone) she says: To me? . . . The same as always.

Starting tomorrow I'll be working as a clerk for a company that makes spoons, forks, knives, and such things. My hours aren't much different than they were before and the salary is a little better. Since I got back, I've been on hiatus from games. (A lie: last week I played cards with Ingeborg and her flat mate.) No one from my circle—because I've been going to the club twice a week—has noticed. There they ascribe my lack of enthusiasm to burnout or long hours spent *writing* about games. How wrong they are! The paper that I was going to present in Paris is being written by Conrad. My only contribution will be to translate it into English. And now that I've embarked on a new stage in my work life, even that is uncertain.

SEECKT

Today, after a long walk, I told Conrad that when you really thought about it we were all essentially ghosts on a ghostly General Staff, forever performing military exercises on game boards. Scale maneuvers. Remember Seeckt? We're like his officers, breaking the law, shadows playing with shadows. You're very poetic tonight, said Conrad. He didn't understand, of course. I added that I probably wouldn't go to Paris. At first Conrad thought I couldn't go because of work and he accepted that, but when I said that at work everyone was going on vacation in December and I had other reasons, he took it personally and for a long time he refused to talk to me. You're throwing me to the lions, he said. I laughed at that: We're Seeckt's trash but we love each other, right? Finally, Conrad laughed too, but sadly.

FRAU ELSE

I talked on the phone to Frau Else. A cold and energetic conversation. As if the two of us had nothing better to do than to shout. My husband is dead! I'm fine, what can I say! Clarita is out of a job! The weather is good! There are still tourists in town but the Del Mar is closed! Soon I'm off on a trip to Tunisia! I assumed that the pedal boats were gone by now. Instead of inquiring directly about El Quemado, I asked a stupid question. I said: Is the beach empty? What else! Of course it's empty! As if autumn had turned us deaf. Not that it mattered. Before we said good-bye, Frau Else reminded me that I had left some books behind at the hotel, and she said she planned to send them. I didn't forget them, I said, I left them there for you. I think she got a little choked up. Then we said good night and hung up.

THE CONVENTION

I decided to go with Conrad to the convention just to watch. The first few days were boring, and although I occasionally did some interpreting for my German, French, and English colleagues, I escaped as soon as I was free and spent the rest of the time taking long walks around Paris. For better or for worse, all the papers and speeches were delivered, all the games were played, and all the plans for a European Federation of players were sketched out and deliberated on. For my part, I came to the conclusion that eighty percent of the speakers needed psychiatric help. As consolation, I kept reminding myself that they were harmless until finally I was convinced, for lack of a better option. The main attraction was the arrival of Rex Douglas and the Americans. Rex is a guy in his forties, tall, strong, with thick, glossy brown hair (does he use pomade? hard to say), who radiates energy wherever he goes. It might be said that he was the undisputed star of the convention and the driving force behind every idea hatched, no matter how random or stupid. As for me, I chose not to greet him, though it would be closer to the truth to say that I chose not to make the effort to approach him, permanently surrounded as he was by a cloud of organizers and admirers. The day of his arrival, Conrad exchanged a few words with him, and every night at Jean-Marc's house, where we were staying, all he talked about was how interesting and intelligent Rex was. Apparently Rex even played a round of *Apocalypse*, the new game just launched by his publishing house, but that evening I wasn't there and I didn't see him. My chance came on the second-to-last day of the convention. Rex was standing with a group of Germans and Italians and I was just fifteen feet away, at the Stuttgart group's booth, when I heard my name being called. This is Udo Berger, our German champion. When I came over, the others stepped aside, and there I was, face-to-face with Rex Douglas. I tried to say something, but the only words I could get out were garbled and incoherent. Rex shook my hand. He didn't remember our brief correspondence, or maybe he preferred not to make it public. He turned straight back to his conversation with someone from the Cologne group and I stood there for an instant, listening, with my eyes half-closed. They were talking about *Third Reich* and the strategies to be used with Beyma's new variants. At the convention they were playing *Third Reich* and I hadn't even gone for a stroll around the games area! By what they said, I inferred that the guy from Cologne was playing the German side and that the war had reached a stalemate.

"That's good for you," said Rex Douglas brusquely.

"Yes, if we hold on to what we've won, which won't be easy," said the guy from Cologne.

The others nodded. Praises were sung of a French player who was leading the team playing the USSR, and immediately they began to make plans for the dinner that night, another "brotherhood banquet," like all the rest. Unnoticed, I slipped away from the group. I went back to the Stuttgart booth, which was empty except for the projects sponsored by Conrad, and I straightened it up a little, adjusting a magazine here, a game there, and left the convention hall without a sound.

Discover more in **VINTAGE CLASSICS** red spine